BROKEN AND SCREWED 2

TIJAN

Edited: AW Editing

Proofread: Kara Hildebrand

Cover Designer: Hart & Bailey Design Co

PROLOGUE

My brother was buried today.

I was standing in the back of the church. There was a special word for it, but we rarely went so I didn't know. I didn't care, either. It was where I stood. People came and said their good-byes. Angie and Marissa, who had sat beside me during the service, were hugging my parents. They were good friends. I suppose. Angie's family came to the funeral. Her mom hugged me, patted me on the head, and then they left. Justin was there, too. He was Angie's boyfriend, but he sat in the back with his friends. He was the one to break Angie away from my hold, urging her to let the next in line give their condolences as he led her to his truck.

I watched from the church as she bent forward once they got inside his truck. Her shoulders were shaking so I knew she was crying. He moved to pull her against him, and I couldn't watch them anymore. My eyes drifted to Marissa, who was watching them, too. She wasn't alone. She was never alone. The new boyfriend had his arm wrapped around her waist and was kissing the back of her neck. It made me sick to watch, but my eyes stayed on them until they climbed into her car and drove off.

Unwilling to turn back to people waiting to talk to me, I let my eyes turn back to Angie, who was still crying in Justin's arms.

"Hey."

Jesse stood next to me and followed my gaze. He grimaced. "Your friends suck."

I frowned. "No, they don't."

"Yeah, they do. But don't take my word for it."

"They're upset."

He snorted, rolling his eyes. "They shouldn't be. They didn't know Ethan, and they should still be here for you. Where are your parents?"

I shrugged. "They're here somewhere." I knew they weren't. They left almost immediately after the service. That was normal. Since the accident, they hadn't talked to me. I knew my mom was grieving. I could hear her crying at night. My dad was with her, but sometimes he ignored her. He spent the nights on the couch. She stayed in their room, and I sat on the stairs, between them. Alone. No one went near Ethan's room. And Jesse had stopped staying over, so his room sat empty as well. I stayed in his room that first night, but I didn't sleep. I had lain there and waited until morning.

Glancing up at him, I saw the frustration in his dark eyes. His black hair had been combed to the side earlier, but since he raked a hand through it and pulled at it when he was really pissed, it was currently a mess. His dark eyes flashed from anger as he scowled. With high cheekbones, his fuck-off attitude, he was lethal.

I asked, "Where's your dad?"

Jesse rolled his eyes. "Fuck. You think he'd come to this?"

"Yeah."

"He wouldn't come." His lips pressed into a tight line and he glanced away from me.

"Did you tell him?"

"No."

I understood. Malcolm Hunt was a big deal in the Hollywood scene, but he was almost nonexistent in his son's life. Hence the reason Jesse had been living with my family since his mother died four years ago. Sometimes I wondered if Malcolm Hunt even knew his son never stayed in their huge mansion, but Mary probably covered for him. She was their housekeeper, but she doted on Jesse. I knew she had more so since Ethan's accident. I saw her at the hospital a few times with him. I'd never admit it, but I was jealous of Jesse. I wished Mary would hug me at times or bring me food like she did with him.

"Screw this shit. Do you want to leave?" He glanced around. The corners of his eyes were stretched tight and his frown had turned to a fully formed scowl. "Go where?"

"To get drunk." He jerked a shoulder up. "I don't care. We can go to the house. No one will be there."

"What about Mary?"

"Are you hungry?"

I shook my head. "No." I didn't remember the last time I was hungry. No, I did. Before the accident. I wanted pizza when we went to Justin's party. Angie and I raided his family's kitchen and baked a homemade pizza. Lots of cheese.

"Why'd you ask about my housekeeper then?"

"I don't know." I was lying. It seemed as if I was doing a lot of that lately. It felt like second nature; though, I didn't know why I had started.

"Let's go. Everyone took off."

I glanced toward the basement. They were serving sandwiches and potato salad, but I wondered who was even going to eat it. Jesse was right. The only people who lingered were the ones who went to this church. We didn't. Some of Ethan's classmates stayed, along with this coach. There was another group of people congregated around the church's picnic tables. I saw their paper plates and a part of me relaxed, but I didn't stop to talk to them as we headed to Jesse's car. At least someone stayed for the food. For some reason, that mattered. Ethan would've wanted people to enjoy a meal for him.

"Hunt!" one of the guys called out.

Jesse ignored them and gestured to the door. "Get in."

As I did and reached for my seat belt, they were still watching us. One girl had stood from the table and stared at me, looking sad. She had long blonde hair and was pretty, like a real life doll. I asked, "Who are those guys?"

"No one."

"Who, Jesse?" I could tell they weren't "no one."

"Jeremy Benson. Stay away from him. He's bad news, Alex."

Nothing more needed to be said. Benson and his friends were known for drugs, boozing, and getting arrested. I was glad that Jesse had ignored him, but why were they here? He drove out of the parking lot and gunned the engine. Jesse had always been a speed demon, but it was worse since Ethan's death. However, no one said anything. Jesse Hunt got away with almost anything he wanted. His dad gave enough money to the local police department that they ignored the black blip of Jesse's car as it flew by. Who else would step in to stop him? Maybe Ethan would have, but he was dead.

My brother was dead.

"What's wrong?"

I'd never get used to it. Ethan was supposed to be next to us. No, that wasn't right, either. Ethan was supposed to be where I was sitting. I should've been in the back seat, and my brother would've been lecturing Jesse on the laws and how he needed to follow the set speed limit. Jesse would ignore him, but he'd grin and slow to a more reasonable pace. Then the two would laugh about something, curse at each other, and we'd head back to my home.

I looked over at his clenched jaw. His knuckles gripped the wheel tight. I sighed, "Are you hoping to join him?"

His foot let up immediately on the pedal. "Sorry." He shot me a rueful look. "I don't think sometimes."

"I wish I could stop thinking."

He glanced over again. "You seem to be holding up all right."

"It's called not feeling. It's the best method for mourning. You don't."

A corner of his mouth lifted, but it wasn't a grin. It wasn't even a half-grin. It was a twitch. "I think I'll try that tonight."

"What?"

"Stop thinking. Stop feeling."

"I want to get drunk tonight."

"It's on the agenda." His eyes flickered with a bit of warmth. "You sure your parents were still there? I didn't see their car in the lot."

I lied again. "They think I'm staying at Angie's tonight."

"Does Angie know that?"

"No."

I got a full grin this time as he turned onto his street. Then he turned up the hill toward his house, hit the button to open the gate, and made his way to up the driveway. When he came to a stop next to a brand new Jaguar, Jesse stopped and stared at it for a beat. The tiny bit of warmth that had been in his eyes turned back to ice. He took his key out and dug it into the side of the car, walking the entire length before tucking the key ring back into his pocket and taking my hand in his. "Fucking new girlfriend's here."

"Yours?"

"My dad's. Come on." He took me down the hill so we entered the house from the back door. We walked through the basement and headed up the farthest set of stairs. A feminine giggle was above us, followed by a man's moan, but Jesse ignored the sounds. He led the way through the back hallways until we got to the farthest end of the house. I knew where his room was, but it'd been so long. I might've gotten lost if I had been asked to find it by myself. As we stepped into his room, it was like a whole other house inside of their house. Jesse had his own living quarters where not even the noises his dad was making could reach.

I perched on his king-sized bed while he rifled through his liquor cabinet. He had his own bar. It still amazed me, even though I knew he'd had it for a while. He was a junior. No, that wasn't right anymore. Ethan had graduated. Jesse would be a senior, and I was going to be a junior. We were so young, but I didn't feel young anymore. I felt old, too old. And as Jesse poured himself a glass of something dark, he didn't look young, either.

Was it possible to age years in three days?

I felt it.

"Here." Jesse gestured to the second glass. "Come over here."

I did. My dress inched up my thigh as I sat down on a stool across from him, but I didn't pay it any attention. I wouldn't even feel it in a moment. I was still new to drinking. My first party had been earlier in the year, but I knew my tolerance wasn't much. This glass and another, I'd be drunk.

Jesse already finished his. He began pouring a second for himself.

Well, maybe not. Maybe I wouldn't feel this, like I didn't feel anything else. I drank it. I had been right and wrong. There was a burn, but I barely flinched as I nudged the glass over for a refill.

"You sure?"

I nodded. I needed it. Tonight, I needed it. Tomorrow, I'd deal with the consequences.

After I sipped the second drink, I cringed. "Marissa told me that you broke up with Sarah. Is that true?"

He nodded as he leaned against the wall behind his counter. He moved his glass around, making the liquid swish in a circle. "I suppose."

"Why?"

"Why not?" he countered, frowning into his glass.

"Jesse."

When he looked up, I saw the agony clear in his eyes, but I could only see it because it was in me. It wasn't about Sarah. It was the same pain I felt. No one else saw it. No one else was privy enough to be allowed past his walls. Why he let me through, I'd probably never know, but I was grateful. He was the only one who understood because he was the only one who loved Ethan as much as I did.

He relinquished, "I broke up with her because it was getting too serious."

That's right. But—I didn't want to go there.

I couldn't stop myself.

"You weren't with Ethan that night?" The words were out before I caught myself.

The 'what ifs' were in my head. What if he'd been with Ethan? What if—but no. He was talking about Sarah.

He finished his glass and poured another. As he settled back against the wall, he shook his head. "No. I was at dinner with Sarah and her parents. The fucking in-laws, or that's what they were referring to themselves as. I didn't give a shit. I didn't even want to be there."

I bit my tongue. Sarah was perfect. She was tiny. She was beautiful. She was kind, and she'd been Jesse's girlfriend for three years. She was opposite of me in most ways. I was normal in height and slender, but unlike her porcelain skin, mine was golden tan. Angie told me it matched well with my dark hair and dark eyes. It didn't matter how I measured up. No one else intimidated me more than she did. I opened my mouth to ask something else but then sighed as he took another sip of his drink, closing himself off a bit more.

I had only seen this look on him a few times, and each time he had snapped. It was never good. A guy had gotten beaten up one time. Another time, Jesse had been arrested for taking a bat to someone's car. The third was when he drove a car over a cliff. I'd been in the car, and he told me to get out before I knew what he was doing. He'd thrown himself out of it before it was airborne, but that'd been the scariest. It was the day his mother had died.

Ethan told me later that car had belonged to Evelyn, Jesse's mother.

That same Jesse was standing in front of me.

Uneasiness prickled down my back, but he wouldn't hurt me. Jesse never hurt me. He'd react around me, but never at me.

"Why are you asking questions about Sarah, Alex?" He watched me over the rim of his glass. His eyes were dark and stormy, sending a tingle through me. It wasn't a bad one. As my lungs filled, I needed to be there. I couldn't be anywhere else. I didn't know what was going to happen, but I wanted it. I needed it.

I tipped my head back and drank the last of my alcohol in one swallow. I pushed it toward him across the counter again.

He didn't move to refill it.

"I want another one."

"Why are you asking questions about Sarah, Alexandra?" He didn't move from the wall.

"Jesse, come on."

"You come on. Answer my question."

"Answer mine first."

"I did." He hadn't. He knew I knew he hadn't.

I sighed and rolled my eyes. "Right, because it's getting too serious makes perfect sense," I bit out. "I'm a year younger, but I'm not an idiot. I know you, Jesse. You dumped her when we were at the hospital. She called to ask if you wanted her there, and you told her to get out of your life for good. Then you hung up. Real classy for a boyfriend. Three years, and that's how you break up with her."

He glowered at me. "Shut up."

"No. I think she deserves an explanation. I would. I mean,

really. Three years, and that's all you have to say to her? I know you haven't talked to her since. You blocked her number."

He raised a single eyebrow, silently asking me how I could possibly know that.

"I watched you do it. I could tell what you're doing. Again—I may be a bit younger, but I'm not stupid."

"You could tell?" He moved then, putting his glass on the counter and taking two steps away from the wall so he was against the counter. "You can tell what I'm doing?"

I swallowed thickly. I had been able to tell, but this Jesse was new to me. He was predatory and scary. He wasn't scary in a bad way, but in a good way, an all-together scary form of a good way. I licked my lips as he stalked around the counter.

My heart began pounding, and I opened my legs a little. I knew what he was going to do before he did it. I think I had always known.

You wanted this the whole time, even back at the church. You little hussy.

I flinched at the voice in my head. Was I really going to do this? I was a virgin, but this was Jesse. And this was me. And I had wanted him for so long.

He reached me and slid his hands under my legs. They went all the way under my cheeks as his body settled between my legs. He didn't even need to nudge them aside. I opened them. I was eager about it. As he bent over me, his lips came down, my heart wanted to explode out of me.

So long.

I had waited for this for so long.

I licked my lips, but he didn't press his to mine. I wanted him to, badly. As he hung there, suspended in the air, I murmured, "Jesse."

"Can you tell what I'm doing now?"

My arms lifted, and I wound them around his neck. I was the one that pulled him closer against me. He fit there perfectly, and I lifted my legs to lock behind his waist. One of his hands fell to my thigh. He burned a trail over my skin as he slid his hand to my core. He was slow and purposeful. He watched me the entire time, judging and measuring me.

My lips brushed against his as I said, "I knew before we came up here."

His chest lifted, and he sucked in a deep breath. "Are you sure about this, Alex?"

I nodded. I couldn't talk. I needed this too much. I needed him. I wasn't sure, but as he lowered his lips to mine—finally—I gave him everything. I wanted to forget the world. There was no brother. There were no parents. There were no friends. There was no loss or mourning or grieving. No sadness. Only heat. That was all there was between us. Even the pain that occurred was minimal to what I'd felt for the last three days.

That night I gave myself to him. I just didn't know the extent of it until later.

1

W hen I went to Jesse's house, I wasn't expecting to find a naked chick on his couch.

I knew it was his house. As I walked in, there was a giant portrait of him and my brother in the foyer. He must've had someone paint it from a picture at some party. Both wore easygoing grins and their affection was obvious. They were happy. Ethan was happy. It stopped me in my tracks and made a myriad of emotions threaten to boil inside me. I pushed them all down. I couldn't handle that. Nope.

I turned the corner into the living room and stopped again. I mentally lifted my foot off the trap door in my mind that I had just shoved my emotions through, and let rage out. Rage was my friend, and every single onc of it was directed at the naked girl on Jesse's couch.

Her back was toward me, but it was clear that she wasn't alone, and her couch buddy was currently tilting his head of black hair so he could neck.

A head of black hair sat underneath her, and he moved to kiss up the girl's neck. As she leaned back with her eyes closed, his hand lifted to cup her breast. A moan slipped from her as he ran his thumb over it. As she gasped, her eyes opened a slit. It was enough. She saw me and horror flashed over her. She belted out a scream and scrambled off Jesse's lap to the couch.

"What the fu—" Jesse whipped off the couch and whirled around. His face was contorted in fury but then shock stopped him.

It stopped me as well.

That wasn't Jesse.

I clamped a hand over my eyes and turned away. "I'm so, so, so, so sorry, Cord. Oh my God! I'm really sorry." Muttering more curses, I tried to run from the room but smacked into a wall.

He spewed a few more curses as the girl cried out, "Who the hell is that?"

I frowned when I heard the snippy tone. She had every right to be pissed. I couldn't fault her.

She continued, "You said we had the house to ourselves. Who is this girl?"

"It's no one." His voice faded for a second. "Here. Put this on, Chandra."

She sneered at him.

"Chandra."

"You owe me for this," she snapped at him.

I waited, still against the wall with my hand over my eyes. I breathed in and out with a brief hope that maybe he'd forget I was there and go after her. This was too awkward.

"You can look now."

He hadn't.

The awkwardness lifted a notch. I could tell he was pissed.

My hands didn't move. "Are you dressed?"

"Yes." He sounded exhausted and a little less pissed, so I peeked. There were bags underneath his eyes as he sat on the couch, leaning forward on his knees. He wiped a hand over his face and regarded me with narrowed eyes. "You're looking for Jesse?"

I nodded.

His head dropped to his hands, and his shoulders hunched inward. He was still shirtless, but his shorts rode farther up his thigh, his very manly thigh. As he didn't say anything for a moment, my eyes roamed over him. I couldn't help it. He had filled out since the last time I saw him, around nine months ago.

"You look good," I remarked lightly as I perched on the end of the sectional.

"We've been training like crazy." His head lifted, and he grimaced, rubbing a hand over his jaw. It clenched under the movement.

I searched for where the girl might've gone. "Who was that?"

"No one."

From the soft tone of regret, I grimaced again. "That wasn't 'no one.' That was someone. Is the infamous Cord Tatum off the market?" I teased, "I know someone who goes to school an hour away that'll be disappointed."

"Who?"

"Marissa." I frowned, though I was slightly unsurprised he would forget about her.

"Oh. Her."

Okay, so no love lost there. I took notice. This was a new guy in front of me.

"Jesse's not here."

"I gathered."

"Yeah. You're coming here then?"

I nodded.

He turned away from me but continued to rub at his jaw, as if mulling over some problem in his head.

I glanced at my lap, unsure what to say. I didn't know this was how it would go down. When Mary gave me Jesse's address, I had every intention of marching in and giving him an earful. He kept secrets about Ethan's death and hadn't returned any of my calls. I just got a letter that gave me the fuck off sentiments from my parents. I had no intention of taking another one from Jesse. I was primed and ready to tell him how it would be since I was going to be attending the same university.

"Look," I began, smoothing my hand down my pants. "It's obvious that I interrupted something special—"

"No, you didn't." He stood abruptly.

I froze from the sudden movement, but he left the room and hollered, "Come on."

Sliding off the couch, I trailed behind him, and he led the way into one of the biggest kitchens I have ever seen in my life. It was half the size of a banquet hall, but then I had to roll my eyes. Should I have expected otherwise? Mary told me that his father bought this house for Jesse. Of course, it would be grandiose. His dad was a movie producer and a jerk.

Cord opened a cabinet and pulled out a bottle of wine. "You want some?"

I hesitated. I did, but I still needed to move into my dorm room.

He flashed me a grin.

My shoulders loosened. There was the cocky son of a bitch Cord Tatum. I reached for one of the glasses that hung from a cupboard and slid it across the counter. "Fill her up."

He chuckled as he did. Then he topped off his own glass. "Instead of talking about the chickadee that was just here, why don't we talk about you?" He picked up his glass and moved toward the large table that could've sat thirty people, took a seat, and motioned for me to join him. As I sat, he asked, "Why are you here to see Jesse?"

Oh goodness.

As I sat, I needed to remember who this guy was. He charmed his way into Marissa's pants—who was I kidding? She charmed her way into his after trying to charm her way into Jesse's pants.

With a scowl on my face, I took a big gulp of the wine. I set the glass back down, roughly, as I scowled at him. "Why'd you sleep with Marissa?"

His eyebrows shot up, but he schooled his face. I had to give him points for that. Not too much shock got through before he contained himself. "What do you mean?"

I scoffed, drinking more of my wine. "Don't act like I'm stupid. I know she was calling Jesse, and you took up the cause." The whole thing settled on the bottom of my gut in a bad way. A pang seared through me. She'd been my friend, and she had been hoping to get Jesse while she knew of our history.

It hurt.

It hurt a lot.

He leaned forward with his arms resting on the table. His tone was gentle, "Look, Marissa was stupid, okay? I don't know how you two are right now, but take it from me. She was a stupid girl. She was selfish."

I swallowed over a knot in my throat. It hurt. It hurt so fucking much.

He continued, so soft and gentle, "And if you think Jesse wanted anything to do with her, you're completely wrong. The dude's barely looked at another girl since you handed him your walking papers and marched last November."

Relief hit me like a ton of bricks. I sat there, stunned. It felt good to hear that. It felt really good to hear that, but he never returned my calls. Why hadn't he if he cared that much?

"Look." Cord sighed and stood from the table. He tossed the rest of his wine in the sink and then did the same with mine. "Have you moved into the dorms yet?"

I shook my head.

"And I bet you have a whole car loaded to the top with stuff, huh?"

I nodded this time.

"All right. Mind's made up. Come on."

He bent to slip on his shoes, pulled a Grant West University shirt on, and grabbed his keys. He dangled them at me from the door. "You coming or not?"

"What are you doing?"

"I'll help you move in."

"You will?" This visit had gone in a different direction than what I intended. "I didn't come here for that."

He shrugged, grinning at me. "I know, but Jesse would want me to do this. He'd do it if he were here."

I stood and bit back my retort. "Yeah, where is he?"

Barking out a laugh, he shook his head. "Nope. Not going to touch that one."

I was even more confused as he put his hand between my shoulder blades and urged me out of the house. Following behind me, he locked the door and then asked, "What dorm are you in?"

"Frasier Hall."

"Yeah? What floor?"

"Sixth."

His eyebrows shot up and he almost missed a step.

I narrowed my eyes at him. "Why?"

He shrugged but turned for his car. "Nothing. I'll follow you."

"Suurree . . ." Something was up. That was obvious, but when Cord climbed into his Jaguar and shut the door, I knew it was too late for me to ask about it.

"Let's go, Connors." He reversed out of the driveway. Pounding the top of his car, he gestured for me to hurry up. So, I got into my car and pulled out. He followed behind, and when we pulled up to the back door of my new dorm, the reaction to his Jaguar was comical.

There were girls everywhere, along with their parents, little siblings, and friends galore. Most of the dads seemed to halt whatever they were doing. Their heads craned for a better view so they could see his car. The girls snapped to attention as well, but their eyes were on Cord as he rounded his car and sauntered to mine. Even though his head was down and he only looked at me and talked to me, he still emanated a subtle cockiness. It was as if everyone knew there was an elite athlete among their mix.

I could only shake my head. If people reacted like this to Cord, how did they handle Jesse?

"Any order?" Cord asked as he opened my car door and bent to haul out a box.

"No order."

"What room?" He straightened from the car.

"613."

"Got it." His head clipped up and down in a brisk nod before he headed for the open stairway. It was as if he knew where he was going, exactly where he was going.

"Was that Cord Tatum?"

I had expected the question from a girl. When it was a deep masculine voice instead, I was thrown off balance for a second. He looked in his mid-forties with a beer belly. Sweat soaked most of his shirt, and he wiped a hand over his glistening forehead, but his eyes were lit up. "Was it?"

I had a feeling I'd be getting this question a lot from the other dads.

"Uh," I wasn't sure what to say.

"Yo, Connors." Cord was already back.

I almost did a double take. He must've sprinted up the stairs and jogged down, but he looked like he could do that twenty more times. He grinned at me from the corner of his mouth as he bent to pick up another box. "You got no roommate. Nice."

The dad moved in his way. "Are you Cord Tatum?"

"Nah, man." Cord gave him a polite smile and jogged back to the stairway. "I just look like him."

The guy's shoulders dropped down. "Oh. I thought—well— he looks a lot like him."

He was still looking at me, but I shrugged and grabbed a box of my own. Locking the door, I went inside and up the stairs. Cord passed me on the third floor. He rolled his eyes as he held his hand out for my keys. "That guy still down there?"

I nodded. "Does that happen a lot?"

"Usually only when we head to a bar. I didn't expect that here, but it makes sense. It shouldn't be a problem."

"Is that . . ." I hesitated. I wanted to know how it was for Jesse, but I didn't want to ask. I kind of just wanted him to offer up the information he knew I wanted.

Cord flashed me another grin. "Don't sweat it, Connors. Jesse comes off as a dick so he usually isn't approached for autographs." He laughed to himself, shaking his head. "And he gets away with it. No one's going to think anything less of Malcolm Hunt's son."

I nodded. I wasn't sure what to think of that.

"Oh, hey."

I turned back on the stairs.

He winked at me. "Jesse will like knowing that your room is right next to the stairs."

"Cord!" I hissed, horrified, excited, and embarrassed at the same time. I didn't want to dwell on any of those emotions, they were too threatening, so I ignored all of them and went the rest of the way to my room. When I stepped onto the sixth floor, I realized he was right and my room was right next to the stairwell.

My room wasn't anything special. There were two beds, two desks, two closets, and two dressers. I had paid for a single after I received the screw-off letter from my parents. I hadn't known my grandfather was wealthy, but I capitalized on it. I had the money so I was going to use it. I'd heard enough horror stories about freshman roommates.

I was stepping out from the room and heading back down-stairs for another load when someone tapped me on the shoulder.

"Hi, there!" A girl waved at me and gave me a friendly smile.

She had bright blue eyes and platinum blonde hair. Dressed in white khaki shorts and a white polo, she could've stepped out of a golfing magazine for the rich and preppy. Then I noticed the GW logo on the top right corner of her shirt in purple lettering.

This girl was my resident advisor.

"Hi."

She held her hand out, tanned like the rest of her with a diamond-encrusted watch wrapped around her wrist. "I'm Kara."

I shook her hand and tried not to grimace at how my hand contrasted next to hers. She was golden and beautiful. I was pale and grotesque, but I drew in a breath and tilted my chin up.

"Alex."

"Yeah." Her smile doubled. "Alexandra Connors, right?" She lifted a clipboard and wrote something on it. A strand of her hair slipped forward to the board, but she didn't notice. She compressed her lips together before she was done and looked back at me. The smile slipped a second, and her eyes widened as they shot past me. "Cord?"

"Oh, hey, Kara." He breezed into my room with two boxes. Setting them down, he came back out and leaned a hand against the doorframe behind me. He was sheltering me. I didn't know if he did it on purpose, but for some reason I was grateful. His hand came down to my shoulder in the next moment. "You've met Alex, huh?"

"Uh . . ."

He squeezed my shoulder. "Treat her right. She's like family."

I was? I sent him a furtive look over my shoulder. His smirk deepened, and then he jogged back down the stairs.

"You . . ." She blinked rapidly. "You know Cord?"

"You know Cord?"

"Yeah, he's roommates with my boyfriend."

The slight enjoyment I was having hurdled down my stomach. I felt it grinding into the ground as I swallowed down the urge to vomit. Roommates? Cord lived with Jesse. Chewing on the inside of my cheek, I had to ask. "Oh. Uh. Who is that?"

"Derek Williams."

My knees buckled underneath me. The relief was overwhelming. I grabbed on to the doorframe Cord had rested against and struggled to keep myself upright. For a moment, I thought a nightmare had occurred in front of me. This girl wasn't dating Jesse. Thank God.

Then it clicked with me. My RA's boyfriend was roommates with Jesse. No wonder she seemed surprised that I knew Cord.

"How do you know Cord so well?"

When my gaze shot to hers, I was startled from the sudden fierceness in them. And then I had a conundrum. Did I tell her the truth? That Cord was just playing with her because I wasn't really like family to him? Or did I tell the other truth, that he was only looking out for me because of my connection to Jesse. My gut was telling me that she'd have an even bigger reaction if she knew that last part.

So I lied.

"I don't. We went to the same high school, and I looked him up. I had a friend who wanted me to keep tabs on him."

"Oh." Her shoulders loosened, and she looked back down to her clipboard. "So he was just teasing me? Because I know Cord does that sort of thing. He's roommates with Derek, after all. I'm good friends with him."

My head lifted up and down in a long, drawn-out motion. I was getting what she was giving. She wanted me to know how well she knew Cord, and I was struck again by how small I felt next to this girl. She was important. I was not. I got her message.

Then she frowned and shook her head. "I'm sorry. That was a really bitchy thing for me to say."

"Um." No idea what to say, but I knew I wasn't going to say anything about Jesse.

"Kara?" An annoyed tone came around the corner and then I heard, "Oh, fuck me. Really?"

I turned and gulped.

It was the girl who'd been straddling Cord an hour ago.

The corners of my mouth lifted, and I said the first thing that came to mind. "At least you're wearing clothes this time."

2

K ara's eyes widened, and she sucked in her breath, but she pivoted to her friend. "Chandra, this is Alex." Her eyes held a special meaning as she stressed to her, "She knows Cord."

The hostility doubled. "I'm aware. How do you know him?"

I opened my mouth, unsure what to say, but Kara forced out an awkward laugh. "They went to the same high school together." She was mum on the rest, which piqued my interest. Her friend must've been a jealous sort.

"Really?" Chandra's eyes snapped to attention. "So you know Jesse Hunt, as well?"

Well, fuck. I hadn't expected to be linked with him this quickly. I wasn't going to hide that I knew him, but I wasn't ready for everyone to know right away how connected I really was to him.

Cord saved the day.

He popped out of the stairwell and handed me his phone. "Call for you." Then he saw who had joined the conversation and groaned. "You're here, too?" Disappearing into my room, Chandra followed him inside.

Kara motioned to the hallway behind her. "I'll leave you be. I should get back to the other girls. Oh, before I forget, we have a floor meeting in my room at six tonight. So, I'll see you in three hours." She started to leave. I started to lift the phone, but her head appeared around the corner. "And we're all going to eat in the cafeteria tonight. I want to show everyone how to get there and register your identification card. That's all. See you in a few hours."

Then I heaved a deep breath. I knew who was on the phone. My stomach took a sudden dip, and I pressed a hand against it. Was I ready for this? The nerves had my hands shaking, but I swallowed tightly and croaked into the phone, "Hello?"

There was silence on the other end.

I closed my eyes and turned into the corner. My forehead rested against it. Though he couldn't see me, a part of me was cowering from him. A storm swept through me and left me shaking. I felt like vomiting as I asked, "Can you please say something?"

"You went to the house?"

There it was. Jesse's voice slid over the phone, smooth and sensual, sharp and cutting. He was angry with me. My chest tightened, and my heart pounded against it. Would it ever lessen? He held so much power over me. Already, even with how he had ignored me for months, a flame ignited in me for him. It was simmering in my depths, and I knew the longer I talked to him, the more it would become.

"Mary gave me your address. Nice place."

I hadn't paid attention, but it seemed like the right thing to say.

"You didn't tell me you were coming to Grant West."

I sucked in my breath. His tone was so biting. "Would it have mattered?"

"No."

I fell silent. My hand tightened its hold on the phone. I was pressing it against my ear so hard I knew there'd be an indentation from it. "What do you want, Jesse?"

"What do you want?" he lashed back. "I haven't heard a word from you since Vegas and now this? Cord texts me that you were at the house? You're the one playing games, Alex."

"What are you talking about?"

He laughed into the phone, harshly. "I might not have been the nicest to you in the past, but there were reasons. What's your reason? Are you doing this on purpose?"

My back straightened and my voice rose, "What are you talking about?"

"Stop it. Seriously."

"Seriously," I bit back. "Tell me what you're talking about. I called you. You're the one who didn't call me back. You ignored me. You don't think that hurt me?" My voice dipped as searing pain ripped through me. I had needed to know what happened. He'd been on the phone with Ethan that night, but he hadn't said a word. There's been no response and that hurt more than I could've imagined.

He grew quiet again. Then he softened his tone, "What are you talking about?"

I bent over and drew in a shuddering breath. It hurt to breathe. "I talked to Barbie. She told me about Ethan. You called him that night, Jesse. Why didn't you tell me that? I called you over and over again. I left messages. I texted you, but you never replied to any of them. Do you have any idea what that did to me?"

Agony stabbed at me.

He choked out, "What? When? Wait—I lost my phone. I had to get a new one. When did you call me?"

I shook my head as I felt tears sliding down my cheeks. "You got a new phone, but not a new number. My calls would've come to your new one. Stop lying to me, Jesse."

"I'm not." His voice rose, and I heard a twinge of desperation.

"I'm not. I swear. It took me almost two months before I finally got one. The guys talked me into it. I didn't want to, but I figured if you ever called me again, I needed to keep that number."

A harsh laugh ripped from me. "You got a new phone because of me?"

"Yeah." He sounded serious. "I see Coach every day. The guys live with me. Who else do I care about? Mary learned how to use the Internet, so that's all she does now. I keep a chatting window up just for her. I don't give a damn about my dad. If he wants to talk to me, he can come see me. I got the phone for you. You don't believe me?"

I wanted to believe him. So much. It was killing me. "Are you serious?"

"Yes," he stressed. "And yes, I called Ethan that night. He was with Benson and Barbie that night. I didn't think he should be with them. That crew wasn't good for him. They were into drugs, and I didn't want him taking any of that crap. We fought, Alex—" He stopped abruptly, but I heard his deep breathing. Then he wrung out, "I've felt so damn guilty about that night. I told him to stay away from Barbie, and he told me to stay away from you." An ugly laugh came from him. "Look at how that worked out. I seduced you the first night I could."

"No, you didn't," I whispered into the phone. "I wanted you, too."

He grunted. "Well, whatever. It's done now."

I bit my lip. I wanted to plead with him, but I held back. I couldn't handle the rejection, if he turned his back on me. I couldn't take that after everyone else had left me.

"Isn't it?" he asked.

My breathing became labored.

"Alex?"

A groan escaped me. My eyes clasped shut, and I could only hold the phone. I was struggling to keep from begging him.

Then he asked, his tone dipped low, "Are you with Eric?"

"No," I wrenched out.

"You're not?"

"I never was." I slid down and bent over my knees. I wasn't on the ground, but I was close. I curled into a ball, right there in the corner of the hallway. I didn't care who saw me. I couldn't do anything else in that moment. The need for him was paralyzing me. "Jesse."

He murmured, "You didn't call on his anniversary."

"I wanted to," I rasped out. "I thought you had turned your back on me."

"No. Never. Where are you?"

"At my dorm."

"Is Cord with you?"

My throat grew thick so I couldn't talk. I nodded instead.

"Alex?"

"Yes," I squeaked out. "Yes."

"Look, I'm coming back right now."

My head rose. Where had he been? I wanted to ask him, but my throat still couldn't work. I grunted instead.

"Give the phone to Cord."

Wordlessly, I went to my room. Cord was sitting on the bed, and Chandra was on my desk. Her feet had been resting on my chair, but she jumped up as soon as I entered the room. Ignoring her, I handed the phone to him. Cord stood from the bed and left the room. I heard him say, "Yeah?"

As his voice faded, my chest lifted up as I struggled to push the emotion away. This was almost embarrassing. I couldn't even speak. One simple phone call and I was close to being a blubbering mess.

"So."

I stiffened.

Chandra gave me another serene smile. I wondered if she

used it on all the people she considered her minions. "You seem close to Cord? I thought you only knew him from high school. That's what Kara said."

I jerked my head in a nod and moved to one of the boxes. Lifting it from the floor, I set it on the desk. She had to jump out of the way, but I was able to stand with my back to her. As I started to unload the pictures and books. "I don't live in the dorms." She said, ignoring the fact that I clearly didn't want to talk to her. "I only came to see Kara. She's one of my best friends, her and Tiffany. We're all juniors this year, with Cord. I was upset. I thought Cord was cheating on me." She heaved a deep breath. "He's not, right? I mean, you're not . . . cheating with him? Are you?"

I didn't say a word. I should've, but I kept my lips shut. When I heard the bed squeak, I knew she had sat down. Her voice rose higher, shrill now, "Not that Cord and I are dating, but I care about him, and you already know that he and I are more than friends. Or, at least, I hope we are. Oh my God. Why am I saying this stuff to a freshman?"

My shoulders stiffened, but I still didn't say anything. She kept talking, which surprised me, but I went with it. As she laughed at herself, the ball of emotion left my throat. I felt more in control of myself, but I continued to listen to whatever she was going to spill.

"You have to admit, I have reason to be thrown for a loop here. I mean, Cord is on the basketball team. He's a starter. He's at the top, and here you are, some little girl that waltzes into his house. He doesn't say a word to me about who you are. He doesn't explain anything. Cord doesn't do that. Ever. Not even with me, he doesn't do that stuff. But you're someone important to him, obviously. I mean, he's helping you move in. He wouldn't even help me move in, and he's done most of the work for you, some freshman. Who the hell are you?"

I whipped around and snapped, fed up, "Ever thought that

I'm none of your business? Maybe that's why he hasn't 'explained' me to you? It's none of your business."

She jerked to her feet. Her eyes flashed in anger. "Are you kidding me? Anyone that's connected to Cord is my business. He's my boyfriend—"

"Chandra!"

I didn't register the tone, but I looked up, expecting Kara. I saw another golden beauty instead. This one was even more stunning than Kara. What was it with this school and all the blondes? Kara's hair had been platinum blonde, but this one was a golden wheat color. Her hair fell down to her waist and she was dressed in similar clothes, with white khaki shorts and a blue polo instead. The material clung to her like a second skin, but it wasn't tight. It fit her perfectly.

I wasn't ready for all these girls. Even Chandra was beautiful, though hers was more from her makeup and tanned skin.

All of them looked like sisters.

"Tiff, what are you doing here?" Chandra stumbled over her words.

The girl's eyes narrowed before they rested on me.

I felt branded. She had scorched me with some meaning behind her gaze. I wasn't sure what it was, but my skin crawled from it. She didn't have a good opinion of me. That much I knew, but I had no idea why. She didn't know a damn thing about me. My chin lifted. My shoulders rolled back, and I rose to my highest height. For some reason, I didn't like this girl, and she didn't like me.

She murmured to her friend, but her eyes hadn't thawed as she stared at me, "I came to check on Kara and see if she needed help with any of the girls. What are you doing here?"

Chandra moved around me to her friend's side. She gestured to me. "This girl walked in on me and Cord. I was upset and came to cry on Kara's shoulder."

any frowned. "She walked in on you guys?" She scanned the room. "And she lives here?"

"Yeah." Chandra seemed miffed about that.

I had no idea why.

"That's . . . odd."

Her entire attitude toward me was odd. I glowered back at her. "Can you two please leave? I need to unpack."

"No, you don't." Cord swept an arm around each of the girls. He squeezed them together and lifted them from the doorway. Chandra squealed, delighted by the attention. The other girl's eyes widened, startled from the sudden movement. As he deposited them back down, away from my door, he motioned for me. He threw an arm around my shoulder. "Well, little Connors. It's been riveting. I'll be seeing you."

My mouth dropped. That was it?

"Where are you going, Cord?" Chandra spoke up.

He shrugged. "I'll call you later, Chandra. Family matters first."

"Family?" Tiff's tone sent chills down my back. Her eyes narrowed as she pierced through me. "Whose family, Cord?"

He stiffened next to me but forced a carefree chuckle out. "Not my secret to tell, Tiffany. See you later." He tapped my shoulder. "And you'll have a package arriving . . . tonight . . ." He scrunched up his nose then nodded to himself, and handed me my phone "Yeah, sounds right."

Before he could leave, Tiffany folded her arms over her chest and stepped forward. "We'll be seeing you tonight. Did you forget?"

"Oh yeah. Forgot about Jamie's thing."

"I'm coming over in an hour to start setting up."

Her tone sounded casual, but I felt like it was more of a warning. I wasn't sure if it was to me or Cord, but he lifted a hand before he shot down the back stairway. "Well, see you two in an hour then."

Chandra's smile relaxed, and she nodded. "Bye, Cord."

One gone. I looked back at the girls. Two more to go.

"How do you know Cord? You're not really his family, and what was he talking about, that he had to go and do something for family? He left you here." Tiffany spoke for the both of them. "Do you know the rest of the guys?"

I swallowed. This wasn't a girl I'd want to meet in a back alley, but then I paused. Who the hell was this girl? She hadn't been in my shoes. She didn't know anything about me and she had no right to intimidate me.

My chin lifted and I stepped close to her.

Her eyelids twitched.

Oh yes. Trying to intimidate me.

"What's your name?"

She frowned but grinned. "Tiffany Chatsworth. Look me up."

"Who are you related to?"

The grin slipped a notch. "None of your business."

"Who are you screwing?"

Her lips were pressed together. "Like I said, none of your effing business."

My eyes narrowed to slits. "Then who are you to ask about my business?"

She leaned closer, barely an inch away, and gave me a chilly smile. "I'm your nightmare. That's who I am."

"Tiffany!" Kara had come around the corner and skidded to a halt. Her eyes were wide and her mouth fell open. "Stop it. This girl is one of mine. It's my job to look out for her."

"Then you better start looking out for her." Tiffany stared her friend down. "Because she just pissed me off."

As she left, the other stayed behind. She'd been biting her lip the whole time but turned her eyes to the floor.

"Chandra? What the hell?"

She jerked a shoulder up. Her gaze never lifted. "The girl talked back to her. You know how Tiffany is."

Kara groaned, tipping her head back. She was hugging her clipboard to her chest. "This is great. Just great!"

3

The floor meeting was held in Kara's room. Since there were thirty girls, half of us were in the hallway as she went over the rules. Grant West was still privately funded, so there were rules, lots of them. Handouts were distributed, and after the sixth question, I slid down to the floor and rested my head against the wall.

We'd be there for a while. My only excitement was a text from Jesse, which turned out to not be exciting at all. He couldn't get away from wherever he was. I asked him where he was, but the response was vague.

Family thing.

A girl sat beside me, except she tucked her head and rested her forehead to her knees. It wasn't long before the snoring sounded. I wished I could've done that. I hadn't slept a full night in a long time. Right around the time my eyelids started to droop, Kara called for the last question, which she gave a short answer and then proclaimed, "All right, everyone. We're a little behind schedule. I wanted to take you to the cafeteria and show you how to get your card registered, but since it's after seven and the cafeteria is closed, I think a better alternative is pizza! Everyone up for that?"

A collective cheer went through the group.

Not me. Pizza was good, but I didn't want to spend any more time with people.

"You think we can ditch?" The girl beside me had woken.

I was tempted to go with her, wherever she wanted.

As we stood and the girls emptied from Kara's room, the resident advisor pulled her door shut and locked it. As she did, surprise came over her again. "Beth, I had no idea you were on my floor."

She wasn't looking at me. I turned my head.

"Hi, Kara." Ditching Girl gave her a halfhearted waved. As her arm lifted, the leather bracelets around her wrist slid down, but they didn't go far. Her entire arm was covered with them. They had an inch until her elbow stopped them. As her wrist was bared, I saw a small tattoo of interloping circles.

"That's wonderful." Kara's delight doubled when she saw me next to her. "You two should be friends."

"Huh?" Beth glanced at me. "Why?"

"Um. Just . . ." She bit her lip. "Just cause. I think it'd be really great. Is Hannah coming over tonight? You could invite her to pizza?"

Whoa. The turn of events had me dizzy. Who was Hannah, and why was she pushing this friendship? Though, I had to admit, this girl was the first in a while that I hadn't minded sitting next to. That didn't mean I wanted to be friends with her.

Still. I was curious. "Who's Hannah?"

"No one." Beth threw me a scowl.

Kara jumped next to her side but realized all the girls were still waiting in the hallway. She motioned toward the doors. "Go ahead, girls. The pizza will be here shortly. I reserved the downstairs lobby until ten tonight anyway."

A few grumbled as they headed down. I stayed behind. Something was going on, and I knew it had to do with me and Hell Bitch from before.

Kara turned back, biting her lip and wringing her hands together. She seemed to be eyeing me up and down, measuring for something, but she switched to Beth. "Call Hannah. Be friends with this girl."

Then she flounced away, hurrying after the rest.

I shifted back to my heel and reassessed this girl. Dressed in baggy jeans, a black tee shirt with a rock band on the front, and she had a lip ring—make that an eyebrow ring as well, she didn't seem like any sort of help against Hell Bitch.

"Who is this Hannah, and why does she want our friendship so bad?"

Beth shrugged as she bent to grab a backpack. Glass clinked together inside, but she put her arm through one of the straps and slung it over, uncaring about whatever was fragile inside. She flipped her straight brown hair over her shoulder. As she did, I caught another small tattoo of a hummingbird behind her ear. "No idea. And Hannah would not come to something like this."

"Still." There had to be a reason. "Who is Hannah to you?"

"She's my cousin." She grew suspicious. "Why?"

"Because when someone throws a girl at me and commands our friendship, I want to know why," I snapped.

"Oh." The suspicion melted away. "That makes sense. I'd want to know, too."

"You're not curious why?"

Checking her pockets, she started toward the stairs. I fell in step beside her and heard her say, "When it comes to Kara and her friends, I don't really give a damn. They're too loony and pretentious for my liking."

"Wait." My arm caught hers. I hauled her to a stop on top of the stairs. "You said Kara and her friends?"

She rolled her dark eyes. "Yeah, I know Kara because she's best friends with my other cousin."

My heart began pounding. I already knew where this was going. "Who is that?"

"You don't want to know her. Trust me."

I think I already do. "No, really. Tell me."

"Tiffany, she's Hannah's older sister."

Bingo.

I knew there'd been a reason. "So you're best friends with Hannah, who is sisters with Tiffany? I'm confused."

"Join the club." She shrugged again and started down the floors. When we would've veered to the left and kept going to the basement lobby, she went to the right.

I paused. For some reason, this seemed important for me to know. I hated to admit it, but Beth wasn't hard company.

She jerked a thumb over her shoulder. "If you want to, we're going to Club T."

"What's Club T?"

She flashed a grin, and it transformed her face. Beth had seemed moody and withdrawn, but with the slight curve of her lips, she was animated. Most guys would consider her plain-looking, but in that moment, I thought she was radiant. She laughed at me. "Come and find out. Hannah's driving."

I didn't need any more incentive. I was out the door in two heartbeats.

A red Camaro was waiting for us with yet another blonde bombshell behind the wheel. She never grinned, waved, flipped us off . . . nothing. Her aviators hid most of her face and her lips never moved an inch. She only spoke to Beth as I crawled into the backseat, and her cousin took the front, "Who is this?"

"Um." Beth glanced at me before she settled into her seat. "A friend. Let's go."

She gunned the Camaro and off we went. I was thrown back by the force of it, but I didn't mind. The girl was thin like her sister, but she was tanner. Her hair held red streaks among the golden blonde of it, and a tattoo was on the underside of her forearm. It was in another language, but in simple and tiny letters. While her sister had been dressed like she was attending tennis classes at the White House, this girl wore tattered jean shorts and a black top that stuck to her.

Beth frowned at me once more before her cousin turned the radio up and the two talked the rest of what ended up being a thirty-minute drive. She pulled into a parking lot outside a warehouse. The tall building, which was built from tin, was decorated with nothing. A lone black sign hung over the side entrance. A guy clad in black was smack dab in front of the door, glaring at the line of people waiting to get in.

"Oh, hell no. This ain't happening."

Hannah parked the car and was out in record time. Beth caught my arm, holding me back, and we watched as she sauntered toward the bouncer. She pressed her chest against his and arched her back. One of her legs lifted in the air, all the while she was smiling and cooing into his ear.

"What is she doing?"

Beth shook her head. "She's getting us in. That guy is new. Hannah's been coming here for three years. She doesn't like change."

Three years?

"How old is she?"

"She's a sophomore this year, but we came to visit Tiffany when we were in high school and she was a freshman at Grant West."

"So Tiffany's a junior?"

"Yeah." Beth couldn't stop grinning as she watched her cousin in action.

I had to admit. I was impressed. She was stroking his arm, putting her boobs on display, and even puckering her lips. Oh yes. This girl knew how to work guys and every movement promised them so much more.

Finally, the guy grinned with lust as he ran a hand over her bottom lip. Then he nodded and stepped aside.

Her eyes lit up in triumph, and she glanced at us.

"Come on." Beth grabbed my arm and pulled me after her.

We hurried through before the guy changed his mind.

When we got inside, it was one large room with a frenzied mass. People gyrated, ground together, did all sorts of dancing to the band on the stage. Some of them wore clothes that lit up like Christmas trees. As we fought our way to the bar, I was entertained by a girl who extended the lights to her hair and neck. She wore eyelashes that glowed in the dark. When she caught my eye and saw that I was studying her, she pressed a hand against her cheek, and then touched it to mine.

Beth grinned. She saw the exchange and leaned into my ear, "You have a glowing rose on your cheek now."

I nodded, happy for some reason.

The girl pressed a kiss to my cheek and lifted her hand to the bartender. After she got her drinks, she turned and disappeared again.

Two glasses were pushed our way. The bartender leaned close over the bar with his elbow braced on it. "That girl paid for your drinks."

I was floored by the generosity, but Beth grunted and flashed a wad of cash. The bartender nodded, and she was given a tray of drinks instead. She added the free ones to it and lifted it high above the heads as we moved out of the crowd. When we got to the edge, she lowered the tray and hollered in my ear, "The girl seemed fine, but don't accept any more drinks from anyone. I like this place, don't get me wrong, but don't be stupid at the same time."

I hollered back in her ear, "Where's your cousin?"

She gestured to the dance floor.

And yep, there she was. She had an arm around some guy who was grinding against her hips. Hannah pressed her chest against the guy's, and he dropped his head to her neck. When she gasped, I turned back to Beth. "You think she's coming back for these drinks?"

Beth laughed. "Maybe. They're for all of us, help yourself."

"What?"

She found a table in the back section and placed the tray on it before setting her bag the chair beside mine. "Have yourself some fun. I'll be back." And with that announcement, she vanished into the crowd.

I was left alone with a tray of drinks and a backpack.

Wonderful.

I didn't even like to drink.

I didn't see either of the girls for a while, but I couldn't really fault them. I didn't know them, so I settled back against the wall, kept the tray in front of me, and watched the people. When it was nearing midnight, Beth returned. Her hair was sweaty and slicked back from her face. Her face was red. When I saw the hickey on the side of her neck, I didn't ask what she'd been doing. I hadn't seen her on the dance floor.

"Did you have fun?" She hopped onto the stool across from me and yelled over the table.

I indicated the tray, still full with the drinks. "Loads."

"Sorry."

She didn't look it.

She started searching the dance floor. "A lot of my friends come here. It's an underground club."

I had gathered.

She kept going, "I'm a big band junkie, and these guys are one of my favorites."

"What's their name?"

"Do Cocktails."

"Nice name."

"Yeah." She flashed me a grin. Her eyes were glazed over and the smile was sloppy. I wondered if she'd been doing more than drinking, but I didn't ask. It wasn't my business, and it wasn't my place to judge. A yawn came over her, and she fought it off before leaning closer. "Listen, you want to leave? I'll call a cab for us."

"What about your cousin?"

She shrugged. "She's with that guy. Don't worry. She's been with him before."

Duly noted. I nodded. "Okay. Sure."

She pulled out her phone. After she called for the cab, she yelled again, "It'll be about twenty minutes."

"They know this place?"

"Oh yeah. All the cab companies do. Sometimes they don't even charge, but we'll get charged tonight."

"Why's that?"

She gestured to me. "Because of you."

Me? I looked down. Why me?

"You look rich."

"I do?" I only wore jeans and a gray shirt. There wasn't anything special about my outfit and I never wore makeup.

"Yep. You might think you're being simple, but I can tell you've got money." When she saw that I was dumbfounded, she waved it away. "Don't worry. Kara and Tiffany are like that, too. They try to look like that, though. You just exude it or whatever."

I wasn't sure how to take that. I didn't want to be like either of them.

Beth's phone lit up and she hopped off the stool. "Come on, cab's here. That was a lot quicker than I thought."

She led the way, weaving through the crowd. When we neared the door, I saw her cousin not far. She was being pressed against the wall by a different guy. His tongue was inside her mouth, and his hand was underneath her bra.

I tapped Beth on the shoulder and pointed. "It's a new guy, and your cousin lost her shirt."

She grinned, not the reaction I was expecting. We both

watched as the guy started to undo her jeans and slide them down.

My eyes bulged out. They were going to have sex, right there, in front of everyone. My hand wrapped around Beth's arm. "Stop them."

"Why?" She shrugged. "That's why she came."

From a different tone in her voice, I edged back a step and gave her another more measuring look. "Is that why you came here?"

She could've gotten mad. She didn't. Another jerk of the shoulder as she mused, sounding bored, "I don't do it in public. Hannah doesn't give a shit. She will in a few months, but she doesn't care right now."

This was not what I expected from a night at the club, and I would have put money on Kara not knowing about any of this.

"Come on." Beth tugged me out the door.

A cab was waiting for us, and she darted into the back door as another group started toward it. They stopped but moved closer again when she left the door open. Her head popped out, and she shouted at me, "I'm sharing with her." She pointed at me. "Not you guys."

"Oh," one of the guys groaned, but their entire group stopped.

As I hurried past them and climbed inside, the cab started forward. It was cold in contrast to the club that had been over-heated with human bodies. Beth started to shiver, and the cab filled with the smell of sweat quickly dissipating.

As her teeth began chattering, she looked at me. "Don't start doing that."

I looked over, but I didn't ask what she meant.

"Don't start judging us." Wrapping her arms around herself, she started to shake. "I know what you're thinking, that we're some sluts or something. We're not. You don't know why we do that, or even what we're doing."

She was right. As she said that, in the back of our cab, a deep

loneliness filtered inside me. People judged me. They became
scared of me because a part of me died after that letter. That
damn letter.

My phone buzzed. It was a text from Jesse.

**Jesse: U at ur room? Sorry, took longer than I thought. Can I
come over? Cord told me how to sneak in back.**

Me: Yes, will be there in twenty minutes.

Jesse: K.

A shiver went through me, but it wasn't from the coldness, or
even the loneliness. I was sitting in the back of this cab with
someone I didn't know but who had managed to scold me. I
wasn't a judgmental person, but I had been with her. I had been
judgmental with Hanna, too. She was right. What they did was
none of my business. It wasn't until I grew to know them and
understand their situations. Then it would come from caring,
and I didn't care about them.

I held my phone tightly. I couldn't let it go.

Someone that I thought had stopped caring still did. I was
going to see him soon, and like Beth's sentiment, I hoped he
didn't judge me. He would learn, at some point, that my parents
had abandoned me. They lost their son, and I was no longer good
enough for them. Instead of forgiving me and taking me as I was,
they chose to start a new life. There was no room for me in
their plan.

I drew in a breath. Pain blasted me, tightening my chest.

I didn't know what I would do if Jesse saw the same defect in
me as my parents did, if he walked away as they had.

I sent a furtive look beside me. For some reason, the cab
wasn't as lonely as before.

4

I hadn't been in my room long when I heard his knock.
A rush went through me. He was here. He was on the other side of the door. As I opened it, he ducked inside. There were rules against having boys in our rooms, but I didn't care. Not at that moment, not as I was drinking him in.

Jesse flashed me a grin as he ran a hand through his hair.

I murmured, "Your hair looks good."

"Hmm, yeah." He grimaced. "I was tired of the faux hawk. Told the girl to buzz it as close as she could."

"You look good." And he did. I chewed on my lip as I looked him up and down. He was leaner. Cord hadn't been the only one working out. Jesse had muscles showing in places he hadn't a year ago. Even as his wrist twitched, a small muscle stood out on his arm, one that I never would've known was there last fall.

He looked really good. I licked my lips. Damn good.

He smirked. "You checking me out, Connors?"

My chin went up, and I narrowed my eyes at him. He was doing the same thing. Suddenly, I was glad that I had changed clothes. I hadn't had the intention to dress for him, but I wore a tank top and lightweight scrub pants. They fell low on my hip

and were tied in a loose knot. I became very aware that I wasn't
wearing a bra and my underwear's strap was visible above my
scrub's waistband.

"You approve?" I murmured, my voice husky with desire. It
had been stirring since his text, simmering, but it was boiling as
soon as I heard his knock on the door. It was a full fire when he
stepped inside.

His eyes centered on my hand.

I lifted it and saw the small burn on the inside of my wrist. It
was from that night when I lit my parent's letter on fire. I hadn't
let go of the last piece quick enough and I hadn't felt the pain so it
went untreated for a while. No one had been around enough to
notice it. As Jesse stepped close and touched my arm, he lifted it
for inspection.

I bit into the inside of my cheek. What would he think? I
already knew I couldn't give him the answers to any questions. I
didn't want him to know, not yet, not on the first night.

Slowly, I eased my arm out of his hold and crossed to my
desk. "I met some of your friends today."

His head bobbed forward. "Mmmm."

My shoulders dropped. He had let it go. Relief had me
sagging against my desk, but I got myself under control. A grin
came over me, but I knew it was half of one. I was still reeling that
he hadn't asked about the burn. "Oh, come on. Chandra, Tiffany,
Kara. I think I should nominate them for a Good Samaritan
Award. Do you guys have that here?"

The corner of his mouth curved up. "Yeah, maybe Kara. Cord
mentioned that you and Tiffany didn't seem to care for
each other."

"Please tell me you're not best friends with her or screwing
her behind your buddy's back. I don't think I could look at you
the same." It came out as a joke, but I wasn't teasing. I meant it.

The other corner of his mouth curved up. "No, but she's
protective of me."

"Great."

He stepped toward me. His voice softened, "She's not you, Alex. Cord's not Ethan. Don't get confused about that. No one can touch either of you guys."

My chest swelled with emotion. He moved another step closer, and my hand lifted to rest on his chest. His heart was pounding, and his gaze seared into me. There was no humor, only dark promises, swirling in his depths, mixing with the same lust pounding inside me.

I asked, feeling raw, "You promise?"

His hand touched my pants. He tucked his thumb inside the band and pulled me against him. Closing my eyes, I felt him. I felt every inch of him. Then his thumb moved to the front of my pants and slipped farther inside. His entire hand went underneath my underwear until I felt him at my entrance. My legs wanted to press together, but I willed them to stay still. I didn't move to give him better access. I couldn't do anything except keep still and stop myself from launching into his arms. My heart was a continuous thunder and I already knew I was wet for him.

His finger dipped inside. I gasped. My head hit his chest as I concentrated on breathing. In and out. In and out.

I clutched on to his shirt. My legs threatened to buckle, but I couldn't do anything. Pleasure rippled through me from the sensations he was building. "Jesse."

He ducked his head down to rest his forehead on my shoulder, and then he turned and kissed my bare nape.

I shook my head, struggling to form a thought as a second finger slipped inside.

Kissing down the side of my neck, he nuzzled under my chin before he started up the other side. His other hand gripped my hip, anchoring me against him.

The edge was nearing. He kept pumping faster, holding himself still against me. When he stopped kissing me, I felt his breathing grow labored as he continued to rest his forehead on my shoulder. My head fell back and my eyes were heavy-lidded, but I saw him from underneath my eyelashes. He was watching us. He was watching as his hand moved against me and the way his fingers kept thrusting into me.

Then I felt myself hurdling over it, and I exploded for him. I trembled against him, but he didn't relent. He kept his fingers in me but pressed his forehead against my neck. A sheen of perspiration had built up. I felt the moisture, and then his lips curved against my skin. He pressed them to me in a soft and lingering kiss as he withdrew his fingers.

A moan escaped from between my erratic breaths. A flush of renewed heat flared through me and lit up my face. As he began to pull his hand away from me, my legs squeezed together. I felt empty. I didn't want him to leave, but he tilted my head to meet his gaze with his free hand. His eyes had darkened until they were black with lust.

Cupping my head with his hand, he ran his thumb over my lips. When it settled between them, my lips parted and my tongue darted out to brush against him.

His eyes fell to my mouth, watching as my tongue sweep against him again and then tasted the end of his finger, he stepped closer. He crowded me against the door. We hit it with a thud, but it didn't stop us. I scrambled to lift his shirt, which he yanked over his head before he shoved my pants down and ripped off my shirt. When they were on the ground, he hoisted me up underneath my arms and carried me to the bed.

When he lowered me to it and held himself above me, he looked at me for a long moment. He seemed to be absorbing every inch of me. I felt ready to burst and reached for him to pull him down.

He blocked my hand and shook his head, a small grin appearing as he held it down on the bed. He positioned my other one above my head, pinning me beneath him.

He still continued to study every inch of me.

"Jesse," I rasped out. I tried bucking my hips up to touch against his, but his grin only grew wider.

"It's been too damn long, Alex. I'm going to make this last a long time."

The throbbing burst inside me again. I gasped out, huskily, "Touch me, dammit."

Then he bent over me, and I closed my eyes.

Knock, knock

"Jess—" I started again, but then the door started to open, and I heard instead, "Alex, I thought I heard some—oh!" It was slammed shut. The sound echoed in my head. Everyone had heard. Everyone would wake up and come to see what had happened.

Then my eyelids lifted. What had just happened?

Jesse had frozen on top of me with his head turned to the door. In slow motion, he turned to look at me. "Some girl came in here."

"Really?" I rolled my eyes, frustrated and pissed about the whole thing. "No shit, Jesse." Shoving against his shoulders, I groaned, "Get off."

He sat on the edge of the bed.

When he made no move to put his shirt back on, I scrambled off the bed and threw it to him. At the same time, I threw mine on and hopped around as I tried to pull my pants up, as quickly as possible. When I was dressed, I bolted out of the door. I figured someone would be milling around, looking for where that door slam had come from, but I came to a halt instead.

Nothing.

The lights were still low. The doors were all closed.

Then the bathroom door was opened and light flooded the hallway before it swung shut again.

Beth strolled back to me with a caddie in hand. She was in a robe and a towel. She saw me and grinned. "I thought you were in bed."

I paused, dissecting her question for a hidden meaning.

I wanted to slap myself. Get it over with. "You saw?"

The grin widened, and she nodded, a sparkle came to her eyes. "Oh yeah. I saw. And I know who that is."

"You can't say anything."

She snorted. "Like hell. You were with Jesse Hunt. Is he still in there? Does Kara know? Is that why she said we should be friends?"

My head dropped, and I wanted to crumble to the floor. "You can't say anything. Please, Beth. That would be horrible for me."

The realization of who Jesse was on the campus and how many knew him was settling in.

I felt like smacking myself in the forehead. Going to his house before had been a horrible idea. I wanted to demand answers about Ethan's death, but if someone else had been there and not just Chandra . . . I gulped. It could've been bad. Really bad. I was starting to think the best way to start life as a student at Grant West was for no one to know about our relationship.

Goodness.

Our relationship.

What was our relationship?

Images of him above me flashed in my head and lust sparked again. My throat went dry, and I knew he was in my room still, waiting for me. What the hell was I doing?

"You okay?" Beth was watching me, a look of concern pulling at her brow. "Don't worry. I won't say anything. I was just playing with you. Sucks to be on the receiving end, huh?"

I nodded. It did. It really did. I shook away the desire and any remaining terror. "You won't say anything?"

"No, but I think it's cool you know Jesse Hunt. It'll be nice to see Tiffany knocked down a peg. Finally." She started back toward our hallway, and I fell in step beside her.

"What do you mean?" Different type of dread formed.

She stopped again before glancing in the direction of my room. "Is he still in there?"

I jerked my head in a nod. My limbs felt like lead.

She touched my arm and tugged me back closer to the bathroom. Lowering her voice, she said, "Tiffany's dating Jamie Striker. Do you know who that is?"

I frowned. "Just that Cord laughed at me when I asked about him. I have no idea why."

"Well," she searched for her words, "let's just say that Jamie's not the brightest bulb in the group, or the nicest, or the one with morals. Okay. Jamie doesn't really have any morals."

"What does this have to do with Tiffany and Jesse?"

"I don't know. Hannah's sick of her attitude, but I think Tiffany mothers Jamie and so that goes to the rest of the guys, too. She'd try with Derek and Cord if they didn't have girlfriends."

"Cord doesn't have a girlfriend." At least not that he would admit to.

"Trust me. He is taken. Chandra's been working him since they were freshman."

"How do you know all this?"

"I grew up with them, duh."

"Oh."

She grimaced then and rolled her eyes. "Look, I'm sorry. When I say that I grew up with them, I mean in their house. My mom left me with them when I was eleven, and I've been living with them ever since."

"Oh." I could relate.

The scowl flared back. "Don't feel sorry for me. Hannah's mom is wonderful. Trust me, I got the better end of the deal."

I scowled back. "Relax. You were dumped by a parent. I understand." My hands went up in surrender. "That's all I meant. You're a bit touchy, you know."

The scowl lessened but didn't completely vanish. "So, yeah. I know all about The Selects."

"The what?"

She waved a hand in the air, as if the answer should have been obvious. "That's what Tiffany calls them, The Select, since they're all on the—"

"It made sense. I just think it's stupid."

"Me, too." A grin lifted the corners of her mouth and her eyes warmed. "And she thinks she's Grant West royalty."

"Why does she think that? Because she's dating this Striker guy?"

"It's because she's been Homecoming Queen every year she's been here."

"Are you serious?"

"Yep."

"That sucks." I was starting to think Ethan had horrible taste with his college choices. I should've thought this through more, but then I remembered this was the only school where I had an academic scholarship. At the time, I hadn't thought I had money to even go to school, so I never considered a different school.

Like you were going anywhere that Jesse wasn't? Be real.

I frowned at the nagging voice, but it was right. I sighed as I was starting to get a better picture on my new life. Jesse was still at the top and there were a bunch of prissy bitches surrounding him. The only problem was that they didn't know about me, and I didn't know if I wanted them to know. Keeping it a secret had its benefits, but they already knew I was "family" to Cord. I wanted to scream from frustration.

There'd been a brief hope of starting over again and living a life as a nobody, which hadn't lasted long at all.

We went back and parted at our doors. When I went inside, Jesse was gone. In his place was a note on top of my cell.

Cord arrested, snuck out. Call later.

It was like Homecoming all over again.

5

I got to my political science class early on the first day of classes. Sunday was spent moving in, Monday was the day for making sure everything was ready to go, and it was now Tuesday. My first class was at eight thirty, but I showed up at eight. It wasn't that I was nervous. I think it was that I was bored. I hadn't slept well and was up early so I got dressed and headed out. After grabbing a bagel and coffee, I found the classroom and took the seat farthest in the back. As others started to trickle in, I put my bag in the chair beside me. I wasn't feeling social.

No one minded.

They trailed in and sat by themselves. A few girls came together and took the row in front of me. At eight twenty-nine, I slumped down in my chair and rested my head against the wall behind me. Closing my eyes, I could've fallen asleep. I was hidden in my back corner, but then I heard something that had my eyes wide open again.

One of the girls whispered in her friend's ear in front of me, "That's Cord Tatum and Jamie Striker. I heard they might take this class, so glad we took it now."

The friend giggled, whispering back, "Super HOT!"

"Jenna was with Jamie at the Kappa party last Friday night."

"Really? Isn't he dating—"

The first one nodded, her excitement was barely contained. "Tiffany Chatsworth. Sucks to be her, huh? He's the biggest manwhore on the team."

"Bad for her. Good for us."

The two shared a knowing grin. Then the first one leaned closer. "I heard they're having a party next Friday. I'm going to try to talk to Jamie after class; maybe we can get an invite."

"We need an invite? We can't just go?"

She rolled her eyes, flicking her hair over her shoulder. "It's at Jesse Hunt's house. You have to have an invite to even know where it is. No one knows where it is unless you're in their circle. I heard his daddy bought him a new mansion."

The friend groaned, giggling at the same time. "Jesse Hunt. Oh my God! Is he going to be there?"

The other one shrugged. "Don't know. I heard he's anti-social. You have better chances trying for Cord."

"Why Cord? Jesse Hunt is way hotter."

The first one blinded her with a smile. "Because I'm going for Jamie. And trust me, Jesse Hunt is out of our league."

"What about Tiffany?"

"Who cares?" She shook her head, a look of disgust flashing over her. "She's a bitch. She needs to be taken down a notch."

Then the third friend leaned over. "Would you two shut up? Everyone can hear you."

"Sorry," one whispered.

"Sorry," the other hissed, but neither looked all that sorry.

I wanted to groan. Cord was in my class. Nothing against Cord, but I hadn't told him about my hope to be anonymous. It hadn't mattered over the last two days. Jesse hadn't texted or called. I hadn't cared. For real. After he left, my head had swollen with questions and doubts.

I didn't know if I wanted a real relationship. And if he did, I had no idea. Jesse wasn't the committed type. It was why I had stopped our arrangement in the first place, but then he was in my dorm room. He hadn't ignored my calls on purpose, and there was no big secret about his phone call to Ethan that night.

All control fled when he was close, but he hadn't been close since, and my sense of reason was back.

I could not do a relationship. No way.

I was barely able to stand saying hello to Beth the past couple days. Kara had been sickeningly sweet when she saw me in the bathroom. She wanted to know if I had hung out with Beth and Hannah, but my mouth had been full of toothpaste. I used that to my advantage and shrugged, unable to talk. She'd been nice and waited until I spit it out and then rinsed my mouth. I hadn't been so nice. I gave her a polite smile and walked out of the bathroom.

I didn't need anyone knowing my business.

Hurt flared in her eyes, but that didn't stop me from snubbing her. She was better off. That was what I told myself, and the next time I saw her, she didn't try again.

An unnamed emotion burned low in my gut, but we were both better off. She hadn't asked how I knew Cord, and I hoped she would let that go as well. No one needed to know any of that information. And certainly not these three girls who sat in front of me.

I tried to slump farther down in my seat, but to no avail, I could see Cord and a taller guy who looked like he could've been a poster boy for any Ivy League school follow behind him. He was tall and built with wavy blond hair, dark eyes, and a smirk plastered over his thick jaw. He knew they were the center of attention, and he loved it.

They approached the back of the classroom. The girls in front of me bristled from excitement. Their eyes were glued to the guys as they trekked all the way to the back to where I was.

The first girl drew in her breath. The second one nudged her friend.

They were openly staring as their heads followed the guys until they were almost completely turned around in their seats.

Oh God.

I closed my eyes. My gut fell to the floor, and I looked up. Cord was grinning at me across the three empty seats. His friend seemed annoyed, shifting on his feet behind him.

"Little Connors." A big smirk came over Cord's face.

The same cockiness had been with him the night he told Marissa to get lost. I bristled with irritation. No way was he going to treat me the same way, even though he had been nice to me on Sunday.

I scowled at my bag. "The seat's taken."

His smirk deepened, and he gestured to the two empty seats next to it. "These too?"

"Yep."

"Alex, come on."

"I have friends coming."

"We're the last ones in, and there are no other seats." He flashed me two dimples. "Sorry, Little Connors, you're shit out of luck. We're sitting here."

"Come on, man." His friend was growing restless. "Let's sit already. Since when do we have to chat about it?" He shot me a dark look. "Who's the chick? Never mind. Sit down, Cord."

The decision was made.

Cord's bag landed on the seat with mine, and he took the closest seat. Our bags were between us, but he leaned over and asked in a quiet voice, "Why you got a stick up your ass? I thought after Sunday night, you'd be happy to see us."

I glared at him.

His friend snickered. "That's what I thought."

Cord ignored him and asked me, "You embarrassed to be seen with me, Little Connors?"

"Stop calling me that," I hissed. I was fully aware of the attention we were receiving. All three girls were blatantly eavesdropping on our conversation. Not that they needed to strain to hear. Cord wasn't quieting his voice. "And stop insinuating we slept together."

"Hmmm." Cord's dimples appeared again. Oh, yes, he was enjoying himself.

"I mean it. It's like we don't know each other, okay?" I wanted to smack my forehead. I had just made it worse. Judging by the smug looks, the girls were certain we had done the deed. The one who wanted Cord not so discreetly turned toward me, measuring me up and down.

I glared at her. "Eyes up front."

Her mouth gasped open, but she turned quickly in her seat. The third friend's shoulders were shaking in silent laughter.

"Were you left unsatisfied Sunday night?" Cord mused. Lounging back, he rested his arm across the back of the seat between us. "Are you mad at me?"

"Yes, Cord. You left me unsatisfied Sunday night. May the decree officially be announced that you didn't measure up."

His eyebrows furrowed together. "Well, I wouldn't put it that way."

"Nope. We should air this out, you know, so other girls have been warned ahead of time. My time with my lover was cut short. A guest arrived, prematurely, if you're getting my drift. Its arrival came early."

His eyebrows shot high, and his arm dropped from the chair, but then he caught himself and chuckled. Shaking his head at me, he put his arm back on the seat. He looked ready with a retort when his friend checked into the conversation. "Dude, you were in jail Sunday night. When'd you hook up with her?"

"He didn't," I snapped at him. "That's my whole point."

The friend glared back. "Sounds like you need to get laid to me. You're a bitch."

"Jamie." Cord gave him a pointed look. "You don't know who she is."

"Yeah, but—"

"You don't know who she is. Watch your tone."

He reared back. "Are you kidding me? She's just some—"

"No, she's not," Cord cut him off again. "I was just giving her a hard time. Relax."

"She was being a bitch to you. Just saying, that's not cool." His friend leaned back in his chair with a slight glower. He grumbled, "Since when do you let chicks talk to you like that?"

"I was baiting her on purpose. She lashed back. It's my fault."

Hearing this, I sat back and had to reanalyze Cord again. This was the same Cord from Sunday, when he'd been nice and helped me move in. This wasn't the old Cord from when he had thrown aside Marissa after their first hook up. I kept quiet since I had no intention of asking. It was interesting to see the change, though.

Cord dropped his arm and leaned close. This time he lowered his voice so the girls couldn't overhear him, "You pissed that Jesse hasn't called? He's got stuff going on right now. I don't know if he told you that."

I shrugged. "I don't care."

Yes, you do.

Ignoring that nagging voice in my head, I scowled at him. "Just do me a favor. Pretend we don't know each other. I don't want the extra attention, you know?"

His eyes narrowed.

I stiffened, feeling the weight of his measuring gaze, but then he nodded. "Sure." A ball of tension loosened in my gut, and I lounged back in my chair again. The professor had started roll call. Cord was true to his word. He dropped the teasing, and it was as if we never knew each other. The only time he violated this was at the end of class when the professor told us that we would need to form a group of three or four.

Cord latched on to my desk. "Partner up, Connors."

I glared. What was he doing?

Jamie had the same sentiment and glowered at me around Cord. He didn't argue.

The three girls had turned around, hoping to become a part of their group, but they stopped when he did that. I realized why he'd done it, and rolled my eyes at him. He shrugged, but gave the professor our names when the groups were recorded. It was then announced we'd be working with the same group throughout the semester on different projects. The first project was for introductions.

Screw that.

Class was dismissed and everyone stood to give phone numbers and e-mail addresses out. Not me. I grabbed my bag and darted past Cord and Douchebag for the door. I heard DB grumble behind me, "Dude, are you mental? That girl is crazy."

I didn't hear Cord's response. I was already out the door.

I had two more classes, and it was after two before I was done for the day. My stomach was rumbling since I'd skipped lunch so I wasn't late to my third class. When I headed to the food court, I spotted Beth and Hannah at a picnic table in the yard. They had books spread across it and Hannah was lying on her side while her cousin was hunched over a book on the other side.

I paused, wondering if I should go over or not, but Beth glanced up and saw me. She waved me over, and Hannah lifted her head to see who was coming. She squinted with a hand over her eyes, but dropped her head back down when she saw it was me.

Drawing closer, I nodded to Beth.

"You have another class?"

A line was forming outside of the cafeteria's doors, but I put my bag on the ground. "I'm done. I was going to grab some food and start studying."

Hannah groaned. "It's the first day. You two are nerds."

Beth shot her a dark look. "We are not. When you're failing all your classes before finals, don't come to me for help."

"Ugh," her cousin mumbled, scowling back as she sat up on her side and pulled a book in front of her. "Fine. Whatever. You suck."

A small grin teased the corners of her mouth, but then Beth rolled her eyes. She turned to me, "Take a seat."

Gesturing to the doors, I started toward them. "I'm going to grab some food. Be right back. Watch my bag?"

She nodded, turning back to her book already.

Hannah frowned at me before I turned all the way around. I couldn't see from the Aviators she was wearing, but I was sure she was studying me intently. I narrowed my eyes back at her, wondering the reason behind her sudden perusal. She hadn't given a damn whom I had been when we went to Club T. When I headed back with a salad, muffin, and water, both girls seemed to be reading again. Neither said a word when I sat, so I ate my food and pulled out one of my textbooks for my own head start.

"Hannah!" a sharp voice called out.

I checked my phone. We'd been there for an hour.

"Oh God," Hannah groaned. Her forehead went into her book. "Maybe she won't see me."

I fought against grinning, but then I didn't have to fight against it anymore.

Tiffany marched over to us with Chandra and Kara behind her.

The three of them struck a picture among the rest of the Grant West students. Royalty, I snuck a look at Beth. She had used that term before, but I hadn't seen it before that moment. These girls were beautiful, all of them.

When Tiffany saw who else was with her sister, her lips thinned, but she ignored me. "Hannah, you never called me back last night."

Hannah groaned in response, muffled from the book.

Kara glanced at me but turned away quickly.

I fought against biting my lip. That was not guilt rumbling in my stomach. That was my food. That was all.

Chandra stood behind their leader, ready for whatever was going to go down, but when she sent me a questioning glance, I knew it was bothering her about Cord. She still didn't know how I knew him. When Beth let out a small sigh, my attention was distracted. Tiffany stood at Hannah's head, glaring down, while her sister continued to ignore her. Beth's shoulders slumped and before she lowered her head back to her book, I caught the pain that flashed over her.

I straightened where I sat. That wasn't the sort of pain where she was being ignored or where she knew there was going to be a confrontation between the sisters. That was deep pain, the type that I felt stirring inside me as a response to seeing it. I chewed on the inside of my cheek, wondering what the hell had gone down in Beth's life for her to react like that.

Then I shook my head clear. What was I doing? I couldn't get involved.

"Hannah, I'm speaking to you!"

Her elbow rotated and her hand lifted in the air. The middle finger was extended next.

Beth and I both shared a look, each grinning.

"You're such a pain in my ass."

Hannah finally looked up, sunglasses still in place, and grunted, "Likewise, big pain-in-my-ass sister."

"You need to call me when you go out drinking. Mom was worried to death about you."

"Mom wasn't worried about me. Mom would've been cheering me on. You were worried, Tiffany. Stop putting your crap on other people." She gave her sister a nice eff-off grin. "I have no plans on reporting to you wherever I go, whenever I go, and whoever I do so get that out of your head. You didn't care last year. You don't need to now."

Tiffany's hands slid from her hips and her voice quieted,

"Hannah, I'm worried about you. Last year, you didn't have—"

She cut her off, "It's none of your business. Back off."

"I'm—"

Hannah shoved her book closed and swept it into her bag as she stood from the table. Pulling her bag onto her back, she was seething at her sister. "Stay out of my business. You do that, and we'll get along fine."

"But—" Tiffany glanced at Beth, who immediately dropped her eyes back to her book.

I frowned.

"And don't look at Beth. Unlike you, she's actually there for me and trying to support me."

"I'm trying to do that, too."

Hannah poked her sister in the chest, pushing her back a step. "No, you're not. You're trying to control me. Trust me. I feel back-doored up the ass every time you talk to me."

Her sister's mouth dropped open, and her friends moved away from the two. Tiffany sputtered, "But—Hannah, I don't—"

"You do." She silenced her with a look. "Do us both a favor and leave me alone. Focus all your energy on making sure Jamie doesn't cheat as much as he did last year."

Tiffany's face flamed, and her shoulders went rigid. Her jaw clenched, but before she could send a scathing retort, Hannah was gone. She jerked toward her cousin instead and clipped out, "Can you make sure she doesn't end up dead by the end of the semester? It's the least you could do."

Beth didn't respond.

When she realized she wasn't going to get a response, Tiffany turned to me instead.

I just held a hand up. "Don't even start. I'm not a punching bag for you."

She rolled eyes and muttered, "We'll see about that," before she left. Chandra and Kara both gazed at me in concern but followed a second later.

"What a bitch," came from beside me.

"Does she always talk to you like that?"

"More or less." Before I could reply, her shoulders went back and her chest rose. "I'm not weak to let her talk to me like that. I used to fight back, but it only made things worse between her and Hannah. If I don't respond to her, she always goes away and things aren't that bad between them."

They looked pretty damn bad to me. "Why are you telling me this?"

"Because I'm not weak."

"You are when it comes to Tiffany."

She had started to turn back to her book, but her eyes snapped back to mine. Anger morphed over her and she lashed back, "You don't know what you're talking about."

I shrugged, but I murmured, "I know enough to know that you're scared of your cousin." Before she could reply, I finished, "And we both know that's not Hannah. Does she remind you of your mother?"

Beth paled. "What did you just say?"

"Tiffany. She's like your mom, isn't she? That's why you don't fight back."

"Shut. Up."

I grabbed my book and my bag and stood before regarding her for a second. "I'm not judging. I was dumped by both my parents, so I get it. But Tiffany is not your mom. You can stand up for yourself against her. She's still here, and it doesn't look like she's going anywhere."

As she gulped, I gave her a small wave and left.

I hadn't minced my words, and I hadn't taken pity on her. That was what she'd been scared about, but that small voice whispered in my head, telling me that I was being a hypocrite.

You're scared, just like her.

I was, but I wasn't going to deal with my parents yet. I wasn't ready for that.

6

Jesse called two nights later. I checked the time and saw it was after eleven before I answered. "Hey."

"What are you doing?"

I glanced at my sneakers I was lacing up and my gym bag was already packed. I went to lay on my bed instead. "Nothing. You?"

"You want to do something?"

I grinned into the phone. "Is this my first official booty call in college?"

"No." I could hear his amusement. "Well, maybe later. Want to go somewhere with me?"

"Where?" I was tempted to tease him and ask if he was going to say his bedroom, but I stopped myself. There was exhaustion in his voice, and my Jesse senses were tingling. Something was up, probably whatever he'd been busy with all week.

"My buddy's in a band. Sometimes I go and listen to their practices."

"Sure."

"Okay. I'm outside your dorm right now."

"The back door?" I didn't wait for his answer. "I'll be down." I hurried to change my shorts into jeans. My shirt was off next, and I pulled a tank with a sweater over it. Slipping my feet into flats, I grabbed my purse and headed out. As I was locking my door, Kara was coming up the back stairwell with a tall guy behind her. He had brown hair, which was long enough to be teased with some curl, but not long enough to look shaggy. He had high cheekbones, almost as chiseled as Jesse's, and keen dark eyes. Their hands were interlocked, so I figured this was the boyfriend.

"Oh, hi!" Kara stopped. He stood just inside the doorway with a hand against it to keep from slamming into him. "This is my boyfriend, Derek. Derek, this is Alex. She . . . knows Cord."

An eyebrow went up, but he didn't comment on that. "Nice to meet you."

When he didn't extend a hand, I was relieved. "You, too. Be seeing you guys."

"Oh, wait." Kara stepped to the side, blocking me. Her smile never moved an inch. "I wanted to invite you to a picnic two weekends from now. Are you doing anything Saturday?"

Yes. I had such a busy life. "Studying?"

"You can't study all the time. The picnic is at Carver Park, eleven thirty. You don't need to bring anything."

"Who else is going to be there?" This sounded fishy to me.

Her smile was strained.

I knew it.

She answered, "Tiffany, Chandra, myself, and another girl, Elizabeth Ives are putting it on. There will be lots of guys, if you want to meet a guy. Oh, and I was going to invite Hannah and Beth, too. They have a Frisbee golf course, and I know some of the guys will probably put together a soccer game. Don't worry, there'll be other girls there. It's just for a fun afternoon at the park."

Derek seemed to frown a bit at the way she was blubbering on, but he didn't stop her.

"So do you think you'd come?"

"Oh. Uh. You think it's a good idea for Hannah to come if Tiffany's going to be there? They didn't seem to get along so well."

She waved that off. "They're always like that. There was another fight last night. So? Do you want to come?" Her eyes were animated as she waited for my answer.

I shrugged as I started to say, "Suu . . ." But I faded. I didn't want to go.

Kara didn't care. Her smile stretched from ear to ear. "Great! I'll come to your room at eleven fifteen. We can walk over together."

With a pat to my shoulder, she jerked her boyfriend from the doorway and past me. I was left unsettled when they disappeared into her room. When the lock clicked, I shook my head. I felt duped but went down the stairs and to the back door. I'd deal with that later.

I stepped outside and saw the black Ferrari, I was thankful Jesse had his windows tinted. There was a cluster of girls on two benches, which had been landscaped amidst foliage. They were eyeing the Ferrari. With a quick scan, I figured they were freshmen like me. Maybe they hadn't heard Jesse Hunt drove the same car. I was hoping.

As soon as I got in, he sped away. For some reason, I wasn't surprised to see he was wearing a black long-sleeved shirt and black pants. The shirt was snug on him. His arm muscles moved underneath, and it accentuated the cut of his shoulders. The warmth from before came back, mingling with lust.

Neither of us said a word. There was a comfortable silence, and I didn't want to break it. Closing my eyes, I leaned back and opened the window a bit. The wind raced against my face, calming my racing heart. Being there with him and not needing to fill the silence soothed an edge inside me.

My chest lifted up and down in a smooth rhythm.

When we were nearing the outskirts of town, he asked, "Are you hungry? Did you want some food?"

"I had old pizza. I'm good."

He nodded and wheeled the car onto the interstate. We were flying away from town with no end in sight. After we had driven thirty minutes, I felt Jesse's gaze on me. "What is it?"

He gave me a rueful grin. "Do you have an early class tomorrow?"

"Nope, those are Tuesdays and Thursdays. I have a ten o'clock class." Which I didn't mind skipping, it was psychology. My head couldn't take that stuff.

He nodded and went back to the road. "Good. It might be a long night."

I grinned to myself as I heard that. Pleasure spread through me and the steady boil went up another notch. This addiction to him was like a drug. I was intoxicated. He pumped adrenalin through me and made me feel as if I were living again.

My head went down. My eyes closed.

My chest filled with searing pain.

He was making me right again. I didn't know what would happen when this was done. Could I go back?

"What's wrong?"

I shook my head, unable to speak. Too many damn emotions were stirring in me. "Nothing. Are we almost there?"

"Yeah." He pointed to a small building in the middle of nowhere. "They call it 'The Shack,' but it's just a place they practice. Sometimes they'll have their friends come and listen and hang out."

"How did you meet these guys?"

Half of his mouth lifted up in a grin. "A bar. Okay. A dive bar in the wrong area of town. Luke and I were both having a drink when some guys picked a fight. We were sitting next to each other so both of us were pulled into it. Afterward, we shared a few more drinks. I was laying low; he was doing the same. We bonded." As he pulled into the gravel parking lot and slid to a stop, he laughed to himself. "These guys know sports, but they don't say anything. I can just be me."

Getting out, I grabbed my purse, but Jesse took it from me. He opened his trunk, tossed it in, and then took my hand in his. "You don't need that in here."

Which was code in Jesse's world for: please don't bring your phone. Little did he know that no one called me anymore. He'd been the only one in my history over the last week.

Loud music met us when we stepped inside, but it was dark. The only light was on the stage and pointed at a guy, who was singing into a microphone, leaning forward with it. He had a smooth tone that sounded like a caress to my ears. He was good. Jesse led me to a back table, and we sat side by side. He leaned back against the wall, and he pulled me against him with an arm curved around my waist. We sat there and listened longer, this band was really good.

When they switched to a different song, one that I recognized, I bolted upright and twisted around. "This is Sustain." Even I knew who these guys were, and I never paid attention, but this band had exploded a year ago. They'd been some of my only company the summer before I came to school. Jesse gave a small smile as he ran his thumb down the side of my cheek before pulling me back against him. Settling back in, his chest lifted as he took in a deep breath.

His hand fell back to mine and interlaced together.

A girl came over and nodded toward Jesse. "You here just to hang out? You want something to drink?"

"Water for me. You want something?" he asked me.

"Uh." I was battling against being star struck. These were normal guys, just like Jesse. Jesse was a normal guy. That last thought helped calm me down. They were normal, and they didn't know me. When I jerked my gaze from the stage to the girl, she was grinning. I wondered how often she dealt with girls like me. "Yeah. I'll have water, too."

"You guys sure? Luke stocked the refrigerator. We have more than enough."

"No, thanks." Jesse's voice sounded close to my ear, and I shivered. It was caressing. His arm shifted, pulling me tighter to him. "Thanks, Bri."

She nodded before she walked away with a sexy saunter to her hips.

I peeked to see if Jesse was watching, but his eyes were closed. His chest lifted back up in another deep breath. It was the first time I'd seen him this relaxed and awake at the same time in what felt like forever. He'd brought me along with him to this place. That meant something. I couldn't hide from that, but he had already told me that no one could mean to him what Ethan and I did.

As the band started another song, I blinked back tears.

Jesse was already doing this to me, and it was only been the second time I'd seen him. My parents had shattered me. I didn't need to go to therapy to know that they killed a part of me when I read that letter. Over the summer, I had survived. That'd been my only thought, to keep going, but since coming to school, things were better. A little bit better at least. With him, though, they were becoming more than a little bit. But with that new hope, new terror had begun to build with it.

He'd leave. They always left. What then?

I gripped on to his hand as if he were going to go right then and there.

What would I do?

When I wasn't with him, I was okay. I was broken, but functioning. I could do that and endure college like that. I'd be fine. And when that would stop, whatever it was . . . that searing pain rattled against my chest. It wanted to burst through every part of me, every cell in my body. I wasn't letting it. I pushed it away and then stopped thinking.

I'd take what I could get. Maybe enough of me would heal so that I wouldn't be completely shattered when he eventually left.

The band played for an hour. They'd stop and discuss sections of a song, then start over again as they implemented the new changes. It was fascinating to watch. We remained at our table without speaking. When Jesse's chest started to rise up and down at a steady rate, I knew he'd fallen asleep, but I didn't move away. Bri came over a few times and had a new water bottle for us. After the third time, I started to ease from Jesse's arm and stood. Bri was talking by the bar with a guy who was stocky and an inch shorter than she was, but he had a scar that ran across his entire face. It started at one corner of his forehead and ended underneath his chin on the other side. He saw me first and nodded in my direction. Bri turned around with a friendly smile. She looked around me, and her grin softened with fondness. She gestured to Jesse, "Is he sleeping?"

"Yeah." She wasn't surprised by that. "Does he do that a lot?"

She shrugged before she slipped behind the bar's counter. She reached underneath and pulled out a shot glass with a bottle of whiskey. Filling it up, she slid it toward the stocky guy. "Drink it, Emerson."

He hadn't looked particularly friendly before, but a small scowl appeared as I watched him. I glanced away. He was terrifying.

He growled at her, "Fuck off, Bri. I'm not drinking that shit."

Her eyes sparkled as a smile lit up her face. She poured another one for herself. "I'll take it with you. You lost the bet, fair and square. You have to drink."

He continued to scowl at the shot glass.

"It's not going to disappear unless you drink it." Bri winked at me behind her hand, and she held her own glass up. "Come on, you big baby. Luke said you were supposed to take five shots tonight. You've got some catching up to do."

"Luke can kiss my ass."

His statement would've only been heard by the two of us, but the music abruptly stopped right before. Everyone heard it, and the lead singer gripped his microphone. "You lost the bet, Emerson. Take your five fucking shots."

The drummer started a roll as he taunted into his microphone, "Em-er-son. Em-er-son. Em-er-son."

"You can kiss my ass, too, Braden," he shouted across the warehouse. "Screw all of you. I'm out of here."

The drummer changed his chant, "Hy-po-crite. Hy-po-crite. Hy-po-crite."

Emerson stalked toward the door and shoved outside.

"Your boy's awake." Bri handed the shot to me and nodded to the table I'd been sitting at. "He looks like he needs this more than Emerson did."

I wanted to ask her more questions, if Jesse did this a lot? When had he started? If they knew anything about him except his name? So many were burning in me, but I took the shot over to him and put it on the table. "That girl, Bri, said you looked like you needed this."

Jesse took the shot without argument.

"Hey!" The lead singer came over as I reclaimed my seat. He nodded to me in greeting, pulled a chair out, twirled it around, and straddled it. "I didn't see you come in."

Jesse grimaced. "Yeah, to get away. You know."

The guy nodded, slid his gaze to me, and held his hand out. "Luke Skeet."

I took his hand, which was firm and polite, nothing more. "Hi, Alex Connors."

He nodded, there was no recognition, no speculation, nothing. He turned back to Jesse, his gray eyes were alert. I felt slightly zapped by this guy's attention, and I could understand why so many girls had fallen in love with the lead singer to Sustain.

I glanced at Jesse underneath my eyelashes. He was friends with them, and he came here to get away. That told me these guys were either important to him or they understood him in a way that no one else did.

Luke was saying, "There's a Feast this Saturday if you and your girl want to come."

I tensed, not really knowing what I missed in while I was zoned out. I knew I was waiting for Jesse to say the inevitable "she's not my girl," but he only shrugged.

"Maybe. Some of the girlfriends are throwing a picnic for the team. You guys should come to that." He grinned to himself. "Tiffany would drop bricks if you guys showed up. She wouldn't know what to do."

Luke's eyebrows furrowed together. "Is there going to be food?"

Jesse's grin turned into a smirk. "Lots of it. You guys should come, the whole band. Brielle, too."

A smile had been growing on Luke's face, but it froze at the last words. "Why Brielle?"

Giving me a tired smile, Jesse seemed oblivious to the sharpness from his friend. "She's part of the band, isn't she?"

"Since when do you care about who's in the band or not?"

Jesse turned, frowning. "What?"

"Nothing," Luke bit out, taking a deep breath and loosening the tight grip he had on the table. "Nothing, man. Sorry. Yeah, maybe we'll check out your picnic."

Jesse started to chuckle.

"But only if you come to the Feast that night." Luke glanced at me. "And bring your girl." From how he stressed that word, he was either fishing for information or he wanted to remind Jesse that he was taken. My eyes slid over his shoulder to Brielle. She was behind the counter again, trying to pour drinks for the band, but the drummer kept poking her in the shoulder. She would swat at him, but he'd dance back two steps, and when she went back to pouring, he'd poke her again. After a few more pokes, she set down the pitcher of beer and whipped around to face him.

Her fist was cocked, and she punched him in the shoulder. Howling, he fell back, but he still couldn't contain a wide smile. She rolled her eyes. When he poked her again, she went back to swatting at him. The rest of the guys ignored the commotion. But then Brielle glanced at us, and her features tightened for a moment before falling back into a friendly grin.

I lifted my hand in a wave.

Luke caught the motion and twisted around to see who I was waving at. When he did, his shoulders stiffened and his hands clenched around the table in a death grip.

Jesse frowned as he saw the same reaction and gave me a questioning look. Luke was still turned away, so I jerked my head in Brielle's direction. Understanding flooded him, and he jerked his shoulder toward the door. I knew what he meant so I started to stand as he spoke up, "Luke, I think we're going to head out."

The lead singer turned back and stood with us. His gray eyes had darkened, but the easygoing smile on his face never gave anything away. He patted Jesse on the shoulder. "It was nice seeing you. I'll let you know about the picnic, though, knowing how Braden works, we might just show up."

Jesse shrugged. "Good entertainment for me if you do. My buddy's girlfriend is something else. She wants everything to go how she wants, but if your band showed up, she couldn't kick you out. Damn funny to watch."

"And we'll see you for the Feast." He nodded to me. "Your girl, too."

Jesse nudged me out the door with a hand in the small of my back. "See you then." When the door closed behind us, I told him, "I don't think they would mind if I didn't go. I think he was only pushing that 'your girl' part so you'd stay away from his girl."

Jesse flashed me a grin as we got into his car. "Nah, he was trolling for information. He probably wanted to hit on you."

I didn't think he was right, but I let it go.

When he pulled back onto the highway, he rolled the window down and asked, "Did I fall asleep in there?"

"Only for a little bit." Screw it. I just asked, "So, what's their story? Do you go out there a lot?"

His eyes remained on the road as he mused, "Not sure about their story. I've gone a few other times. It's interesting."

"Why do you go out there?"

"To relax." The corner of his mouth curved up. "They don't give a shit who I am. Luke likes me because I had his back that night before I knew who he was. When he found out that I didn't care who he was, he told me about The Shack and invited me out whenever I wanted. He sent me a text tonight saying they had a few more practices before they go on tour."

"Yeah, they're huge."

Jesse answered both my questions without knowing it. "I shouldn't have invited them to the picnic. Everyone would flip if they knew I knew them. I knew you wouldn't care, but the other girls and Jamie?" He shook his head. "I'm going to have to text him that the picnic was canceled. I don't want Jamie latching on to those guys, he'll think he's King Tut being on the basketball team and knowing those guys."

I wasn't special. I was . . . easygoing? That didn't feel any better. I couldn't contain the annoyance anymore, so I tried to divert it. "Are you going to tell me where you've been all week?"

"What?"

I bit out, "You fingered me in my room Sunday night, and I don't hear from you for four days. Then you take me to some hole-in-a-wall bar and fall asleep. What's going on with you?"

The air sizzled with tension as he shot back, "Are you kidding me? We don't have the type of relationship where we hold hands and have deep conversations on the phone. Now you want that? You told Cord you didn't care that I hadn't called you. Are you going back on that, too?"

I felt slapped in the face, but I bit back, "I didn't think I cared. I just need to know the rules here."

"I didn't think we had rules."

"We did. We fucked when we wanted to forget everything else, but that's not what tonight was."

He swerved his car to the side of the road and slammed on the brakes. He was out of the car and rounding to my side before I could even start to open my door. He wrenched it open and hauled me out with a tight grip on my arm.

I was seething.

He was livid as he rasped out, "What is your problem? I've been keeping it cool with you, especially when you're the one who walked out on me. Remember that? I don't hear shit from you for almost a year. Ethan's anniversary—nothing. Then I hear from Cord that you're at the house and you're going to school at Grant West. Fuck me in the ass and finger me sideways, huh? Is that what you intend to do for the next three years? I can't take this crap."

"You didn't call me back! I was told that you knew something about Ethan's accident, then I called and left how many messages and you never called me back!" I shouted back.

His eyes bulged out. "I lost my phone! I would've come to you if I had known, but I didn't. You left me, Alex. It wasn't the other way around. I didn't leave you."

"But you would've!"

I gasped as I heard what I said. I hadn't meant to let it slip. Clamping a hand over my mouth, I twisted away and stumbled to the back of the car. My heart raced, and I felt the world pressing against me. I couldn't believe I had said that. But then, I waited . . .

There was silence.

One.

Long.

Moment.

Of.

Silence.

My eyes were pressed tight, and I bent down. Touching my forehead to the cool metal of the Ferrari, I wanted to take it back. I couldn't. The words were out. He could see into me with them. I had exposed myself with those three words.

Then he asked, quiet and strained, "What did you say?"

I shook my head. Nothing. I said nothing. Please let it go.

The gravel ground under his feet, and I closed my eyes tighter, unsure what he was going to do or say. When his hand touched the back of my elbow, I pulled away and rounded to his side of the car. Running away was stupid. I'd need to deal with this, but I couldn't look at him. There'd only be rejection in his eyes. I couldn't see that, rejection and pity. My heart withered. It would completely shatter me if I saw it, but I already knew that he pitied me. He had to.

I was pathetic.

"Look at me, Alex."

My shoulders stiffened. I couldn't do it. Nothing would be the same after I did.

He stepped closer. I heard the gravel once more, but I kept myself firm. I couldn't keep running. He was going to see what he was going to see. If he rejected me, if he pitied me, I'd deal with it. I had to. Going in circles around the car was only putting it off.

Slowly, so slowly—as my heart pounded and tore through me —I forced my neck to turn. Then I saw him, but there was nothing.

He was bristling in anger. His hands were in fists pressed to his legs and his jaw was clenched tight while his eyes were glistening with repressed emotion. He wrung out, "You must have an extremely low opinion of me if you think that."

This wasn't right.

I shut up. What the hell?

My heart was pounding like crazy, but what he said didn't make sense. "What do you mean by that?"

He threw his head back and barked out a laugh. "Are you kidding me?"

"No."

"You think I'm going to leave you. You've always thought that. What'd your friend say, that I'm not going to treat you right? Oh, wait. That's right." His eyes hardened, and he clipped out, his tone ice cold, "That I'm not going to be patient with you, that I wouldn't go the extra mile. The best one was that I'm not boyfriend material." He frowned as his jaw clenched. "No, I have a better one. That I wasn't a good guy, your friend, Angie, said I wasn't a good guy. I might not say nice things, and I might not do nice things all the time, but I don't think that makes me a bad guy."

Oh. Goodness. My heart began thumping against my chest. I knew he had heard, but I hadn't thought about it. He was right. Angie had said all those things about him, and I hadn't defended him.

I hung my head. "I'm sorry, Jesse."

"No, no. Don't do that. Don't apologize to someone like me,

who'll treat you like dirt. It's a shame I'm not like Eric Nathan, right? He's the good guy. He's going to treat you right." He took a step closer. His eyes were gleaming at me. "He's boyfriend material. He's going to be patient with you. He's not going to do the shit things I did to you. Right?"

He bit out that last word, and I flinched from the intensity behind them.

My throat started to burn as I remembered that day. I couldn't bring myself to defend what I had done or defend what Angie had been saying. She'd been wrong. I'd been wrong.

The burning turned into liquid pain. It flowed everywhere in me.

Jesse wasn't done. He ground out, "What the hell did I ever do to you?"

My head snapped up then. Baring my teeth at him, I couldn't hold back the anger anymore. "Are you kidding me?"

"No." He never flinched.

"You ignored me."

He flinched. "I didn't—"

"You did!" I took two long steps and shoved at him. The small ball of control in me snapped. I kept shoving at him. "Ethan died, and a week later you took my virginity. You never called me after that. You never called at all. You fucked me, and you walked past me at school. You didn't even look at me, you asshole. You just walked away."

The pain was agonizing. I wanted to bend over, maybe that would ease it. I pushed past it, so much damn hurt blazing inside of me. I reared back to shove him again, but he caught my hands. Trapping them against his chest, he turned so I was pushed against the car. Then he crowded me in, his thighs were on either side of me and his chest pressed against me. I tried to shove him back, but the fight was leaving me.

An image of that day was on repeat, playing over and over again in my head.

We were in the hallway. Angie had been talking to me, and I looked up. He was there with two of his buddies. I opened my mouth to call out to him, but he went past. I was air for him to walk through, a ghost that he couldn't see. He made me feel like that for the rest of the year until Ethan's birthday.

The fight suddenly left me. I was weaker because of it.

He came to me the second time. His touch made me alive. I'd been starving for it. I continued to hunger for him until the next summer, until the anniversary of Ethan's death. Jesse found me again. Then again in August. He came to me. And again. And again. He kept coming for me, but I hadn't been the only girl. He told me there'd been others, and I had heard about the ones in high school. He told me about the ones during his freshman year at Grant West.

I couldn't handle that, not again.

"Hey." He captured the side of my head and lifted up. "I'm sorry. I was a mess that first year."

"So was I," I said.

"I know." His chest lifted up and down. "Shit, I know. I'm sorry." Pressing a soft kiss to my forehead, he moved to my eyelid and pressed another one. The other eyelid got a kiss, then my nose, and then both sides of my cheeks. He lingered above my lips, whispering against them, "I was trying to do the right thing. I was trying to stay away from you."

My heart clenched. I couldn't believe him. It'd hurt so damn worse if I did . . .

His lips moved against mine. "Your friend was right. I wouldn't have been a good boyfriend. I was hurting. I was stupid. I was an asshole. You're right about all of that, but it wasn't because I didn't care. I did care. I cared too much." His hand pressed against my hip as he ground into me. He began to breathe heavily. "I still do. Only you can reduce me to this."

"To what?" I asked, my breath held in my throat. My heart

was a continuous pounding rhythm. I wondered if he could feel it. I could feel his. It was racing.

A dry chuckle left him. "To trapping you here. You make me crazy. You might not know it, but you do."

Hope kindled in me. It was starting to build. I couldn't let it so I shook my head. "Stop, Jesse. We should stop this before it gets worse."

"Worse?" He cupped the back of my head and pulled away. His eyes held mine, searing into me. "I tried to give you space. I did. I stayed away from you after Vegas. I was tempted not to get a new phone just so I would have to leave you alone. But you came here, and all I have wanted to do since is see you every single night."

I closed my eyes. The hope had mingled with another emotion I didn't dare let myself feel. It was too dangerous. "Stop, Jesse."

"No. It can't get worse than it already is. I'm not trying to be crude, but my dick's been twitching since I heard your voice on the phone. I've been hard for six fucking days."

Everything went flat for me. "That's what this is about?"

"What?" He edged back a step. His eyes widened when he saw the anger in mine. "No. I meant—my dick has been hard, but this is more. I promise."

I shoved him back. Damage done. "Can you take me back?"

He didn't argue but watched me warily. "Are you okay?"

"No." Why lie? There was nothing to lose.

"Really?" His voice hitched on a note.

I almost looked at him. Almost. That couldn't have been panic. Jesse Hunt did not panic. He did not grovel. He did not feel anything except lust. The memories of two years ago flooded back to me. Every time he looked away, every time he walked past without a hello, every time I saw him touch another girl, all flared in my memory. I cringed and clenched my teeth to keep from sobbing before I could stop the memories. They were haunting me.

"Alex?"

"Just take me home." I'd been put through the emotional wringer. I wasn't about to sign up for round two.

For the ride over, he kept looking at me. Every look set my nerves on edge. My blood was already boiling, but if he kept that up, I was going to snap again. The only thing that held me back was the car. I didn't want to die in a car accident like Ethan. A harsh laugh ripped from me at that last thought. Just like Ethan. God, Ethan.

Paralyzing pain filled me again. I hadn't thought about Ethan in so long. He'd been buzzing around me at home. All day long, every day, every night, I felt his presence. I hadn't felt him once since coming to Grant West.

I missed him.

Closing my eyes, I bit down on my lip and tried to keep from crying. I hadn't let loose tears over him since coming here. I knew that if I did, I wouldn't be able to stop. Too much else was going on. I was barely holding it all in.

The ride took too long and not long enough. When Jesse got to my dorm, he had to go to the front door. The backdoor was locked from midnight to six in the morning.

He parked and started, "I know that I haven't—"

I clambered out of the car and shut the door before he could say anything more.

Hurrying into my dorm, I ignored the startled front desk clerk and shot up the stairs.

8

I avoided everyone for another week. Or, I thought I was avoiding them. The truth was that no one probably cared. I hadn't heard or even seen Beth in the hallways. Since the professor hadn't given us a group project, there was no reason to interact with Cord. I caught a few glares from his friend, but after the third one, I realized they were directed at the girl in front of me. She still snickered together with her two other friends, but that was the only interaction between them and Jamie. It'd been quiet from Jesse, too. I didn't know if that was good or not. I didn't want to contemplate that.

Hannah broke the week of isolation.

My books were spread out on a table in the outside food court when her bag landed across from me. My head jerked up, but before I could look around, Hannah plopped down next to me.

She began riffling through her bag as her blonde hair slid over her shoulder, masking her face from me. When she glanced up, the same aviators were covering her eyes, and she grinned at me. "Hey-a, stranger. I heard some interesting tidbits about you this weekend."

I stiffened.

Her lips curved up in a smirk. "Relax. It's nothing real juicy."
She paused for a second, her mouth pursed in thoughtfulness. "Is
there something juicy? I'm intrigued . . . no. No, I'm not. Never
mind. You're all closed off and sheltered. I'd have to kiss your ass
for you to spill. I don't care enough to do all that work."

Did she dismiss me?

I wasn't sheltered.

The strap of her top slipped, showing off her bare shoulder
and a tattoo design of birds flying down her collarbone. "You can
stay all elusive and shit. Fine with me."

I frowned. This girl was something else, but my own interest
was piqued. "What'd you hear this weekend?"

Her lips curved in a sultry come-hither smile. "That you told
my sister off. High marks for that one."

I let out a breath. I thought she was going to say something
else, maybe about Jesse, but it was about Tiffany. That wasn't
something I cared about. "Oh."

A deep chuckle came from her.

As she laughed, her head tilted to the side and her shirt
slipped farther down her arm. The girl was oozing sexuality and
didn't even seem to notice. The guys around our table had taken
notice, though. A few seemed ready to join us. I sent them a glare,
which stopped them in their tracks. Nope, I saw one reinforce his
smug grin as he strode toward us.

"Heads up. Pick-up Line at three o'clock."

Hannah glanced over and the sultriness went up a notch.

The guy stumbled in his footing. He almost tripped and fell,
but caught himself. Normally, this would've ended the approach.
Not with this guy. His smile never budged. His shoulders rolled
back and his cockiness rose.

He was a determined little bugger.

A low deep-throated chuckle came from her again. It was
loud enough so I heard, but no one else did. I had to give her
some credit. She was good.

When he stopped at the table, I heard one of the worst pick-up lines I could imagine.

"Do you come here often?"

I snorted.

He shot me a glare. It was gone in the next second when Hannah teased, "You mean to this exact table or to this school? Because I do. I go to this school."

"Oh." A flush spread from underneath his shirt.

Hadn't thought that one through, buddy? I shook my head. I was betting he used that one at the bars. We were in a city with three other colleges. His chances were better off campus.

"Hannah, this guy bothering you?"

Her sister's boyfriend to the rescue. From the gloating in his voice, I could imagine his entrance. White horse, metal armor, and maybe even a javelin? I shook my head. When I snuck a peek from underneath my eyelashes, he wasn't alone. Cord was with him, along with Kara's boyfriend. No Jesse. Why did I never see Jesse with them?

I ignored the disappointment that fluttered in my chest.

"Keep going, guys," Hannah clipped out.

She was annoyed and glaring at both Cord and Jamie.

"Walk, numbnuts." Jamie warned the guy with a dark look. "She's off-limits."

"Shut up!"

If the kid could've run without looking like an idiot, I knew he would've. Instead, his power walk rivaled some housewives I had witnessed in the mall. They wanted to burn rubber in bright spandex and would've been envious of his speed.

"You shut up, Hannah. I'm not going to listen to your sister bitch at me because I didn't stop another guy from climbing in your bed. That's all she complains about now. You! I'm getting sick of it."

Derek clapped him on the shoulder. "At least she's not bitching about you, man."

Some of the tension lifted from Jamie, but not much. He continued to glower down at Hannah. "Stop being a whore on campus."

My eyebrows shot up. The guy had balls.

Cord frowned. "Hey, man. We should get going."

Hannah slammed her hands on the table and shoved to her feet. She glared right back. "Are you kidding me? You are a bigger whore than I am. Why don't you stop dicking around on my sister?"

He moved back a step, but the glower never left. "Whatever. You're such a bitch."

"And you're an asshole. We're even."

Derek stepped between them. "I think it's a good draw. Let's call it, hmmm? Jamie, march." He jerked his head in the opposite direction. "We have to meet Jesse anyway."

Jesse? My head shot up and tingles zinged down my spine.

Cord had been watching me, and a knowing look came over him. I tried, and failed, not to scowl at him. I didn't want anyone to notice and start to wonder, but he seemed smug. Why the hell did he seem smug? My eyes narrowed. He had nothing to be smug about.

"Yes, run along." Hannah waved her fingers at her sister's boyfriend. "Go play patsy for the real star in your group. No wonder he's a recluse around campus. Who'd want to be seen with you? I bet you use him to pick up even more chicks to cheat on my sister with." Her lips thinned. "Is that what you do when you guys go out?"

Jamie snapped, and he jerked forward a step. His hand rose in the air, already fisted.

Cord drew him back. "Stop it. Now." He turned to Hannah, "We didn't come over for this."

"Why did you come over?"

"To say hi to you and Alex." At her disbelieving look, he held both of his hands in the air. "I swear. That's all. The guy cut us off when he was coming over."

"My business is none of yours." She swept them with a cool cold indifference. "None of you."

Jamie looked ready to argue, but Derek pushed him forward with his hands on his friend's shoulders. "Yeah, we're leaving. See you both."

Cord went after them, lifting a finger in a good-bye salute.

Hannah extended her middle finger. Before they disappeared into the crowd, Cord laughed back as he shook his head.

I had to give it to the guy. Nothing seemed to faze him.

Hannah folded back down on her seat with a huff. She asked, heatedly, "How do you know those guys?"

I wasn't completely honest. "I'm in poly sci with Cord and Jamie."

"Oh." She seemed surprised. "Never mind then."

What'd she think? I was hoping to use her to get to them? My anger was on a simmer as I asked, "Why?"

"Because I thought you screwed my sister's boyfriend." She didn't mince her words. Then she shrugged, turning back to her bag. "That would've made sense why my sister hates you."

"Does he still cheat?"

"Oh yeah. All the time."

I was blown away. "Seriously?"

"Yep." She pulled out a different book, along with a high-lighter. "It's my sister's idea of being modern. She's such an idiot."

"What do you mean?"

"Technically, he's not cheating, but I don't care. Cheating is cheating. Jamie's allowed to sleep around for another year. Tiffany has it in her head that if she doesn't let him do his thing now, he'll do it later. And she won't let him cheat on her when they're married."

"When are they getting married?"

"The summer after his first year at law school." A yawn

stretched over her, as if she were bored with our conversation. "Anyway, Tiffany locked him down when they were freshman. Now that he knows Jesse Hunt, she thinks that Jamie can use his connections and run for the senate or something."

"Huh?"

I hoped my jaw wasn't touching the table. It had dropped so low. I was too dumbfounded. I couldn't be hearing this right.

"Yeah," she shrugged again. "Jamie's dad owns a firm, so once he's done with law school, he'll have a job there. She has it all mapped out. After he's a lawyer for two years, he'll start hobnobbing with the Hollywood crowd. She thinks that'll help him get noticed. Anyway, when he eventually runs for office, he'll be a shoo-in."

"You're kidding me."

Nope, she wasn't. I could tell from the irritation in her eyes. They flashed whenever she spoke about her sister. They'd been on full blast with her entire explanation. She pressed a hand to her chest and pretended to double over. "She makes me want to gag. She's so hypocritical. I can't sleep around, but she allows her boyfriend to bang anyone he wants. And she thinks he's going to stop. Jamie's not going to stop. He's never going to stop sleeping around. He can't stand her. He can barely stomach the sight of her."

"How do you know that?"

"Because he's told me." She gestured to her phone. "He's been trying to do me for three years. He sends me text messages all the time."

Holy shit. "Does your sister know that?"

Her lips pressed together. "I'm not that stupid. I'm never going to give it to him, and I'm not opening that can of worms with my sister." Another shoulder went up in a shrug before she hunched over her book. "Anyway, I need to study. Can we postpone this chat session till after I fail my cultural psychology quiz?"

I fell silent, still reeling from everything she'd exposed. I wasn't sure if I was more shocked by the relationship Tiffany had with Jamie or because they assumed Jesse would help them out. I figured they were hoping to use his dad's connections, but did they not know Jesse? Or maybe it was Tiffany that didn't know him. Jesse hated Malcolm Hunt. I didn't know what family stuff had been going on, but I knew Jesse hadn't enjoyed it. Malcolm Hunt could never be considered a candidate for Father of the Year.

It was an hour later when Hannah called it quits. She shut her book and stretched, yawning all the while. If I had cared, I might've been insecure next to her. The girl was gorgeous. She must've noticed my look because her arms dropped from the air and she grinned. "Wanna go for dinner somewhere?"

My eyes narrowed. "Why are you talking to me?"

"What do you mean?"

"Beth isn't here. You don't have to talk to me."

Her eyes widened a fraction. "That's some chip you have on your shoulder."

I scowled at her, though, I couldn't argue. "I like my chip. I've named it."

"Oh yeah?" Her grin grew. "What's the name?"

With a blank face, I said, "Hannah."

She barked out in laughter. "Beth said you were cool, not that you were funny. Back to my first question, want to go somewhere for dinner?"

"Like the cafeteria?" I glanced around at the fast food shops around us.

"Nah. I mean off-campus. There's a nice dive bar with two-dollar burgers. They're pretty good. Plus, I wouldn't mind a pitcher of beer."

"I'm underage."

She shrugged. "So am I. They'll let us in. The owner has a boner for Tiffany, so all the staff's been told to be nice to me." She rolled her eyes. "Little does he know that I hate my sister and he has no shot."

"If your sister lets Jamie cheat, does she cheat, too?"

"No." She shook her head as her lips tightened against each other. "She should. She thinks she's practicing for marriage, and she doesn't want any evidence spread around campus. Tiffany believes that if she ever cheats, it'll get caught on video and there goes her stellar reputation."

"What's her reputation?" High-class bitch?

She grinned. "You've seen the wicked side of her, but trust me. There are girls who would kill their mothers to be friends with my sister. It's nice to be Queen Bee in high school, but this is Grant West. Tiffany's got connections to the crème of the crop."

"Who's that?" But I had a good sense who it was.

"The jerks who were just here. Slap in their leader, Jesse Hunt, and Tyler Kurtis, and you've got the starting five for our NCAA championship bound basketball team. Tell me you haven't noticed that they're celebrities on campus?"

Oh yes, I had noticed.

"There are a *lot* of girls who would love an 'in' with those guys. Derek's the only one with a steady girlfriend. You know Jamie's story. Cord hooks up with Chandra, but he still doesn't like a title on it. I know he enjoys sleeping around. Tyler's the same."

My heart began to pound in my chest. "What about Jesse Hunt?"

Her eyes grew thoughtful. "I don't know much about Hunt. He's gorgeous, but the guys are pretty tight-lipped about him."

"Does he party with them?"

"Sometimes he's out with them, and sometimes I'll see him talking to girls, but I haven't heard much about him. I don't think he hangs out around campus much. Since he's the big shot now, people crowd him. Can't say I blame him for hiding out. I saw him in the quad once last year, it was after the NCAA championship game, and he was almost mobbed. He had to hide in the bathroom until people finally left him alone."

"Is that normal?"

"No. People aren't usually like that, but I think it's because he's rarely seen around campus. So when people do see him, they want to go and talk to him. There's a girl on my floor who has a class with him. She says he always sits in the back and leaves right away. He's not too social."

My heart began beating at a fast pace, and a fluttering sensation grew in my chest. It wasn't anger this time.

9

I learned a pitcher of beer and cheap burgers didn't end with one pitcher of beer and good conversation. Not with Hannah. When we got to the dive bar, the owner came out to schmooze her. She was right. He gave off the impression of dirty sex mixed with stalker. We were shown to a back corner booth between the pool table and the dart games. As dive bars went, it was the prime seating area. As soon as the owner left, she drank the first pitcher.

A second was ordered. When it arrived, she poured a glass for me with the order, "You're drinking tonight." I started to tell her that I didn't drink, but she shook her head. "Nope. I don't care. Getting drunk is a freshmen right of passage. You get to do it the right way, in a hole like this. Others have to do it in a filthy house party, so drink up, Elusive Bitch. You're getting wasted tonight."

Another argument was on the tip of my tongue, but I swallowed it. She was right. It was a normal thing to do. I might as well get it out of the way. I reached for my glass. It was empty when I put it down. Hannah went nuts. Her eyes lit up, she filled both of our glasses again and began doing a drumroll on the table while I finished another.

We were wasted by the third pitcher.

This was also when the music started and a group of guys sat in the booth across from ours. It wasn't long before they were at ours and we had a party going. A game of pool was suggested, and Hannah enjoyed being taught how to play. Well, she probably enjoyed the guy she'd been eyeing being curved around her to help her "learn," anyway. I was willing to bet on the next pitcher of beer that she knew pool. After she sunk her third ball, she gave me a wink. Oh, yes, she knew how to play the game just fine.

Most of the guys had joined the game of pool, but the quieter one stayed behind. He was in the booth with me. I knew where this was going. When he scooted closer and tried talking to me, I moved farther away, closer to the end of the booth. He scooted again. I was at the end next, but he didn't get the hint. He draped an arm around my shoulder and crowded against me.

Hannah saw my dilemma. I waited for her help, nope. She laughed and pointed instead. The rest of his friends turned as well. All of them started laughing at my situation. It seemed to give the guy more encouragement, and he pressed harder against me. However, this was the time when two more arrivals showed up.

A girl and a guy were holding hands as they paused by the pool table. She had sleek black hair and striking dark eyes. The guy next to her had a similar look with black hair, dark eyes, and a physique that showed he enjoyed lifting weights. The guys who had been flirting with Hannah saw the couple first. Some of them checked the girl out in a blatant manner, which she seemed to enjoy. Her perfect small lips curved up, looking smug. The guy frowned at her and shot a glare around the table.

When Hannah caught sight of them . . .

All hell broke loose.

Hannah started cursing at them. The girl cursed back. The

guy clamped a hand around his girlfriend's waist, but he had a few harsh words for Hannah as well.

As I listened to both sides, I started to piece together the puzzle.

The girl had been Hannah's best friend. She went to Grant West with her, lived with her—my eyes bulged out when I heard Hannah yell, "You two are always screwing in the room. It's my room, too!" Bombs went off. They still lived together. The roommate yelled back, "Don't blame me for enjoying sex with my boyfriend, at least he can get it up for me." Hannah tried to lunge for her. The guy who had "taught" her how to play pool held her back. He shared an uneasy glance with his friends, and I knew they were going to bail. They had started to ease back when the shouting began. It wouldn't be long before they completely left.

I glanced at the guy who'd been crowding me. He was still there. He gave me a smile that I assumed was supposed to be charming and reassuring.

My stomach protested, and I clamped a hand over my mouth. I wasn't sure if it was the beer or the guy's cheesy smile, but I darted for the bathroom. I lost it. My stomach emptied out, and I was bent over the toilet for the next ten minutes.

Gross.

When I was done and a whole lot more sober, I searched my purse for a breath mint and then I headed back out.

I heard them, but I didn't see them anymore. When they weren't by the pool table, I followed the shouting. They were in the parking lot, and Hannah had a death grip on the girl's hair, who was trying to claw Hannah's eyes out. The big guy was yelling at Hannah to let go but was tossing in some curse words and a few derogatory terms as he did so.

No one had Hannah's back.

It might've been the beer. It might've been the deliriousness that came with vomiting or nostalgic memories from other friends, but I joined in. Angie and Marissa would've been proud.

The girl was swinging her hand around, her nails ready to rip into Hannah's face when my fist blinded her. I punched her in the cheek and she fell to the ground. The guy gaped at her before rounding on me with a snarl.

Hannah stood with a clump of black hair in her hands. Dazed, she looked at the hair, at the girl on the floor, and then at me. The guy started for me, but she threw the hair at him and grabbed my hand. "Run!"

She didn't have to say it twice.

Holding hands, we took off down the block. We kept going, panting and giggling. We went down two more streets before we slowed to a stop outside of a grocery store.

Panting, Hannah swiped her hair from her face and swept it back into a ponytail. As she did, she kept shaking her head at me and laughing. "That was awesome, Alex. I didn't know you had it in you."

I shrugged, unable to hold back my own grin. It had felt good, and I had the urge to call Angie and Marissa. They would've laughed their asses off, but then I remembered reality. Angie and Marissa were no longer my friends. And Hannah wasn't really a friend, either.

The grin fell from my face.

The situation was no longer so funny.

Hannah's grin faded, too. "You okay?"

"Yeah. Who were those two?"

"Oh." Her lips pressed together, and her shoulders stiffened. "They're no one."

I frowned. "Are you kidding? I punched her for you. Who were there?"

"No, I meant they aren't even worth talking about. Trust me. It's all stupid drama."

I remembered some of the shouts and asked, "She's your roommate?"

Hannah visibly cringed and her jaw clenched as she wrapped

her arms around herself. She sat on a bench outside the store. I sat beside her. When she didn't say anything, I asked the next theory that was mulling in my head. "And he was your boyfriend?"

Her eyes closed. Her head hung down, and her shoulders drooped beside me. She was withering before my eyes. In a broken voice, she whispered, "Yeah."

A light bulb went off for me.

Hannah was broken, just like me.

My hand found hers, and I squeezed it, patting it at the same time. "Trust me. I understand."

"Your boyfriend cheated on you for a whole year, broke up with you because of the long distance relationship, and ended up transferring to Grant West so he could date your roommate/best friend?"

"Well," I let go of her hand, "no." I patted her shoulder instead.

"Oh. Because that's what happened to me. I dated Dylan forever. He went to Cal U, I went to Grant West, and you know the rest." She sounded defeated. "They got together over the summer after he broke up with me. Angelique didn't tell me until the day we moved in together. She said she had some news to tell me, and then Dylan strolled in. Fuck me. I thought he had come to beg forgiveness, but then they started kissing."

Bitch.

"Thanks for punching her. I've wanted to do that for so long."

"Eh." I waved my hand in a dismissing motion. "Not a problem."

She grinned at me. "We're a mess. Sorry about ruining your first drunk moment."

"I've been drunk before."

"You have?"

I nodded. "But that was the first time I've hit someone. It was satisfying."

"Oh." She began to laugh. "Beth's right. You're cool. I'm glad my sister hates you."

"Me, too."

We began laughing together then, unable to hold in the hysterics of the evening. When an elderly couple walked past into the store, a fresh wave came over us again. The old guy seemed intrigued while his wife grabbed his cane and hurried him inside. I wasn't sure how long we sat there. It was a while before Hannah sighed, hugging herself. She ran a hand over her hair, trying to calm the mess, and shuddered. "We should go back."

"Sure."

We didn't move.

Hannah asked, "Do you know how to go back?"

"No idea."

"Oh. Okay."

We remained sitting. The elderly couple came out, followed by a grocery clerk with their purchases. When he wheeled his cart back in, his gaze lingered on us, mostly on Hannah and her hair, before he went back inside.

She glanced over. "I have a feeling if we don't leave they're going to call the cops on us."

"You're right. Probably think we're drug dealers—" I started.

She finished with a wicked grin. "Or prostitutes!"

I nodded and pouted my lips so I'd look full of knowledge. "You're right. I'd go with the hookers. They think we're hookers."

She eyed my outfit before she leaned over, took hold of my sleeves, and ripped them off.

My mouth fell open. "That was my favorite shirt."

"It was?"

Doubling over with more laughter, I shook my head. "No. I think I'm still drunk."

"Me, too." She pressed a hand to her forehead. "But you look more like a hooker. Maybe we can get a ride."

"Or call for a ride." I pointed at her pockets. "Call Beth."

"Oh yeah!" More giggles spilled from her as she fumbled with the buttons, but by the end of the conversation, Beth was on her way for us.

We didn't have to wait long. She pulled into the parking lot in the red Camaro from before. Hannah bounced into the front seat, exclaiming, "You got my car. How'd you do that?"

Beth seemed less than happy to see us. She skimmed a hard look over both of us as I got into the back seat, then she turned out of the parking lot. "I got a ride to Mitch's. You left your stuff there so I found your keys. They were going to call the cops on you, but then you ran."

Hannah scrunched her face up. "Were they still there?"

"Angelique and Dylan?"

Her lips pressed even tighter together.

Beth gentled her tone, "No and Mitch said they've been banned."

"Oh Mitchy." Hannah slumped down in her chair, a sloppy grin on her face. "He wants my sister so bad, doesn't he?"

"He asked me to tell Tiffany that he was looking out for you."

Hannah snorted and pumped her hand in the air. Her middle finger was extended to the ceiling. "Fuck you, Mitch Carinns. He ain't getting anywhere near Tiffany. He didn't do crap for me, told me to take it outside. That was all. And they were going to call the cops? He's pathetic." She jerked upright. "We should trash his bar tonight."

Beth shrugged. "If you want."

I kept my face schooled, but damn. I wasn't sure if I was ready for vandalism.

"I want." Hannah was heated.

"We'll have to do it after hours, around five or so in case anyone stays after closing."

"Four should be okay."

The two nodded—a crime couple in the making. I was waiting for the fist pump, but it never came. Instead, Hannah slumped back down and Beth kept driving. That was when I realized they'd done this before. I had newfound thoughts on these two. Hannah had always struck me as a loose cannon, but I understood a little bit more why she was that way. I wasn't sure about Beth. However, unless they were killing people, I wasn't fearful of any friendship with them. I was more inclined. I didn't understand it, but I knew that these two made me feel stronger.

Hannah was still drunk. I was sobering up, and Beth didn't care, so we went to another party. This time, instead of a dive bar, we parked on the street for a house party. Cars were lined up and down the block, so we had to walk from two blocks away, but as we drew closer, the bass got louder. It was nearly ear splitting by the time we walked up to their open garage.

Either the neighbors were gone or sleeping. All the lights were off in the houses surrounding.

"Chitty!" A guy opened his arms and Hannah leapt for him. Her legs wrapped around his waist as he caught her, and buried his head in her hair. Some of his friends laughed, swatting Hannah on her butt as the guy disappeared inside with her.

Beth touched my arm, gesturing inside. I nodded. The music was too loud for conversation. She weaved through the crowd, glancing up a few times and waving at people as we passed by. I noted that each person would've gained Angie's disapproval. They either had tattoos, piercings, or both all over them. Some of the guys were large and intimidating, but they nodded at Beth with kindness.

It was like she instantly knew where to go because she never lingered as we went through the house. She led us right to where the keg was and passed a cup to me. Leaning close, I asked in her ear, "What about Hannah?"

She shook her head, sipping from her own cup. "She knows the owner of the house." She gestured to the ceiling. "She's probably upstairs with him right now." Nodding with her head farther inside the house, she said, "Come on. I'll introduce you to some of my friends."

We went to a back closed-in patio room. Couches lined against the walls with three large beanbags in the middle. People sat everywhere and stood against the wall. Two girls, nearly naked, were lying across the beanbags with two guys rubbing them. One had his hand inside the girl's pants, which had been loosened and pulled down, while the other was openly caressing the girl's breasts.

I touched Beth's arm and gestured to the girls. She leaned in again. "Don't worry, those are both couples. Those girls are known for this thing, they get off on the attention."

Still. Live porn?

Angie would more than disapprove. And because of that thought about my ex-best friend, I plopped down next to Beth on one of the couches. I didn't care.

"Beth!" A big bald guy crossed the room, lifted her up, and settled her on his lap. He wore a ripped shirt over a muscular chest. His arms were covered in tattoos, as was his chest from what I could see. A large hoop hung in the bottom of his earlobe and he had a large cross tattoo that extended from the base of his skull and disappeared underneath his shirt on his back.

"Sal, this is Alex," Beth introduced us. Sal was short for Sallaway. He owned a tattoo parlor and had known Beth for two years.

The two whispered to each other over the next hour while I sat beside them and drank my beer. When my cup would get empty, I'd go and fill it again. Beth did the same, taking mine with her a few times until some of Sal's friends showed up. They brought two coolers into the room, sat them beside the beanbags, and opened them to show an impressive display of hard alcohol. Bourbon. Rum. Whiskey. Bacardi. As the two couples continued to be the room's entertainment, a bottle of Wild Turkey was opened and passed around.

Beth took a drag and handed it over.

The stuff smelled foul and I was full from too much beer so I passed it.

"Hey, you need to drink." Sal grabbed the bottle from the guy next to me. He gave it to me. "It's a bonding thing."

I stared him down.

Beth had frozen on his lap. His hand was tucked on the inside of her pocket, but her eyes were glued to me.

I glanced at her in questioning. Was he serious? Then I shook my head. What did I care? Coolly, I handed the bottle away and said, "I don't have to do a goddamn thing."

His eyes narrowed. Despite the music still blaring, the room fell silent. Sal must've been a big deal with these people.

Lifting my chin, I still didn't care.

Beth whispered something in his ear as her hand started rubbing up and down over his chest, through a rip in his shirt. After a moment, he broke out in a grin and relaxed back into the couch. "Yeah, whatever. Don't get your panties in a twist."

The guy next to me took his swig of the alcohol and continued passing it on. Everyone went back to what they'd been doing. The couple progressed to complete nudity.

When Sal didn't pay me any attention, I went back to my beer.

It wasn't long until I'd gone from being buzzed to being wasted so it took me a while to register that Beth was pulling on my hand. She was saying something to me, but the beer had given me tunnel vision and tunnel hearing. It mixed with all the other noises in the house. She kept yanking at my hand and her face was masked in concern.

I rolled my head over. Sal wasn't paying any attention to her. He was chatting with another girl, with his hand inside her front pocket.

Was that why she was upset?

I started to point at him, but my arm was so heavy.

Beth kept tugging on my other one and I fell off the couch.

Stumbling to my feet, I shook my head. Everything spun around me. Had the couches turned upside down? Ugh, no. That was me. She kept tugging at me and I tried to follow, but all the people kept getting in my way. Bumping into someone, I turned to apologize, but Beth grabbed my pants and literally dragged me behind her. She was going at a breakneck speed. I wanted to tell her I was sorry about Sal, but she was better off. He didn't seem like a good guy. I never got a chance. When I'd open my mouth, she'd yank me through another group of people. The words kept getting swallowed as I tried not to hit anymore people.

And then she pulled me through a doorway. The house had been overheated, but a rush of cool air blasted me. Being sweat-soaked, I began shivering and wrapped my arms around myself. It was fucking cold. I could hear a chattering and looked around for the sound, and then I realized it was me. My teeth were chattering against each other.

"Hannah!" Beth yelled next to me.

I clamped my hands over my ears and fell down. She was so damn loud. Glaring at her, she didn't seem to care. She rushed forward and I swung my head to follow her direction. From the ground, I watched as she ran to a group at the end of the driveway. There was a girl with white hair, grappling with another girl with blonde hair. That hair was familiar. I frowned, scrunching my eyes together and saw it was Hannah. Ah, Hannah! She must've been done with the party owner. Good for her.

Beth reached over and grabbed the white hair, then yanked the girl backward. She began dragging her away from Hannah, who was on the ground. Why was she on the ground? Oh, I saw the blood next.

"Hannah," I croaked and began to go to her. When I pushed back to my feet, everything spun around me again. I took a step forward, but my body went to the right. Crashing into a chair and people, I tried to apologize again. Nothing came out. I could only mumble words. Even in my drunken state, I knew I was a mess.

I tried to say I was sorry for that, too, but someone caught my elbow and spun me around.

Oh, the world.

I felt vomit rising in my throat.

Hannah. Hannah had been beaten up. I needed to help.

Muttering a thank you to whoever had stopped me from falling, I stumbled forward, wavering. I waited until I regained my balance and took another step, then another step. I kept going until I reached Hannah's side and knelt down. She was wiping blood and tears from her face.

Oh, her poor hair. A big chunk had been pulled out. Her eyes lit with anger. She put the hair in my hands and darted off.

"Alex?"

I turned, hearing a familiar voice, and squinted at Marissa.

No. Not Marissa. She couldn't be here.

But she was. She took my arm and lifted me to my feet. Then she wrapped an arm around my waist, asking, "What are you doing here?"

I gave her the hair. "That's Hannah's."

"Oh." She looked at it with disgust. "But Alex, what are you doing here?"

"What are you doing here?"

"Sarah and I drove down. Cord said he was having a party, and we came here to pick up Sarah's cousin."

I looked around, feeling a little bit sober. "Beth and Hannah are cousins, too."

"Who?"

I couldn't see them. "They were here. I think they were fighting someone."

A guy was walking past, but he turned and pointed down the street. "Your friends took off. That one fucked Robbie. No way Kari was going to let her get away with that."

Who was Robbie and who was Kari?

I sighed and turned to Marissa. "What are you doing here?"

She heaved a deep breath, frowning at me. "You're a mess, aren't you?"

I nodded. It wasn't a big secret. "Angie would not approve of my new friends."

She gave me a sad smile. "No. No, she probably wouldn't."

A girl came over, annoyed. "She's not here. That bitch. She probably took off with her friends already." Then she frowned at me. "Alex?"

Oh hell. Sarah Shastaine. Anger, jealousy, and other emotions swirled up inside of me. Then I frowned to myself. I was drunk. I wasn't supposed to feel. That made me not like Jesse's ex-girlfriend even more. I scowled at her. "You took my friend from me."

She rolled her eyes. "Don't talk, drunk girl."

I muttered to Marissa, "She's not very original."

Patting me on the arm, she said to Sarah, "Let's go to the party."

"Not with her."

"Yes, with her. She's drunk. We're not leaving her."

Sarah pressed her lips together.

Marissa corrected, snapping at her, "I'm not leaving without her."

"Whatever! We can't even get to the party. My cousin knew how to get there."

"Sarah."

"This sucks!" She threw her hands in the air. "My cousin is going to die. I bet she went ahead without us on purpose. She's such a bitch."

Marissa's arm tightened around me. Her chest rose and she rubbed a hand over her face. "Alex probably knows where Cord lives."

Sarah's gaze snapped to me. "Do you?"

I was stuck. I did. I didn't want them to know. "No."

I could see the disappointment.

"This sucks!" Sarah yelled again. "We drove an hour for nothing. My cousin won't pick up her phone. Hussy."

"Well, whatever," Marissa lashed out at her. "I didn't come just for the party. I wanted to see Alex anyway."

"Congrats. She's wasted and can barely stand."

"I know, which is why we're taking her home. Alex, where do you live? We'll give you a ride back."

"At the college."

A small grin graced her features before she patted my arm again. "Okay, you give us directions and we'll take you there." We turned and began to walk down the street.

As we went to a car and drove away, I wondered if I should tell Marissa about Chandra. I kept quiet. Something told me she wouldn't care. She had never cared before about cheating, she definitely wouldn't care about Cord having a maybe-girlfriend. And I didn't even want to think about why Sarah Shastaine was there. More bad feelings would overwhelm me, and in my state, I knew I'd say or do something I couldn't take back.

She'd just better stay away from Jesse.

I closed my eyes. I'd wake up the next morning and all of this would be a dream. Marissa being here didn't make any sense. She'd left me like Angie, like my parents. They all left me.

10

When I woke, I was a hung-over mess. Stumbling to the bathroom, showering, dry heaving, and trying to dress took two hours. There were lots of breaks and a few of those where I had to rest my head on a cool counter-top. Beth ran into me as I was going back to my room and asked where I had disappeared to after the party. They'd returned to search for me. This information was welcomed. I hadn't liked the feeling that they had abandoned me, since they were the only two people I spent time with. Beth also gave my bag back. I'd left it in Hannah's car. When I went inside, I checked my phone.

Zap me twice and kick me in the arse.

I hadn't imagined Marissa's presence the night before. She called and left me two messages, along with a text saying she was heading to town. She wanted to meet up for coffee or a drink.

I erased the text. There was no way I wanted to have that awkward conversation, especially after she saw my wasted state the night before. I didn't regret getting so drunk, but I wasn't signing up for another round in the near future.

Then I scrolled through the rest.

Jesse called a bunch of times and left six text messages.

Jesse: Where are you?

Jesse: Can we talk?

Jesse: I'd like to talk. I'm sorry.

I thumbed a response back, feeling my ego get a little boost.

Me: Crazy night, didn't have my phone. Did you know Marissa and your ex-gf are in town?

I didn't wait long. My phone buzzed back right away.

Jesse: Yeah, M called the house phone. We moved houses, but same number. Want to meet for lunch?

I checked the time. It was just before noon.

Me: Sure.

Jesse: Will pick you up in twenty.

Me: K.

Instead of waiting in my room, I finished dressing and grabbed my book bag. I wasn't sure what Jesse had planned, so I brought my laptop and enough homework to last me the entire weekend. Then I went downstairs and parked my bottom on the curb. Before he showed, the back stairwell door opened behind me.

Beth plopped down beside me. Kicking her legs out, she leaned back and yawned. "Who are you waiting for?"

"Jesse."

"Ah. The mystery man."

I frowned as I heard the amusement in her tone. It wasn't amusing to me. "Who are you waiting for?"

"Who do you think?"

I grinned at her. "Your hunky Sal?"

She snorted. "He's a good guy."

Really?

She added, "Rough around the edges, but he's loyal to the extreme. He was surprised by you last night."

"Because I wouldn't drink the Wild Turkey?"

"That, and because you didn't give a damn who he was or even where we were." She laughed as she readjusted and hugged her knees to her chest instead. "Most people piss their pants when they step foot into a party like last night. You didn't seem to care at all."

"Because I didn't. Your crowd doesn't scare me. I could tell they all cared about you, and I was there with you. So . . ." I let the sentence fade.

In the silence that hung afterward, I could feel her studying me. After another few moments, she sighed in surrender. "You're a different bird, aren't you?"

I glanced at her. "What do you mean?"

It was at that time when Jesse pulled into the parking lot and wheeled to a stop in front of us. Beth gestured to him. "Not many would keep a relationship secret with the biggest star at Grant West."

Standing, I gave her a crooked grin. "Not many know who I am here. I'd like to keep it that way."

She frowned, and I knew the wheels were going again. I hadn't meant to sound mysterious, just that I didn't want people pitying me when they heard about my older brother's tragic death or my parents' neglect. Too many stares and too many whispers hadn't helped my grief back home. Coupling that with the target on my back that'd be there once people knew my connection to Jesse sounded like my worst nightmare. I wasn't stupid. I knew it'd get out, but I had every intention of prolonging that as long as possible.

As I got in, Jesse flashed me a grin. Those black shades on him were lethal to my hormones. Beth was a forgotten thought as he peeled out of the parking lot. When we passed Hannah's Camaro, I was grateful his windows were tinted.

"Isn't that your friend?" Jesse asked, turning onto the road.

I nodded and twisted around. Beth hopped into the Camaro and Hannah wheeled the car around to follow us. If I'd been driving, they would've been behind us within seconds. Jesse went fast. They were a speck behind us before long.

"Where are we going?"

He ignored that question. "I'm sorry I haven't called."

I wanted to tell him I hadn't cared, but I was trying to keep the lying only to myself. I said nothing instead.

"There's a lot of shit going on with my dad. I can tell you, but I don't want to. I don't even want to think about it."

"Why are you telling me this?" We weren't a couple. I wasn't his girlfriend.

"Because the press might get wind of it, and I don't want you hurt that I never said anything. I just," he let loose a deep breath, "I just don't want to deal with it."

"Cord said something was going on."

"Yeah." He smirked at me. "He also said you didn't seem too worried about me, said that you told him not to talk to you in classes, too. Are we your dirty secret?"

"More like I'd be yours."

The smirk flattened. "Are you fucking with me?"

"No, but you two are the basketball celebrities. I'm a nobody."

His hand clenched around the steering wheel. As his chest loosened and he let out a constrained breath, his hand never unclenched. "You're not a nobody. I don't ever want to hear you say that again."

I wanted to be a nobody. It was easy that way. But I forced a bright smile. "Where are we going?"

"I'll tell you when you tell me about your crazy night."

Ugh. I groaned just thinking about it. "Don't make me sick. Recounting it makes me want to vomit."

"You were sick last night?"

I nodded. "I was sick after the first stop in our crazy night of adventures."

"First stop?" His grin widened, so I was graced with his dimples. They were rarely seen, and only two people knew of their existence, one of them was dead. Laying my head against the seat, I felt his gaze on me. He was studying me, much the same as Beth had done, but I felt warm under his perusal. Anyone else and I would've been prickly and ready for a fight if the scrutiny lasted too long. Not with Jesse. Everything was different with Jesse.

"I'll tell you if you tell me where we're going."

He wheeled the car onto the highway and took a left. "Tiffany's throwing that picnic."

Oops. I'd forgotten.

Darn.

"And since my roommates are all going to be there, that means the house is going to be empty . . ." He glanced over as he left his statement hanging. His eyes darkened with lust, and my own sparked up in answer. One look and that was all it took.

I'd forgotten how much power Jesse had over me. "I thought we were in a fight."

He shrugged. "We fight. We make up. Always have."

My grin mirrored his. Always will.

With that shared look, everything else melted away. I wasn't a freshman. He wasn't a sophomore. He wasn't even my brother's best friend. It was only him and me, and my heart picked up its pace. The car couldn't get to his house fast enough.

Jesse reached over and slid a hand between my legs. I leaned back, closing my eyes, and concentrated on breathing as his fingers began working their way around. It wasn't long before he had my button undone, and I helped him move my pants for better access.

He murmured, deep throated, "Scoot down."

As I did, a moan escaped me. What he could do with his fingers. Then they dipped inside me. I grabbed on to the seat belt above my head as he began going in and out. When he slid two in, my hips moved with him.

His breathing became labored. I wasn't the only one affected by this. As I rolled my head and opened my eyes so I could see him, I knew mine were nearly black. They were wanton. I didn't care that he could see how he affected me or how fast one touch from him could render me a puddle mess.

"Jesse," I murmured, my voice husky with need.

He bit out a curse. His own was hoarse. "We're here. God, we're here."

I was ripped from his car. My legs wound around his waist, and his lips slammed onto mine as he carried me inside. He held me with a hand behind my head and one under my ass, urging me closer against him. My hips started moving up and down, sliding against him. A deep growl came from him as his tongue demanded entry. Pressing me against a wall, his hand slid underneath my shirt and moved to cup my breast. I gasped from the sudden sensation, arching against him. It mingled with the throb that was making me crazy as I melted.

Our tongues slid against each other's, savoring the feeling, as he lifted me from the wall. We were moving again. It seemed too long until he lowered me to a bed, and then his hands reached for my shirt and it was off. The bra was next. Then my jeans. As he bent over me, his hands paused on my hips before he drew them down slowly.

My eyes widened. I was ready to burst. A warning growl from me was all he needed. He flashed me a smile and whisked off my pants. When he pulled my panties next, I reached for his shirt. It was off in a flash—oh Lord—I gulped. I had missed that pack of muscles. Jesse didn't have a six-pack, he had a twelve-pack. Every muscle stuck out as he bent over me, his lips claiming mine again.

His pants were next, which left him in just his boxer briefs.

He was drinking me in as I was doing the same. My hand twitched to touch him all over. I didn't hesitate. I reached forward and pulled him down to me. He grinned, a delicious and sinfully melting sight as he caught himself just before he would've fallen on top of me, but that was what I wanted. I wanted to feel his hard body on mine, heavy and commanding, as he slid inside of me.

Jesse had other ideas. He propped himself up by his elbows and bent low to my lips.

Good gracious.

He touched my lips softly, so softly and so tenderly, I was writhing underneath him. "Jesse," I rasped out.

He slid his nose across my cheek in a caress. "Mmmm?" Then his hand slid up the side of my ribcage and cupped one of my breasts.

I was panting. "Please."

"Wait."

He bent low again, this time his lips touched where his hand was. His tongue swept around my nipple. I gasped, arching my back, and grabbed on to his shoulders. I pressed him against me, but his shoulders bulged underneath my touch as he held himself away. His entire body, its weight, was a tease.

I wanted more.

Twining my legs around his waist, I jerked down. He came into contact between my legs, and both of us let out groans. He gasped against my breast, moving up and then licking my neck. "I'm trying to take this slow."

I used my legs to push down his boxer briefs. "Fuck going slow."

His eyes jerked up to mine.

I licked my lips.

He closed his eyes, and his hand became rough on my breast. "Fine. A hard fuck, Alex. That's what you're asking for."

My heart lurched. My hunger grew insatiable for him.

Then he swept off his underwear, had the condom on in seconds, and grabbed underneath my hips. I had little warning before he jerked me down and then slammed into me.

I gasped, coming alive in his arms, but he wasn't waiting. He reared back and thrust farther inside, then again and again. The hunger in me rose, and I moved with him. Hanging on to his shoulders, I synched with his movements. It was wild and fast, and we were both bristling with pent-up aggression and need. It'd been so long. As he pounded into me, gripping my hips in his hands, he nestled his face into the corner of my neck. His lips began trailing kisses down and then up until he met my lips again. His tongue slipped inside and moved in rhythm with us.

White-hot pleasure coursed through my body. I felt it building.

Jesse grunted and braced himself against his headboard. Clenching on to it, he used it for a deeper access. His chest was above my head, and I bent forward and licked over him. His body shuddered underneath me. Grinning and drunk off him, I leaned forward as far as I could to taste as much as I could of him.

"Alex," he gasped above me.

I looked up. He'd been watching me. His eyes were molten black, holding me suspended in their chaos of lust. He kept thrusting into me, each one building the heat in my core a bit more, and then he grunted with one last push, tossing me right over the edge.

Crying out, he joined me. His body jerked in pleasure before he collapsed beside me, pulling my back against his chest and wrapping his arms around me. I was enclosed within his shelter. Running a hand up and down my arm, he pressed a kiss to the back of my neck.

"You okay?"

My heart was still fluttering in my chest. "Yeah . . ." Holy hell. I'd forgotten what it was like with him. "I'm going to be sore."

His hand caressed over my thigh and dipped between my legs. His lips moved against my shoulder as his fingers started to rub me. He didn't slide inside. He just slowly rolled around in a soothing circle. It was relaxing, tender. He asked, quietly, "Has it been a long time?"

I heard the soft question and rolled over. Wrapping my legs

tightly around him until we were flush against each other again, I tilted my face so I could gaze up at him. "Since you."

"Good." It was a whisper of a word before he dipped back down and met my lips with his.

I curled a hand around his neck, holding him close until he settled all of his body weight onto mine. When I grew heated again and moved against him, he chuckled as he pulled back. "Shit, Alex. Why didn't we do this the first night?"

"Because Cord got arrested. Again."

"Oh yeah." The small smile was gone, and his eyes grew somber. He moved to lay on his side and looked down at my body. As he ran his hand up and down, touching every inch of me, he murmured, "And then we got into that fight."

I remembered what he said before. He was right. Jesse had always been a dick, but when we got into bed, it didn't matter. It was only the two of us. Toward the end, I was starting to feel maybe he was ready for more than that, but I hadn't been sure. I had listened to Angie. Why had I listened to Angie?

I gazed up at him. "Are there others?"

His hand froze, and his eyes found mine again. He knew what I was asking.

"Jesse."

"No." The word was so soft, so quiet.

I strained to hear it. My heart was pounding against my chest. "Are you sure?"

"I wouldn't lie to you. Never to you."

My throat was suddenly full, too full to speak, and I moved my head in a nod. I couldn't tear my gaze away. His hand moved to cup the back of my head, and his thumb rubbed against the base of my neck. "Are you still in contact with Eric?"

I shook my head. My heart kept pounding, harder and harder. Eric Nathan had been so long ago, a faint memory compared to Jesse.

"Good," he whispered as he bent for my lips again.

His hand slid across my stomach and between my legs as he turned me to my back. With his lips against mine, he positioned himself above me. When I began to writhe around, needing him against me, he held himself up. Only his lips touched me. I was a wanton mess, reaching for him. "Jesse."

He chuckled against my lips and then slowly moved to slide into me. After a few slow, deep thrusts, he stilled and gasped against my lips, "Are you protected?"

I nodded. "Are you clean?"

He groaned, "God yes." Then he began moving in me, slow, so goddamn slow.

Closing my eyes, all thought fled as the sensations took over.

11

B *AM!*
   BAM!
      I jolted awake, sprawled out over Jesse's naked chest. His hand was resting on my back and his head had been nestled to my neck under my hair. His hand tightened in reflex, and a sleepy curse spilled from him as he lifted his head. "Striker, if that's you, you're going to get hurt."

"Whatever," Jamie's muffled voice came through the door. "You ditched the picnic. Not cool."

Jesse's head fell back to the pillow with a groan. When I started to get up, his hand held me in place. He murmured in my ear, "The door's locked. He can't get in."

I relaxed. Slightly.

"Come on, man," Jamie whined. "Listen, we're doing an after-party. You coming out of your hole for that?"

"No."

I lifted my head enough to get a good view of Jesse. There was no regret in his voice, but he was giving up time with his friends for me. He had never cared before, but this was college. These were his roommates and teammates. I needed to make sure.

When his gaze caught mine, there was nothing there. No hesitation. No torn emotions. Nothing. He just looked back and asked, "What?"

I shook my head as something close to relief spread in me. Then I laid back down where I'd been in the first place. My head went to his chest and his hand cupped the side of me again to hold me in place. As his fingers started to rub through my hair, my eyes closed, and I felt real relief go through me. This was the type that went to the bone, it mingled closely with feeling content. I should've stirred as I realized that, but I didn't. Jesse was weaving a spell for me, one that felt intoxicating. I was being pulled down to the abyss, and I didn't want to fight it. It felt good. It felt right.

Jamie wasn't taking no for an answer. He banged on the door again. "Come on!" His frustration came across loud and clear.

"Jamie, what's your deal?" Jesse sat up this time. He had a bit more bark this time. "Leave me alone."

"What the hell! What are you even doing in there? Come to the after-party."

"No. Leave it alone. You've never given a damn before. Why today?"

"Because—" He stopped abruptly but then mumbled, "Never mind. You're right." There was a moment of silence before he asked, "You got a girl in there?"

Jesse leaned over, picked up a shoe, and hurled it at the door. It smacked against the wood with a resounding *thud*.

We heard a mutter from the other side, "Shit. Fine. Jesus. Have it your way."

When we finally heard him leave, I bit my lip from laughing as I saw Jesse's stormy expression. My hand splayed out over his chest where I could feel his heart beating fast, and I frowned. "Are you okay?"

"Hmmm?" His eyes jerked to mine. "Yeah, I'm good. You?"

"I'm fine." Why was he asking me? It was obvious he wasn't good. "What was that about?"

"Nothing. You sleepy?" He didn't wait for my response as he slid out of bed and grabbed some clothes. "Want to get some food or something?"

"Uh . . ." I was confused. Something had occurred that I wasn't privy to. He hadn't cared about Jamie banging on the door, but then it changed. It was swift and suddenly he wanted to get out of here. But I swallowed my words. His movements were precise and quick. I knew this Jesse. This was the one who didn't want to talk about whatever was bothering him. He'd get snappy, even a little bit rude with me, but he'd be fine later. It had taken me two years to understand that he still wanted me around him, even though he wasn't a big sharer. I wasn't, either, so it worked.

There was nothing left for me to do except shower and change. Jesse had hopped in first and was out within record time. I had only grabbed half of my clothes by the time he strolled back out. Toweling his hair dry, his chest glistened with water and his jeans were pulled haphazardly over his lean hips. They weren't zipped so they hung open, exposing his black boxer briefs underneath.

"Are we racing someone?"

The corner of his lips curved up. "Sorry. If Jamie's here, that means the rest are, too. I just want to get away."

"Okay." Trailing into the bathroom, I couldn't tear my gaze away as he turned and grabbed his phone. His back was bare to me. It was curved and muscular. A droplet of water slid down his spine before being absorbed by his boxer briefs. We'd spent the entire afternoon in bed and lust was stirring in me again as I couldn't look away from where that water had vanished.

Then his back stiffened. "What is it?"

He glanced over his shoulder. "That Feast is going on tonight. You want to go to that?"

"Feast?" My stomach rumbled, but food was the furthest thing from my mind. "I'm not that hungry."

Not for that.

He caught my meaning, and his eyes darkened from response. A slow grin came over him, curving until it promised me so many sensual things. The lust kicked up a notch. The guy was going to be the death of me.

"Remember that band?"

Sustain. How could I not? I cleared my throat and nodded.

"Remember they invited us to the Feast? It's a small private event with a bunch of local bands. They're playing, but it's a quiet thing. They only told some of their biggest fans. And there's going to be a ton of food. You want to go?"

"Sure." Food. Bands. Jesse. I'd be stupid to pass that up. Hurrying into the shower, I couldn't break Jesse's record of cleanliness so it took me longer. He had made the bed and tidied his room by the time I emerged from the bathroom. He looked up from the book he was reading and licked his lips as his eyes trailed all the way down to my toes and back up again. He lingered on my lips as he stood and drew near. In a husky voice, he murmured, "You're going to kill me, Alex. I want you already."

The lust from before had diminished to a simmer. It flamed again at his words, and his hand touched the side of my hip to draw me against him. It was like he had read my mind. I closed my eyes as his head bent. His cool lips touched against my neck and his hand clamped tighter on me, pulling me flush against him.

As his lips trailed to my mouth, his free hand slid down and rested on my jeans. His fingers slipped inside, but he didn't make any other move. He kept kissing me, and I returned the kisses, slow and deep, as if we had all the time in the world to just be there together.

No matter the nosedive into hell my life had taken, I still needed this man.

I pulled away. My heart was beating like crazy and I gazed at him in shock.

The need I had for him wasn't superficial. It wasn't an itch to scratch that would eventually go away. It wasn't on the surface, like a crush. This went deep, way deeper than I wanted to think about at that moment.

"What's wrong?" He was watching me again as his hand touched my throat. "Your pulse is going crazy. What's going on?"

"Nothing." My senses screamed at me to tear away from him, but I stopped myself. I pulled away in a gentle fashion, one that wouldn't alarm him of the chaos going on inside me. "Let's go. Right? That's what you wanted."

"That was until you came out here all wet. My dick's never sprung up for someone like it does for you."

I shook my head. Those were the least romantic words I could ever want to hear.

I tugged on his hand. "Let's go."

"All right." His hand went to my butt, and he squeezed. Crowding close behind me, he wrapped an arm around my waist so he could find the best fit. "But we're not staying long." He rose against me. As he started to grind against me, I closed my eyes and almost missed his next promise. "I'm going to lay you bare all night long, Alex."

We slipped from the house unnoticed.

I'd been a little worried. I didn't want to run into any of the girlfriends, Tiffany, Chandra, or my RA, but as Jesse led the way, I realized he had his own entrance and exit. Even though he lived in the basement, the house was built into a hill. A separate driveway and patio was connected to his level. I wasn't sure how that was possible, but when we stepped past the patio doors and into his garage, I saw the deck had rock walls all around it.

Backing the black Ferrari out, Jesse turned onto a small gravel path that wound around the hill and connected to the road. He drove past the driveway leading to his house, and we saw that a bunch of cars had arrived. People were climbing out and heading inside, but I saw Cord pause when he caught sight of us. He lifted his hand in a wave as we shot past.

Jesse let out a deep breath once we were out of their sight.

Taking a deep shuddering breath, I ignored the knots in my stomach. My time with Jesse was just that, time with Jesse. I didn't care about any after party or if that would stop my time with him.

Liar.

"Where's this Feast?" My voice hitched, but I cleared my throat as if to hide it.

Jesse glanced over with a small frown. "You okay?"

"Yeah." I just needed to clear my throat again. That was it. "So where is this at?" My chest lifted in a deep silent breath and prayed it would calm my stomach down.

"At Grace Park."

"Oh." Never heard of it. "That's nice."

Jesse grinned at me. "Yeah, it is. It was a smart move on their part. The back part is surrounded by trees, and it's on the river. I used to go there for basketball. Some local guys get together for a friendly game every Sunday."

"You don't go there anymore?" I asked, noting a twinge of longing from him.

He shrugged. "The friendly stuff is just that, friendly. Coach put a stop to it when he found out, said we could get hurt."

"We?"

"Cord played with me."

"You and Cord are close now?"

He shrugged again. "Close as two guy friends can get."

I didn't know how I felt about that.

"He's not Ethan, Alex."

I jerked my head in a nod. I knew that. No one could take Ethan's spot, but it felt good hearing that from him.

"Okay. Here we are." Jesse pulled onto a small road. Trees lined both sides and it went up a hill to a clearing with playground equipment and basketball courts. He paused the car by them. "I'm going to park on the other side of the hill. The bands should be set up in the back section, so wait for me. Luke said it was a small thing, but with these guys, you never know. Their drummer sometimes goes on a tweeting spree. They had three hundred show up for a private gig one time."

I nodded and got out. As I found a bench to wait on, I listened to the music I could hear playing in the distance. It wasn't long until I heard giggling.

I knew those giggles.

Sick dread speared me, and I turned around.

Marissa and Sarah Shastaine were walking toward me. When they saw me, both faltered with mixed expressions. Marissa's eyes rounded while Sarah's narrowed to slits. A sneer came over her, and her hands shot to her hips. She lifted her chin as if to look down her nose at me, which was exactly what she was always the best at doing. "What are you doing here?"

Marissa sent her a quick glare before she moved toward me. "Hi. I set you a text about us having brunch. You didn't get it?"

Sarah followed her until they both stood closer to me. She snorted, "Yeah, right. Why do you even care, Marissa? This one's a freak now. She became a freak last summer, and she's always going to stay a freak."

Jesse's ex-girlfriend had never been my fan, but I wasn't expecting the venom she just spat at me. "You're drunk."

Her hands flew up and flattened together in a praying motion. She lifted her arms to the sky before she nearly fell over, but she blasted out, "Hallelujah. The girl is not dumb. Besides," an extra sheen of hostility came to her, "like you can sit there and judge me. You were wasted last night. You couldn't even stand. And great friends, by the way. Real class act, running off after a fight and leaving you there all alone."

I grinned at her. "I almost wish they were here because Hannah would rip into you for that." I glanced at Marissa, who seemed annoyed at her friend. "They came back for me but couldn't find me at the party."

She jerked her gaze to me and put on an expressionless mask. The annoyance was gone. She even tried to smile nicely at me. "I know. I mean, I don't know. But—" Sarah gasped beside her and she sent her another scathing look from the corner of her eye.

Sarah grabbed on to her arm. "That's Jesse over there. I'm going to go say hi."

Before Marissa could comment, Sarah scampered down the hill and after his disappearing figure.

I glared at him. Bastard. I knew he came up, saw Sarah, and decided to avoid the entire scene.

"Uh." Marissa chuckled to herself. "Imagine that. You show up and minutes later Jesse Hunt's in the background."

I turned back. She knew.

She smirked at me. "You guys are together again?"

"Were we before?"

She lifted a shoulder. "I don't know. Yeah, I think you were. Angie hated it."

I know. I remembered how much she hated that I was with Jesse and how easily I'd let her own feelings sway mine. "She just didn't want me hurt."

A dark look stopped any other words from spilling. Marissa shook her head. "I cannot believe that you're defending her after what she did to you."

I shook my head. Nope. I wasn't going to do this. "I'm going to go." The tornado was back in me, and it was picking up speed. I could not be here, not with her and definitely not with Jesse's ex-girlfriend so close to prey on him.

"Okay. Stop." She grabbed my hand. I pulled it away and started in the direction Sarah ran after Jesse. "Please, stop. Alex. Come on. I really do want to talk to you."

"Why?" I rounded on her, a strangled note in my voice.

She braked and her eyebrows shot up. From my intensity, she

fell back, then her eyebrows bunched together and a determined look came over. Her shoulders squared back and her chin steadied itself before she nodded. "Okay. I get it. I messed up as a friend. I ditched you—"

"Twice."

Silence fell between us like a heavy blanket. It was suffocating and sweltering. I wanted to fold underneath it and disappear into the ground. I forced myself to keep calm. My insides were twisting and turning, but I drew in a deep breath and hoped it would calm the chaos down.

"Okay." Her voice had dropped to a soft whisper. "And I'm sorry for both of those times."

I shook my head. This wasn't even right. Marissa had dumped our friendship, but she hadn't been the one who ran like I had grown horns. That'd been Angie. A tremor went through me as I remembered that last day. They had come to say good-bye. Justin had been there, alongside his girlfriend, but he had stayed in his truck that day. He couldn't even muster a good-bye in person. Angie hadn't taken two steps inside my house. She seemed ready to crap her pants at an invitation from me.

Their good-byes had lasted five minutes. Five minutes from the two who I had considered as close to my family as I could get.

"Stop, Marissa."

I wasn't going to hang my head in shame. I had done nothing wrong, but I knew she was getting ready to unburden her soul and that wasn't right. Marissa had just gone away. That was all she had done. She'd been my best friend. She dumped me when she fought with Angie, and then she apologized at a party toward the end of the school year. That'd been it. Nothing more from the second person I considered a best friend all my life.

"What is it?"

"Just stop. You don't have to do this."

"Do what?"

"Apologize. That's what you're doing, isn't it?" A bitter taste was in my mouth, and I couldn't get rid of it.

Her lips clamped shut and she gazed at me, studying me and trying to figure out where I was going with all this. It was an uncomfortable feeling and one I wanted to shed. Like a second skin, I wanted it off me.

"Stop," I snapped this time.

She blinked. Once. Then she murmured, "You think I'm apologizing for ditching you, don't you?"

"Aren't you?"

One shake of the head.

My heart dropped. There was so much more in her gaze and my chest squeezed. I didn't know if I was ready for whatever else she was going to say.

The wind shifted. It grazed against my cheeks, but there was moisture on them as well. I glanced up idly, had it started raining? There were no drops in the sky.

She started out, cautious at first, "I knew what was going on last year."

My heart plunged all the way to my feet. She knew. I hadn't thought anyone knew.

"I worked in the counselor's office as a teacher's assistant." At my look, she explained, "I never said anything. I didn't want you guys to make fun of me or, God forbid, be proud of me. I know. I know. Stupid of me, but I know you and Angie thought I was only some party hussy who could hold her own. I wasn't. I was messed up. I know that much, but I wanted more."

She'd gone after Jesse. She slept with Cord instead. Then she dated Eric, only to cheat on him with Cord. Again.

She was right about some of it.

I tucked all that away. That wasn't the same girl in front of me. Marissa had changed. Sarah had always seemed perfect, and she turned into just another catty bitch. Even Cord changed.

I had changed.

Did nothing stay the same?

"Look," Marissa kept going. "I was unhappy last year and I was jealous."

"Jealous?"

"Of you and Angie. You two are so close—you two were so close. I was left out all the time. I know Angie called me a slut behind my back. She said it to my face all the time. I messed up. I went after Jesse when I knew you two had a thing. And then Eric was going to ask you out, and I got to him first. Then I became friends with Sarah." She waved in her direction. "And look how she's turned out."

I frowned. "Yeah, she seemed so perfect last year. Now she's . . ."

Marissa grinned. "Vapid? Shallow? Insecure? Because she's all three of them. I think she thought if she stayed nice and perfect last year then Jesse would come back."

I shifted on my feet and shoved my hands into the front pockets of my jeans. Turning away, I muttered, "Yeah, well, they dated for three years."

"Three years that he hated her."

"What are you talking about?"

She gave me an incredulous look. "Come on, Alex. You had to have known. I thought you always did, and it hurt my feelings. I could never figure out what I'd done so you wouldn't confide in me. Then, last year, I stopped caring. I stopped caring about a lot of stuff."

Scratching at the back of my head, a foreboding sensation settled in the middle of my shoulders. It wouldn't go away as I tried to figure out what she was talking about.

"Jesse." Her head inclined a notch. "Are you serious?"

What?

"He's liked you since forever. You never knew?"

"He was with Sarah. Three years, Marissa. He was with her for three years."

"Yeah, but he didn't want to be." She lamented, "Okay, he might've liked her in the beginning, but he didn't for a while after. I heard them fighting one time."

"Sarah and Jesse?"

"Ethan and Jesse."

This was the second person to talk about a dispute between my brother and his best friend. It sent daggers through me when Barbie had first said it, and it sent daggers through me again. Ice-cold daggers with tips of steel. I didn't like hearing about any discord between the two, and I really didn't like hearing that my best friend had known. She hadn't said a word.

My lips were stiff as I demanded, "What are you talking about?"

"Jesse wanted to be with you. Your brother told him to stay away."

He'd said the same thing to me, but there was a missing piece. I knew it. It was nagging me from the back of my mind. The puzzle wasn't complete, and I was determined to figure it out. With my lips pressed together, I gave her a pointed look. "Thanks for telling me."

She flushed. "I'm sorry. Again. I was jealous." She rolled her eyes. "He told Ethan he wanted to break up with Sarah and be with you, but your brother wasn't having it. He threatened Jesse that if he broke up with Sarah, then he'd say something horrible to you. He was going to turn you against him." Her laugh was hollow. "Your brother was hardcore, huh?"

Not the Ethan I knew.

Pain tingled at the tips of my fingers and toes. It was slowly working its way through me, all the way to send my heart into a tailspin.

The brother I knew would've never kept me from someone I loved.

Oh shit.

I drew in another shuddering breath.

I had loved Jesse then.

Had I stopped when he hadn't returned my calls? Because I didn't still love him. I couldn't.

Liar.

"You okay?"

I jerked my head in a nod. "Yeah."

She wasn't convinced.

"Look," edging closer to me, Marissa glanced over her shoulder as she spoke, "I know Jesse's going to ditch her soon, and she's going to come back. I won't say anything. I know you two were secretive before, and I'm figuring you are now since you didn't tell us where his house was." She bit her lip and kicked at some dirt before her head came back up. "It's no secret. She wanted to come down because she's still obsessed with getting Jesse back. She's dropped the perfect act. She's hardcore, like your brother."

Anger flared in me. Ethan wasn't hardcore. She must've heard wrong.

"I've gone through a lot of my issues, and I have a lot to say to you. I'm sorry about your parents. I knew what they were doing to you."

"It's ok—"

"No, it's not okay. I should've said something or done something, but I didn't. I was a shitty friend to you, no matter what you think. I wasn't loyal, and I didn't stand up for you." Her frown deepened when she saw Sarah in the distance. "I hate feeling rushed. I wished you had met me for brunch. Listen, don't trust Sarah. Don't trust Angie."

Angie? Her name was a lightning bolt. "What are you talking about?"

"Angie's going to contact you."

I sensed her withdrawal. Sarah was almost upon us, and this new Marissa would disappear again. My hand latched on to her arm. "Did she tell you that?"

Startled, she looked up from my hand to my face. I felt the blood drain from me and knew she was seeing a ghost. Good. I was starting to feel like one again. She shook her head. "No, but I know Angie. She'll take a semester off, see me at some party at Christmas, and I'll tell her that I've seen you. She'll hate that. She's going to contact you, just for her conscience probably. She'll think she's the bad friend, and she'll hate that." A smug grin came over her. "On second thought, maybe I won't say anything at all. I like thinking of her as the bad friend."

I was getting restless. Marissa was talking too much about the past. It was a year of hell, and I wanted it remain behind me. She was dredging up past hurts, past feelings, and memories. All of them were better left buried. I snapped, "Shut up, Marissa!"

She jumped back.

"Just shut up. Stop talking about shit you don't know anything about."

"What?" Her mouth hung there for a moment. "But I do. I know what I'm talking about. Don't trus—"

"Stop it!" My voice rose, and I knew the last was a shout.

Sarah had halted a few feet from us, but she edged closer. When Marissa jerked away, an evil grin came over Sarah. "Not so perfect now, Alex? I'm glad we ran into you at this pathetic picnic. I can't believe my cousin told us hot guys would be here. Other than Jesse, I didn't see anyone. They're all freaks."

Taking a few deep breaths, I tried to settle my pulse down. I couldn't believe this was the same girl Jesse had been with for so long. She'd been shy. She'd been dainty. The version standing in front of me was ugly deep into her damn soul.

"Let's go." She gave me a pointed look as she spoke to Marissa, "Jesse told me where the real party is at. He said Cord's there, and he's coming right behind us."

Marissa had been watching me. When I didn't react, her lips thinned. She knew Jesse had been lying. "Sure. Why not?" Her eyes never left mine. "I'll see you later?"

I didn't answer.

I didn't care.

When they left, she gave me a sad smile while Sarah hurried off. Her hand was clutching on to Marissa, as if claiming her, and she went along like a dutiful friend.

Whatever had changed, I knew Marissa would never be my best friend again. She'd never be merely a friend either.

I squared my shoulders and lifted my chin.

That was just fine with me.

All you do is lie.

I went in search for Jesse, and I shut that nagging voice down. It would only bring me heartache.

12

When I approached the group at the bottom, no one paid me attention. This was why Sarah hadn't liked them, because they hadn't cared about her. A few others were behind me and were greeted by a group to the side. It was obvious this was a tight group. Sidelong glances were cast at me. I felt the suspicion from some of the members, but others were merely curious.

Jesse lifted his arm. He was sitting in one of the lawn chairs around a campfire. As I drew near, I saw it wasn't a real campfire, but one that stood in the air. It was an expensive looking piece of metal that would've looked at home on a millionaire's patio. It stood out, nestled in the middle of its group with ripped and fading lawn chairs.

Jesse patted his lap. I sat in front of his feet. I sensed his confusion, but then his hands came to my shoulder and he began to rub them. When they paused, I dropped my head forward and let him rub out the knot of tension he had found. Biting my tongue, I hoped he wouldn't comment on what took me so long. I didn't want to talk. As his thumbs started to press into another knot and he began a massage, my shoulders lifted up in a relieved breath.

Thank God.

A girl from across the campfire waved. She had a baseball cap pulled down to cover most of her face. Her jean shorts were ripped at the ends with a white tank underneath a baggy flannel shirt. I was surprised as I recognized this girl from The Shack. She'd been the one tending the bar. Brielle? Was that what Jesse had called her? No, he called her Bri. As I looked around the rest of the campfire, I was even more surprised.

The entire band of Sustain sat around it. All of them had on baseball caps, all pulled low over their faces. They were unrecognizable.

No wonder Sarah thought this Feast was a joke. I knew without a doubt that she hadn't known who else was in attendance.

The drummer was beside Bri, and he was tapping her foot with his. She glared at him before kicking his leg back. A goofy grin slid over his face as he continued to bob his head to the music's beat. After she settled back down, he began tapping her foot again.

"Braden!" she hissed at him.

"Shut up," a low warning came from beside me.

A guy was on the ground with a guitar in his lap. His shoulders were being rubbed how mine were, but instead of Jesse, he got a blonde bombshell. Her hair was sun streaked and instead of the flannel shirt Bri wore, this girl only wore a black tank top. It resembled more of a tube top as it rested high on her stomach and barely covered her cleavage. Tight black shorts disappeared in her lawn chair as her golden legs wrapped around the guy in front of her.

Jesse chuckled, and gray eyes shifted over to us. A menacing look was in them. I felt blasted with his coldness, but it didn't have the same effect on Jesse. He cursed at him, "Stuff it, Luke."

The drummer, identified as Braden, pumped a hand in the air. He held two drumsticks in it. "Yeah, Hunt! You tell him."

Bri's lip curled up. "Just what we need, two superstars getting in a fight."

A guy in the back commented, "It'd be good publicity."

As they continued to tease Jesse and the guy beside me, I was even more jolted to recognize the lead singer of Sustain. I hadn't put two and two together. My gaze had skipped over him and I assumed Luke Skeet was elsewhere.

As I studied him, he sent a withering look across the fire to Bri, whose gazed coolly back at him as she lifted her beer. An eyebrow went up, defiantly, and she took a long slow swallow from her can. His head moved down a notch as he glared at her, but he seemed riveted by what he was seeing.

She caught me staring and winked.

Maybe I should've been flustered. Maybe I should've been embarrassed. I wasn't. I grinned back and then caught a beer that was tossed in my lap.

"Jeezus, Hunt. Your date's probably parched by now. Good manners."

His fingers dug into my skin, but a low chuckle was his only response.

I risked a peek over my shoulder, but found myself in my own riveted state. His gaze had darkened and smoldered down at me. My throat went dry. My core began to throb in answer.

I didn't know who moved first. It might've been me or it might've been the shift in his fingers, but we moved as one unit. I was transferred from the ground and into his lap. As I laid my head against his chest and his arm wrapped around me, one of the guys asked, "Hunt, you ever going to introduce us? This is the second time you've brought her around."

His arms tightened protectively around me. "You've got a girl in your own lap, Emerson. Pay attention to that one."

"Yeah, pay attention to me."

"Fine, Hunt. Rude, but fine."

I grinned as I settled in Jesse's lap. Bri sent me another wink from across the fire. She lifted her beer can in salute. Reciprocating the motion, we both broke out in grins. Jesse's chest lifted up and down underneath me in a big yawn. As the night wore on, we didn't talk much. I remained on his lap, and the guys continued to talk around us. Bands changed for background music, and every now and then, one of the guys would disappear from the group. They'd come back with a tray full of food. I realized each campfire made their own food and people were encouraged to share with each other. It wasn't until the end of the night, after I'd had too many beers, that the guys began to grow restless. A break in bands started and they stood, one by one.

It was their turn.

Jesse pressed a kiss to my forehead and soothed some strands from my face.

And then Sustain took to the stage.

It wasn't fast and energizing like most of their usual music. When Luke gripped the microphone and started singing, it was new music. His voice was a smooth and gravelly. It was caressing and seductive in the same manner.

His eyes were trained on our camp, on Bri, who was looking down at her lap the entire time. Her eyes were closed tight, and she was biting her lip. She glanced up once, saw me staring again, and brushed away a tear before she turned to the side in her chair.

In that look, I understood. It resonated deep in me for reasons I didn't want to acknowledge. This girl was in love, and it was haunting her.

I drew in a shuddering breath as my own pain sliced me, and Luke's voice pulled me deeper.

With tears streaming down, I looked up with my head tilted to the sky. Looking, searching, eyes on a quest, but I was unseeing, the clouds everywhere.

Marissa had said.

"She's going to contact you, just for her conscience probably."

"She's hardcore, like your brother."

My heart started pounding. It wanted to push its way out of my chest, and I drew in a gaping breath. I pressed a hand there to keep it in, as if I could do that. I tried to stop from hearing more.

"He was going to turn you against him."

I failed. They kept coming at me.

"I was a shitty friend to you, no matter what you think. I wasn't loyal, and I didn't stand up for you."

I was curled in a ball on Jesse's lap as the memories assaulted me. She'd only said those things to me, but they stemmed from the years before. The history was my undoing. I couldn't hold up against the past. It was weighing me down.

"Hey?" Jesse nudged me with his shoulder.

I didn't respond. I couldn't.

"What's wrong? You okay?"

With tears streaming down, I looked at him.

My heart was reaching out in pain, in anguish, in agony. Wondering why, wondering the reason. Where are you? I wondered.

Luke's voice picked up again. I felt those words, and looking over again, I saw a mirrored torment in the girl across from us.

I shook my head and sat up. "I have to go. We have to go."

"What?" Jesse cast a cursory look to the stage. "I wanted to stay and chill."

Scrambling off his lap, I ignored my pounding heart. "You can stay. Whatever. I can call someone to pick me up."

He scowled at me and shoved up from the seat. "Don't be dramatic, Alex. I brought you here. I'll take you home."

I ignored the rapt audience we had around the campfire. In the distance, the band moved to their next song, which was the same haunting melody as the first. The words were different, the notes were altered, but its meaning was the same. Pain. Whoever had written that song and the last was under the same kind of mountain of agony I held inside.

I couldn't be there to hear any more of it. "Are we going? I'm leaving."

Jesse was grumbling behind me, but I left and didn't wait. As I walked up the hill, I realized that I didn't know where he had parked the car so I went to the playground instead. Taking a seat on one of the swings, I tried to desperately calm my racing heart.

When I finally managed to open my eyes, Jesse was waiting in front of me. His voice was chilling to hear, so soft against the harshness inside me. "Are you going to tell me what that was about?"

I dropped my head as fresh tears pricked my eyes. There was no way he was going to see the tears threatening to spill.

"Fine. Whatever. I'll go and get the car."

Good.

I meant to say that aloud, but my throat failed me.

I was primed and ready for the fight. When Jesse was like this, when I was like this, we always fought. Okay. That wasn't true. We never fought because I had been too weak and too sad to stand up for myself. During that first year, I let him treat me how he did. I never said a word against him. The only thing or the only person I ever stood my ground for was Ethan.

That person was gone. I didn't mean my brother.

I had changed, so I waited the entire car ride back to my dorm. I waited for him to say something, but he didn't. His jaw was clenched tight, and he gripped the steering wheel until his knuckles were white, but he never said a word.

As he pulled to the front door of my dorm, I reached for the handle.

"Wait."

My shoulders tensed. Here it was.

"I'm sorry for whatever I did to make you uncomfortable."

I could only blink at him. What did he say?

He fidgeted under my stare. "Was I acting too couple-y? I

know we're not like that, and I know we don't talk about things, but can you tell me what I did?"

My hand let go of the handle. I sat back in the seat. He was self-conscious. I had never seen Jesse self-conscious. It was a different look, one that pulled at my heartstrings, and I couldn't have this conversation because of that. One word, one touch, all of it would come crashing down on me.

I looked at the door. I should go.

It was like he sensed it because he said, "Please, Alex. Can you tell me?"

I shook my head. "You didn't do anything."

"Did I say something?"

"You didn't say anything, either."

"Then what? I wanted to spend time with you. You and those guys, you're the only ones who don't care who my dad is or what I do on the court. That's sad, isn't it?" His hands were curled into fists on his lap. "I really needed some time with you. If that makes me a loser or pathetic, whatever. Fine. I'm pathetic. I want to spend time with you. I want to be with you. Please don't go."

Oh my God. He was almost begging me. A vulnerable look was in his eyes. I felt him stripped and raw in front of me.

I was struggling.

I wanted to go. Badly. I didn't. I couldn't get myself to leave. Then I sighed, "You didn't do anything, Jesse."

"Then what? What happened? You were fine, and then you weren't. I could feel it from you. You wanted to bolt, but I don't know what I did."

"You didn't. Honest."

He blew out a breath in annoyance. "Then Sarah or Marissa. What'd they say to you?"

"Nothing."

I tried to lie, but my voice broke on that word. That wasn't true.

His eyes flashed. He knew. "Which one?"

I heard the savagery in him. This wasn't good. "Your ex is a bitch."

"I know. That's why I broke up with her. All that saint stuff was an act. I couldn't stomach it anymore." He frowned. "Was it Sarah?"

"No." My head went down. My gut bottomed out as I whispered that word.

"So Marissa then?"

I couldn't confirm it. He knew. We both knew, but when he reached for his phone, I grabbed it from him. Shaking my head, I was horrified to find some tears on my cheeks. "Stop."

"She made you cry."

I blew out a calming breath. "Stop, Jesse. Marissa didn't mean any harm. She said a few things and old wounds opened. That's it. I'll be fine. I promise."

He wavered.

I clenched his phone tighter. I knew he could grab it lightning fast.

"Fine."

My shoulders sagged in relief.

"Just to be clear, I didn't do anything?"

A grin broke free as I shook my head.

"And I didn't say anything?"

"You did call me dramatic."

"I'm sorry."

I blinked at the automatic apology. That wasn't a normal Jesse comment. Had he changed as well, like everyone else? I held my tongue on that one. "So what's going on that you needed to get away from your friends?"

This was the second time in two weeks. He liked to hide with those friends and bring me along. Well, this time was different. We'd been doing other things before he took me along to hide with them.

He grew still. "I don't want to talk about that."

The old roles clicked into place again. We were back to that. Neither of us talked about anything real in our lives. The only topics allowed were Ethan or sex. It had always been like that.

"Oh."

His head tipped back and a deep groan escaped from him. "I'm sorry. You should know what's been going on and why I haven't called you that much."

Oh.

Were the rules changing?

"This has nothing to do with my friends, but there's a girl suing my dad. She claims that she's his daughter, he knew about her, and he ignored her as she grew up. She's claiming emotional damage." He'd become a statue. The words fell from him, his tone so cold, "She's probably his kid. You know how he was, how he still is with a different girl every other month. Fuck. Two months after Mom died and he had some eighteen year old in the house."

Reaching over, I slipped my hand within his. Our fingers wrapped around each other. "I'm guessing that the lawyers said you couldn't talk about the case?" Was that why he was avoiding his friends?

Jesse sighed, "Yes and no. They told me I should warn my friends against this girl, in case she reaches out to them. The other side is trying to bring me as a character witness against my dad. I don't even know if they can do that, but they're claiming he's damaged my life. I don't want that shit out there. It's only a matter of time before the press gets wind of this."

The question of whether Malcolm Hunt had damaged his son wasn't a question. He had. It was the reason why Jesse moved in with my family from eighth grade until his junior year. He moved out after Ethan died and lived in their huge mansion. Malcolm was rarely around by then, so it was him and his housekeeper. Mary was like a second mother in some ways to him. And I knew he considered my parents as his own.

Pain swelled in my chest.

Hell, my parents considered Jesse to be more of their own kid than I was. Blinking back more tears, I remembered when my mother tried to kill herself. Jesse had been with me so he went to the hospital as well. My father hadn't said a word to me as he embraced Jesse like a long lost son.

I wondered if they took the love they had for Ethan and myself and channeled it into the son they could be proud of—Jesse?

Flicking a tear away with a thumb, I refused to think about them anymore. Except that Jesse was lucky in some ways. He still had two parents who loved him, even though they weren't his by blood. They were still his.

Hoarsely, I asked, "Have you said anything to your friends about her?"

A bitter laugh wrung from deep in his throat. "Are you kidding? Of course not." The laugh faded, and his lips pressed into a flat line. "They think Malcolm Hunt is awesome. Cord's the only one who remembers a little bit, but he doesn't remember much, and you and Ethan never spread it around school. I was always grateful for that."

My hand squeezed his.

"Anyway, can we not talk about this anymore?" He tried to give me a reassuring smile. It didn't reach his eyes. "I think the party moved somewhere else. We could go back there and just hang out? I'll show you my place. You haven't seen it yet."

My emotional wheel of misfortune was on a constant spin. As the arrow started to fall on STAY AWAY, it went past and landed on RUN AWAY RUN AWAY, but I found myself smiling back. "Sure. That'd be nice."

13

I guessed Jesse and I had a called a shaky truce, but I did know I couldn't tear myself away from him. Not anymore. I wasn't ready to take the plunge into an actual relationship, so we did what we did. We spent the night together, not every night, and we hung out in secret. The only two people who might've guessed about our situation were Cord and Beth. She caught me on the curb again when Jesse drove to pick me up, and Cord had been in the basement one time when we slipped through. Other than those two, I didn't think anyone knew. Jamie knew Jesse had someone in his room that day, but he didn't know that girl was me.

We had to write a paper for our group project, and he grumbled the entire time we were in the library about the chick Jesse was banging. Cord stared at me the whole time. I ignored both of them.

The first time we met to work, Jamie had complained the whole time, only breaking when he spotted a leggy blonde or a hot brunette. His words, not mine. Then he'd talk about them the whole time, rating them on his scale. A few times he even left the table to score a date.

I was listening to the same rant from him as we met for our last time to go over the paper. We had to plan a presentation, but my part was in the beginning. It was the easiest, and I just introduced the group. Cord and Jamie wanted to do the rest. Jamie boasted that they had the most charisma. Cord told me Jamie wanted to be a news sports anchor after college. I asked him if Tiffany knew about those plans, but he only shrugged and went back to typing on the computer.

"All right. I'm done." Jamie dumped his book on our table and stood to stretch. His massive arms touched some girls as they were walking by us, but he paid them no attention. When I caught a small grin on his face when he sat back down, I knew he'd done it on purpose. The two girls who'd been targeted giggled together as they took the table behind us. They recognized the two basketball players.

Apparently, they didn't hold much interest for Jamie, though, because his next words were, "Let's go to the cafeteria. I'm fucking starved."

Cord frowned from the computer. "Dude, I'm still typing our bibliography."

"I'm hungry."

"I'm not."

"Come on, man." A five-year-old child's whine came from Jamie's throat. He lifted his shoulders in a huff.

I waited, expecting his foot to stamp or for him to cross his arms over his chest as he pouted.

He did neither, but I wouldn't have been surprised if they were on the way. Instead, he rolled his eyes in an exaggerated motion. "You hear my stomach? It's like Hurricane Murphy in here. It needs to eat, or you don't know what damage will be done."

Cord jerked his head toward the door. "Go eat. We'll still be here."

Jamie turned his surly gaze to me, but my attention had gone back to my book. No way was I getting pulled into this tug-of-war.

"Fine." Jamie shoved back his chair. "But this sucks, man. I don't like to eat alone."

Cord glanced at the two girls still giggling together. "I think you could get company if you wanted."

"I have a girlfriend."

"Not on Friday and Saturday nights according to you." Cord said in a bored voice.

"Oh yeah. And sometimes Thursday and Tuesday nights, too."

As he left, he lifted his arm and hit the doorframe above his head with a thumbs up in the air.

Cord only shook his head.

I asked, "Why not Sunday, Monday and Wednesday nights?"

"Caught that, huh?"

I nodded. I wasn't sure if I wanted to know, but I was intrigued. There was a meaning behind their statements to each other.

Cord grinned as he kept typing. "Because those are the nights Tiffany's over."

"They don't see each other on the weekends? Just Sunday?" I was starting to think their relationship was more screwed up than whatever I had with Jesse.

"Sometimes, but rarely. Tiffany likes to spend her time with her friends." Cord snorted to himself. "She thinks this will be worth the pay-off later, and that Jamie will get all his partying out of his system. She thinks by the end of college, he'll want to spend time with only her and no one else."

Judging by his sarcasm, I knew Cord wasn't a subscriber anymore than Hannah. "I was told that she thinks he's going to law school and in five years will run for political office. Does he really want to be a sports news anchor?"

"Yeah, but don't tell anyone."

"Who'd I tell? Jesse?"

"I know you have some little friends. Hannah. That other girl who's always with her."

Oh yeah. I was friends with them. We ate together most nights, and as I thought of that, I glanced at the clock. I was running late. "I have to go."

"You're leaving, too?"

"Sorry. My part is done. I wrote the first section of the paper. Remember?"

"I thought you'd stay for moral support."

"Nope. I'm outta here."

"Alex."

"See ya, Cord!" Stuffing my books and papers back in my bag, I flashed him a quick grin and waved as I hurried to the door Jamie left through. I really did have to meet with Beth and Hannah. The daily supper date had become a tradition for us, and it was highly anticipated every night for me. They didn't ask questions about the years before, bring up names, or ask about things that happened to me. They were comfortable to be around, unlike Marissa, who had emailed me every day since her visit.

She was determined to be friends again. I had no interest. That ship had sailed. Accepting her friendship was the beginning of a slippery slope. I just knew it. Then Angie would be in contact. Justin might be with her. Even Eric might give me a phone call.

They had all ditched me, and I wasn't signing up for a second abandonment.

Going through the doors that led to the mess hall, I stopped abruptly before I rounded the corner. I heard Jamie saying, "Come on. Seriously. You're killing me, Chatsworth."

Expecting Tiffany's comeback, my eyes popped out when Hannah spoke instead. "Lay off, Jamie. I mean it. I have a crap load of texts to show my sister if you don't leave me alone."

"She said I could be with other girls."

"Not her sister. She didn't have me in mind, and you know that. She'd go ballistic if she knew you were doing this."

"Come on," his voice lowered to a husky soothing murmur. "Doesn't that feel good? I can make you feel really good. You know I can. Just say the word. You can feel this all night long."

A slapping sound came next before Hannah rasped out, "I told you to stop touching me. I mean it."

"Bitch!"

Gritting my teeth, I tightened my hold on my bag and threw my shoulders back. Cued my entrance, and I rounded the turn. He had Hannah pressed against the mailboxes. The rest of the room was empty, not a surprise. It was Friday night. Most didn't eat in here if they didn't have to. Plastering a bright smile on my face, I marched up to them. "Sorry I'm late, Hannah. I got caught up with a group project."

Jamie turned. His glare doubled from the usual one he kept for me. "You're everywhere."

His hand hadn't moved from under her shirt and Hannah slapped at it, pushing him away at the same time. "She's my friend."

"She's weird."

My back stiffened, but I couldn't argue. I was weird.

"She's my friend," Hannah stressed again. "Leave me alone, Jamie, and leave her alone, too."

"She's in my group for class." His eyes chilled. I expected frost to start forming on them. "I don't know what you've got over Cord, but it's not cool. I'm going to find out."

I blinked. "Excuse me?"

"You heard me." He raked a disdainful eye over me. "You're not hard on the eyes. I'll give you that one, but I know you're not banging Tatum. So, I figure you're blackmailing him."

"You think the only reason he would like me would be if I were blackmailing or sleeping with him?"

He wasn't far off, but it wasn't Cord who was sharing my bed.

"You're not giving it up to him. You're a damn prude if I ever saw one." A cocky smirk came over him. "You can't stand the sight of me, I know that, too. Most girls love me. Hell, most girls put the moves on me within five minutes of meeting me."

Hannah groaned, muttering, "Oh my God."

He kept going, his gaze harsh as he stared me down. "Your social skills suck, too. Only people I can tell that like you are Cord, this chick, and her freak cousin."

"That's enough!"

Ignoring the outrage beside us, my eyes narrowed to slits, and I took a step closer. His eyes widened just a fraction before the same cocky arrogance slid back in place. Oh yes. He saw the anger in my eyes, and he'd taken notice of it. It wasn't the type of anger he'd dealt with in Hannah, his girlfriend, or any other girl.

They were normal. I was not.

I had banked this rage for so long, but it was there. It was why my friends had left. They'd been afraid. Jamie wasn't, but he had fallen silent. He knew he'd stepped into something that maybe he wasn't sure he should've.

As I continued to stare at him, only him, Hannah moved to stand behind me, and I let the rage grow. I let him see what was inside me.

It had gone beyond the bristling stage. It was full-on raging.

I was loving it. It made me feel alive.

It made me feel powerful.

Then Jamie backed away. "Whatever. You're a freak."

An evil grin came over me. He was right. A part of me was freakish. It was the part that'd been given life when my parents dumped me. I'd been scared of it, but I was starting to embrace it. No words had left my lips, but an unspoken knowledge was there. I would do anything to get back at him. He only had to give me a reason. I would enjoy it. No, I would thrive on it. Jesse and everyone else be damned. In that moment, as I was feeling my rage, no one could stop me.

Jamie saw it all. He backed down from it.

Wise choice, my friend.

"Jamie!" Hannah smacked him in the chest. "Stop talking to my friend like that. I mean it."

He scoffed at her, shaking his head as he backed away from us. He treaded in reverse until he hit the door. Reaching behind, he fumbled for the handle and pushed the door open as he slipped through it.

"I'm so sorry. He shouldn't talk to you like that. He's such an asshole."

I shook my head and pushed the rage down. It was still simmering, but I had it under control, enough to look at my friend. She wouldn't know.

She gave me a shaky grin. "I'm really sorry."

She didn't. I shrugged. "It's okay. I've grown used to his attitude. What isn't okay is him touching you after you told him to stop."

"Still," she sighed. "He shouldn't be able to talk like that to you. I'll say something. I'll make him stop."

"It's okay." When she tried to continue arguing, I stopped her. "I mean it. I'll handle him." I already had, though she'd been unaware of it. Jamie would be a bit more cautious of me, and I highly doubted that I'd have to deal with the same type of callous treatment again.

"Hey, guys." Beth joined the conversation. She glanced over her shoulder. "I almost got bowled over by Jamie. Why's your sister's boyfriend shaking like a leaf out there? He looked ready to piss his pants."

"What?" Hannah was taken aback. "What are you talking about? He was just in here, being an asshole to Alex."

"Oh." Beth swept speculative eyes over me. "Maybe I got it wrong."

She hadn't, and I knew she knew she hadn't.

Hannah muttered more derogatory names at her sister's boyfriend as she led the way inside the cafeteria. After placing our bags on a table, we separated for the different buffet lines, but I felt Beth's knowing gaze on my back the whole time. When my tray was full, I headed back to our table. She was already there, waiting for me.

She placed her glass on the table and leaned over it. "What'd you do to Jamie Striker?"

"Nothing."

We both knew I was lying.

"What'd you do? I didn't get it wrong, but I don't know how Hannah is clueless. You did something. I know you did."

"No, I didn't."

"Stop lying to me."

Okay. Well. How was I supposed to explain it to her? That I opened a compartment inside myself and let him see the darkness my parents had created? That was what had happened, but it would sound crazy. Lying was the best option. I'd been doing a damn good job of it since coming to college.

Beth sat back, defeated. "Fine. Don't tell me. Just don't do anything to hurt my cousin."

"Tiffany?"

She gave me a disgusted look. "Hannah. I don't give a shit what happens to Tiffany."

"Oh."

Apparently satisfied, the corner of her mouth curved up. "What are your plans with boy toy tonight?"

"He's not a boy toy."

"What is he then? You're screwing the hottest guy at school, and you won't say a word. I know only because I walked in on you two."

"What's your point?"

She gave me an incredulous look. "That you wouldn't have

told me, either. He's not your boyfriend—you'd tell people if he were. That leaves boy toy."

I frowned and starting picking at my salad with a fork. "Your logic sucks."

Laughing, she reached for her glass again. Her knees were lifted and she settled back against her seat with her feet propped up on it. "Say what you want. I think I'm right. And you never answered my question."

"What question?" Shifting in my seat, I looked to see where Hannah had gone. She should've been back already.

"What are your plans tonight?"

"We haven't discussed it. Why?"

"Because we're going to Club T again if you want to come."

"The club you ditched me at so both of you could have sex with people? That one?"

With her straw in her mouth, she grinned around it. "That's the one. Wanna come?"

I sighed, "Sure." I refused to let myself sit at home, twiddling my thumbs in case Jesse called. I'd never been that girl before, but I had felt like it at times. When he said jump; I asked how high. I wasn't going back to that. I couldn't. I'd be destroyed if I did.

However, after we ate and went to the dorm to dress, my phone started buzzing in the car. I ignored it. Not the most mature move, but I knew if it were him, I'd read whatever he sent and I'd go to him. The last month had been like a slow drug. I was becoming more addicted to him the more time we spent together.

It was when we after we all got inside and my phone had buzzed for the seventh or eighth time that Hannah snapped, "Just answer it already. Whoever's calling isn't going to stop. It's annoying."

Taking a deep breath, readying myself, I was prepared to keep my hormones in check.

I didn't need it. It wasn't from Jesse. It was from Cord.

Cord: Call me back. Entire damn paper is gone. Come to the house, we have to work on it tonight.

Fuck me. My night was over.

"Who was it?" Hannah asked, throwing her elbow back as someone bumped into her. "This place is crazy packed tonight. What band is playing?"

Beth, who had been watching me, ignored her cousin. "What'd he say?"

Interest sparked with Hannah. She forgot about the crowd. "Wait, what? He who? You have a boyfriend, and you haven't said a word about him?"

Glaring at Beth, I replied, "No boyfriend, and it was Cord. Something happened to the paper. He wants me to go to their house to work on it tonight."

"It's Friday."

"I'm aware."

"You don't do homework on a Friday night."

Beth started snickering.

Hannah had a point. I texted Cord:

Me: Why tonight?

Cord: Have something going on. Need to get it done tonight, proof it Saturday, and do other homework Sunday night.

I shared the text with the girls.

Hannah's face scrunched up. "That sucks."

"Wait, doesn't Cord live with Jesse Hunt?"

My foot ached to make contact with Beth's butt. I settled for glaring instead.

Hannah threw her cousin a confused look. "Yeah. So?" A light bulb clicked on. "He's way out of our league, Beth. Although, I like the way you think."

It was her cousin's turn to grow wary. "What are you talking about?"

"We have homework to do, right? Let's go with her. Besides, I don't want Jamie to talk to her like that again."

"No, wait. That wasn't what I meant—"

It didn't matter. Hannah was starting to gain speed. "Yeah and Cord will be there. Obviously. So, when you guys need a break, I can be there ready to give him a massage. He won't turn that down. I bet Chandra won't be there, not if Cord's doing homework. She hates it when he studies. I think she gets a rash and goes crazy. She itches all over. We should go."

Beth's mouth joined mine on the floor.

This night had gone a different direction than I anticipated.

14

"Surprise!" Hannah flung her arms in the air when the door opened. All three of us stood on the front doorstep, but Beth and I wore sheepish grins while Hannah was poised as if she were in a photo shoot.

"Uh ..."

The guy stared at her for a moment. His lips were pursed together and moved in a fish movement, confused, as he scratched at his head. He was dressed in blue scrub pants and a white shirt and his dark hair was messed and sticking up, as if he'd just come from bed. I was racking my brain trying to remember why he looked familiar. Then we heard someone ask from inside, "Who is it, Derek?"

Beth and I shared a glance. This was Kara's boyfriend. I had actually forgotten he lived here too.

No drinking for us tonight.

A wide grin stretched over Hannah's face, and she pushed her way in. We followed, giving Derek an uneasy look. He waited, holding the door open and nodding to us, being polite. Beth gestured to me. "She's here for a group project with Cord and Jamie. We came to keep her company."

He nodded and didn't say a word. This could've been a normal thing from how he was reacting. Gesturing around the corner where Hannah had disappeared, he closed the door, and I couldn't help but grin as he made sure to lock the door before he moved around us.

We moved into the kitchen and into the massive dining room where we got our own shock.

It wasn't just the three of us girls or only Cord and Jamie.

Kara was at the end of the table, and Derek took the seat beside her. But at the opposite end was Jamie, and in his lap . . . Tiffany. She was currently drilling holes in her sister's head, but there were two other occupants at the table. On one side was Cord and across from him was Chandra.

Visions of her flashed in my head again. I cringed as I snuck a peek at the living room where the offense had taken place. Never again. I did not want to see her naked and straddling Cord again.

Beth dropped her bag on the floor between us. She muttered, "So I guess it's a study night for all of us."

The entire table was covered with books, papers, pens, high-lighters, and laptops.

Yep. They had the same idea as Hannah. I wondered if it'd been Tiffany. Did the two sisters think alike?

I moved to set my bag down and the basement door opened, revealing Jesse. He was barefoot and in gym shorts. No shirt, judging from the soft gasp I heard beside me, there was plenty of service ready for him. I couldn't blame Hannah's reaction—her eyes were wide and her lips were slightly parted, as if she couldn't quite catch her breath. I'd seen him without any clothing on at all many times, but it never got old. He had just worked out. I could always tell. His muscles were more enlarged than normal. His body was more sculpted, and his hair was wet. He was fresh from the shower. A lone droplet of water fell from his forehead and crashed to his chest. It made a solitary trek all the way down until it disappeared underneath his short's waistband.

My throat went dry, and I licked my lips. The same lust as always was smoldering in me. It was waiting for the opening, the word from him, the gesture to follow him. None came. So, I held myself still and tried to keep my pounding heart from being heard by anyone else in the room.

"Oh my," Hannah whispered.

He heard her and stopped. His gaze jumped from her to me.

I was given a swift kick in the gut when his eyes narrowed and hurt flashed in them for a moment.

Swallowing over a lump in my throat, I knew I should've texted. I shouldn't let him know ahead of time. He could've been prepared, but then Hannah would've missed the vision before her. I wouldn't have minded that. My gut clenched as a sultry smile came over her. She tilted her head to the side in a sexy poise and strode over to him with her hand outstretched. "Hello there. I'm Hannah, Tiffany's sister. We've never formally met before."

I flinched. Even her voice was husky and seductive.

Jesse was still watching me. A dark look appeared, and he scowled before turning his attention to my wanton friend in front of him. Ignoring her hand, he clipped out, "I know who you are." Then he moved around her and went back down to the basement, slamming the door behind him.

I jumped from the fierceness.

Hannah rotated back to us. "What a dick."

Jamie shoved Tiffany off his lap but stayed in his seat. His scowl matched the one Jesse had worn. "Maybe if you'd stop being a slut, he would've been polite."

Tiffany frowned at her boyfriend but crossed her arms over her chest. She said to Hannah, "Jamie's right. Don't hit on Jesse. He's had his share of whores trying to use him for his dad."

Hannah snorted, "Or just for him. He might be a dick, but he's hot. I'd forgotten from the few times I saw him in person before."

Holding still, I was aware of the two pairs of eyes trained on me. Beth's and Cord's. They were both silent, just watching, just waiting, just judging. I felt ready to burst.

Everyone else was fixated on the sisters, who seemed ready to rip into each other. Kara came to the rescue as she gave Beth and me both a friendly wave from her chair. She pointed to the empty chairs around the table. "Cord and Jamie told us about the computer eating your paper. Have a seat. We figured it'd be a fun night if all of us stayed in for a study night. These are some of the best times I've had at the house." She glanced at Hannah. "Don't worry about Jesse. He's not a fan of new people."

Derek leaned over and pressed a soft kiss to her forehead. She melted into his arms but continued to smile our way.

They were out of place, happy amidst a room full of wolves. I could imagine Tiffany and Hannah sharpening their fangs as they stared 'em down.

"Yeah." Chandra shoved back her chair and stood awkwardly. Her entire demeanor was forced. "Sit. Get comfortable. Do you guys want some food or something to drink?"

Beth and I shared another look, but Hannah spoke up, "Are you serious? Playing hostess again, Chandra? This isn't even your house."

"It's more hers than yours," her sister snapped back.

Hannah's eyes went feral. A snarl came to her lips, and she was ready to lunge, her hands were already forming claws to go around Tiffany's throat.

"Hey. Whoa." Beth grabbed Hannah's arm. She sent a warning to her other cousin. "Stop it. Both of you."

The tension rose another level in the room, but my mind wasn't in there. My mind was downstairs. He looked hurt. I had hurt him. How was that possible? He had told me before that he cared, that he had wanted to be with me. Marissa has said pretty much the same thing, too. Slowly, it was sinking in. Maybe Jesse really did want more. But . . . panic flooded me.

I still wasn't ready.

My eyes jerked up to the portrait of Ethan and Jesse by the front door. I felt him beckoning to me. I'd purposely avoided looking at it when we first came inside, but it seemed I couldn't do that this time. God. My throat trembled as agony spread in me.

I missed him. So damn much.

"Alex?"

Jolted back to the room, I looked around. Dazed. "Huh?"

Beth's eyes darted to Cord from underneath her eyelids.

Oh. I turned to see that he had risen from the table. He knew. How did he know? I brushed a hand over my eye and took a deep breath. I couldn't break down in this room, not with these people. "What'd you say?"

"Do you have to use the bathroom? You can use the one downstairs."

I caught the extra meaning and nodded, grateful.

"What? Hell no," Jamie interjected. "Downstairs is off-limits to chicks. What are you thinking?"

Beth hastily stepped in. "I have to go to the bathroom, too."

Hannah sighed and plopped down on one of the chairs. She grumbled, "This is going to take a while. She can pee forever."

"See. Jesse won't care if she uses the bathroom. It's not like she's going to use his personal one."

Another furtive glance. Another furtive meaning. Caught it and understood. I was bursting at the seams to get to Jesse, but I held back. Jamie opened his mouth again, another argument on the tip of his tongue.

"I think she could wait," Tiffany offered, frowning at me with suspicion lurking in her depths. "Or she can use the one upstairs."

"Which is filthy." Cord pointed to the door. "Go ahead, Alex. You're not going to get murdered down there. I don't know why they're freaking so much."

"Rules are rules, dude!"

Hannah held a hand in the air. "I'll use the one upstairs. If they're going, I'm going."

"Oh my God!" Tiffany threw her arms in the air. "Pee break for everybody?"

Kara stood. "I don't know about a bathroom break, but I wouldn't mind pouring some more wine and maybe ordering a pizza?"

"These are your residents. You can't drink with them."

Kara frowned at Tiffany and then shrugged. "I don't think Beth or Alex will say anything. They're kind of related to our group of friends, aren't they?"

"Go, Alex."

Cord's statement was soft and all the clearer against everyone else.

A ball of emotion was in my throat. I couldn't speak because of it, but I nodded at him, gratefully, and didn't wait for another chance. As soon as I was through the door, I shut it behind me and heard the automatic lock click in place.

Hurrying down the stairs, I didn't turn on any lights. I knew the way by memory.

His door was open, and I knew he'd been waiting. He knew I would come. Turning into his door, he lifted his head. He was sitting on the edge of his bed with his elbows resting on his knees. Just waiting. No other lights were on, only what could be seen from the moon as it filtered through his opened windows. A breeze wafted in, caressing against my cheeks.

Right there, right then in that moment, I felt beautiful.

My heart jumped to my throat. I was moving before I knew it, and I was in his arms. He caught me and fell back on the bed with me on top. Pressing a kiss to my throat, he whispered against my skin, "You think I'm mad at you, don't you?"

I nodded. My throat was still too thick for words.

"I'm not. I promise."

"You looked hurt." My tongue was so damn heavy and big. It was constricting me. That was why I couldn't talk.

"I was."

"What?"

Moving to the side, I propped myself up on an elbow as he mirrored my position. He grinned and traced a finger down my side profile, down my neck, to my shoulder, down my arm, my hand, my waist, all the way over my stomach, and back up.

I was breathing heavy by the end, when he paused at the corner of my lips. With my eyes closed, I waited and tried to memorize every touch from him. I wanted them in my permanent memory for when we wouldn't be like this. Huskily, I asked, "Why were you hurt?"

He pressed a kiss to the corner of my mouth. His hand flatted over my stomach with his thumb rubbing in a circle. "Because you were in my house with my friends, and I wasn't the reason you were here."

"What?"

More heavy breathing. His damn thumb was talented.

He chuckled against my skin, lingering over my lips. "I was jealous, Alex."

"What?" I shoved him back enough so I could stare at him. My heart was throbbing in me. I felt every beat pulsate through my body. He must've felt it as he was pressed against me.

His hand moved up the middle of my back and splayed out in a possessive hold between my shoulder blades. The tips of his fingers gripped my skin like he didn't want to let go. Ever. A primal thrill swept over me, and I sank back down over him. My body melted against his as I forgot what we were talking about. Nothing mattered. Jesse swept the demons away. I wanted him to sweep ours away, the one the two of us had created. It was dark and looming, wrapped with fear because I didn't know what was going to happen with us anymore.

I was too far gone.

Holding my hips with his hands, he rolled us to the side and kept going so I was on my back. but he positioned himself so he wouldn't bear all his weight on me. His lips nibbled up my throat, and his hand skimmed over my hip and back to my stomach. Two of his fingers began caressing again, making the throbbing between my legs stronger. It was taking me over. I was becoming blind to anything except the need to have him inside me.

Why were we still talking?

Urging his head up, I pulled him so our lips met. When they did, he didn't apply the pressure I wanted. I wanted him. I wanted him to take control how he always did. Groaning, I felt the tension in him and knew he was going to speak again. Enough with the talking. My hips pressed up against his. Hearing his swift intake of breath, my lips curved against his in a smirk.

"Shit, Alex. Your friends are upstairs."

Reality crashed over me, and my eyes snapped open. I shoved him back and shook my head, needing to clear all the sensations and lust from me. I needed to think clearly.

He chuckled, but I saw the same struggle in his eyes. His hand reached out to my arm as he murmured, huskily, "I was saying before that I was jealous. You're involved with my friends through Cord and not me. I wanted to introduce you to the gang, but as mine. You're Cord's friend to them."

"I'm not Cord's anything."

He lifted a shoulder, frowning. "You are in their minds. Not as his girlfriend, but I know they think you were a hook-up. Cord doesn't keep his hook-ups around. He drops 'em right away. They don't know why he's looking out for you."

"Is he?"

Jesse nodded. "Yeah, he is for me. But maybe he shouldn't have to anymore."

My breath hitched in my throat. My heart slowed. "What are you talking about?"

"I don't know. Maybe he shouldn't have to look out for you."

I frowned. "He doesn't, not really. I would've been fine in someone else's group. He did that for him. Trust me. The hyenas were circling until he pulled me in."

"I know, but I'm just saying . . ." A darker frown appeared, and he started picking at his bedcover. What was going on? A sliver of panic started in me. It grew with each breath I struggled to take until I heard him say, "Maybe we should go public about us?"

Ice cold panic blasted me.

I couldn't handle this.

All those girls knowing. All those girls hating me. So many ways they could take him away from me.

I stood up, my legs numb and headed for the door.

"Hey!"

I fumbled for the handle, but Jesse was there. His arms trapped me in. The door wouldn't budge. Instead of turning me around, he pressed me against the door. His hips pushed into my backside, and his mouth fell to my throat. He rasped out, against my ear, "That sends you into this? Are you fucking kidding me?"

The fury was back. Unease clawed into my gut as I knew I'd awakened his beast. I needed to settle this. We couldn't explode.

"Jesse." My voice trembled as he continued to move his hips against me. Oh God. In two seconds, I was writhing in his arms again. But this time, he wouldn't turn me around. He wouldn't do what I wanted. My head tipped back, and his lips seared a path up. Sucking on the corner of my lips, he slid his hand into my pants and worked his fingers between my legs. In one motion, he tipped his hips into me, lifting me up as his fingers took advantage of the slight opening. They went inside of me.

He'd been gentle at other times. Not this time. As his lips moved up the arch of my jawline before going back to my lips, he pumped his fingers furiously into me. He was pissed at me. He was taking it out on me. I groaned, searching for his lips with mine greedily. I wanted him in me, but his fingers kept thrusting, going harder each time.

I tried turning again, but his hips slammed me back in place. He didn't care about hurting his own hand. Reaching behind me, I clamped a hold on to the back of his head and anchored him to me. His lips were fighting against mine. We were both trying to hurt each other as we fought to fulfill our insatiable hunger. As it began rising in me, a whimper left me, and I couldn't move. Another finger went inside. He kept going. My hand and head fell away to the door. I could only gasp for breath as he continued assaulting my body. My forehead rested there. Wave after wave crashed over me. I was unable to control the attack of it, and then I crested. Hurdling over the edge, my body lifted in the air from the climax, and Jesse's arm went around me and held me suspended in the air as he flipped us around.

He threw me on the bed and shucked my pants down the rest of the way.

Then he was inside of me and I gasped. My body hadn't stopped trembling from my first climax before he was working me back up once again. Thrusting into me, his body was rigid and determined. This wasn't for me. This was for him. The coupling was rough. His hips pistoned into me until both of us tensed together. He shot himself into me as I climaxed, again.

Then he was off me. His shorts were pulled up, and he was gone in the next second. I heard his car's engine as the lights flooded into his room. He reversed his car and gunned the engine, soaring away.

Shit.

I couldn't move. I couldn't even think. What had just happened?

15

Beth came to check on me. I'd been gone over thirty minutes. Still weak from the explosion from Jesse, I was mortified as well as angered when she told me. I didn't ask what Tiffany and the other girls might've been thinking from my long absence, but then Beth said that Jesse called when he left. He told Jamie that some girl was sick in the basement bathroom.

He covered for me.

Beth had volunteered first to check on me, and everyone was already grumbling. They didn't want to get sick so when we went upstairs, Tiffany and Chandra gave me a wide berth. Even though they had moved into the living room, leaving Cord, Jamie, and myself in the dining room, I caught the sidelong glances they sent my way. The glares were bordering close to a mean girl snub. I wouldn't have been surprised if they asked that I leave, but they kept quiet. However, later in the night after Hannah and Tiffany got into a yelling match, she was asked to leave. Beth went with her.

It was late in the night when the other girls finally started to leave. Chandra went to her place, wherever she lived, while

Tiffany and Kara both went to their boyfriends' rooms. Drunk from wine and full from pizza, Kara whispered loudly to me that she couldn't be seen in that state at the dorm. I wasn't supposed to tell anyone, but I shrugged. I didn't care. I didn't think RAs were supposed to always be in their rooms. They had lives, too.

Derek gave me a polite nod as he ushered his girlfriend up the stairs. Jamie slapped him on the ass when they moved past, but Derek didn't react. It must've been a common thing among this group of friends, so at one in the morning, I was left alone with Cord and Jamie. A box of wine had been opened and left on the table, alongside three opened boxes of pizza.

That was when Jesse returned home.

His headlights were visible as he pulled inside his own garage. A car door slammed, and it wasn't long until the basement door was shoved open and he came through.

Jamie lifted his hand in the air. "My man! Where the hell have you been all night?"

Jesse's eyes flashed to mine, pinning me in place, but he turned to his roommate. He shrugged, grabbing a glass from the kitchen before he took a seat at the table across from me. He said to Jamie, "Out and about."

Jamie's head bobbed up and down. "Cool. Get laid?"

I lowered my gaze to my book, but I felt his gaze on me, burning into the top of my head when he murmured, "You could say that."

"You always get the best ass, too," Jamie grumbled, lifting his hand in the air. "Pound it, Hunt. You're my hero."

I heard the fists meeting before Jesse replied, "You're slow in the head, Striker. What's your deal tonight?"

Cord snickered behind his laptop. "Tiffany was here all night. Jamie's going through withdrawals."

"She never puts out. Is that what marriage is going to be like? Never having sex? It's been since the end of sophomore year, five months of abstinence."

"From her."

"So what? The other girls are good, but Tiffany's talented in bed. You don't know." A long pregnant pause. "Right? You don't know, right?"

Cord dissolved in more laughter. "He thinks you got laid by his wife."

Jesse's tone was dry. "I've never touched Tiffany. You're safe."

"Oh good." Jamie's relief was strong. "Cause I know she'd do you if she could."

"I'm not interested."

"Yeah, but you might one day. Can you refrain on that day, please?"

Cord spoke up, "Dude, why do you care? You get laid every night Tiffany's not around."

"I don't know," he grumbled. "I don't love them. I love her."

"Are you asking me to stay away from your girlfriend? If this weren't so entertaining, I'd be pissed at the insult. I don't touch my friends' girls."

"No, but friends' sisters are another thing," Cord piped in.

That—yeah. That hurt.

"Tatum," Jesse snapped.

Jamie's eyes went wide. His mouth formed an O leaned back a bit, looking between Jesse and Cord. It'd been easygoing with undertones of tension, but that tension was loud and couldn't be ignored. It rose to the top and there was no going back.

His eyes darted around the table. "What's going on?"

"Take that back." Jesse spoke to Cord, but his eyes caught mine. His head moved in the tiniest of shakes.

He was eyeing me, trying to get a reaction from me, trying to see what was going on with me.

Nothing.

Nothing was happening.

I could feel myself closing in, pulling away, retreating behind so many walls.

A soft curse left Jesse's mouth before he shoved back his chair. "Come on." He stood beside me. "I'll take you back."

I didn't go. I didn't even move.

"What's her problem?" Jamie griped.

"Her name's Alex," Cord spoke, glaring at him.

"Whatever her name is. Look at her. She's like a zombie. We should get her out of our group. Fuck this. I'll call the professor tomorrow."

"Jamie, shut up." Jesse half-dragged me from my chair. Instead of heading out, he began to take me upstairs. He spoke over his shoulder, "Cut her some slack. Being in a room with you, I'd either snap or go zombie, too."

"Ha ha. Not funny, Hunt." As Jesse started up the stairs, he called after him, "Where are you going?"

But he wasn't listening.

He kissed my temple, whispering, "Not far."

He knocked softly on a door. When it opened, Derek was there in only a pair of boxers. He rubbed at his eyes, his hair sticking in the air. When he took us in, his eyes lurched awake, and he stepped through, closing the door behind him. He asked, a low murmur, "What's going on?"

"I need the codes for the backdoor from Kara. I have to take her girl home."

Derek frowned. "Why you?"

"Because," he clipped out. "What does it matter?"

"Chill. Jeez." He nodded before going back inside.

Derek emerged again, shutting the door once more as he joined us in the hallway. He handed Jesse a piece of paper. "She said it'll open the back door, but don't go until the hour mark. I guess they have a security guard that makes rounds. She doesn't know when he walks through, but he always has to be at his office on the hour mark."

"Thanks." Jesse took the paper and glanced at his watch. "We can go now. I'll get her in right away."

"Hey, man."

Derek stopped him, a twinge of concern in his voice.

"Yeah?"

"Secrets get out, Jess. This one will get out, too. I don't know who she is, but I know that's her brother downstairs."

I began crying. I didn't know until Jesse stiffened. His hand cupped the back of my head and he bent low to my ear. "Ssh, Alex. Hold it together, just for a little while."

I tried. Drawing in a deep breath, filtered through his shirt, I tried to quench the sobfest unleashed inside me. No avail. Tears trickled from my eyes, and I couldn't stop them.

"She okay?" Derek asked.

There was no response.

Jesse picked me up and carried me back downstairs. When he stepped through to the kitchen, I heard, "Oh shit. What the fuck's wrong with her?"

Cord's voice was closer, quieter. "What happened?"

"Breakdown."

"Dump her on the streets. Why do we have to take care of all the emotional chicks?"

"Jamie!"

"What? I'm just saying. Make sure there are no pictures on her phone. I can see her turning around and claiming rape or some other crazy shit. Look at her. She's nuts."

"Go to bed, Jamie." The irritation settled in Jesse's chest as he went rigid against me. His hands tightened on me. I knew the signs. He was gearing up for a fight. His roommate had two seconds before Jesse was going to let loose on him.

Pushing past the pain that was blinding me, I looked up and touched the side of his face. When I felt moisture on his cheek, I withdrew my fingers. Surprised, I saw what must've been tears on the tip of my finger. Jesse had shed a few of his own tears. He looked down, a mirror of my agony clouding his face. I held my breath. He understood.

"Go to bed, Jamie. Go and get laid by your woman," Cord seemed to have finally broken his silence.

"Get laid?" He smirked back. "More like get shot down you mean."

"Go."

"All right, all right. Why are you two worked up? You're like girls. Seriously."

"Jamie."

"I'm going." He lifted his arms in the air, surrendering his defeat as he left the room and disappeared up the stairs.

Cord came closer and softened his voice, "I'm sorry for my dig. I didn't realize you'd get hurt by that, Alex."

"Too late, asshole. You go to bed, too."

"Yeah, yeah. Alex, we'll finish the paper tomorrow night." He chuckled. "Maybe at the library instead."

I wanted to say something back. I wasn't sure what.

The emotions were too fresh and raw inside me so I laid my head back down and stayed still. The agony that blasted me had lessened, just a bit, but enough so I wasn't crying so loudly anymore. But when Jesse glanced down, his concern didn't let up, and I felt more tears sliding down my face.

I wasn't going to be normal.

The realization sunk down, like an anchor to my soul. As Jesse turned and started down the stairs for the basement, I knew that I would have to pretend to be normal. People couldn't see the mess inside me. They'd want nothing to do with me.

When Jesse went to his room and put me on the bed, I knew he intended for us to sleep together that night. I couldn't let that happen. He'd seen too much. He couldn't see the rest, not when I was in this fragile of a state.

"Take me home." My throat was hoarse.

"Stay. Please."

I shook my head, more tears slipped free. "Take me home."

"Alex," he sighed. "I'm sorry. Is this because of before? I'm sorry I was so rough. I just—I'm sorry. I won't do that again."

"It's not. It's . . ." I hesitated. "It's because of Ethan. I want to go back and be alone."

His arms tightened around me. "But that's not what we did before. When it got too much, we were together. Remember?"

But we weren't. Our old tradition had stopped when I left him in Vegas. Ethan's anniversary passed by, and I'd been alone. Since coming to school, there was no routine for Jesse and me.

I shook my head as my heart was breaking. "I just want to go home."

Expecting more of a fight from him, I was surprised when he gave in. I followed as he took us out to his car. The ride to my dorm was quiet. And when he parked in the back lot, we waited until the hour mark before getting out. As he climbed out of his side, I looked over. "What are you doing?"

A thin smile graced his features. He tossed his keys in the air and caught them in a swift movement. "Oh. I brought you home. That's fine and dandy."

There was a but. I waited for it.

"But I'm not leaving you alone."

"Jesse."

"Nope. If it comes to it, I'm prepared to walk through the front lobby. I don't care. I certainly don't care about keeping this secret anymore. I'm going up there with you, whether you want that or not."

I glowered at him, but I couldn't deny the pitter-patter my heart was doing in my chest.

"Alex."

"Fine." Glaring at him, I felt like baring my teeth. Why did he push me so much? Why did he care so much? "You're going to be the death of me."

"Yeah, well, I think Ethan would want us to be together, and I think it's time I stopped fighting whatever this is." He waved a hand in the air between us.

"That's not what you said before."

He shrugged, falling in step beside me as we went to the back stairway. He thumbed in the passcode Kara gave him and opened the door for me. His hand touched the small in my back as we started our way up the stairs. He murmured, bending close to my ear, "I think he would've come around and realized he was being stupid."

"Is that so?"

His hand applied pressure on my back as he nipped at my earlobe. "I think so, yeah."

We snuck into my room. When I took my caddie to the bathroom to get ready for bed, a tingle was spreading inside me. It was tickling me, sending me into something that might've resembled being happy. But that wasn't me and it wouldn't last. This was the first night Jesse was sleeping in my room, in my bed, and I tried to convince myself that this was what we had before. There was nothing new here.

We weren't boyfriend/girlfriend.

When we had an itch, we'd seek each other out.

Yeah. I was lying to myself.

Stepping back into the emptied and darkened hallway, I went to my room and then took deep breaths. I was a mess. And he had no idea how much of a mess.

Closing my eyes for a moment, I took one more deep breath before I went inside. As I did, I saw him waiting for me on my bed with an easy grin on his face, and I knew that he was going to learn how screwed up I was.

Was it too much to hope that he wouldn't leave when he realized just how far I'd fallen?

"I'm horny." He said it with a straight face. "Come on. Crying women speak straight to my loins, Alex."

The last shred of resistance I had shattered.

I was in love with him. I had never stopped.

16

Jesse never pushed for the reason of my emotional breakdown at his home. He thought it was because of how rough he'd been earlier. That time with him had touched me in ways he'd never know. He had made me feel alive, in ways that I hadn't felt since before Ethan's death. That was also the night my floodgates opened again.

I felt Ethan everywhere I went, but it was different. Instead of the grief from before, or the hole that he'd ripped in me, it was a better feeling. Maybe this was the acceptance stage of mourning. I didn't know, but I did know I was still angry. Ethan shouldn't have died. I shouldn't have lost my brother. We should've still been a family.

I also realized that night that even though what my parents had done to me was awful, I couldn't just stay numb to my hurt. I was angry with them. Duh. That was a no-brainer, and I didn't need a therapist to tell me that, but I'd been numb to their damage. Since Jesse's house, I couldn't do that anymore.

I felt my rage toward them, but it was banked. It had always been there, in the bottom of my gut, simmering but manageable. Because of that, I snapped at people more. Beth got it a few times when we had dinner in the cafeteria. Jesse got it, too. Hannah just snapped back at me. It didn't seem to faze her. The only benefit was that Jamie watched how he talked to me. I knew most of it was because of that time in the cafeteria, when I let him really see the storm warring inside of me, but I lashed out at him a few more times before we finished our project.

Cord was quiet around me. Jesse told me that Cord blamed himself for my outburst. It happened after his dig at Jesse, so he figured two plus two equaled him. It didn't. The truth was that I didn't know why I snapped, but I had and things hadn't been the same since. For me.

"This blows. Let's go."

I stared across the table. Hannah threw her leg up on it and leaned back. Stretching her arms up and wide, she arched her back and sent a wink at a table of guys behind us.

"Shhh!"

She flipped off the girl who hushed her.

"Do not get us banned from the library," Beth warned her cousin, slumping down in her own chair as she peeked over the edge of her book. "I need this place to survive the midterms this week."

"Whatever. Robbie's having a party. Who wants to go?"

I became engrossed with my laptop while Beth jerked back down underneath her book cover.

Hannah sighed in disgust. "You guys suck."

Beth smirked back. "We may suck right now, but we're going to have passing grades next week. You won't, and you'll be crying your misery to me over a beer."

"At least I'll be drinking."

"Drinking and failing. Do you want Tiffany to have more ammunition over you?"

Hannah pointedly ignored that last curve thrown to her. She straightened in her chair, arched her neck out, and sent another flirty glance over her shoulder as the edge of her shirt slipped down to bare her arm. She didn't pull it back up as she muttered to us, "I'm more in the mood for Club T."

I glanced over. Beth was sitting next to me and she froze at the club's name. I'd gone back a few more times with them. Each time, Beth searched for someone—I assumed it was the same someone each time—and disappeared with for an hour. Hannah would go to the dance floor and grind against guys. I would hold down the base at a table nearby with our drinks on a tray, ready for Beth and Hannah to grab. When Beth was done with whatever she did, she'd return and keep me company. I had been told that Beth had an itch to scratch when she went there, but it was more than that. Beth was seeing a guy, who was always at Club T, who was only at Club T. I could imagine Hannah in my place as she'd pump her cousin for information, and when none was given, she'd smirk as she taunted, "Growing more and more curious. Who's the dick you crave?"

But Beth didn't rise to the bait. She slunk back in her seat and Hannah's disappointment was noted. She snapped, "Jesus, you are pissing me off. I never took you guys for being nerds."

Beth sent her cousin a dark look. "Do not start quoting your sister at me."

"Oh. Sorry."

So Tiffany called Beth a nerd. I wasn't surprised.

"Alex."

Hannah had turned her mission my way. I glared at Beth, who gave me a smug look back.

"Wanna go to Club T?"

"No."

"You're just like my cousin! Losers." But the grin Hannah was sporting negated what she said. "Fine." Standing up, she winked at the guys one more time. "I'm going to roam. See you two in a bit."

As she left, one of the guys darted behind her. They disappeared around the corner to the restrooms.

"Great. I wanted to go to the bathroom."

Beth had been watching, too. She nodded in the opposite direction. "There's a bathroom in the back section of the library. I use that one sometimes. No one goes back there so no one knows it's there."

"Yeah, all right."

Our library had six stories with nrooks and crannies all over. To be honest, it could be a scary place to walk around. People could hide for days if they wanted, and I heard stories where people did. So after I found the bathrooms Beth had been referring to, I shouldn't have been surprised to hear Jesse's voice behind a bookshelf in the very far section.

We hadn't seen much of each other over the past week, both of us studying for midterms coming up. A thrill went through me as I started for him, but when I heard a soft feminine voice, I careened to a stop. There were two bookshelves between us, and I hunched down. I was eavesdropping. I wasn't ashamed.

I heard the girl saying, "I just saw my sister in the front section. And guess what she was doing?"

Jesse murmured, distracted, "Studying?"

She snorted. "I wish. She was flirting with an entire table of guys. Can you believe that?"

Oh. My stomach settled with a crash. Tiffany Chatsworth. And she was alone with Jesse, in a very private corner of the building. A rollercoaster started inside me, but we weren't exclusive and she was dating his roommate . . . there was no rule that said they couldn't talk to each other.

"Yeah." Jesse didn't sound riveted.

Tiffany sighed from exasperation. "I'm just so sick of how she sleeps around. I get it. She's heartbroken. Dylan fucked her over, but she has to stop spreading her legs for any guy. It's so hard to sit and watch her do this to herself. Beth doesn't help. She lets Hannah go off and do whatever. What if my sister gets sick? What if she gets AIDS?"

He yawned as he replied, "I'm sure she uses protection."

"Yeah, if she's sober enough. They go to Robbie Haskill's house, you know. All three of them. You know what kind of a crowd he runs with. I know Hannah sleeps with him. I've gotten threatening texts from his girlfriend. She's always warning me to rein my sister in and keep her away. I think they even got into a physical fight."

"Wait. What?"

My stomach lurched. The rollercoaster went back at the interest in Jesse's voice. "What'd you say?"

"About Robbie Haskill's girlfriend?"

"No, all three of them go to his parties?"

"Yeah." A thick moment of silence before she asked, "Why?"

"Who's the three of them?"

"My sister. My cousin. And that weirdo girl who's always hanging around them. Do not tell me you have a thing for her? She's been hooking up with Cord. She's why he dumped Chandra."

I shook my head. All of that was news to me.

"I didn't think Chandra and Cord were dating."

"Hooking up. It's the same thing."

"Not for Cord." I could hear the amusement in Jesse's tone. "Chandra knew that."

"It was exclusive for her. She wasn't seeing anyone else—"

"She should've been. Cord doesn't date. Chandra knew that."

"What's your problem? Why are you harping on Chandra's heartache? She really loved him."

Jesse snorted, yawning again. "And that's the problem. Cord's not been quiet about who he is. Chandra knew that going in, and she decided she could change him. She couldn't. No big shocker there. What is it with you girls? Why do you always think you're going to change the guy you're with? He'll only change if he wants to. You can't do a thing about it."

She grew quiet before asking, "Are you talking about Jamie?"

"What? No."

"You are, aren't you?" She grew more insistent. "Are you trying to tell me something about him? Is there something I should know?"

"Tiffany, stop."

Her voice grew muffled. A sob hiccupped from her. "I know he texts my sister, you know. I pay for his phone and I see the records. I've tried to search in it, but he's got it password protected. Are they hooking up? You can tell me. I won't say anything. I just need to know."

He groaned. "Come on. We're supposed to be studying."

"Are they?" Her tone rose again, sharply. "I don't know if I could take that, my sister and my boyfriend."

"Your whole thing is messed up. If you want to keep Jamie, an open relationship is not helping you."

"It's not open on my end." She paused again, there was a soft shuffle of papers, and then her voice sounded, a husky laden promise, "But it could be."

My eyes snapped open. The rollercoaster went flying again, and I waited, my heart pounding as I waited for his answer. I knew a proposition when I heard one.

"Stop, Tiffany. I didn't agree to study with you for this."

And this hadn't been the first proposition. Judging by Jesse's wariness, this wasn't even the second or third. He sighed again. Books were closed. A chair was pushed back. His voice sounded again, more authoritative, "You've been a great study buddy, but our friendship needs to cool off."

Another chair was shoved back. "That's not what you said this summer."

A knife went into my chest. My insides were spilling out. They'd hooked up.

"And that was a mistake. Trust me."

"How about last fall? That was another mistake?" She lowered her voice so it was a seductive whisper, "Jesse, it was good with us. You're the only guy that I'd leave Jamie for. You know that. You know how I feel about you."

"Stop. I mean it."

A harsh intake of breath and then she demanded, "Are you seeing someone? Jamie thinks you are. I thought he was being an idiot, but are you? Who's the girl?"

"I'm not talking about this anymore."

"So there is. Who? I'll find out. You know I will."

"Tiffany."

"You know I can find out, and you know what I'll do to that girl when I find out. It'll be better if you just tell me right now. I'll even promise to leave her alone. Just tell me, Jesse. Come on."

He hesitated but said, "I'm not seeing anyone. You're crazy."

I heard something being shoved into his bag, and I stood from behind my bookshelf. He hadn't told her. He hadn't said a word, but her threats stung. It was worse than I thought. I knew if we went public, it wouldn't be good for me. Girls were obsessed with Jesse Hunt. I'd heard the giggles in the bathroom, from rooms with open doors, behind girls in line at the cafeteria. Basketball star that everyone already figured would go pro and the son to movie producer Malcolm Hunt. There was a reason Jesse kept a low profile around campus, but hearing the lethalness from Tiffany made my hair stick up.

Jesse rounded my bookshelf and braked. His eyes went wide, but he didn't say anything. My pulse raced. This wasn't good. Backtracking, he caught Tiffany by the shoulder before she saw me, too. He herded her the other way, muttering, "I forgot something."

Trembling, I made my way to the table, but I knew I was pale as I sat down. Beth frowned, but didn't say anything. Jesse and Tiffany swept behind us a few seconds later. Both ignored us, but her frown cleared and the corner of her mouth dipped down in disapproval.

I couldn't take it. Grabbing my backpack, I stuffed my books

and laptop inside before I hurried out of the library. When I
rounded the corner, headed to the back of the library where my
dorm was located, an arm grabbed me. I was pulled into a group
of trees and bushes. It happened so quickly. I couldn't react
before I was pushed against the library's wall and Jesse clamped a
hand over my mouth. He hissed, "It's me. Don't scream."

The scream was swallowed deep in my throat. As he pulled
his hand back, I hit his chest. "Are you kidding me? Do you want
me to have a heart attack?"

He grinned, so damned cocky. "That's what you get for eavesdropping."

Touché, but I wasn't sorry. I glared at him. "You slept
with her?"

His smile dropped. "Yeah. You knew there were other girls
before."

"Her boyfriend's your roommate." I didn't say anything about
us. I couldn't. There was no exclusive contract, but it stung.

He sighed, leaning away to rest on the back of his heels. One
of his arms was braced against the wall beside me. "He wasn't at
that time. It was a dick move; one that I'm ashamed of. But I
didn't like Striker last year, and I still didn't when Cord asked if he
could move in. He was in Camden's corner and gave me hell
last year."

Remembering when I had hidden in his hotel closet and the
fight he'd gotten into, I was impressed by how Jesse had turned
everyone around. He took them to the championship game. They
hadn't won, but everyone was looking Jesse's way for another
journey there. This time, a win was expected.

"You haven't done anything with her since?"

"No." He gave me a dark look. "And she caught me when I was
really drunk, both times. If anything, she took advantage of me."

Not surprising. Sighing, I relented and wrapped a hand
around his arm. Just feeling the touch of him again made me a
bit warm.

He thought the same thing as he tucked a finger into my waistband and tugged me against him. My head rested on the wall as my back was arched, my body pressed into him. He watched me the whole time, his eyes darkened at the same time my lust started swirling in me. It was always there, just waiting for the next time I was with him.

He bent low and nuzzled underneath my ear as his hand pressed flat against my stomach. His thumb began rubbing again. Each stroke made me forget where we were. As his ministrations grew bolder and slipped inside my pants, I was panting, holding his head against me as his lips nibbled the underside of my jaw. He whispered, "I want to go public."

I froze.

He pulled back, his mouth in a flat line. "Why do you do that? You did it the last time, too."

"Come on."

"Yeah. Come on," he snapped. "I'm sick of hiding. I'm sick of the sneaking around and picking you up late at night, making sure my roommates are sleeping. I want you to come over so I can study with you during the day and not have to deal with Tiffany always asking. What's your problem? Are you embarrassed?"

"Yeah, right," I bit out. "Me, a nobody, being embarrassed at being the campus basketball star's fuck buddy."

His hand went to my shoulder and he pushed me against the wall. He bent so he was eye-level. "You are not my fuck buddy. Shit, Alex. You've never been. You know that."

"That first year—"

"That first year nothing. I felt guilty. Ethan hadn't wanted me to be with you, and you were the first thing I did after he died."

I flushed at the literal meaning behind his statement.

He continued, vehemently, "I'm serious. I'm sorry about that first year, but I was trying to stay away. I was trying to respect your brother's wishes, but screw Ethan. If he were alive now, he'd know he was wrong. I mean, hell, he knew first hand that being perfect wasn't what it was cracked up to be. He tried to do everything your parents wanted, and when he messed that up—" His eyes widened and he stopped himself, but his chest rose from the effort. He backed away from me, watching me with guarded eyes.

I was slammed from what he'd said. My parents. Perfection. Ethan messed up. "What are you talking about?"

"Nothing." He shook his head.

I stepped closer to him. I knew enough. Something had happened. Something my brother had done and somehow it included my parents. "Explain yourself. Now."

"I can't." All fight left him. His tone was soft, defeated. "I'm sorry, Alex."

"What are you talking about?"

He shook his head. That was all he did.

"Why can't you just tell me!" Agony and long-forgotten grief broke free. It was sweltering, overwhelming. I couldn't push it away. The old Ethan was there again. His ghost was next to me, pressing against me, pushing at me. I was being suffocated. I couldn't get away from him.

"Alex," Jesse grabbed me. "This isn't the right time, but to hell with it—" He kissed me.

He continued to kiss me, and he walked me back against the wall. His hand slipped under my shirt and he cupped my breast. His fingers wrapped around one and he began to caress me. His tongue commanded his entrance. Helpless, I opened for him. His tongue swept in, and he melted against me. Every inch of him was plastered against me.

Desire battled away the panic. Then my body came awake and I gasped, wrapping my arms around him. One of my legs lifted on its own accord. He caught it and held it up, using the angle to press even more against me.

I felt him between my legs. I knew he wanted me as I kissed him back. My fingers unzipped his pants. They went inside and I found him. Gasping, he hissed against my lips, rubbing against my tongue as I began to stroke him. He was already hard. He grew even harder.

"Your room," he whispered.

I nodded.

Before we left the hideaway, he tried to adjust himself. His shirt was pulled out to cover him and then we slipped from the bushes. As we did, a large group had congregated outside the library's doors. They spread over the yard, and it wasn't long before the whispers started. Jesse Hunt had just been seen coming out of the bushes. I knew this would be all over. A few cell phones were raised, but he ignored them. Taking my hand, he led the way toward my dorm. As we went up the back stairs and into my room, I knew the damage was done.

Jesse wanted to go public, and we just had, whether I wanted it or not.

Yet, when he locked the door, took me in his arms, and kissed me, I stopped worrying. For the moment.

17

I t was an hour later when the knock came. I threw on some clothes, made Jesse do the same, and opened the door to find Beth standing there. She closed the door behind her and locked it before turning to us.

My gut dropped. I remembered the cell phones. I remembered the whispers. I knew where this was going.

"Hi, I'm Beth."

Jesse nodded, coming to sit on the edge of the bed. His jeans were on, but no shirt. Her eyes lingered over his broad shoulders, and I couldn't blame her. "Beth."

"Oh." She took a deep breath. "It's all over. You know that, right?"

My butt made contact with my chair. I wasn't consciously aware of sitting, but I must've. I was also looking up at her. Faintly, I nodded. "People saw us come out of the bushes."

"Yeah." She frowned at me. "Those pictures are on a website. I even got a few sent to me, and you know how social I am with the gossip mongers at this college."

I nodded, but I was reeling.

She perched on my sofa's arm. "What are you going to do?"

Jesse snorted, rolling his eyes. "Are you fucking kidding me? Who gives a shit if I'm banging you. It's none of their business."

"Jesse," I started.

"I'm serious." He stood, just gaining momentum. He grabbed a bag and started stuffing my clothes in it.

"What are you doing?"

"I'm packing you a bag. You don't want to deal with this? Fine. Live with me. Problem solved, but damage is already done. You can't go back on this. Hell, I won't let you."

Frowning as he grabbed my favorite things and put them inside the bag, I could only sit there. Had he not heard Tiffany's threat? And she was only the first one. I knew it'd get bad after this. It never got better. There was always a valley of hellish moments I'd have to wade through. But then Beth came over and she started grabbing my books. "What are you doing?"

She took all of it. My textbooks, my notebooks, all of my laptop cords, even my highlighters and pens. "What do you think? It's a good plan. Do you not know what girls live on this floor? I heard the stories. Kara took them to their party, and they broke into his room."

"They did?"

Jesse shrugged. "Worse shit has happened."

Another soft knock came at the door, followed by Kara's voice, "It's me, guys. Can I come in?"

Jesse was closest. He opened the door and locked it as soon as she slipped under his arm. Glancing up at him, she was flushed in the cheeks. "Oh, hi, Jesse. I didn't realize you'd be here."

"Hey." He started grabbing my shoes.

Giving me a warm smile, she came over and touched my arm. "You okay?"

I was still dazed. What was going on with my life?

Beth answered for me, "She's behind. We're packing so she can live with Jesse."

"Oh! That's a great idea." She looked around. "What do you want me to do?"

Jesse gestured to my mini-fridge. "She's got her favorite foods and sodas in there. You can put them all in a bag."

"Stop! Stop, you guys."

His bag was dropped by the door, but he bent for another one. Underwear, socks, and bras went into that one. He drew out a piece of black lingerie and raised his eyebrow at me before flashing me a smirk and tossing it with the rest.

"Jesse, stop." I tried to take the bag from him, but he shook his head and nudged me out of the way with his hip. "Jesse."

Kara had squatted down by my fridge and she blinked up at me from the floor. "I think it's a good idea, Alex. Kate and Amanda are outside your door. I know they're wondering if Jesse's in here."

"Who are Kate and Amanda?"

Beth snorted as she zipped up my bag. "They're tarantulas. Icky and full of poison. I hate those girls. They're friends with Hannah's roommate."

Noted. Jesse nodded at the bed. "You want your pillow and blanket, too?"

"I don't like this." I plopped back down. This was all too much. Was this really necessary?

Beth said to him, "Better take it, just in case."

"Oh my God."

"Okay." Kara stood, a grocery bag bulging in her arms. "I'm done. Anything else?"

Jesse looked at Beth, who shrugged. "I think I got all her stuff."

I was moving out. It was final. The revelations were already starting, and I knew there was more to come. I couldn't believe any of this. Then panic started in. I would be living in a house with four guys; one that I would be sleeping with every night. I'd had the house to myself over the last year. My parents moved out after her suicide attempt. Then that summer, there hadn't even been friends around.

My chest tightened. My vision grew blurry. My head started to pound.

I couldn't do it. I couldn't live with all those people.

"She's freaking," Beth spoke over my head. "Shouldn't you say something to her?"

Jesse replied, "Nah. Let her stay in this state. She's easier to move around. When she wakes up, she'll start fighting. I won't get anything done then."

Someone patted me on the head.

Kara soothed, "It'll be okay. Jesse's like a celebrity here, and now everyone knows you're connected. Once they get over the shock, they'll start not to care. The smart ones will realize that pissing you off will piss him off, and then everyone will fall in line. You can come back then."

"Why aren't you mad?"

"Derek told me. He said Ethan was your brother." She turned to Jesse. "That was your best friend, right?"

"He was my family," he said softly.

My heart constricted. I was his family, too. So was Mary. Wiping a tear away, I stood on trembling knees, but I ignored them and reached for a bag. "I can carry something."

My purse was slapped into my chest. Beth grinned. "You can carry that. You have to lock the door, don't forget."

I flushed. I would've.

When we went into the hallway with our army of luggage, some girls squealed. I heard the sounds of cell phones taking pictures, and one girl even asked for his autograph. Jesse plowed through them and led the way for Beth. Kara waited until I locked the door and went behind me. Once everything was in his car, Beth patted my shoulder, saying, "This is the best good-bye you'll get from me. I don't do personal contact."

Kara threw her arm around her shoulder. She beamed at me. "I'll bring her over to visit."

Beth threw her arm off before darting back inside.

"If you need anything else, let me know. I'm coming over for the night. The RA from fifth floor is covering for me."

"Because of me?"

"Because I want to be with my boyfriend. So, call if you forgot anything. I'll be here for three more hours."

"Oh. Thanks."

Jesse waited until Kara had stepped away before he turned the car out of the parking lot. The same girls who were always outside the door smoking, watched the entire spectacle, but this time they waved their good-byes. I wondered if they had known the whole time. They always seemed to be outside.

Derek had the garage door open and waited until we parked. He came over, nodded to me, and bent to grab the bags from the back of Jesse's car. Everything, the little I had, was transferred in minutes. It was then that I remembered my car.

Jesse already had my keys in his hand. He dangled them and gestured to Derek. "We'll go get your car."

This was so stupid. It was as if some trauma happened and they were treating me with kid gloves, like I was ready to break. Sighing from disgust, I went up the stairs to put my food and soda away. As I stepped into the kitchen, Cord was coming from their garage. He was holding hands with a tall and leggy blonde. She giggled, running her hand up and down his arm. He nodded to me in greeting. "Heard what happened."

I grunted.

"That bad?"

"What do you care? You don't have to look out for me now. It's out in the open. I can handle it from here. Thank you."

His eyes narrowed, but he shrugged. "Fine, but I wasn't being nice cause of Jesse. I liked Ethan, too. Thought we were friends, but if that's not what you want, so be it."

And the Bitch of the Moment Award went to . . .

I sighed as they started up the stairs. "I'm sorry. I don't have a great track record with friends."

"I know. Why do you think I don't give Marissa the time of day?"

"You did that for me?"

He flashed me a smirk. "Nah. I did that because it showed me what kind of girl she really was, well, that and how she cheated on her guy with me. Once a cheater, always a cheater."

I snorted and finished putting all my food away. I was still in disbelief at the turn of events. Maybe everyone was overreacting. They could be blowing this entire thing out of proportion. *I* could be blowing this whole thing out of proportion. I was turning back down the stairs when the front door opened again.

Keys were tossed on the counter and someone walked into the kitchen. They hadn't spotted me. It was someone familiar with the house, so, holding my breath, I figured I should get it over with. It must've been Jamie. And I didn't want to imagine his reaction.

"Are you fucking kidding me?"

Nope.

Tiffany Chatsworth stood before me, rigid and furious. Sadly, the look agreed with her. The ice-cold beauty queen seemed even more stunning before me. All her hatred was directed at me. She said it again, "Are you fucking kidding me?" Waving her phone around, I guessed what was on it. "I thought this was a prank. Had to be, because who the hell are you? You're no one. You may be pretty, but you've got to be blackmailing him. He kept his mouth shut, for you?"

A door was opened and footsteps hurried down the stairs. Then Cord was there, standing between us. He held a hand out to Tiffany as if she were going to attack me, but she knocked it down and twisted around him.

The first dose was only her warm-up. Her face scrunched up

as she threw out, "You're a freak. Hannah told me about you. You don't think she didn't? She said you're not normal and something's off with you. She said things don't compute right with you. She's right, but I can't believe Jesse has anything to do with you. He must be—"

"Enough!" Cord screamed down at her.

Her words stung, but I knew they were true. She was right about all of it. What was Jesse doing with me? But it wasn't the first time I'd thought that. I had always wondered, but Tiffany was wrong at the same time. My gut kicked in, an emotion spread through me. It was—I couldn't name it, but it felt right. It felt normal. Then I knew what it was, and I looked her dead in the eye. Softly, I started, "You're wrong."

A bitter laugh wrung from her. She threw her head back, and it came bellowing out. She didn't look very ladylike, not how she always tried to be. "Okay, little girl, why don't you tell me what I'm wrong about. Please enlighten me! I would love to hear this."

"You're the one who doesn't fit in."

She scoffed in disbelief. "Please."

A calm settled over me, and I spoke clearly, "I heard you."

She frowned.

"In the library. I heard what you said to him. You're the one who wants in. You want Jesse, don't you? It goes both ways, you know. Your sister told me things, too, about you this time. I know you want your boyfriend to use Jesse's connections to help Jamie run for office. Does Jamie know that? Or no, do you not know about his dream of being a sports news anchor? Because that's what I heard his plans are after college, not law school."

Her frown deepened, but it didn't cut her.

She didn't care. I realized that, and then I knew the real reason she liked Jesse's connections. "Or no, you're using your boyfriend to stay close to Jesse."

Her eyes widened.

Bingo.

I shook my head and took a step closer, softening my voice, "You want him. You want to use him to become famous, don't you? Or do you just want to be with Jesse? Do you think you love him? You think he could ever love you?"

"And you think he loves you?" she spat out.

I shrugged. "I don't know. Maybe. Probably not, but I know one thing."

She rolled her eyes.

"I'm his family."

They snapped back to mine at that statement. Oh yes. I saw the different assessment. I wasn't the crazy one. Wariness flooded in, as if she were just realizing that perhaps she had misjudged the situation. I could see all the thoughts playing over her, and then dread settled in along with loathing. The bitch loathed me. Well, welcome to the club.

"I grew up with him. He lived with my family. I'm his family. Alex, always Alex. That's what Mary said. Do you even know who that is?"

Her eyes shuttered, closing and turning away from me. The bitch was being knocked down a peg. It was damn time. The smug smirk on my face wasn't pretty. I knew that. I didn't care. As she looked me in the eye again, she saw some of the crazy rage, a gift from my parents. It was the least I could give her. "I have been in his life longer than you, and I will remain in his life, well past your expiration date, so don't get comfortable in this home. Your boyfriend lives here. He's the only reason you're allowed."

"Alex!"

Jesse's shout didn't startle me. I heard the gravel on the driveway outside. I was aware of the door opening and how Kara followed Derek inside. Stepping back, I glanced at him idly. He was chalk white, but his eyes were riveted on me. He looked sick.

I frowned.

Tiffany's voice seethed at him over my shoulders, "Nice new girlfriend you got here. She's a complete whack job."

Taking two steps, he wrapped an arm around my waist, but he frowned down at her. "Do everyone a favor and just stay away from Alex. She's going to be living here a while." He turned for the stairs, and I knew our time was up with playing house.

She stopped him at the door. "Was she right?"

He was stiff behind me. "She's family, yes. She always will be, too." Then he went down and before the door was closed behind him, I waved my fingers at her. Toodles, Bitch.

18

Round two happened in the middle of the night, but it wasn't with Tiffany. It was with her boyfriend and her sister.

After taking me downstairs, Jesse informed me that he didn't want to hear it. Then he gave me a lecture on getting along with his roommates, when I tried to interrupt, he included the girl-friends as well. That'd been the last of our discussion, and we remained in the basement for the rest of the evening. I'll admit. It was nice. We studied in the living room section of his private basement/apartment.

After Cord sent the random girl home, he came down for a while to study with us. Kara had stuck her head over the stairs and said good night. And it wasn't long until Jesse started rubbing at his eyes, so I took his hand, put both of our books away, and led him to bed.

Our lovemaking was nice and tender that night. Maybe it was because we were living together or because we didn't have the stress of having to hide this thing between us. We still hadn't defined our relationship, but he said the words I longed to hear. I was family.

I hadn't been family to anyone in so long.

As he fell asleep after, I gazed at him for a while. There was a heavy feeling over my chest. It was pushing me down, anchoring me in place beside him. I didn't want to move, but I couldn't sleep. My blood was singing, zipping around in me and I couldn't stay. I'd wake him up. I'd done enough to him already so I snuck from the bed.

I couldn't sit still in the living room of his basement so I went upstairs. As I was going to the main living room and searching for the remote controls, I heard the front door open again. This time no keys were tossed on the counter. A person was tossed on the counter. Moaning. Groaning. Gasping. A zipper was heard, I held my breath as I was about to hear my first porno in living color. Live and 3-D.

Then I heard a female voice rasp out, "Jamie, oh God!"

"Hannah," he murmured back as his voice grew muffled again.

Oh whoa. I was frozen in place. If they turned the light on, they'd see me. I'd be caught red-handed, but if I moved, they might hear me, and I'd be caught for certain. I was still debating when Jamie pulled away from her, muttering, "Hold still, baby. I'm going to get some of the good stuff. I know where Hunt keeps his stash."

When he went into the kitchen, she could see me. The foyer attached to the living room, and I saw the shock on her. The horror came next. Guilt was the third, and she clamped a hand over her mouth, a sob hitched in her tone. She slid off the counter, "Oh my God."

"I got it." Jamie came back to the foyer and turned the light on. He had a bottle of tequila in his hand.

Hannah couldn't look away from me. I grew flustered and tried to cover myself. I'd forgotten that I only wore a pair of boy shorts and a tight tank top, no bra. Then he followed her gaze and the storm surged forward. His eyebrows furrowed together and his lips went into a tight line. His jaw hardened before he clipped out, "What the hell? Tatum didn't wear you out? You better fucking get back to his room. And don't you say a word of this to anyone."

I opened my mouth, "Um—"

"I swear." He took a menacing step toward me. "If you say one word, I'm going to cut you. I don't give a shit whose bitch you are. I will make your life hell if you breathe one word. So keep your trap shut, you hear me, girl?"

"Jamie," Hannah started. She slurred at the end.

Oh no. I knew what he'd done. I was revolted as I asked, "Is she drugged?"

He had turned to her, but his head rotated back to me. His massive bulk was a frightening sight when it was filled with hatred and violence, and all of that was directed at me. I shivered, but not from being cold. My shoulders lifted as I took a deep breath. Hannah was drunk. I could smell the liquor from her. He couldn't do this, not when she was wasted. That wasn't right.

Hoarse, I tried to speak up, "You can't—"

"I can't?" His voice went over mine. His chest started heaving, and he clamped a hand over Hannah's. She winced behind him, but he didn't care. "You don't know how long I've worked to get this piece of ass. You're not going to ruin it for me."

"I'm not going to ruin it?" I shouldn't laugh at him, but I couldn't stop. He was delusional and he was an asshole. "You had to drug her! That is rape, asshole."

"She's not drugged."

"She's drunk." Pointing to the tequila in his hand, I added, "And you were going to keep her that way, weren't you? I was going to do you a favor, but by all means—have at it. Take her to your room." Wake the beast in his bed.

He scowled. "Are you messing with me?"

"Alex." Hannah pressed her hands to her head. "I'm really drunk."

"I know." Oh God, do I know. "Maybe you should call Beth. She can come and pick you up."

"She's not going anywhere."

"And you're not forcing her to do what I think you're hoping to do."

"Where the fuck's Tatum? Why aren't you screwing him? Use that mouth for something useful or shut your trap. This is none of your business."

Who the fuck did this guy think he was? "It is my business. I'm here. You're here. She's here. She's my friend. I know that she doesn't want to have sex with you when she's sober, and she's drunk right now, so you do the math."

"Bitch." He took another menacing step toward me with his hand raised in a fist, but then he was slammed against the far wall. Punches were exchanged and everything happened after that in a flurry of activity.

Jesse threw him against another wall and rained punches down on him. Jamie tried to fight back, but there was no use. Jesse knocked him dazed with the first few. He couldn't lift his arm to even block after a while, but then lights were switched on and footsteps stampeded down the stairs.

Jesse was tackled off him and thrown against a far wall, clear across the living room. Derek stood over Jamie as Cord held Jesse back. Jamie flung himself to his feet and started for Jesse. Derek held him back, though. Then a sob was heard from the stairs.

Tiffany stood in a flimsy nightgown. Kara was beside her, a comforting arm thrown around her shoulder. She was in her pajamas, which were a top and shorts like mine. Tiffany's gaze wrenched from her boyfriend to her sister, who was still dazed in the foyer. "Oh my God." She breathed out a hissing sound before her chest jerked up and she held firm. All the blood had drained from her face, but she turned to watch her struggling boyfriend. He was trying to throw off Derek, who seemed to have a firm grip on him.

"What the hell, man? What the effing hell!"

"Stay away from Alex!" Jesse shouted back at him. He pushed Cord off, shaking his head at the same time. Cord only moved a foot away with a hand kept on his arm.

"WHAT?"

"You heard me."

"Tiffany," Hannah groaned. "I can't—I'm drunk."

"Let's hope you are," her sister snapped back. "You were going to screw my boyfriend. My boyfriend, Hannah!"

"I wasn't. I'm sorry. I'm drunk."

Tiffany looked at Jamie, who had grown still by that time. Her eyes narrowed, and the same venom she had spewed at me was directed at him. "If you would check your phone, you would've known I was here. You would've known that she's not screwing Cord, you idiot. She's screwing Jesse!"

The fight drained from Jamie, and his body slumped as Derek pushed him back against the wall. "She's what?"

Cord cursed. "Man, you're so stupid sometimes. I told you I wasn't sleeping with her."

"Yeah, but you never keep a girl around and then Chandra was gone. You're not sleeping with her?"

"No."

Dumbstruck was the only word to describe the look on Jamie's face as he swiveled his eyes from me to his roommate. Then the same horror I'd witnessed on Hannah appeared over him. "Oh man. That's worse. Serious?"

Tiffany rolled her eyes. "That's the least of your problems right now."

"Oh yeah. Um," biting his lip, he turned to me, "I'm sorry, Alex. I really am. I had no idea—"

"Obviously," his girlfriend ground out. Then we heard crying from the doorway and she sighed, "Hannah."

"I'm so sorry, Tiff. I'm so, so sorry. I can't believe I was going to do that. That's—"

"I know you guys have been texting each other."

Hannah hiccupped on a sob and wiped a tear from her eye. "You do?"

"Wait, how?"

Tiffany sent another scathing warning look to her boyfriend to shut up. The message was delivered and received. He slid to the floor, cradling his head in his hands. A soft "oh, man" could be heard underneath his breath. He kept repeating that phrase, no doubt seeing his life flashing before his eyes.

"I pay for his phone." She'd gone over to Hannah and peered down. "You're really drunk, aren't you?"

Hannah wordlessly nodded, more tears falling from her. Then she lifted skinny arms and wound them around her older sister's head, hugging her tight and mumbling, "I'm so sorry. I'm so sorry." Wrapping an arm around Hannah, Tiffany rocked her back and forth, brushing her hair down her back and murmuring, "I know. I know you are."

Cord was the one who cleared his throat and suggested, "Jamie, you might want to clear out for a while."

"Because I was rude to his girl? Jesse, I'm sorry. I didn't know."

"Shut up!" Jesse whipped back at him. The fury caused even me to jump back. He jerked forward, pressing against Cord again, as he drilled holes into his roommate on the floor. "You stepped wrong, Striker. I walked up here to find this shit? My fucking girl. I want you out."

"Hey, whoa." Derek and Cord both turned at the same time. Cord spoke up first, "You're kicking him out, for real?"

Jesse didn't care. I saw the cold in him and shivered, he was beyond not caring. "It's my house. I want him out. Get your shit tomorrow and don't come back. I don't want to hear it, either." He sent me a scathing look. I knew he didn't blame me for what happened, but the anger was barely checked. I was scorched by it, but I knew this Jesse. He wanted time alone so when he stalked downstairs, I stayed put. I'd go in a little bit.

Kara had sidled up next to me. "Should you go after him?"

"No. I need to wait."

Tiffany glanced over, confused, but she didn't comment as she continued to stroke her sister's back. Hannah was full-on sobbing, clinging to her sister. The guys helped Jamie to his feet and he went to his room. It wasn't long before he came back down, a bulging bag over his shoulder. He paused in the doorway, but he didn't say anything as he left. He looked ready to apologize or say something to his girlfriend, but she shot him a dark look and turned her back to him. So he left with a defeated heaviness in his shoulders.

He deserved it.

Derek and Cord went back to their rooms, leaving the girls around the sisters. Kara had gone over and was stroking Hannah's back as well. She kept crying. It was the deep sobs, the ones that come from a person's gut. Flinching, I could sympathize. I'd experienced the same gut-wrenching emotion.

"I'm so sorry, Tiffany."

"Ssh. Just let it out. This is good, Hannah." Tiffany pressed a tender kiss to her sister's temple, moving her hair aside. "You need to feel this pain."

And this wasn't about Jamie anymore. This was about Dylan, her ex-boyfriend, who she'd been with for six years. I stood there, unsure what to do. The Hannah I was used to wasn't this one. She was crass, bold, sexual, carefree, or maybe careless. I knew she was hurting. I knew she was broken, but it was always covered up. This version of Hannah was letting it out. Feeling a tear threatening, I swiped at it, annoyed at myself. It's been so long since anyone needed me for emotional support..

I found myself scared. I wasn't sure what to do, and I couldn't mess it up. I may not get this opportunity again to show that I cared. But then Kara suggested, quietly, "Maybe you should just take her upstairs."

Tiffany nodded, leading Hannah up the stairs with her friend following behind.

Standing at the bottom of the stairs, I opened my mouth. What did I say? Should I do something? And Kara turned back, a small smile on her lips. "You can shut off the lights. Thanks, Alex."

Oh. Yeah. I could do that. Reaching out, the house plunged to darkness again. Myself included.

Jesse was pacing in the room when I went back down, pissed off and ready to do damage. As I stepped inside, he swung his piercing eyes to me, pinning me down. "What else did he say to you?"

"I think you heard most of it."

"Cord said he's been rude, but not like that. That wasn't being rude. That was being a dick to you."

"He didn't know—"

"He shouldn't have to know!" He punched the side of his closet door, and it broke off. The hinge cracked open.

I rushed over to inspect his hand. There was blood, wood splinters, but I didn't see anything too damaging. His hand would be black and blue by tomorrow. It was already swelling up. Caressing his rigid arm, I helped him ease it from the door and then touched the side of his face. He was struggling. His breath was wheezing.

"Hey," I murmured, softly.

His eyes opened, and I saw the storm inside.

"Thank you for defending me."

"God." He swept me against his chest and tucked his head beside mine. He breathed out, haggardly, "I'd do more than that. No one should talk like that to you."

Pain pierced me, and I had to blink back my own tears. Jesse had defended me. He stood against his roommate, did serious damage, and he'd do it again. He'd done that for me. My throat was thick with emotion and I couldn't talk, not then and there, but I was so touched. Turning my head, I nuzzled into his until he moved to meet my lips with his.

My body quivered with emotion.

He had created a hole in my armor, and it opened farther that night. It was big and gaping and I wasn't scared for the first time in a long time. I was becoming okay again.

19

"She was crying?" Beth sat across from me with a dumbstruck expression on her face. She had pulled her feet up to her chair so her knees were against her chest. With one arm resting over them, she reached to pick up her coffee.

We had met the next morning for breakfast. Jesse asked if he should come with, but it'd be worse if he had. The attention was going to be there, it'd be ramped up ten notches if he were with me. As it was, I had already been propositioned three times by guys in the parking lot and approached by a handful of girls. They were giggling freshmen and wanted Jesse's autograph, if I could hook that up. I caught a few speculative gazes from other girls. I was being sized up. They were figuring out the best angle to go through me to get to him.

To be honest, I had been expecting worse than this, but it was the first morning. And it was early. There was an entire day to look forward to, though I'd get a break. Jesse wanted me to meet him for lunch. He explained where he ate, but it sounded complicated. He said to keep up with Cord after our class. That explained where the guys went that one time. They had lunch with him.

I nodded at Beth. "Yup."

"Like a breakdown sort of crying?"

"Yup."

"Huh." Beth bobbed her head forward, munching on her breakfast sandwich. She seemed dazed at the turn of events. "I never saw that coming. I thought it'd be longer, in three months yet."

"She was with Dylan since seventh grade?"

"Yeah."

"Now he's with her best friend?"

"Ex best friend/roommate still. She's been trying to get out of that room, but Housing said there were no other openings."

"She could take my room."

Interest flickered in her gaze. "Yeah, you're right. She could."

A table beside us was filled with girls. All of their heads were pushed together, and we could hear loud whispering from them. At the glances, I knew they were talking about me. I sighed and put my toast back down. My appetite had waned suddenly. "How bad is it on the floor?"

She grimaced at me. "You don't want to know."

I didn't think it would bother me, but I was surprised at the lengths the girls went. A few approached Beth, hoping to get to me, and that path always led to Jesse. My door was covered with invitations to parties. A few sorority girls had stopped by to extend in-person invitations to their tea parties. The only part that angered me was when she said Kate and Amanda tried to break into my room. I still had things in there, photographs of Ethan that I hadn't even told Jesse about. If any of them were damaged, I'd be livid. By the end of breakfast, it was decided that Hannah would move into my room. I knew the other girls wouldn't be a problem when she opened the door.

We just had to fill her in on the plan.

Leaving for classes was another ordeal, or it might've been because more students were arriving on campus. When I checked my mailbox, a group of girls just stood and watched me the whole time. They didn't interact, just watched me. A path opened for me as I left. Stepping out onto the quad, clumps of people were all over. I was painfully aware of heads turning, conversations stopping, and then starting with renewed vehemence as I passed. Ducking my head down, I gripped my bag tight and plunged onward.

Seriously. Jesse was this big of a deal? When I got to my class before lunch, Cord plopped down in the chair beside mine. He flashed a grin, glancing at the girls who had turned around in their chairs to openly stare at me. Leaning forward, he pretended to bite my arm and beamed at them. He picked up my arm and held it out to them. "If you want, you can have a bite, too. She's right here, no pens or cages. She's free for the taking."

Two of them flushed and jerked around. The third girl chuckled before she joined her friends. With their backs to me, I saw more girls were looking over from the other side of the classroom. Cord leaned close and said for my ears only, "Jesse's the closest thing to a celebrity they have here, so you're like prime rib to them. They're hungering for you, thinking they can take what you have. You can't be weak, or they'll eat you alive. I've seen it happen to other girls. Jesse went on a date with one girl last year, but she was stupid enough to announce it to everyone. They never went out again, but she said she was his girlfriend. She used him to get in some prestigious clubs on campus."

"So they don't even want Jesse."

He shook his head. "They want what he has, his connections, his power, whatever they can get. Some girls just want that attention."

It made sense, but it sickened me. I couldn't help but wonder about that girl who was claiming she was Malcolm Hunt's daughter. I wondered if she knew about Jesse or wanted what he had because of his father. Jesse hadn't been called for any more lawyer meetings, but I knew the court case was coming up. It was scheduled for the same time as the NCAA tournament. It had already been hard on him, but it was going to get worse.

Then Jamie slunk in. He took the seat at the end of our aisle, shoulders hunched, a glower in place that matched the bruises on his face. Cord turned and grew quiet. He was waiting for something, and then I knew what it was.

Jamie swiveled his head to me and held out a hand. "I'm sorry for talking to you like that."

He expected me to shake his hand? All was forgiven? Just like that? My eyes narrowed to slits. I don't think so, buddy.

He grimaced and withdrew his hand back to his side. "Fine. Whatever. Look, just tell Jesse that I apologized. All right?"

Cord smacked him in the back of the head.

"What?"

"You talk to Tiffany like that?"

He flinched. "No."

"You apologize to her yet?"

"No, but I have a whole apology list." Jamie slumped down in his chair. "It sucks."

"It's good for you. You can't talk to girls like that. And I'll do you a favor. I won't tell Jesse about your half-ass apology."

"What?" Jamie's head jerked around. "Oh, come on. I apologized."

"That wouldn't fly with Tiffany, and you know it."

"She ain't my girlfriend."

"No, but she's Jesse's. You better turn your mind around. You're not getting back in the house like that."

"I'm already going to have to grovel to Jesse. Come on. Give me a break. And the sisters. They're pissed at me."

Cord sighed, shaking his head. "If that's your starting point, you've got a long way to go. Good luck and nice knowing you, Striker."

Jamie huffed in response, a scowl seemed to be a permanent fixture on his face. "This sucks!"

"Deal with it. You screwed up. Big time."

I grew fond of the day Jamie had been scared when I let him see my inner rage. That lasted a week. A deep sigh left me. Jesse had changed me. That rage was going away, and I couldn't let it out on command anymore.

Class seemed to take far too long. Lunch with Jesse was located in the back of a building, overlooking their stadium. Cord showed me the way with a reluctant Jamie behind us. As we got closer and as I saw the small cafeteria, Cord whispered to me, "The best athletes eat here. Boyfriends, girlfriends, close friends are invited, but only if it's kept a secret."

As I got inside, I could see why. The buffet had a carving station with a private chef behind. There was another grilling station. A salad buffet was set up on the far side, along with a pasta bar. As I passed by, there was whole grains, tofu, items that I'd only see in the organic section of a grocery store and certainly too pricey for me to buy. This was all for them, the elite athletes.

Jesse waved from a table in the back corner. He was surrounded by other guys, a few girls, and all of them moved down to make room once we filled our plates and grabbed some drinks. Jamie pounded fists with a few of the guys before he sat, eyeing Jesse at the same time, warily. Cord filled in next to him. Wrapping a hand around my wrist, Jesse tugged me beside him. Derek and Kara came in not long after and sat across from us. Glancing around, I wondered if Tiffany would show. Kara must've guessed at my thoughts. She gave me a brief shake of her head, leaning over the table. "She's with Hannah. They stayed at the house today."

"Jesse's?"

She nodded. "It's become a retreat for some of us."

I could understand. I wasn't even sure if I dared invite Beth over, the study session being an exception. But I made a note to ask Jesse about it. She had proven her loyalty more than a few times already to me.

"How was your day?" Jesse had been waiting to ask.

His eyes pierced mine, trying to shift inside and read my thoughts. I caught the concern in his and wanted to lean against him. Merely shrugging instead, I murmured, "It was interesting."

"I had a ton of girls ask about you. They wanted to know who you were and how you guys met." Kara smiled, her eyes sparking from warmth.

I wasn't sure what to say to that, so I just took a sip of water.

"What'd you say?" Jesse spoke for me, frowning slightly.

"I didn't say anything except that Alex is a very nice girl."

I wasn't sure why I'd been tense, but Kara hadn't thrown me to the wolves. She added, "I'm not being nice because you're one of my residents, Alex. Jesse's a good friend, one of Derek's best friends, so you can reach out for anything. I mean it."

"Even though Tiffany hates me?"

Her eyes shifted down the table, to where Jamie wasn't hiding his own eavesdropping. Her lips pressed together. "Even if Tiffany hates you. She knows better than to act on it, especially after Jesse handed Jamie his own ass last night." She ducked down, but I caught the pink flush and small giggle that escaped her lips.

Derek gazed fondly at his girlfriend, rubbing her back. "You're good for Jesse. We've noticed a big difference from this summer."

"Yeah," Jamie surprised everyone by speaking up. He cleared his throat as he straightened in his seat. "I've noticed that, too. And," he caught Cord's meaningful look, "I want to apologize for last night. Again. I should never have spoken like that to you."

Cord coughed once.

Jamie added, "Or to any girl like that. I wouldn't want my sister to get treated like that."

"I still don't want you around."

"Oh, come on! Why not?" The polite charade was gone. A

sulking five-year-old came over the big jock. "I apologized to her. Twice."

"Words are cheap. Find a new place to stay over the season."

Outraged, Jamie's mouth hung open. "Are you fucking with me?"

"No," Jesse snapped back. "I've been getting tired of your shit anyway. Last night was the last straw."

"So this isn't even about your girl?"

I fidgeted in my seat as new pairs of eyes turned my way. The argument had taken center stage in the small cafeteria. No one else even pretended to be having a conversation. They all shut up and were waiting with open ears.

"Some of it. Some not."

"This sucks. Come on. What do I have to do?"

"Not be such an asshole. How about that?"

"Why are you riding me? You trying to grow big balls for the team now?" As soon as those words left him, Jamie knew he'd stepped wrong. His mouth clamped shut and a tense silence filled the room. A pin could've been heard dropping. I knew I quieted my quick gasp as Jesse had clenched his jaw. His body grew rigid like stone, and I didn't dare look in his eyes. I knew the deadly threat that would've been in them.

Jamie tried to backtrack immediately. "Hey, I'm sorry, man. I didn't mean—"

Jesse cut him off. His tone was soft, but even more lethal because of it. "It's comments like that. It's because of that attitude that I don't want you in my home. If it were up to me, I wouldn't even have you on the team. You were in Camden's corner all last year. You think I don't know about the shit you said about me? That I was weak, a Hollywood pansy, mooching off my daddy's strings?" He rose from the table, his arms so clenched that his veins stuck out. "If you even fucking knew one real thing about me, you'd know that I'm anything but those things."

As Jesse was lashing at Jamie, I recognized the tortured look

in his eyes. I knew what he was feeling. Jamie wasn't Ethan. No
one was. Cord wasn't. Derek wasn't. Jesse was surrounded by a
bunch of people who thought they knew him, but none did. It
was only me, and I'd just gotten there. A mirrored emotion came
up in me.

"Jesse," I touched his hand. "Let's go somewhere private."

He wrenched his arm away, but glared, keeping himself in
check. Barely. Then he sighed, "Fine."

I led him down a hallway until I spotted a room that resembled a conference room. Plush leather chairs surrounded the
table with an expensive-looking projector in the middle. It slid up
from the floor. Two speakers were in the corners. No matter how
many hours I might've trained at a sport, I knew I'd never be good
enough to be in that room again. But this was Jesse's world.
Private cafeterias. People trying to get to him for what they imagined they could get from him, and he had ripped into one that
might've been a friend. I wasn't sure about Jamie so I held my
tongue. At times, he seemed genuine. Other times he was just an
ass. But it wasn't Jamie that Jesse was mad at. I understood that. I
also understood that I was the only one who could help him.

"Hey." I took a deep breath.

Jesse slumped into one of the chairs, gaze lidded, and shoulders hunched forward. Everything about him was screaming for
me to shut up.

I couldn't. "I'm mad at him, too."

"You'd be crazy not to be." He snorted, rotating the chair to
level me with a dark look. "He was bordering on abusive
last night."

"Not Jamie."

Ethan's presence was there. I felt him so strongly. A chair
moved an inch. It could've been from the wind, if there was any,
but I imagined him there. I wanted him to be there. In fact, I
wanted it so badly that I was struggling to keep my emotions
in check.

"Oh."

All the fight left him.

I sat beside him and leaned back. I was going on instinct here, but touching would take us into a different dimension. This was about Jesse. This was about my brother. Biting the inside of my cheek, I started, "He was supposed to be here."

A ragged breath left in a whoosh. "You're damn right he was supposed to be." He shoved his chair back again. It went crashing into the wall and he was pacing around the table, twisting his hands together. "He was supposed to be on the fucking team with me. He was supposed to be my roommate. Him and me. That was it. He was supposed to have my back, not go off and get killed going to— He was supposed to be here. Instead, I got Cord. And Derek. They're both good guys, but they're not—"

He stopped and gripped the chair in front of him. His jaw went rigid and he was swallowing his words. He was fighting the emotions that had rushed out.

I sat rooted in my seat. Holding my breath, I thought that would've taken longer, but I didn't dare mess it up.

I began praying for him to keep going.

One. Two. Three. I counted to six before he started again, saddened, "He was my best friend and my brother. And he's not here."

"But he was supposed to be."

"He was supposed to be."

"I came for him."

Jesse had turned toward the wall, but he looked over again. A slight shimmer was over his eyes. He never moved to brush it away or pretend it wasn't there. He let the moisture build as he nodded. "I know you did."

Nodding, I didn't know what else to say or even what else there was to say.

Then he added, "I came for him, too."

"You did?"

"Yeah." He let out a deep breath as he sat down His voice was calmer, stronger. "I was offered at six other places. I came here because it was where Ethan dreamed of playing."

We were in the same boat.

"Your family was like my only family. Hell, my dad might've had tons of kids, but I didn't grow up with them. I don't know any of them, and this girl, I can't reach out to her. The lawyer went nuts when I said I was thinking about talking to her. And you know the messed up part?" A strangled laugh rose from his chest. "I don't even know if my mom's my real mom."

"Jesse?" I rose from my chair and went to him. Sliding into his lap, I waited as he leaned back in the chair. His hands rested lightly on my legs.

"I saw a file. It'd been left open."

It hurt to hold his gaze. There was so much pain.

"It said she was barren, she couldn't have kids. I don't know if she was like that after me or . . ."

"You think another woman had you and your dad passed you off as hers?"

He nodded, swallowing thickly. "I loved her, but what if she wasn't even who I was supposed to be loving?"

"Oh, Jesse." How could I answer that? I couldn't. Resting my head against his chest, he tightened his arms around me and rested his cheek on top of me. I felt him take another deep breath.

I used to do that, to lessen the pain. It never worked. The pain always won out. It always suffocated me.

"I'm so sorry, Jesse," I whispered.

"Yeah," he bit out. "What do you expect, though? I should've thought of that growing up with him. You have no idea how grateful I am to your family for taking me in and letting me live with you guys. Your parents have been so good to me."

My own agony stirred. My parents had abandoned me, but I knew they would never do that to him. Jesse was the son they wanted to replace Ethan. He just didn't know that. Biting my tongue, a familiar heaviness came over me. I couldn't tell him about my parents. I knew Jesse would be upset, but he'd be hurt. He'd be disappointed and there went his ideal image of what parents should be.

I couldn't do that to him.

20

T here were a few changes in the house after that first night. Jamie wasn't allowed back, but Tiffany started living in his room. After an apology for her stupidity, Hannah moved into my room. Everything was approved through Housing so it looked like I had a roommate on paper. The girls stopped knocking on my door the day she moved in. Since I refused to bring more of my stuff over to Jesse's, I had to stop by every other day for clothes or random things. The other girls on the floor tried to become friendly with me. When I ignored them, which I would've done anyway, they started getting nasty. Insults were heard from opened doors when I'd pass by. These were followed with more of them lingering in the hallways. It was a mean girl situation. They'd whisper about me, not quietly anymore, and shoot me death glares as I was forced to walk around them to my room.

After Hannah witnessed a few of these moments, she made me promise to text her whenever I would come over. When I did, Hannah was in the hallway, in a lawn chair with a table beside her. Most times, she had a book in her lap and a drink on the table. The location of the lawn chair moved. The first time was outside her (my) door. By the third week, she sat outside the doors of the mean girl leaders. No one won against Hannah when the insults flew.

The other change was at the house.

After our first fight that had almost turned violent, and after she saw how Jesse defended me, Tiffany began to ignore me. It was the most passive aggressive tactic, but it didn't bother me. I could ignore her as well, made my life easier. After one night, when I went into the kitchen and Tiffany left the table to go upstairs, I took her vacant seat. Kara rolled her eyes and asked, "How are you handling that?"

I shrugged and popped one of Tiffany's grapes in my mouth. "I don't really care. I think she thinks this is getting to me, but it's easier. I don't want to be her friend, so I don't know what she's getting out of this."

Kara grinned. "Tiffany thinks everyone wants to be her friend."

"Not me."

"I know. She doesn't know that."

Eyeing her, I asked, "Why are you saying this stuff to me? You're not being loyal to her."

"I'm loyal to Derek, and he likes you. Plus, I still consider you one of my residents. I've told Tiffany she's being dumb. It's obvious how much Jesse cares about you. You're not going anywhere. She needs to accept that and move on. Even though she doesn't see it that way, I'm trying to help her in the long run."

"Oh." That made sense to me.

"In her defense, she's never met a girl in Jesse's life before. Those two were close last year, as close as I think he'd get to another female as a friend."

I nodded. Jesse had explained it to me one night, but he made sure to reinforce that he never saw Tiffany as more than a friend. I wasn't too sure about that. He had slept with her. Twice. But she wasn't his family. I was.

"What about Chandra? I thought she was friends with you two."

Kara looked down at the table. "Cord doesn't want her here, so she's not allowed to come over."

"Yeah, but you guys are friends with her."

She looked up. I caught the sadness there before she masked it. She shrugged, forcing a smile to cover. "It doesn't matter. We can still be friends with her outside of this house, but she has to respect Cord's wishes."

Remembering that first day, I thought there'd been something extra between the two. I said as much to her, but she shrugged again. "If you haven't noticed, Cord doesn't like getting close to any girl."

"Yeah." I had noticed. I had witnessed it a few times. Marissa had emailed me one time, asking if Cord was mad at her. He had never responded to her emails, phone calls, or text messages. My old friend was getting the snub. She knew it; she just needed to accept it.

"You know, you can have your friends to the house. That'd be okay."

"My friends?"

"Beth and Hannah."

"Oh." I frowned. "Isn't that weird? I thought Hannah was fighting with Tiffany again?"

"They're always fighting. They're sisters, but Jesse said you live here, too, so you can have your friends over."

"Yeah, I guess." It felt weird. There was an unspoken rule to keep the house from people. I knew Beth and Hannah would be fine, but I didn't want to get comfortable. When I did, something bad would happen. So, I kept being there without really living there. It would be safer for me in the end when that bad thing did finally happen. I loved Jesse, but I was still trying to save myself from other attachments. It'd be hard enough to lose him. I knew it would happen. Nothing good happened to me, nothing that lasted.

<small>THANKSGIVING CAME AND WENT.</small>

I still lived with Jesse, but our time had dwindled because of basketball practices. It'd been a month into the new season until they had their first home game. Even though Kara mentioned having Hannah and Beth over to the house, I never did. Instead, the three of us began hanging out at a diner off campus. We were leaving the place when I invited them over. It was my first time ever. Jesse and the guys were gone. They'd be at their game. And Tiffany and Kara had already left to watch it, and the thought of being alone for the rest of the night, didn't sit well with me.

Hannah shrugged. "Sure. Can I get drunk?"

Beth hit her on the arm before she frowned at me. "Aren't you going to the game?"

"And sit by myself?"

"Oh, come on. There must be lots of fakeys that will keep you company. You could have fake friends all you want. Think of the possibilities." Hannah spread her arms out, laughing at her own joke. "Fake people everywhere!"

"Yeah, I get it." Beth waved off her cousin's theatrics.

"I'm down. Let's throw a rager." Hannah caught my look. "Kidding, Alex. Chill."

"Oh." Relaxing, but only a little, I didn't know what I was so tense about as we drove in our separate cars to the house. I led the way, Hannah and Beth behind me. When I pulled into the driveway, a visitor was waiting for me.

She'd been waiting on the stoop.

Angie. She and Marissa had been my best friends. Marissa had been smart. She checked out earlier, but Angie had tried to hang in there. Even in my darkest days, it hurt. I hadn't heard from her since the day she left for college, but it didn't look as if she had changed much. She looked like the same Angie.

I saw the silver Prius in the driveway. "You retired the truck?" I didn't even bother with a hello first.

Angie relaxed a little. She grinned, a little, and eyed Beth and Hannah warily. "No. My little sister's driving it now. I bought this last weekend."

"That was a nice Thanksgiving present to yourself."

She shrugged and wrapped her arms around her middle. "Yeah, well, I'm modeling now. I can afford it."

"So can Alex." Hannah stepped closer with her hands on her hips. She drew her chin down, leveling Angie with suspicion. "She won't say a word, but I can tell. I can smell money on people, and Alex has it. You're not here for that, are you?"

"Hannah," Beth groaned, "let's go inside."

"Can't. The Missus here has the keys."

Rolling my eyes, I dangled my keys in the air.

Hannah snatched them but cast a warning eye over Angie. "She's my friend. Just so you know."

Angie's slim shoulders lifted up and down in a deep sigh. "Yeah, well, she's my friend, too."

"I haven't heard about you." She raked her up and down.

Beth grabbed her cousin and dragged her away, saying, "You didn't know about Jesse, either."

We heard Hannah grumbling when the door opened and shut behind them, "You think you're so special because you did—"

Angie bit her lip, smiling nervous at the same time. "They seem like good friends."

I shrugged. "They're like me. We get along."

"They're like you?"

I caught the sincerity in her voice and my gut dropped. Just like that, I was reminded of the last summer. It was only four months ago, but so much had happened. There'd been so much distance by the end and there was even more spanning between us. I didn't want to lie anymore. I didn't see the point to it. I shrugged. "They're broken like me."

She sucked in her breath and jerked to the side. Her throat started trembling and she was biting down on her lip, hard. As she glanced back, she flicked a tear away. "You were broken."

I frowned. "You knew that."

She shook her head quickly, one brisk movement. "You never admitted it. I felt it. I knew something was going on, but you never said."

"I told you about my mom."

"Because I knew! I knew about your mom, and you never told Marissa. Your brother died and your mom tried to die the next year."

There was so much emotion in her voice. I heard the sob in her throat, but I refused to feel sorry for her when I was one who had been shattered. I heard the unspoken insinuation. If I had spoken up and told them what was going on she would have helped. That still wouldn't have made it better. Heaving a deep breath, I said, "I know you're going to say otherwise, but you couldn't have handled what was going on in my life."

"You didn't even let me try!" Pressing a hand to her mouth, she tried to quiet her sobs. "Marissa told me that she saw you. I went home for break and stopped at your house a few times, but I ran into her at Eric's house. He had a party. She said you looked good."

"She did?"

She nodded, more tears falling free. Her chin kept quivering. "She did. She said some things hadn't changed. You and Jesse were sneaking around again." Glancing around, her smile was shaky. "I guess that's not true anymore. You're living here, huh?"

"Yeah." I frowned. "How'd you find this place?"

"Oh." Her cheeks flushed. "There's rumors about where Jesse lives. I was driving around, guessing. Please don't think I'm a stalker. Just, desperate, I guess. I emailed you a few times. I should've called, but I couldn't bring myself to do that. I just, I don't know what I wanted."

"I don't check my personal email that much. It's been mostly my school email. I have the same cell phone."

"I know. After Marissa told me how cold you were to her, I figured the element of surprise was the best course. I don't know. Stupid, now that I think about it. Whatever." She took another deep breath. Her voice didn't tremble so much. "I emailed Jesse, can you believe that? He told me that you'd be here and he said this was the best time to come. We came to town for the game. Justin wanted to watch Jesse's game, you know, an old teammate and all."

"Justin's here?"

"No. I dropped him off. I told him I'd wait for you to come home. He's at the game."

"So you're missing the game?"

She nodded. "God, Alex." She shook her head, "I can't believe it. You look . . . like your old self."

"I do?"

"Yeah." A tentative smile started to grow over her face. "You look good. You look almost like that party girl from our freshman year. Remember that year?"

The hole in my chest closed off. It went to shelter where it was safe and protected. "No," I answered. "I don't want to remember that year. It was my last year with Ethan."

"Oh." Her smile was wiped clean. "I'm sorry. I didn't think about that."

I was growing tired of this. "What do you want, Angie?"

"I wanted to see you."

I continued to stare at her. She was lying.

Her shoulders drooped. "I wanted to see how you were doing."

There was more. I felt it from her.

Finally, she admitted, "I wanted to apologize for last year."

There it was. I bit out, "Why?"

She flinched from my tone, it was so cold. "I don't think I was a good friend to you. I *know* I wasn't a good friend to you. I made you break up with Jesse, then that last summer when . . ." Her words faded. She still couldn't talk about it.

No one could. No one understood it, not even me. "Did Eric ever tell you about that night in my kitchen? When he came in, and I was burning something?"

She jerked a shoulder up.

So he had.

She couldn't look at me, which I didn't blame her for. People always hid from hard truths, too scared or feel uncomfortable or exposed. Hannah understood it. Beth understood it. I didn't know how, but I knew they did. I knew something so atrocious had happened in their lives that they were changed. They would always be changed and that was how it was for me. That letter shattered me, and people didn't want to admit that could happen. Because if they had to accept that it could happen to someone else, they would have to entertain the idea that it could happen to them.

Angie grew up in a good family. She had good parents who loved her and a family that would be there for her, so it made sense why she didn't want to hear what happened to me. Why would she? Why would a person like that want to experience the pain that I had? Even if it meant being a good friend?

I understood why Eric had been scared. I understood why Angie and Justin had shied away from me. They didn't want to know the amount of pain that I'd been feeling, so I kept to myself. They knew, but when I got that letter from my parents, I couldn't keep it checked and hidden anymore. The pain was too much. It had started to mingle with rage until the two became one and the same. It made me look different. It made me walk different. It made me act different, think different, feel different. It was like my damn arm had been cut off. I kept going, but I couldn't grow another arm. Couldn't grow another set of parents, another brother, anther family.

"You're off the hook."

"What?"

"You're off the hook, Ang. I know you tried to be a friend to me last year, but let's just admit this. It was hard being my friend. I get it."

Her tears started falling again. She crumpled to the ground and began to rock back and forth. She just kept crying.

I knelt beside her. I didn't touch her. I wasn't going to comfort her, but I knew she needed to be released. "I know you tried to be my friend. I think you did a good job, but with the whole mess of my family, I wasn't a normal person. I'm still not a normal person. Pain and grief, loss and mourning, then being abandoned . . . a person can only take so much. Eventually, if they don't get support or love, they're going to fall under all those strikes, you know?"

She started sobbing, deep gut-wrenching sobs, and she buried her head in her knees. Her shoulders jerked forward with each sob.

Frowning at her, she was the one crying while I had been the one hurting. It didn't make sense to me, but I still said, "You have a good future ahead of you. I know that I was holding you back. I was like an anchor with all my stuff. I get it. I do. Beth and Hannah, they're like me. They get it, and they're not scared to be around me. Neither is Jesse. I get him, no one else does."

She looked up and wiped at her face. "Have you told him?"

"About?" But I knew. It had never been put into words. I was still scared of what would happen.

"Alex, I was at your house. Your parents were never there. I mean, come on. Stop playing dumb. Just say it," she snapped.

Reeling, not from her tone, but that she really knew. She actually knew. My heart began racing, pounding in my chest, and panic started again. It was rising.

"We live in a small town, Alex." She kept going. I tried to shut her out, but I couldn't. "My mom's cousin works at the law firm your parents used. I know about the stipulations on their stipend for you. That you can't communicate with them. That you can't even call them or visit them. That if you want to hear how they're doing, you're supposed to send an email to your dad stating your reasons for even asking in the first place. Are you kidding me?"

I couldn't hear anymore.

I knew about them. I'd read them in an email they sent me later, but I wanted to box my hands over my ears. My heart was trying to claw its way out of me.

"I know, I know. Blah, blah, your fucking parents blah. They're horrible people. They've been horrible to you. I saw them last weekend, and I couldn't stand it. I wanted to go over and smack your dad. I wanted to shake common sense into your mom and ask why they could do this to you? You haven't done anything to them!"

"I could've . . ." I couldn't have. A storm was inside me. I could've peed my pants and I wouldn't have felt it, but I forced myself to stay there. Everything in me screamed to run, to hide, but I couldn't. I stayed put. I stared straight ahead, and I made myself hear what else she was going to say. Angie was going to rip off the Band-Aid of denial I had put over myself. I had started to peel the ends away, but she was about to rip it all clear.

All the agony from last year and summer was about to come flooding back. My hands curled into my legs, and I held on, waiting for it.

"You were the most perfect daughter they ever could've asked for. Your brother died. You worshiped him. You gave your virginity to his best friend, and I know some of that was because of Ethan. It wasn't all about you and Jesse. I don't know how, but I know some of that was about Ethan. Maybe you were trying to connect to another person who loved him like you did, I don't know, but your parents should've been there for you. They weren't, Alex!" Angie was shouting through her tears. She was still sitting in the driveway and she was yelling, but it wasn't at me. It was *for* me. "And your mom, come on. You really think she tried to kill herself? I don't. I think she wanted attention. I think she wanted a reason to leave and to justify it in her head that she couldn't care for her daughter anymore. I know those nurses who took care of her. They said she was the one who called the ambulance. She told the 911 operator to call her husband, but her daughter could not be told a thing."

I was faintly aware of a door opening, but I couldn't look. The tears were blinding me and all I could really do was try to breathe through the pain of it all.

Angie's disgust came out, loud and clear, as she continued, climbing to her feet now. "And you never said anything! Why didn't you say something? I would've been there for you. I would've gone to the counselor if I knew for sure. I didn't know for sure. I thought maybe, but it took all last week to ask around. Finally, people started talking about it, but I knew. I knew something was going on. They were never home. Every time I came over, they were never there. And you could go anywhere. You came over all the time. You never had to call your parents for permission for anything. And that depressing house. I mean, seriously, Alex. They left you in that house? All alone in that house?"

I shot to my feet now. "I wasn't alone." My chest was being split open once that Band-Aid was gone and now the hurt and pain and sorrow were leaking everywhere, spilling around me in tidal waves. "Ethan was there!"

"Ethan's dead!" she shouted back. "News flash, Alex! Your brother's been dead for two and a half years now. It's time to move on!"

"What do you think I'm doing here? I'm trying, Angie."

Her face clouded over and more tears came. She began

shaking her head, "I can't. I just, I tried to be a good friend to you, but I knew something was wrong. I knew it, but you never said anything. I couldn't be there for you if you didn't tell me. Why didn't you tell me?"

"Because you couldn't handle it! Your parents love you. Your boyfriend worships you. You don't know what it's like to feel as much pain as I did and to watch everyone else have what I didn't. You don't know what that was like."

"Because you didn't let me," she whispered, pressing the back of her hand to her mouth again. "You didn't let me in. Why didn't you let me in?"

The truth slid free in me. I hung my head as I whispered, "Because if you had known, you would've left me, too. I only had you."

"Oh my God," she gasped, wrapping her arms around me. She jerked me against her and hugged me as if her life depended on it. "I am so sorry. I am so, so, so sorry. I really am. I am so sorry, Alex. You'll never know how sorry I am."

Slowly, I hugged her back. I was clinging by the end.

She began to rock me back and forth, smoothing a hand down my hair and back. "I don't know if I would've been there for you, but I think I would've tried. You never told anyone. No one knew, not really. You got good grades. You were so damn perfect. Too perfect, but I knew something was wrong. I felt it, and they were never home. I'm sorry I didn't know until now. I really am sorry."

She held me, and we both cried. I wasn't sure what I was crying for, but it was the good kind.

21

Angie had left not long after our crying session, and I had been relieved. It wasn't that I wasn't grateful for her visit, but I could only handle so much. When I went back inside, Hannah and Beth acted as if they had never snuck outside or overheard anything at all, but I knew they had. I was okay with that. This was why I was friends with them. When the game was over, Hannah got an invite from her sister to an after-party. She made a crack how this wasn't going to happen again, so they went. When Jesse came home later, I could tell he wanted to go too, so I went with him. It was then that I learned their after-parties were something else. We drank out of gold-rimmed glasses. I got one with sparkles inside. That was also where I learned how much I didn't fit in with the other basketball girlfriends. Was I one? Jesse and I hadn't talked about it at all, we weren't official, but I was family. I contented myself with that. I was Jesse's family. No one else could take that claim from me.

The night ended without any great event happening, which I was thankful for. My drama meter was full and tipping to the overfull capacity.

The next morning, I woke up to the realization that it was Ethan's birthday.

The knowledge came at me and it felt as if a truck had run over me. Still, I rolled over, my hand searching for Jesse, but he wasn't beside me. The pain doubled, and was lying there, wishing I had some damn booze, when the door opened and he came in. He was shirtless, and his chest was glistening from sweat.

"Hey," he said. "We were shooting hoops outside."

"Yeah." I slid from bed and headed to the bathroom. My senses were screaming at me to escape, to get drunk, to do something so I couldn't feel anymore. Jesse would've understood. He was the only one, but it was too much. I missed Ethan. The sense of being cheated railed inside me. He should've been alive. He should've been playing hoops with Jesse, not whoever had been. The anger in me was bitter. It was starting to boil up.

I wasn't in the shower long before Jesse came in. I felt him before I saw him. His hands touched my hip and he moved me back against him. Pressing into him, need surged within me. I gasped as he kissed my shoulder and trailed up my throat. My skin sizzled from the path he left. As his mouth lingered under my chin, I began panting. Molten lust was swirling in me, taking me over. I turned around so my breasts were flush against him. He pushed me to the wall and swiped a kiss over my lips. It was the faintest of feather touches. I was throbbing between my legs, needing him inside me, so I pulled his hips closer, grinding on his leg. His lips moved over mine as I felt him grinning. He enjoyed making me squirm. I tried to nip at him, but he chuckled and moved back. His hands anchored me in place, still to the wall, as he bent low. My eyes closed, I knew where he was going. As his lips touched my stomach, I gasped from the onslaught of new sensations. Desire pulsed in me, one with my heartbeat. It grew with each beat. His lips moved farther down, and I arched my back out. I needed him. I needed him in me.

"Jesse," I groaned. My hands held to the back of his head,

keeping him in place and just holding on at the same time. "Please..."

He was unyielding. Gripping my hips with both hands, he knelt down and his tongue dipped into me. A strangled cry came from deep in my throat. It was gargled, and I was panting heavily for him. My lips were pressed to keep any more sounds from escaping, but I couldn't focus. My hands moved and gripped on to his shoulders. My fingers kneaded into his corded muscles. I couldn't do anything against the torrent of pleasure coursing over me. He was working me closer and closer. A moan slipped from me, and then my body jerked. I shot over a last wave, climaxing as his tongue laved around me. He rolled back to his heels with a wicked grin. Gazing down at him, a feeling of elation glided through me, I couldn't do anything more as my body continued to tremble.

His eyes darkened as they swept up my naked body, lingering on my lips. Shooting back to his feet, he held me against the wall, jerking my hips towards him and he slammed into me. I gasped again at the sudden push, but renewed need took over and my hips moved with him. He began thrusting, working both of us into a frenzy.

This was what I needed.

This would always take place over feeling or thinking. I just needed Jesse. I just needed him in me and all else flew away. He tensed as he grew closer to coming, then he gripped my legs and pushed us both over the edge together. A second explosion burst forth, and I was helpless against it. Wave after wave came over me. I could only tremble underneath their power. Jesse held me up. His own body was trembling as well as he pressed a soft, lingering kiss to my lips. He breathed against me, labored and choppy from what we had just done.

He picked me up and carried me to the bed. Then he gazed down at me. He was solemn, and I knew he could see into me. He saw the anguish before he dipped down and took my mouth again. So many pent-up emotions were in that kiss. Grasping my hair in his hand, he fell down on top of me. I felt his need. I felt his anguish. Then I began kissing him back, and I gave him everything.

He had taken the lust before, my physical need for him, but this kiss was different. This was the baggage kept locked away. It was unleashed, along with Ethan's ghost that I had never freed. The haunting, the turmoil of being left behind—all of it was given to Jesse. I felt his own ghosts being let go, then he rolled us over and we lay there, side by side. Our legs and arms were intertwined, but I couldn't let go of him.

Jesse pressed me into him. He had hardened again and he slid into me. He rocked against me, this time slow and tender. He went deep and touched the bottom of my core. Tears fell free from me as he showed me his love. I gasped as I felt it.

We never said the words. But Jesse loved me. It reached inside me and took root where the bad emotions had been. He made love to me, and afterward, I felt scraped raw on the inside. Everything hidden and stored away had been cleared away.

He cupped my cheek and whispered as he curled on his side beside me, "I know what day it is."

Ethan was there. He was beside us. I could feel his presence.

Jesse spoke again, "Do you want to go somewhere?"

I nodded. I couldn't talk anymore.

He pressed a kiss to my forehead and then got up from the bed. We dressed in silence. My eyes were trained down. I couldn't see into him. New dams would break free, but Jesse didn't seem to mind. He packed a light bag for us, disappearing upstairs and coming back with two bottles of liquor. He put them in the bag as well. Then he drove us to a hotel. It was a ritzy place, and as he checked us in, I realized he had made the reservation ahead of time. When? My eyes shot to his, but he only held them in a long drawn-out gaze. He was going inside again. I felt him seeping into me, and I turned away.

We had always come together, but this was different. It was on different ground. The rules had changed. I no longer knew the expectations, but then I needed to admit to myself, I hadn't known for a while.

Getting into the elevator, Jesse swiped the card for our floor. The access was otherwise restricted. And then we went to a larger suite. We stepped into a large apartment structure, but Jesse went into the back bedroom. He put our bags on the couch and pulled out the bottles of liquor. One was put in the refrigerator, and he poured the other into two glasses. Handing me one, his eyes held mine captive again. I flinched under the weight but held firm after that. He could see all he wanted. I knew it was the same inside of him.

My chest lifted with a deep breath.

We spent the day and night in that hotel room. We did what we always did on Ethan's birthday. We drank, and we had sex. Unlike the time in his bathroom, this wasn't romantic. There was nothing sweet about it. It was what we did on those two days of the year, except we had missed Ethan's anniversary the summer before. We made up for it this time. We pushed all the demons aside, all the emotions of missing him, and we used each other to fill that void.

It wasn't until after another coupling and on my third glass of liquor when I looked over. Jesse was frowning to himself. I recognized the look from our first year, and my gut kicked. That look wasn't good. It meant there was more. Jesse was keeping something else from me.

I sighed.

I thought we had gotten all of it out, but that nagging voice in my head reminded me that I had secrets, too.

Ignoring it, I sat up and pulled the sheet to cover me.

Jesse rolled his head against the headboard to look at me. "Hmmm?"

I put my glass on the nightstand. I was already drunk. I didn't need to spill the booze.

"Alex?" He sat up as well. "What?"

"You said some things before." Frowning, I tried to remember what they were. Tapping my finger on my forehead, I searched and searched. "You said . . . what did you say?"

"If he were alive now, he'd know he was wrong. I mean, hell, he knew firsthand that being perfect wasn't what it was cracked up to be. He tried to do everything your parents wanted and when he messed that up—" Another one plagued me; he thought I hadn't noticed. *"Him and me. That was it. He was supposed to have my back, not go off and get killed going to— He was supposed to be here."*

He got killed going to . . . to where? I wanted to ask Jesse that. I wanted to know what Ethan did, how did he know firsthand that being perfect wasn't what it was cracked up to be? Those questions were burning in me, but I knew Jesse wouldn't tell me. He hadn't before, and he had distracted me successfully.

"What did I say?"

I swallowed the questions. Because if he told, if I made him tell, then I'd have to tell him my secret. I couldn't do that. And as I shook my head and leaned over for another kiss, there was a part of me that didn't want to know. I wasn't sure if I could handle knowing a secret about my brother, not after everything I'd been through. My world fell apart the day he died and it had just started to mend. I wouldn't be able to pick myself up a third time.

Because of that, I slid down and pulled Jesse on top of me. As his body started to move against mine, I tucked that part of me away. I should've faced it head-on. I should always be willing to dig into the shadows, unearth what other lies have been told, but I couldn't this time. I chose to pretend we were fine. I needed for us to be okay. Maybe I just needed Jesse while I had him, while that secret was still buried between us. And not just his secret, but my secret, too. Maybe secrets weren't that bad.

IT WAS LATER when I was reminded how damaging they could be.

I checked my email after my class with Cord and Jamie. Cord was fine. Jamie was still a jerk, pouting every minute he was around me. He thought I had influence over Jesse and could grant him permission to enter the house again. I had no influence, so I ignored him. The other girls in the room were less curious about me, at least outwardly. I still caught looks from them, but I was certain they were more stressed about next week's final exam.

It was a relief.

When I saw an email from my dad, my relief fled.

Everything fled.

ALEXANDRA,

I am writing to you with a heavy heart. While your mother is doing well—the life coaches have done miracles with her—we were contacted by our lawyers. There is a concern regarding the inheritance Ethan left you. You were named in his will and testament, but they require additional documentation from you. If you could please contact Mr. Benson at the Benson, Filler, and Associates, I am certain that their questions will be answered. Please and thank you for your time fulfilling this matter. Your mother talks about you often. She has expressed an interest in visiting you. Her life coaches seem quite hopeful that reconciliation is possible, but I will express my concerns surrounding this situation. I fear your mother may suffer a relapse, and this is a matter I think upon daily. I will contact you again if your mother should decide to pursue this avenue. Until then, my thoughts and prayers are with you.

Sincerely, your father

P.S. We will be visiting Jesse Hunt this weekend. Your mother wished to attend one of his basketball games. We both miss Jesse so much. He was like a son to us. I would be appreciative if you do not create a scene, if we were to run across paths.

I SAT THERE as a familiar numb sensation spread throughout me.

My mother talked of me often.

Her life coaches wanted reconciliation.

My father was uncertain.

Lawyers.

Ethan's will.

Documentation.

Questions. Concerns. Thoughts. Prayers.

The numb feeling began to give way. Rage was filling in. As I sat there, my jaw clenched together, my teeth ground against each other, and I reached forward. Grasping the computer with both hands, I lifted the screen from the table and threw it against the farthest wall.

There were gasps, a few screams, but most of people in the room just turned and stared.

Jerking down, I picked up my bag and left, but I knew the whispers had started. It'd be shared around school that Jesse Hunt's girlfriend lost her shit in class. My name would take on a different undertone. Alex, Alex who, they would ask. Others would tell them my full name. Alexandra Claire Connors would be known as a violent freak within an hour.

As I stalked out, I didn't care.

I didn't care about a goddamn thing.

22

I went home. The driveway was filled with cars, but one stopped me in my tracks. *Their* car was in driveway. A fleeting question flashed in my head. When had they sent that email? But it didn't matter. They were here.

They were in Jesse's house.

My house.

I wasn't supposed to create a scene. As I remembered that part of the email, my eyes narrowed to slits, and my jaw firmed. I got out of the car and slammed the door shut. As I walked into Jesse's house, I didn't expect a crowd around them. Tiffany. Cord. Some girl whose hand he was holding. Derek and Kara. And at the same table, across from my parents was Jesse. His grin couldn't stretch wider.

He loved them. They were his idealized image of what parents should be, but they weren't real.

I lost what every teenager should have. Parents.

There were no words to describe the burn inside me.

My breath rattled. My heart went nuts, but I couldn't feel it. Everything dimmed for me.

My parents were in Jesse's house. They visited him while they emailed me. They missed him, but I was a concern?

Jesse noticed me first. He waved me over. "Come here. You didn't tell me they were coming."

Even Tiffany was grinning. I didn't know she could. I looked at them, then. Both my parents lost their expressions of happiness. That was all it was, because they weren't happy.

They weren't joyous.

They weren't real.

They were fake.

What people saw was all they saw. That was all there was. There was nothing more in them, certainly not love.

"Alexandra." My father started to rise.

"Don't."

My mother sucked in her breath, "Alex..."

I shook my head. They had gone wrong, so far wrong and they knew it. Guilt flared in both of them before they remembered their best course of action: denial.

Pathetic.

I looked at my parents and saw them as nothing more than pathetic. I said as much, "You act like you love him."

Jesse frowned.

My parents shared a look, and I stepped forward. My hands gripped a chair in front of me. I held on so hard, I thought my fingers would snap. I didn't care if I broke the chair in two. "You don't love him. You want to use him. You want to replace Ethan with him."

"Alex," Jesse murmured.

I laughed, bitterly and loudly. The louder, the better. It boiled out of me, but I held on to that chair. I couldn't move from it. It was my anchor. "I wasn't supposed to make a scene, right? If I 'crossed paths' with you, I wasn't supposed to make a big deal out of it. This is my home, Dad."

He paled.

I grinned. "Mom thinks of me often. Are you kidding me?" I pinned her down with my gaze. To her credit, she didn't squirm. She raised her chin, and her shoulders lifted as she took one small breath. Oh yes. She was getting ready for me. I started, "We're supposed to reconcile? Is that what your life coaches want to happen? Did I do you wrong, Mother, at some time in my life?"

My father pounded his fist on the table. "Alexandra, you will not speak to her like that. Your mother is fragile."

"My mother is a fraud!" My head swung back over.

She sucked her breath in again. It was loud and dramatic. Just the way she wanted, I was sure of it. My father gripped the table, mirroring my stance with the chair. He held on to keep from doing . . . what, I wasn't sure? Hitting me? I frowned to myself. Would my father harm me for speaking the truth? Was it that essential for him to protect their lies? But it was. I knew it was as I saw him fighting for control.

"Alex," Jesse murmured again. He had circled the table and stood beside me. His hand touched the back of mine.

I shrugged it off. I didn't need support, not then, maybe not ever again. I needed restraint because I was losing mine fast.

"The nurses didn't think you really tried to kill yourself."

Her eyes threatened to pop out while I heard someone gasp behind me. My father shoved against the table, the same rage in him that I felt. Welcome to the club. He spat out, "You will not speak any longer. You shut up. You will do more harm than ever before."

I sucked in my breath. "Ever before? What damage did I do before?"

Jesse tried again, "Mr. Connors—"

"You weren't the only one grieving, Alexandra. Your mother was as well."

"And you were, too. We all were." I rattled the chair. I wanted to lift it up and throw it across the room. "Why are you two more important than me? You left me. I'm your daughter, and you completely left me. You wouldn't even talk to me when Mom was in the hospital. You talked to Jesse. You hugged him, but you couldn't even look at me. Jesse, Jesse, Jesse. That was all you cared about then."

"Alex." Jesse moved even closer to me.

"Stop." I shifted away so he wouldn't touch me. "This is my secret, Jesse. My parents. They dropped me after Ethan died. I got a fucking email from them this morning. They warned me they were coming to see you, and told me that if I 'would run across their path' I wasn't supposed to make 'a scene.' A scene! Can you believe that?" I lifted my wrist and showed him the burn. "I got this after I burned the letter they sent me. A fucking letter that told me they were starting a new life without me. Without their daughter! How can parents do that? How can you justify that in your head and abandon your own blood, your last kid? You lost Ethan. You think you'd want to keep me closer because you already lost a kid, but no." I swung to face both my parents. "You cut me loose. Fuck you. Fuck you both! I burned that fucking letter, and I didn't even notice my own burn until weeks later. You did that to me. Do you know how screwed up I am because of you? What did I do to you? Nothing. I didn't do anything! Nothing! I got perfect grades that last year. I stopped partying. I did everything a perfect daughter could do, but none of it mattered. I should've gone the opposite. I should've partied or tried to kill myself. Good one, Mom. Maybe you knew what you were doing. If I'd done that, I might've gotten something from you. Maybe even a fucking hello in the morning!"

"Alexandra," my father barked. "Get ahold of yourself."

"I have." I shook my head. The rage was in there. It was flying around, but it was starting to leave. Telling them how I felt was somehow freeing. Cathartic. Then I felt Jesse's hand over mine. He interlaced our fingers. When my parents saw the movement, their eyes widened and they both went still. They had no idea, but did it matter? I lifted our hands and asked, weakening by the second, "Does this make things different? Am I worthly of your love now because he loves me?"

My mother asked in a quiet tone, "He loves you?"

I shrugged. "Does it matter if he does or doesn't? I live here. We've been together—"

"When?" my dad demanded.

I frowned, tilting my head to the side as I regarded him. "Does that matter, either?"

"When?" he shouted, leaning forward on the table.

"Ethan's funeral," Jesse spoke for me. He drew closer. I felt him trying to nudge me behind him, but I stepped to the side. He wasn't going to take them on for me. No way. This was my fight. I'd see this to the end.

My mother sucked in her breath. Again.

A fierce frown came over my father.

"Then Ethan's birthday."

"The anniversary of Ethan's death," Jesse added, throwing me a grin.

"After that it was more frequent. I was with him in Vegas last year. You guys ditched me to go his game, remember? I was there, too. I stayed with him in his room." My parents seemed to shrivel before me, and I grinned. I was loving this effect on them. Any effect, any sign that I mattered, I wanted. It didn't mean they still cared. I was a pest to them. It concerned my father that I could've been brought back into the family. He wanted me gone. My mother told the 911 operator the same sentiment. Her daughter was not to know anything. That was when I asked, targeting her, "Did you really try to kill yourself?"

She flushed. Her head jerked down.

My father covered her hand with his. "Alex," he warned me.

I ignored him. "You told the 911 operator that your daughter wasn't supposed to know anything about what happened. The nurses said you hadn't taken enough to kill yourself, only to go to sleep. They think it was a cry for help." I frowned, trying to figure out her reasoning. "Want to know what I think? I think you were giving yourself an excuse. Dad jumped on board. He whisked you away for your safekeeping. You left me in the house alone with Ethan."

Her head lifted again. Her eyes searched mine, a hope rekindled.

I shook my head. "His ghost, Mom. Only his ghost. He's there, you know. He's everywhere. I used to feel him all the time. I don't anymore, not as much. Some days I do, but other days . . ." I couldn't feel him anymore. It was as if he didn't want to associate with this event. Regret flared in me. I didn't know what that meant. Maybe I shouldn't have reacted? Maybe I should've let my parents go. It was what they wanted. They wanted to forget everything.

My father cleared his throat. He still looked pissed, but he only turned to Jesse.

He'd never change.

"Is that true? Is my daughter living with you?"

Jesse frowned. His eyebrows furrowed together, but he lifted his chin in response. "Yes." He didn't stutter. He didn't falter. He was standing against my father.

"Are the two of you sleeping together?"

"Every time she'll let me."

My mom flinched in her seat.

My heart began picking up its pace again. Something close to hope fluttered in my stomach.

"This has been happening from the start?"

Jesse nodded. His frown deepened, but his hand clenched tighter over mine. He pulled me back to his side so we were touching.

"And if I asked for this to stop?"

"Not a chance."

The frown turned into a scowl on my father and he turned away, nodding to himself.

"Are you happy?"

The question came out of nowhere. I turned, shocked, at the soft voice that came from my mother. It wasn't a tone I heard from her, not in so long, not since before Ethan's death. She sounded like a mother, like she cared.

"Are you?" Jesse asked me.

A lump settled in my throat, but I nodded. I couldn't talk and tears threatened to spill, but I nodded again. "Yes," ripped from me.

She smiled. "I'm glad then."

"Shelby!"

"Don," she lifted a hand and placed it on the table. "Leave it be. I don't think you've thought this through. Do you want to hurt Alexandra? Or Jesse?"

He fell silent.

"We've been hurt enough. Going off and leaving our daughter wasn't the right thing. My life coaches were right. We should've rallied together as a family. Instead, we fell apart."

He sucked in his breath. His jaw clenched.

I couldn't watch any longer. I knew what was going to happen. My father wouldn't listen. He had rallied for her, not for me. He had kept her from falling apart, but he cut me loose because of that. No matter the change of heart in my mother, if it was real or not, wouldn't matter.

"It's okay, Dad."

He turned to me, searching my eyes. I tried to lift the corners of my mouth. "I'm cutting you loose. You don't have any obligations to me." Jesse pulled at my hand. He was trying to get my attention. I ignored him. "You can do whatever you want. I'll contact the lawyers and clear whatever it is with them. After that, you don't have to see me again."

His shoulders dropped.

He was relieved.

He was fucking relieved that he didn't have to see his daughter anymore.

My mother stood. She'd lost weight and was wearing a shawl over a cashmere sweater as if she was never really warm. My mother looked like someone Tiffany would've loved to have as a mom. I glanced over, wondering if she was looking at an older version of herself, but I saw tears instead. That made me pause. Why was Tiffany crying? I assumed they would've loved this. My own parents loathed me. That was right up her alley. She could use that for years to torture me.

"I'm glad that you are in Jesse's life," my mother started but stopped as my father stormed from the room. The door swung shut behind him, and we watched as he went to their car. Getting inside, he turned the car on, but it didn't move. He was waiting for my mother. They were leaving. Again.

Her shoulders lifted for a deep breath. There was so much pain in her eyes. It struck my own, bringing tears to mine, but I wouldn't shed them. Not for her. She took a step toward me, but I moved away. She stopped. Her head hung down. "I am sorry about how your father and I have behaved. I know that I cannot ask for your forgiveness—"

"Because you don't want it," I cut in. I saw it was true.

Shame flashed in her gaze. She didn't mask it. It remained as she nodded. "You're right, Alexandra. I don't want your forgiveness, because I don't deserve it. There is no excuse for what we have done to you. You didn't do anything wrong. There was no reason for us to leave you. I want you to know that."

The tears slid down my cheeks, but I didn't care. They hadn't come here for this. They came to see Jesse and not reconcile or apologize to their daughter.

She turned to Jesse, "Have you told her?"

He shook his head. His entire body tensed at the question.

"You can, if you'd like."

"It's not my secret to tell."

"Oh." My mother frowned. "So, you've had contact with her?"

He jerked his head in a nod. He pulled his hand from mine and moved away, avoiding my gaze.

"Oh."

My mind was reeling. Her? Secret? This was it—the secret Jesse had been holding back from me. Every sense in me was tingling. My secret was out. It was his turn. He had to tell me.

My mother looked torn, as if she wanted to ask something more of him. Jesse cast a wary glance at her. He shook his head. "Don't. After what you did, you can't ask that from her." He looked at me. "And after what you've done to Alex, you don't deserve to see her."

My mother seemed to crumble before my eyes. The momentary kindness she had shown me was gone. Even her coldness was gone. She looked broken instead, just like me. She nodded to herself and left. No one said good-bye. No one followed her to the door. She paused there and looked over once more. Her eyes caught mine. I stiffened, pain searing me again, but I didn't look away. I wanted to, but I held firm. She said, "Losing your brother changed our family. I am sorry for my part. I know that I've not been a good mother, but I lost that ability when I lost Ethan. He was my first baby and—" She cut off, her voice shaking from emotion. "There's no excuse. I just wanted to say that I'm sorry, Alexandra. You've become so beautiful. Do you know that?"

I swallowed over a lump. She thought I was beautiful?

"So beautiful," she whispered to herself as she left. The door closed behind her, leaving the room in a shocked silence.

I was beautiful? I never thought of myself as beautiful.

23

I was reeling from everything that had happened. Somehow, I ended up in a bathroom with Tiffany. She pressed cool washcloths to my face. For what, I wasn't sure, but she was being nice. I frowned as she patted my forehead. "Why are you being nice to me?" Then I remembered she'd been crying out there. Why the tears? Did Tiffany Chatsworth actually have a heart? This wasn't foreseeable.

Her lips pressed together as she drew the washcloth down the side of my face and wet it again. "Don't get all worked up about it. This doesn't mean we're going to be friends. I just," she frowned and lifted a shoulder, "I dunno. I guess I can relate, in some way. I suppose."

"You can relate to being dumped by your parents?"

She took the washcloth to my face again. "You've never asked Hannah about our parents?"

"I don't ask anyone about anything."

Her eyes found mine.

"I don't usually want to know the answers."

She gave me the washcloth and sat back on the toilet. Then she shrugged again. "Our dad left us. He left my mom when we were teenagers. I always wondered if it was because of us, if maybe we were too much to handle or something. I didn't know." She leaned forward and pressed fingers to her temples. She began to massage them as she continued, "And it wasn't even because he had an affair or another family. He just left. He didn't want to deal with having a family. That's what my mom said. I guess I took it as we were too much or something."

I frowned at her through the mirror. She was hunched over, but I wet the washcloth again. My mind was still reeling.

"We all have a story, don't we?"

"Hannah loved our dad. She was his little girl. Not me, I was more into baking and makeup and doing girl things. He took off when she was in seventh grade. That was when she started sleeping with guys."

"Isn't that when she started dating Dylan?"

She shook her head as she continued to massage her temples. Her fingers were working harder, faster. "They started at the end of the summer. She started sleeping around the beginning of the year. That was why I knew it wasn't going to be good when they broke up. The asshole. He did the same to her that our dad did. He just left her. His excuse wasn't even a good one because now he's with her roommate and he transferred here."

"What about Beth?"

She looked up now, genuinely confused. "What about her?"

"I get why Hannah's broken. Why's Beth? What happened to her?"

She took a breath and stood. Crossing to me, she took the washcloth again and pressed it to the crook of my neck. "I don't know. Beth and I aren't close."

I frowned, but then went with my hunch. It helped to think of their problems. My problems were bad, but in a way, I didn't feel like such a freak. "What's your mom like?"

"Before Dad left? She was happy. After he left, she became a stoner. She was like a hippy." Tiffany dropped her hand and looked at me. "I think she was one when she was younger before she met our dad. Maybe that's why Hannah's like that, I don't know. I took the mother role. My mom couldn't handle it. She hasn't handled much since, except some guy's dick or pottery. She's a genius at making pots. Go figure."

My eyebrow arched at that one, but left it alone.

She jerked her head back up. "Why'd you ask about Beth?"

"Just curious."

"Oh." She stood and moved to the door, leaving the washcloth on the counter.

I grinned at her. "Don't worry. I won't tell anyone about your momentary lapse in judgment."

"What are you talking about?"

"You." I gestured to her before gesturing to myself. "Being nice to me. I know we aren't friends."

Her hand fell from the handle. She leaned against it and crossed her arms over her chest. "You have a really horrible opinion of me."

I shrugged. "You've been a bitch, so . . . yeah."

A corner of her mouth lifted up before she dropped her arms. "I'm not a bitch because of my sister or whatever reasons you might think. And it's not because I want Jesse—"

"But you do."

She stopped.

"Want Jesse. You do want him."

Her shoulders lifted as she took a breath. "Yeah, maybe, but I care about him."

"So do I."

"I know. Trust me, I know." Her hand gestured toward the door. "I got it. I heard the history of you and him. I've seen how he is with you. He's not like the Jesse I met last year. You and Jesse, and him and your brother had some bond that I'll never compete against. I'm getting it. Trust me. Hearing all that was hard."

I wasn't sure what to say to that.

"And you're right."

I looked back up.

"He does love you."

"Did he tell you that?"

"No, but it's obvious. He loves you, so you don't have to worry. I can tell he didn't know about your parents. That's what you said, right? That your parents dumped you, and you kept it a secret. People don't keep secrets unless they're scared of something, maybe about the other person reacting, but I'm telling you. You don't have to worry about Jesse. It pissed him off, hearing what your parents did to you. I could tell that, too."

"Oh."

She sighed. "I don't want to be your friend, but I'm in a position where I have to be."

"That's a great endorsement."

She rolled her eyes and brushed her platinum hair over her shoulder. "I don't give a damn. I'm just saying how it is. I care about Jesse, and it's not because of his money or his Hollywood connections. I really do just care about him, but I can see that he genuinely cares about you. You're not going anywhere. I get it. Not happy about it, but I get it. So . . . I figure I should call a cease fire? I'm not proposing that we be friends, but maybe not enemies?"

"I thought that's what we were when you were ignoring me."

She grimaced. "I did that to piss you off. It didn't work, did it?"

"I liked it."

"Yeah." She blew out a breath. "That's what I figured. That pissed me off instead."

I shrugged.

"All right. Well, I'm going to go. You're better?"

I nodded. As she reached for the handle and opened the door, I reached for her. "Hey."

"Yeah?"

"Shut the door." As she did, I took another deep breath. My heart began picking up again. This could blow our truce, but whatever. This was what not being an enemy and not being friends meant to me. Maybe. I had no idea. Oh well. Here it goes. "You should know that Jamie was the one who sought your sister out."

A scowl formed over her face. "What are you talking about? Jamie said she's the one that came on to him."

"No. I heard them one time at school. He was pushing her, and she was trying to say no. I know it's not a ringing endorsement, as you said before, but it is what it is. She was really drunk that night, and he got a bottle to make sure she stayed drunk. He was taking advantage of her."

"My sister's not exactly a saint."

"But it was important to her. Your boyfriend was off-limits, and for what it's worth, I don't think your sister enjoys sleeping around. She's hurting."

"I know," she said quickly. "I know that. I just worry about her."

I fell silent. My message had been given. It was up to her what she did with it. I hoped she'd break up with him, and stand by her sister.

"Thanks." She tried to give me a smile. It didn't quite make it. "For that, thanks."

"No problem."

Before she left, she said one more thing. "Your parents are assholes."

"I know."

Then she left me alone in the bathroom. Kara popped in a second later and gave me a hug. She wrapped her tiny arms around me and held me for a while. Pulling away, she brushed my hair back and took a deep breath. I saw the tears before she left as quietly as she appeared. When I followed behind, the house was silent. It was such a contrast from the shouting earlier.

I heard giggling from the living room and turned the corner. Cord and his girl were on the couch. She was on his lap, and he was tickling her so she'd squirm. His grin faded when he spotted me.

"Hey." The girl muffled her giggles. When it didn't work, she pressed her arm into her mouth, but more split through the air as Cord must've continued to tickle her side.

"Hi."

"So those were the parents, huh?"

"Yep."

"For what's it worth and from what I remember, your brother wasn't treated any better."

That got my attention. "What are you talking about?"

What had my parents done to him?

Oh my God.

An anchor dropped to the bottom of my stomach. Did it have anything to do with the reason he was in the car that night? Jesse said something about going somewhere, but he recanted. He said he didn't want him with Barbie and those guys. But why was he with them in the first place? Was that because of my parents, too? Were they pushing him too hard to be perfect? I took a calming breath, but it didn't work.

"Nothing. You should talk to Jesse. He knows more about it than I do."

The girl started giggling again and fell to her side, off his lap. Cord twisted around her as he continued to tickle her. As I left the room, her feet were kicking in the air, and she was shrieking in laughter, panting at the same time, "No, Cord. Stop. Oh, Cord. Don't. Yes."

His deep chuckle was the last I heard as I went downstairs and shut the door.

It was time. My secret was out. He now knew about my parents. I wanted to know his secret and I knew it was about my brother. I had every right to know. I crossed the basement to find his door open and him sitting on the edge of the bed. His elbows were resting on his knees. His head was down, but he looked up as he heard my arrival.

He'd been waiting for me.

I reached for the door, ready to pull it behind me as I stepped inside his room. But I stopped. My hand fell away from the handle, and my gut dropped to my feet. Whatever Jesse had to say to me wasn't going to be good. I saw the warning in him, and knew I was going to hate it, whatever it was. So I left the door open and leaned against the wall behind me.

He stayed on the bed.

I stayed in the hallway.

It was time.

"Why didn't you tell me about your parents?"

He looked down at the ground. My lips parted. Why was he looking down? Why wasn't he looking at me? Alarms went off in me, but I pushed past it. He felt bad. That must've been it. He felt bad because he didn't know.

I shrugged, even though he couldn't see that. He still wasn't looking.

"Alex?" He looked up.

I didn't relax. He was still guarded. "What's going on with you?" His eyes closed, but I saw the guilt. My voice rose. "What did you do?"

"Nothing."

"Then why do you feel guilty?" I stepped toward him but stopped again. An invisible hand pushed down on my chest. I couldn't go any closer. "What is going on right now?"

"Nothing." Jesse stood but there it was again—dread.

I saw it. I knew that was what it was. This wasn't how it was supposed to be. I whispered as I looked away and pressed a hand to my mouth, "You were supposed to take me in your arms. You're supposed to tell me that everything will be fine. You're supposed to make it right." At least that was how it was supposed to go in my fairy tale dreams. Jesse saved me. He'd been there from the beginning. But that wasn't how this was going. I wanted to rewind time. I wanted to figure out where this started going wrong and stop it. Change it. Take it back.

His voice wrung out, "You should've told me about them."

"Why?" I gasped out.

Confusion flared over him. "What do you mean?"

"Why? You loved them. They were your ideal parents, not mine." My gut kicked again. I went with a hunch. "And not Ethan's, either."

His hand jerked. There it was. I'd been right, but I felt no victory. "It's the secret, isn't it?"

"What are you talking about?"

My hand lifted and I gestured to him. "You. This whole thing. You're not comforting me, Jesse. That's your job. That's what you're supposed to do, but you're closed off." It hurt to say, but I did. "This is you for the last two years."

His eyes closed.

He knew what I was getting at. I kept going, even though I felt like I was being strangled, "What did they do to Ethan?"

His head went back down.

"Jesse."

No response.

"Jesse." My voice rose to an authoritative bark. He had to tell me. He just had to.

Finally, he looked back, but there was a fucking cement wall between us. He wasn't letting me in and my stomach dropped. He wasn't going to tell me. He had to. He had no other choice. Didn't he know that?

Why was this going so wrong?

"Stop this, Jesse. You can stop this right now."

His chest heaved up as he let out a dramatic breath, shaking his head. "I can't. God, I want to. I really do, but I can't. It's not my secret, Alex. Trust me," his voice sounded strangled, too. "I want to. I really do, but I can't."

The wall lifted. There was the same agony. My own came alive again as it felt its twin flare up. Why couldn't he see? He could end both of our pain, if he'd just tell me. He turned away and his shoulders hunched forward. There it was, the look of defeat. He wasn't going to tell me, ever.

This was it then. He couldn't know my secret and not tell me his. I needed to know. It was about Ethan. I had a right to know, but I didn't ask again. He wasn't going to tell me. So instead, I cut out, "I'll pack."

His head snapped around. "What? No."

"I can't be here if you won't tell me. Ethan was my brother."

"He was mine, too." His hands jerked into fists at his side. "He was my fucking brother, too. Don't start rewriting history."

I flinched. There was the old Jesse again, the one who lashed out. I swallowed over a lump in my throat and started grabbing my clothes. My eyes were stinging with tears. They wanted the release, but I wouldn't allow it. My heart was pounding against my chest as I threw my clothes into a bag and then started for my books.

He watched me as I moved around his room. I was blind as I rushed to get my stuff and get out. I was grabbing at things, not thinking. I could only feel his gaze on my back. It was burning into me, drilling a hole.

"Stop, Alex."

"No."

"Stop." He reached for my bag.

I twisted away to keep it. "NO!"

He wouldn't let go, and instead, he used the bag to pull me into his arms. Lowering his forehead to mine, he said urgently, "Please don't do this."

I shoved him away. "You can stop me."

"How?" But he knew. It was clawing at him. I saw the guilt flaring up again in his depths before he looked away.

"Tell me about Ethan. What did they do to him?"

"I can't." His eyes closed tight. "I wish I could. I do. I really do, but I can't."

It was done. No matter what I did, he wasn't going to tell me and I couldn't stay there knowing there was something about Ethan I should've known. A bitter laugh wrung from me. "This is fucking poetic."

"What is?"

"You and me. Ethan wanted us apart when he was living, and he's dead and still keeping us apart. Guess he won."

"Alex, no." Jesse dropped to the bed and caught his head in his hands. His elbows went back to his knees and his fingers grabbed hold of his head. He started to rock back and forth. "Don't say that. It's not like that. If I could tell you, I would. I promise I would. There isn't anything I haven't told you—"

"Except this!"

He visibly flinched.

I swallowed back more tears. They were there, ready to spill. I couldn't, not then. But I would. I promised myself, as soon as I got into the car, I could let them spill all they wanted. My voice wobbled, "Jesse, please just tell me."

"I can't," he whispered back. His eyes were filled with misery.

"This is really what you're doing? You really can't tell me? I'm going, Jesse. This can't keep happening, not if you don't tell me."

I felt Ethan again. He was in the room with us, haunting us so much. Would he have been happy by this? I'd never know.

"I can't tell you, but I'm going to try to make it up to you." Jesse grabbed my arm and hauled me onto his lap. He wrapped both arms around me and buried his head into my shoulder. I felt his lips against my skin. "I'll make it right. I promise."

"You can make it right by just telling me."

His arms tightened. He didn't say the words, but I heard them spoken in silence. He couldn't. It was all he'd been saying from the beginning and now I understood why this moment hadn't happened how it should've been. My secret was out. Jesse's should be out. He knew I would leave. It's why he had kept it hidden for so long.

My heart splintered in half as I turned and pressed my lips to his forehead. Then I slipped from his hold. I didn't say good-bye. I just left, but it was the same as the last time I left him. A part of me stayed in that room with him.

24

When I returned to my dorm room, I knocked. I wasn't sure what was going on inside and I'd been glad I did. Hannah opened the door. Her jaw dropped, but then a guy rushed from her bed and out the door. She'd only had enough time to yell at him about a Kari girl before he was gone. The alarms went off in the next minute. Guess he'd gone through the backdoor. After that, everyone had woken up and we were called into a mandatory dorm meeting. Kara had been surprised to see me, as I was with her. I thought she had spent the night with Derek, but I never explained myself. When they saw my bag, it was all the explanation they needed. I wasn't sure what Jesse said to the guys, but I never asked either.

Cord was the one who answered that when he saw me in class the next week. Jesse hadn't said a word to anyone. No one would've even known I had left if it hadn't been for Kara. I wasn't sure if I was happy to hear that, or hurt even more. Then things took another turn. The girls on my dorm spread the word about the breakup, if that was what it had actually been, so the girls in our class started to throw insults my way.

At first, it was just a word I caught in their conversation, like whore, or skank. It was loser most of the times. They were outright calling me pathetic by the end of the week. Surprisingly, Jamie was the first to rip into them. He chewed them out, followed by a quick appraisal of how they fit into those descriptions based from his first-hand knowledge. Then he followed that by one phrase, "Back off, bitches."

Cord cast me an amused look.

I would've shared the same feeling if I hadn't been painfully aware that Jesse still hadn't called to tell me the truth. He hadn't texted. He hadn't emailed. He hadn't even sent a message through Kara, who checked in on me daily.

Finals passed. Everyone left for Christmas break. I had been planning to stay at Jesse's during the holiday break, so I never considered going home. They still had games so everyone was going to celebrate the holiday together, but considering my situation, I was shit out of luck. The dorms shut down, so I went home to an empty and cold house.

I expected to be alone for the entire break.

I was wrong.

Angie came over the day after Christmas. Marissa came the next day. Even Eric made an appearance. Things were better with my friends, but there was still a strained tension. I never told them about Jesse. Angie never asked and Marissa had never known I was living with him. Eric asked if I could go for dinner one night, and I went, but it was just as friends. I made that clear. Toward the end of the first week home, Angie's boyfriend had a party. It was a small one at his family's cabin. She made me go, and being back at Justin's family cabin had been weird. Marissa was there with Sarah Shastaine, who hated me even more after Marissa told her that Jesse had been sneaking around with me again. After Sarah got drunk, she followed me around and asked questions about Jesse. The entire night went like that. I was asked what he was doing, if he had a girlfriend, if we were still fuck buddies, if he told me why he broke up with her, if I thought she could get him back. It was exhausting. I had a few drinks just to handle her.

Angie eventually kicked her out.

I was grateful.

And because Marissa was still roommates with her at their college, she drove her home. Though, Marissa did apologize for Sarah's behavior the next day over brunch.

It was the second week when I got more visitors. Hannah and Beth showed up on my doorstep. They announced they were moving in for the last week. They didn't say anything about Jesse, but they did share that Jamie was back in the house, and that he and Tiffany were back together. I hadn't known they weren't. Apparently, Kara had wanted to come with them to see me. I was glad they hadn't let her. Kara had seen Jesse every day over the holiday. I wouldn't have been able to handle that.

Eric had a party at the end of the week before everyone went back to school. No one knew how to react to Hannah or Beth. Hannah hit on Eric and Justin within the first hour. Marissa thought it was hilarious. Angie hadn't known who to get mad at —Hannah, Justin, or me. Then Beth grabbed her cousin and told her, "No Sex," in front of the group.

Hannah glared at her but grumbled, "Fine," but ended up sleeping with Eric before the night was out.

Jesse texted me that Saturday night. It wasn't much. He only asked if I was coming back the next day. I shouldn't have responded, but I did. My chest was heavy and pain seared me, but I told him I was.

Me: I hope you had a good holiday. I'm sorry I never said Merry Christmas.

There was nothing else.

I turned my phone off for the rest of the night. He wasn't

going to text me anymore, and it hurt too much. I would've been listening for an alert for the rest of the night.

~

I WAS HEADED TO ANTHROPOLOGY, which was the only class I was taking that was nothing but upperclassmen. At first, I didn't pay attention, but when I heard Jamie's voice, my stomach rolled over. Not again. I looked up and there he was. Again. And Jamie wasn't alone. He was followed inside by Cord . . . and Jesse.

Both guys stood in the doorway. I was in the back row, but I knew I'd been spotted.

I couldn't look away from him. His hair had been cut short again. As his jaw tightened, his eyes flashed an unnamed emotion. It glimmered in him before I pulled my gaze away. As I did, my chest lifted up as I tried to catch my breath. I shouldn't have been surprised. Jesse was gorgeous. And the sight of him, after so many weeks apart, sent sensations through me. Not the good kind.

It seemed that everyone else in the room felt the tension. All eyes trailed from Jesse to me and back again. I looked back. I couldn't keep my gaze away as I watched, as if in slow motion, as he made a decision. He led the way and took the seat beside me.

I couldn't speak. I wanted to say so much, to ask him about the secret, to ask him why he was doing this to us, but I couldn't do any of it. Instead, I slunk down in my seat, and I didn't say a word. Jamie took the seat on Jesse's other side and Cord took the seat on my side. I felt everyone watching, and then the whispers started again.

Just as the professor was coming in, Jamie barked out, "Ya'll shut the fuck up. You don't know shit."

"Mr. Striker." The professor placed his briefcase on his table. "Will you enlighten me to the reason behind your profanity?"

"Sorry, Mr. Cates. Just putting a stop to the gossip mill before it got going. That's all." Jamie leaned around Jesse and flashed me a grin. "New leaf here, Alex. I've got your back."

"Thanks," I muttered.

Cord was trying to muffle his laughter beside me.

The professor took a breath and skimmed our group in one long and silent scrutiny. Then he sighed again, "I'm going to have problems with you four, aren't I?"

Jamie spoke for us, "No way. Model students here."

"Athletes are rarely my model students."

"We are." Then Jamie jerked a hand off his desk. "At least Hunt is."

"Shut up," Jesse hissed. "You're not helping."

"Sorry." Jamie leaned around him again. "Sorry, Alex."

I was mortified. I tried hiding behind my books.

"If you four are done, may I assume my responsibilities as the professor of this classroom?" His sarcasm was duly noted.

"Yeah, sure. No problem."

"Thank you, so much, Mr. Striker."

"No problem. Thanks professor. I'm keen to learn about this stuff."

"Shut up, Jamie," Cord spoke this time.

"What? What'd I do?"

The professor cleared his throat and gave us another meaningful look. "Please refrain from talking for the rest of the class period. All of you."

Not a problem for me.

After class, I sped out of there. Or I tried. Jesse was on my tail. He grabbed my elbow and pulled me into an empty classroom. As soon as that door was closed, I twisted my arm free and shoved at him. "Get off."

He chuckled but stepped away. "I need to talk to you."

"That's surprising."

"I'm sorry. I was trying to fix things before I came to you."

I stopped. My eyes lifted and I felt my chest fill with hope.

"I couldn't. I'm sorry, but I'm trying, Alex. I really am."

Shaking my head, I started for the door. "You're wasting our time. Let it go."

"I can't."

"Spill whatever you know or stop playing with me."

"I'm not playing with you." He took my arm again.

This time, I couldn't pull it away. My heart was racing. I was struggling to breathe. Good God, it felt so good to have him this close again. I turned it off when I left him. Again, I became the numb monster that I'd been after Ethan died. It was like nothing existed. I watched the world happening through a television screen with no sound, no smell, no taste, no color. As soon as he touched me, the world became high definition. My senses were on overload.

"I'm not," he insisted. Gently, he moved even closer until I was tucked against his chest. I felt his own heartbeat. It was racing like mine.

"Just tell me, Jesse. Please."

It was as simple as that.

He let out a ragged breath. "I can't because it's not my secret."

"It's Ethan's."

"It's Ethan's and someone else's."

I frowned. What did that mean?

"Look, I have to talk to you about your parents."

I shook my head. "I don't want to talk about them."

"They're coming to my game this weekend."

"Now I really don't want to talk about them."

He tugged at my arm again. "They're coming with my dad."

"What?"

"My dad and my . . . that girl. She's coming, too."

"Your sister?"

He nodded, finally letting go of my arm to rest on a desk.

Except my arm yearned for his touch again. It tingled where

he'd held it. I rubbed at it, hoping that maybe it'd stop. It didn't. It intensified. My entire body wanted Jesse.

"She dropped the case. He paid her off."

"Your sister?"

"No, it was her mother. She was using her kid to get at my dad, but after seeing what your folks did to you, I talked to my dad. I met the girl. She's sweet, kind of."

I grinned. "Another ringing endorsement from Jesse Hunt."

He grinned back. "It's still weird."

"So you met her?"

"Once. She seems sweet. Her mom's a whack job, so we'll see how far the apple falls from the tree, you know?"

"Yeah, look at my parents and me. I didn't fall far."

He groaned, tipping his head back and raking his hands through his hair. "I didn't mean that at all. I just meant, oh to hell with it. I want you to come to my game."

I opened my mouth, a hot argument on the tip of my tongue.

He stopped me. "You haven't been to one game. We've been playing for a couple months now. You owe me."

"You owe me the truth."

He slouched forward again. "I told you. It's not my secret to tell, but trust me when I say I'm trying." He reached over and drew me to him. His voice softened, "Believe me, Alex. I am trying. My fucking bed is too big for me. It feels empty now. I can't believe I'm even saying that, but whatever. That's how I feel. I want you back. I want you to move in. I want you with me again."

My body melted. I sagged forward, wanting the same thing, but the back of my throat was burning. It was so fucking painful to pull away from him. The tears were there again, threatening to spill as I shook my head. "I can't. You can't keep something about my brother from me. I can't come back until there are no secrets."

He cursed under his breath.

Since I was at it, "And we define what the hell we actually are."

"What do you mean?"

"What am I to you? Or what was I to you? A body to keep your bed warm? Fuck buddies? That's what we were before—"

He jerked me back and bit out, "We were never that. You were never that to me." My hand went to his chest to push him away. It lingered, instead. It curved against him, and I felt his heartbeat.

"You were my fucking sanctuary, that's what you have always been to me. You were my guilty indulgence. I should've stayed away from you, but I couldn't. I still can't. Jesus. Look at me. I'm damn near on my knees here."

"Jesse."

"Stop. I don't want to hear it. I get it. You want the secret. I'll deliver. I have to, but when you find out—don't be mad at me. This wasn't my secret. This was what Ethan wanted. I was just trying to do what he wanted from me."

The pain doubled in me. "Ethan wanted this kept from me?"

"I was left fucking instructions from his lawyers." A threat of violence mingled with his tone. It was low and heavy. It sent shivers down my back. If Ethan had been alive . . .

"Will you come to the game? Please come."

I broke. I heard myself saying in surrender, "I won't sit with my parents. I can't do that."

"Fine. But they want to do dinner after the game. Your mom emailed me. She wanted me to ask you, but . . ." Sensing my resistance, he pulled me close again. "I want you to come for me. Be there for me. My dad's going to be there. No doubt some whore will be with him and my sister. I can't get through this damn dinner alone. I need you."

"Jesse," I murmured. My head fell to his chest. The fight was leaving me. Every second he touched me, it was becoming harder to pull away.

His hand cradled that back of my head. His thumb moved

back and forth against my neck in a soothing manner. "Please, Alex. I don't usually ask for much."

"You don't ask for anything."

"Except sex." I felt the rumbling in his chest from laughter before he added, "I really, really enjoy screwing you."

What every girl wants to hear.

25

I refused to sit with my parents or Jesse's family so I asked Hannah and Beth to go with me instead. Our seats were across the gymnasium and higher up. The view was perfect for me to spy on Jesse's new sister. I already knew what to expect with my parents, avoidance, and I knew Malcolm Hunt was a douchebag most of the time. I also had met enough of the women he brought around to know they were all pretty much the same. Model thin, big breasts, and an aspiring actress/supermodel/singer/take your pick. A few had even made sexual advances toward Jesse when they were bumped off the line by his father.

Hannah put her binoculars down and sat back. "Jesse's dad is hot. He doesn't look like some big-time movie producer. He looks like an actor or someone who'd be in front of the camera."

Beth grabbed for the binoculars and shoved them into her bag.

"Hey!" Hannah tried to grab for them again.

"No." She moved the bag out of reach. "I can't believe you brought those. I'm emo, and even I think it's embarrassing. That says something."

"What do you mean by that? I can't see. This place is huge." Hannah dove for the bag again.

Beth threw it on my lap as she held her cousin away with a hand on Hannah's forehead. "That I usually don't give a damn what people think about me, but that's too much. I'm embarrassed on Alex's behalf."

I shrugged. "I don't care." I was tempted to use them myself.

"See. She doesn't care. Only her opinion should matter." She reached over and snatched them from my lap. No one stopped her this time.

Beth glanced over. "You really don't care that Hannah has binoculars to scope out Jesse's family?"

"I don't. Really. I'd like to use them, too."

"Oh. Here." Hannah had pulled them out and held them across Beth's lap. "You were spot on about the girlfriend. I think she's a Playmate. The sister looks weird. And your parents are still bitches. They won't talk to the sister or the girlfriend."

"The sister looks weird?" As I put the binoculars in front, I was able to follow along until I saw a girl sitting between Malcolm Hunt's girlfriend, or I figured because of the long legs and big cleavage, and my mother. Ignoring the tension that came over me, I skipped over my parents and centered on Jesse's father. He was striking, just like his son. He had a similar build, tall and lean with broad shoulders that tapered down to a slim waist.

However, unlike his son, who had inherited his mother's dark eyes, Malcolm had green eyes. It'd been years since I had spoken to Jesse's father, and judging from the confident authority that clung to the movie producer, I wasn't looking forward to it.

I backtracked to Jesse's sister. She was petite with golden-brown hair. It looked lightly curled, and I could tell it was long. Sitting down, it covered her shoulder and fell to her waist. It was then that I caught a slight movement. She had a hand wrapped around her hair. It was hidden underneath her other hand, but as her arm tensed the strand of hair tightened as well.

She was nervous. I understood.

"She looks weird."

I lifted a shoulder. "She's scared."

"I don't know what about. She's set for life. Didn't you say that he paid her off?"

"He paid off the mother, not the daughter."

Hannah snorted, fixing the binoculars on them again. "Yeah, right. I'm sure she got a nice settlement."

Beth punched her in the shoulder. "Stop that. He's trying for a relationship with his daughter."

"You don't know that."

"He brought her to this game."

"Yeah, his legitimate son's game. If he wanted a relationship, don't you think he'd meet her in private for a while, father-daughter bonding and that crap? My bet, it's some guilt manipulation to work on Jesse. And why are your parents here as well?"

I sighed. I gave them some explanation, but like my falling out with Jesse, they had heard from Tiffany about my real relationship with them as well. Finally, I murmured, "I have no idea what my parents are doing here. But they like Malcolm. They went to one of Jesse's games last year with him, too."

"Yeah, but that was before it was out of the can. Right? That they had dumped you."

Swallowing over a tight knot in my throat, I willed my body to relax. I couldn't dwell on what they'd done, or even the last time I had talked with them. I'd been healing since coming to Grant West. I intended to keep healing. My parents would not have that power over me anymore. I refused to allow myself to relapse back to the slightly crazed state I'd been over the past summer.

Beth punched her cousin again. "Hannah, you're being really rude. Watch what you're talking about."

"What? I'm just trying to get all the facts straight. Mute Girl here doesn't say two bits to us all year. She finally opened up, and I'm capitalizing. She knows all my embarrassing stories."

I grinned. "You and Jamie. Fond memories."

"Shut it."

Reaching over, I snagged the binoculars from her. "Not that I don't understand, but like Beth said, I'm a little sensitive with some of this information being talked about like it's the weather."

"I'm being a friend."

"You're being nosy and you know it. Stop it."

Hannah stuck her tongue out at her cousin before she slumped back in her chair.

Hip-hop music blared in the gymnasium and the crowd stood. Excitement started to build. The players would be coming out. They didn't do grand entrances, not like some teams, but I knew when they came the place would go crazy.

I was right. Jamie was the first on the court. Not a shocker. Jesse trailed toward the end. His head was bent to the side as he was listening to something a coach was saying. His hand was on Jesse's shoulder. The two passed where my parents and Jesse's family was sitting without any acknowledgement of them. I knew that'd been intentional. He never enjoyed when Malcolm came to his games.

Hannah fanned herself with the program. "Holy, Alex. Why are you not sleeping with him again?"

"Sssh!" Beth hushed her, looking around us.

"No one can hear over the screeching." Hannah shook her head at the crowd.

"You don't want your stuff broadcasted, so stop broadcasting Alex's business."

Her cousin rolled her eyes. "You just don't want me to talk about your stuff. And you're scared because I'm happy."

Beth explained to me, "When she's happy, she's chatty. About everyone else except whoever she's screwing."

"I'm happy. So sue me."

I frowned at both of them. I was starting to think I should've come alone, but then I tuned them out. They bickered throughout the entire game—when it started, during the half-time, and toward the end. It wasn't the normal dynamic. I was used to Beth's silence and Hannah's anger, but now Hannah was happy, giddy almost, and Beth didn't like it. As Hannah kept asking me questions about my relationship with Jesse, I was starting to understand her cousin's reluctance. She was nosy.

We won the game by ten points, ten of which Jesse shot.

"That was fun. I'm excited for this year." Hannah was all smiles as we followed the crowd from the stands. When we got through the stairs that opened to a wider area behind the stands, I started for the players' door. Hannah called after me, "Hey!"

I turned around. This was the part I hadn't shared with them. "Hey, uh, I'm going to go and say hi real quick."

The two gave me similar looks. They were dumbfounded.

Hannah frowned. "You're going to what?"

Beth was smarter on the uptake. "What are you really doing?"

Well, here we go. "Jesse didn't ask me to come to the game. He asked me to go to dinner with them."

Hannah's mouth dropped while her cousin prodded, "With them . . . them?"

"His dad. I'm assuming the girlfriend."

"And your parents?"

"Holy fuck! I can't believe you're going to do that. Are you kidding me?"

I'd been asking myself the same question, but then I remembered the pain in his eyes. I succumbed every time every time I saw it. They wouldn't take that as an explanation. "I have to. Jesse and I are family."

"You two are so confusing." Hannah spun around in a tight circle before she stalked off.

"Forget her." Beth moved closer so we weren't crushed by the crowd.

"Is she leaving you?"

She shrugged. "Dorm's two blocks from here. I'll be fine."

"Well." This hadn't gone how I expected it. "Come with me. Maybe Jesse got more people to go to dinner."

"Sure."

I grinned as Beth fell in step with me. With her suddenly chatty cousin gone, she seemed to have returned to her quiet ways. This was the friend I was comfortable being around. We turned the last corner and went down the back hallway toward the waiting area, and I was glad she'd come. I hadn't admitted to myself all week, but seeing my parents again was threatening to send me into another cycle of pain and misery.

When we stepped through the last door, I was surprised to see Tiffany and Kara beside my parents.

My gratitude for Beth's presence went up another notch.

"Alexandra!" Malcolm threw his arms out and swept across the room to me. He embraced me in a tight hug and squeezed. "It's so good to see you again. It's been years."

When he let me go, I nodded. "Yep. The day after Ethan's funeral."

"That's right. His funeral."

"You weren't there."

"Oh." His welcoming smile fell, and he took a step back. "That's right. I was . . ." His eyes widened as he remembered. It'd been the next morning when his girlfriend found her car had been keyed. She went to Malcolm, who stormed into Jesse's bedroom. We'd still been sleeping. "Well." He twisted and glanced at the new girlfriend, who stood with my parents. "Well then. It has been a while."

I nodded. That'd gone exactly how I expected.

"What are you doing here?"

I glanced over, surprised at the hostility in Tiffany's tone as she addressed her cousin. I spoke for her, "I asked her to come."

"Why?"

Blinking at the scathing look she gave me, my eyes then narrowed and my chin tightened. "Because I wanted to."

"Jesse said you were coming for dinner." Malcolm's smile resurfaced. His eyes twinkled as he nodded. "That's wonderful. Have you two continued ... your ... um ... you know?" He moved closer and lowered his voice so my parents wouldn't hear.

"They found out before Christmas." Jesse spoke for me. Unlike his father, he was tense and trying to drill holes into his father from across the room. He was dressed in a Grant West blazer over jeans. Freshly showered and tired from the game, his cheekbones were more striking than normal. He gave off an air of danger. It sizzled among everyone and they grew silent, watchful as Jesse jerked forward a step. His hand was clenched around his bag.

"Oh. Well." Malcolm laughed at himself. "Cat's out of the bag, hmm?"

Jesse narrowed his eyes, and his mouth clamped shut. I watched as his jaw clenched and knew he was two seconds away from yelling at his father. Hurrying over to him, I glanced around and was surprised that no one else witnessed what I had. Everyone seemed unaware of the potential explosion, but as I touched his hand and moved him away from the group, Jesse seethed, "Don't worry. I never lose it around my friends."

"Yeah, well, you have around me."

He forced out a breath, trying to calm himself, but he muttered, "I can't fucking stand him."

"Keep it together." I skimmed a hand over his jaw, tapping it so it loosened. As it did and he tried to smile at me, I shook my head. It was a poor imitation. "Introduce me to your sister."

I started for the girl, who had been keeping to herself in a back corner, but Jesse caught my arm and dragged me farther away. He took me in the opposite direction until we were out of earshot of the group. Then he caught my face in his hands and made me hold his gaze. "Stay with me tonight."

"What? No." I tried to pull away, but he wouldn't release me.

"Please. I'm going nuts. Stay with me."

"You know the deal. Tell me the—"

"Yeah, yeah. Tell you the secret, and what then? You'll come back? You'll stay with me?"

I opened my mouth, but nothing came out. We never defined us. I had no idea. I finally moved my shoulders in a movement that I hoped looked like a shrug. "Tell me Ethan's secret, and we can figure it out."

"I told your parents to fuck off."

"What?"

"Your dad came to a game over the break. He tried to talk to me afterward, and I told him to fuck off. I didn't want to hear anything."

"Oh." I was really spinning inside. Jesse had stood up for me. He'd been loyal and stood against my parents when so many hadn't stood beside me. I had no idea what to do, or feel, or think, or . . . I had no idea.

He pulled me close and pressed a kiss to my lips. "Your parents were shitty to Ethan and they were shitty to you. They've been nice to me, but if they don't make it right with you, I told him to take a hike. They're trying to make things right with you."

"Oh my God," I whispered.

"What?"

"Oh my God." I couldn't say anything more. I already knew what they were going to do. My parents were going to force themselves to be nice to me. They were going to "make things right" so they could still have Jesse in their lives. The information about Ethan confused me. They'd been horrible to him as well? But I thought they wanted to replace their son with a new one? That had been Jesse's purpose, hadn't it? I couldn't grasp a single thought anymore. I was spinning out of control.

"Just come to dinner and hear them out."

I was still in shock when Jesse pulled me back to the group. He kept a hand in mine as he introduced me to his sister. I hoped that I was nice because I didn't remember anything I said or did until we got to the restaurant. Beth must've sensed something was more off than normal, because she stuck close the entire ride there.

I didn't know what my relationship with him was anymore, but he kept a hand on my leg the entire time.

alcolm had the back of a restaurant reserved for us. As everyone took their seats, Jesse's roommates were at one end of the table along with their dates. Tiffany was the closest to us and she sat beside her cousin, who was beside me. Jesse was next to the head of the table, where his father was located. The model girlfriend was across the table from Jesse. My parents were next, directly across from me, and his sister sat between my mother and Kara.

So far, my parents hadn't said a word to me. I was thankful, but I whispered to Jesse, "I thought this was supposed to be a small thing."

"It was until my dad showed up at the house before the game. He invited everybody else. I'm sorry."

This was way easier. He had nothing to be sorry about. I shrugged as my wine was poured. "I'll need more of that stuff."

He grinned and nodded. "Noted."

"So, Alex," Malcolm boomed, drawing everyone's attention to us. "Your father mentioned on the way over here that you've been seeing my son for a while now. I wasn't aware the two of you were official as a couple."

"Dad."

"What?" He turned an innocent eye to his son. "From what I gathered, it was a casual situation with you two. When did it become more?"

"Stop it, Dad."

"You were aware of the two of them?" my father spoke up, watching Malcolm closely.

"I walked in on them."

"Dad, stop. I mean it."

"What? Come on, Jesse. You must remember. You keyed Laurel's car that day."

"Who's Laurel?" Malcolm's girlfriend spoke up. She'd been eyeing Jesse since we sat down. The soft seductive tone wasn't meant for his father.

Jesse stiffened but clipped out, "It was the day before, but you two were so engrossed with each other you didn't even know when we came home."

"Because you snuck in. You knew I wouldn't have approved."

"You had no idea," Jesse tossed back. "And you wouldn't have given a shit. You never did. Alex had been around the house long before that."

His father pinned me to my chair with his eyes, but he spoke to his son, "You mean this had started before that?"

"No, but I grew up with Alex. You wouldn't have given it a second thought. That was my point."

"I would've appreciated a heads-up, Malcolm." My father was still frowning fiercely at his friend, sharing Jesse in the look. "But I would like to know the same as your father. When did this become more serious?"

Jesse shrugged as he leaned back. One of his arms came to the back of my seat. I sucked in my breath and hunched forward, but his hand caught my shoulder. He pulled me back so his hand could rest more comfortably there. He patted me when I did as he wanted. As he responded, his fingers began to trace a light circle over my skin, "It's always been serious for me. I stayed away because of Ethan."

Malcolm nearly choked on his wine. He sat it down forcefully. Some of the liquid spilled out from the movement. "Ethan knew?"

"Ethan knew I had feelings for her. He always told me to stay away from her." Then Jesse pinned my father with a look. He was unusually calm as he discussed my brother and I didn't think my father expected it because he shifted uncomfortably. "His lawyers delivered a letter to me that he'd written before his accident. He wanted his little sister to be unharmed. He felt that included me. I was supposed to stay away from her, so she wasn't hurt by any additional emotional stress."

I sucked in another breath as I saw my father pale. The blood drained from him and he jerked a hand forward for his wine. He drank the entire thing in one gulp.

Malcolm seemed impervious and obviously tired of the current topic. "Jesse, I have a few movies coming up. You'd be perfect for some of the roles. And I've already checked with your coach, it won't interfere with basketball or your training schedules at all."

"Dad. Stop."

"Extra exposure is good for you. It will never hurt to get your face out there. You're already known in your basketball circles, and people are starting to take notice because of your relation to me, but I really think it would be wise if you capitalized on this. Hollywood's knocking at your door. You could be famous, more than your old man."

"Stop," he hissed. His hand had stopped moving and gripped my shoulder, as if holding himself back. "I'm pursuing basketball as far as it'll take me."

"But the endorsements would help—"

"No, they wouldn't. I have to prove myself before the endorsements. I have years to still prove myself."

"Oh, come on. I can name a ton of athletes who have endorsements."

"Not in college. Are you kidding me?"

"Alexandra," my father interrupted them. The chill from him sent shivers down my back. "Since Jesse isn't answering my questions. You will. When did this become serious with you two? Did you give him your virginity?"

"Don," my mother joined the conversation. She placed a hand to her husband's arm. "Not here."

"No, Shelby. We need to know. We were ignorant the last time. I want to get on top of this one before it grows into something like before."

My mother fell back against her chair, ashen. She looked down and drew her cashmere sweater tighter around herself, but I caught the trembling in her arm.

Jesse bit out a laugh. "Like last time? Are you kidding me?"

My father looked ready to reach over the table and strangle Jesse with his bare hands.

Things had definitely changed between him and my parents. And I sat up. He wasn't going to take them on alone.

"Last time?" Malcolm was in the dark. "What are you talking about? This has happened before?" He swept his gaze over me. "I thought you said you weren't together before that day?"

"Not us, father." Jesse's gaze never left my father's. "Ethan."

"Oh." He frowned. "What are you talking about?"

Then Jesse's eyes shifted to me, urging me to see what he was doing, then he looked to my father again. He hadn't said a word, but I knew he was trying to tell me something. I sat up farther. Jesse's hand fell to my back. He trailed a finger down my spine. He was the epitome of calm and calculating while my father was squirming in his seat. I felt it in my gut. He couldn't tell me, but then a light bulb went off in me. My parents could. My parents knew.

Determination kicked in. I was going to find out Ethan's secret, one way or another.

"I don't think this is like the last time. From what I recall, I doubt my mother had been sleeping with you."

My mother sucked in her breath. Her trembling started up again.

My father didn't move. He didn't say a word. Malcolm, who had been reaching for his water, jerked his hand and accidentally sent his glass to the side. All the water spilled onto his girlfriend's lap. She screeched, pushing up from the table and dabbing at her lap. "Malcolm!"

"Oh." He blinked rapidly but only turned back to Jesse. "Your mother and Don?"

"No, Dad." Jesse never tore his gaze from my dad's. "That's the point. Mom was faithful to you."

"Oh Jesse," my mother whimpered. "You went there."

Then my father erupted. He burst out of his chair and leaned across the table. His hand reached out, but Jesse never moved. He didn't bat an eyelash and my father was forced to retract his hand, but he shook his finger in Jesse's face. "You stop this. Right now. I won't have you drag my name through the mud."

"Not like last time, right?" Jesse's tone had cooled. My father was boiling mad, but I grew wary. I knew my father would never touch Jesse, not the son of Malcolm Hunt, but that didn't go for Jesse. He would punch my father without a second thought.

I looked to Malcolm. This was the son he had grown used to over the years. We shared a look, both concerned, but I didn't say anything. Jesse was making my father like this. He was doing it on purpose so I could hear the truth. My gut was telling me that was what was going on. He added, so cold and disdainful, "Not like Ethan did."

A vein popped from my dad's throat. His hands slammed down on the table and a pin could've been heard. I glanced toward the end of the table. All eyes were on us. Cord was watching Jesse, as were his other roommates. Kara had a hand to her mouth. Cord's date seemed confused, but Tiffany surprised me like last time. She was watching me. There was no fear. She looked ready to handle anything.

I took a deep breath. If Tiffany was cool, calm, and collected, by damn that I wasn't going to be. I met Jesse's gaze. He'd been holding my father's in a standoff, but he caught my gaze. I felt his push then. He wanted me to take over, so I put my napkin on the table and stood. I felt everyone's eyes shift to me, and my father stepped away from the table. It was a small movement, but enough for me.

My mother lifted a hand to her husband's arm. She began to shake her head and her fingers tightened.

"Stop." There was guilt and fear in her eyes . . . in her voice.

She was so damned guilty. How had I not seen this before? This wasn't about me. This was about Ethan, whatever secret there was. I remembered Barbie's revelations. Ethan had become friends with her and Jeremy Benson. They were known for using drugs. She told me that Ethan had been with her on his last night before Jesse called.

I shook my head, trying to clear my thoughts. "I blamed Jesse, but I was wrong."

My mother's chest lifted as she took a deep breath.

"Wasn't I?"

She tore her gaze away and stood beside my father. "Don, honey. We should go."

"Not before you tell me!"

"Jesse, what is going on?" Malcolm hissed under his breath.

Jesse didn't answer. He didn't move. He remained in his seat— a lurking predator that chose to stay crouched down. I knew he would spring up if I needed him, but this was my time. This was my fight. He laid the path for me.

"What happened with Ethan, Mom?"

"Oh, honey."

"Dad?"

My father was taking deep breaths. I could hear him wheezing as his lungs were rattling inside of him. Jesse had said it wasn't the same because his mom wasn't sleeping with my dad this time, which means...

"Who did you sleep with? And Ethan knew about it? You said like last time. What did you mean?"

"Stop this, Alexandra," my mother pleaded.

I swallowed the last bit of sympathy for her and pressed again, needing answers. "Who was it, Dad? How did Ethan know about her?"

"Shut up." Finally. My father snapped. His face grew red and his Adam's apple was bobbing up and down. It wouldn't stop. He seethed at me and I saw that his teeth were grinding against each other. "You shut up now."

"Don!"

No one else spoke. This was a family moment, in front of an audience, but I heard Jesse lean forward behind me. His hand touched the back of my leg, and my father lashed out, "You stop touching her."

"Then start telling the truth." There was no fear in Jesse's tone. It was even keen.

Malcolm cleared his throat before slowly putting his cloth napkin on his plate. "I think this dinner has moved past social etiquette. Don, Shelby, I'd like to thank you for coming. It was a pleasure, as always."

Jesse laughed, "Are you shitting me, Dad? Isn't this what you wanted?"

My father's icy gaze never left mine, but he asked Malcolm, "What is your son referring to?"

"Nothing, Don. Nothing at all. Jesse, you stop this right now."

"No."

"Jesse."

My dad was teetering. He wanted to lose his cool. He wanted

to yell at me, but he kept himself restrained. He was right there. Only a small nudge and I would have him. I could taste all the secrets.

I drew in a breath, ready to deliver a taunt, but then I heard, "Oh, for goodness' sake. Don, tell her. It'll come out someday."

"No!"

"Tell her." My mother lifted her chin to him. The trembling was gone and defiance had taken over. "Or I will. This is your secret. You should be the one to tell her."

"Not here." He scanned the entire table. "Not in front of their friends."

I half expected a flippant remark from Jamie, or even Tiffany. None came. I relaxed slightly, but dug my fingers around the table's edge. They couldn't leave. Not like this. I was so close. "Who did you sleep with? What does that have to do with Ethan?"

"Everything." My mother gave up. Her shoulders went down in defeat, and she hung her head. "It has everything to do with Ethan and everything to do with his accident."

"Shelby." My father twisted and gripped her arm. His hold tightened and she whelped from pain.

"Stop it, Dad," I cried out.

"Don," Jesse started.

"You don't talk to me anymore. You don't have that right, Jesse." My father looked ready to murder. "You have lost all privileges with my family and with my daughter. Remove your hand at once."

"No." His hand moved to my back and he took a possessive hold now. "I don't have my privileges anymore? Are you fucking with me?"

"Jesse," Malcolm admonished.

He ignored his father and addressed mine, "To cover your ass, you've hurt the one person who was innocent in all of this."

"Stop it!" His fist hit the table again. A glass tipped over from the reverberations.

Malcolm's girlfriend scrambled from her chair again, squealing as she fled to the bathroom.

"Tell her. This is ridiculous."

"Tell me."

"Your father had an affair." The words came low and swift from my mother.

"Shelb—"

"No, Don." She touched his arm, but her hand was gentle. He tore away from her. My mother never flinched. "I tried to lose myself because of everything you put our family through. I won't lose my daughter. She's my last living child. This has gone on long enough. You wanted to shield her from this, but we've done the opposite. We've hurt her. It has to stop."

"Mom?"

"NO!"

"Then leave," she snapped at him. "But I'm staying. I am staying with my child. You can go, and keep your 'good name.' That's all you care about. Your name. You don't even care what you did to Ethan. My son killed himself because of you. It was all because of you."

My son killed himself . . .

My son killed himself . . .

I shook my head, trying to make the words rearrange themselves.

She couldn't possibly have just said what she did.

My son killed himself . . .

They kept repeating. Over and over, I heard them. They wouldn't stop. Someone stood in the distance and a faint voice said, "I think we should go home." More people rose from the table. People were murmuring their good nights. A few touched my arm, but I couldn't get past what had just been said.

Ethan killed himself?

I looked at Jesse.

Guilt.

He knew.

My gut kicked in as I realized that he'd known the whole time. Sucking in my breath, I started to move away. Why hadn't he told me? But no, there was more. I lifted my head and saw my mother was still there. She had taken her seat again, looking composed despite the evening's events as she watched me. Jesse had sat as well. I kept looking around. No one else remained. It was the three of us, and both of them were waiting for me.

Slowly, I reached behind me to feel for my seat. As my fingers found it, I sat, but I never looked away from my mother. She picked up her wine and sipped it. Setting it back down, she leaned back in her chair again. She was still waiting.

I choked out, "What?"

"Your brother killed himself. The car accident wasn't an accident."

Jesse spoke up, "We don't know that."

My mother sucked in her breath, only to release it at once. The trembling was gone, and instead, she looked broken. I recognized the look because I'd had it. It was then that I got my second shocking realization for the evening.

I wasn't broken anymore.

I didn't know when it happened, but it had. I breathed in and out, trying to get over that surprise and I tried to clue in. This was about my brother. I feared that I wouldn't hear this again so I shoved everything aside, and only listened to my mother.

She started again, swirling her wine around in the glass, "All of this started, well, it didn't start with the girl, but it did for me. Earlier in the year, Ethan brought a girl home to meet us. I believe you were at a party with the girls. He wanted us to meet her first. You know how Ethan was with you, he always wanted to protect you and make sure you only knew the tiniest bit of information. He did it out of love."

"I never knew Ethan had a girlfriend."

"He didn't. Not for long."

Jesse leaned forward beside me. His arm touched mine. I knew he did that on purpose, but I pulled away.

"Her name was Claire, and imagine my surprise when I realized who she was." My mother tipped her wine glass toward me. "Her mother used to be my best friend. She worked with your father. I even named you after her daughter."

My middle name was Claire.

"I thought they had moved away. That was what Stella told me all those years ago. I think they did move away, but I never knew they came back during the summers. I had no idea, but Stella's husband, Claire's father, still worked with Malcolm on a few projects."

Jesse spoke up, "I took Ethan to a party that summer before. I was bored. My dad was making me go so I asked him to go. I had no idea what would happen, Alex."

"Anyway," my mother took center stage again. She had finished her wine so she reached for the bottle in the middle of the table and refilled her own glass. She was looking over my shoulder as she picked up her glass and took a sip. The pain filtered in, and I knew she wasn't seeing me. She was seeing Ethan. I could feel him. He was always there. "You can't even know the bomb that she dropped that night. Little Miss Claire recognized Ethan from the beginning. She got close to him because she knew the real reason why her parents had split from us." She laughed to herself, a sad and lonely one. "She walked in on her mother and your father. They were having an affair. Don never wants to talk about it, but I think it had been going on for a long time. He won't even tell me when it started, just some time when you and Claire were little. I think they only stopped because her daughter caught them. Afterward, your father threatened Stella. He told her to go away, to stop our friendship, everything, or he was going to tell her husband. I still don't know if Jacob ever knew. He was a good man."

So much was swarming my head. I was struggling to get all the information correct.

My mother continued, "I think I'm drunk." She giggled to herself as a tear slid down her cheek. "I think that's the only way I could tell you all of this."

"Mom," I whispered, not knowing what else I could possibly say.

"Your father made them break up. I think he scared Claire away, and I think she stopped talking to your brother. It wasn't good, honey. It wasn't good at all. We found later that the reason Ethan wanted us to meet her that night was because she was pregnant. I was going to have a grandchild." She stopped and bowed her head. The wine was pushed away, and she began weeping into a cloth napkin.

Jesse found my hand under the table.

I didn't push him away this time. I clung to him. It was all I could do.

We listened as she continued to cry. As we sat there, I lost track of time until she had regained control. When she looked back up, I barely recognized my mother. She was broken, but she wasn't the mother who had raised me. She wasn't even a shadow of that woman. This person was a stranger.

She gestured to the wine bottle beside Malcolm's seat. "Jesse, pour me a glass. I need it tonight."

He did and when he handed it over, her arm had the shakes. She didn't care. She didn't flinch as she guzzled more of the alcohol. "As I was saying," her eyes grew haunted. "That was the beginning of the end. For me and for your brother. Ethan got a letter. She was trying to keep him away from her and the baby. I didn't know about that letter until later, but it broke my heart. I think it broke him, too. He got depressed. He got really depressed. I think he was doing drugs. He started hanging out with new friends." Her eyes glanced at Jesse. "I know you two started fighting."

"Benson wasn't a good influence on him."

She nodded, her hand trembling as she lifted the glass again to her mouth. "He gave me the letter at his graduation. I didn't open it until that night. They were his instructions. He said, 'Mom, don't open this until tonight. You'll know when.' I got so scared, but then I thought maybe it was a good thing. I think I didn't want to read what he wrote. I was scared. I failed him as a mother. If I had read it, I could've stopped him. If only I had read that damn letter ..."

Jesse leaned forward. His hand dropped from mine. "He gave you a suicide letter?"

She couldn't talk so she only nodded. Her tears were cascading down her face.

A look of horror came over him.

I frowned. "What is it?"

He looked over but gave me the slightest headshake. He didn't want to tell me, not then, not in front of my mother. She didn't even notice. She had crumpled forward over the table. Her shoulders shook as she wept into the table, the sounds muffled from the tablecloth.

My mother was done for the night.

We both knew it, and we both had to help her to the hotel. She was so thin, I wondered if she ever ate anymore. Her legs were wobbly from the wine, and she grabbed a hold of me. Mumbling apologies the whole way to the car and to the hotel, she kept repeating the same thing as she clung to me. "I lost my marriage, my son, and my grandchild. I lost them all. I'm so sorry, honey. I lost everything."

When we finally got to the hotel and learned my father had checked out and left, Jesse brought my mother to his house.

Derek and Kara were still awake.

She gasped softly when I helped my mother into the house,

but it only took one look between the couple before she nodded to me. "She can stay in Derek's room. I'll sneak him into the dorms."

"Are you sure?"

She reached out and pressed a hand to my arm. She was fighting back her own tears as she squeezed my arm. "I've never been so sure of something in my life. Your mom can stay as long as she needs to."

And then I broke down.

My mother went to Jesse, still mumbling the same phrase, and Kara gave me the tightest hug I had ever received. She pressed me close, and her hand cradled the back of my head. Then she rocked me back and forth, as I finally let my own tears fall free.

27

M y mom called a cab for herself the next morning. She was gone by the time I woke, so I assumed she had gone back to my father, who blocked me from his email, his Facebook, his phone, his everything. I felt dead to him.

Jesse asked how I was every day, but it was the same answer. I was fine. If I were being honest, I'd tell him that I hadn't processed anything. I didn't think about my brother killing himself. I couldn't imagine the letter he gave my mother. I didn't want to know about the extent of his depression. And I really couldn't handle knowing that there was a little Ethan in the world somewhere that I couldn't hug. Most days, I would find myself staring off at my brother's portrait, lost in thoughts my brain blocked from my recollection.

It hurt.

My brother had hurt me. Again.

"Hey, girl." Hannah shoved her head through the bathroom door. Her voice echoed around the empty space and six stalls behind me. "I'm buying shots tonight."

"Uh, sure. No. What?" I answered, not really knowing what they heck she said, just that she spoke.

"Shots." Hannah stepped inside, two girls I didn't know following behind her. "Lots of them. You're drinking tonight." She winked at me and made a clicking sound at the same time before she turned a cold glare to the two behind me.

I didn't look, but I knew they were there. They were always there. Even though things seemed on track again with Jesse and me, I still hadn't moved back to his house. I spent nights, but most of the time, I returned to the dorm. Hannah was gone most of the time. Things had continued to heat up between her and her still unnamed rock star boyfriend. She called him Scarred Baldy so everyone else in the group went with the name.

An image of Ethan flashed in my head again. That damn portrait. I used to love it, but it seemed to be haunting me. Literally. I hadn't admitted it to Jesse, but he was part of the reason why I hadn't moved back in. He was a reminder of Ethan and a reminder of what my brother had done. Maybe it shouldn't have changed things for me, but it did. Along with the renewed mourning and pain, resentment was stirring inside of me, too.

No.

I took a deep breath and stopped myself. Again.

I couldn't deal. I wasn't ready to, so I jerked my gaze up from the sink and found myself staring into two snooty girls from my floor. Kate and Amanda? I think those were their names. Hannah had backed up so she was beside me, resting against a sink and locked in a stare down against the two. When her hand rose to her hip and her chin lifted, I knew sparks were going to fly. Then she started, "You got a staring problem, honey?"

One girl sighed in disgust and flounced into a bathroom stall. Her friend wasn't as smart. She narrowed her gaze and pointed to me. "Just looking at Jesse Hunt's reject. That's all."

Oh, snap.

I wasn't sure who was more surprised, Hannah or me. They weren't scared of her anymore.

"Let's go. I'm ready." I grabbed my stuff and tugged on her arm.

"Yeah." Hannah twisted around as I steered her out the door. "Reject, my ass. Jesse Hunt's coming to pick her up tonight. That's right. The only one who got rejected was you when you hit on him last weekend." I pulled her the last of the way, but she hollered as the door swung shut, "Don't think I don't know about that. You're the reject, not her."

We heard the snort inside.

I had to laugh. It was too ridiculous. "What's going on with you? I like that they think we're not together anymore."

"You're so weird."

I shrugged. "I'd rather deal with that attitude than when they're being fake and trying to be friends with me."

"You're right. Having friends is horrible."

"They are when they're not real. Who wants to surround yourself with people like that?"

"You do. You're buddy-buddy with my sister now?" Hannah pushed open the door, and Beth sat up on the couch. She put her book on the floor.

I set my stuff in my closet and went to my desk and clicked on my email. "I'm not buddy-buddy with . . ." I frowned to myself. I should've seen this coming. Since my mother's departure and the revelations from that night, Tiffany had extended an olive branch to me. We had come to a cease-fire after my parents' first visit, but it was currently bordering on a civil. Hannah hated it.

"You had lunch with her yesterday."

"Because she eats with Jamie in that private cafeteria and I eat with Jesse. We walked together. That was it."

Beth rolled her eyes and laid back on the couch. Her book was open again, and I knew she tuned us out. Hannah scrunched her eyebrows together as she shook her head.

I gestured to her closet. "Are you ready? The guys will be here in five minutes."

She groaned, stripping her shirt off in one smooth motion. It was lifted over her head and her jeans were unsnapped and flung across the room in the next second. With matching black bra and panties already on, she grabbed a dress and shimmied it over and down her body. The thong fell to the floor and she kicked it into her closet before shutting it and sitting on the couch.

"Hey!" Beth scrambled to keep from being sat on.

Hannah ignored her as she leaned forward. Her hair was flipped over and she wound it together in a twisted up-do. Snapping it in place with a clip, she straightened. Her hair fell down, framing her face with curls that looked professionally done.

Bitch.

I sighed and turned back to my computer. "Things have thawed between your sister and me, but we're not friends. You do not have to worry about that happening."

Hannah snorted as someone knocked on the door. "Whatever. If you come home with a friendship bracelet from her, I'm moving out. That's all I'm going to say." She went to the door and swung it open.

Instead of the guys, Kara gave us a friendly wave. "Are you ready? The guys are downstairs."

As we traipsed through the hallway and the lobby, we had expected Derek and Jesse. They were there, along with Jamie, Tiffany, Cord, and a new date. He held hands with a girl that looked Armenian with dark eyes, black hair, and pale skin. Like the others, she stood in the background. She was chewing her lips as she eyed Tiffany.

Go figure.

Hannah put the brakes on. "What the hell? You cannot come."

Tiffany tossed back her golden locks. "Like hell. You're getting serious with this guy. I'm checking him out."

"No, you're not."

"Yes, I am."

The two squared off, and Jamie eased away from them. He stepped sideways and around Derek and Kara before he spotted me. "Looking good, Connors."

An arm came around my waist and Jesse pulled me against his side. "Are you hitting on her now?"

"No." Horror flashed in Jamie's eyes. "No way, man. No way at all. Just saying, she looks good. You're a lucky man." Leaning forward, he patted Jesse on the shoulder. It was the most awkward exchange I ever witnessed between the two.

"Thanks."

"Oh hell no."

Beth and I snapped to attention. That was Hannah's war cry. As we turned around, the two girls from the bathroom were there. They were dressed to go out in tight, short dresses. But when I expected them to leave, they didn't. They stayed. That was when I clued in to what Hannah had realized right away. Even though they didn't come over to the group, they lingered close enough to overhear the conversations.

Hannah stepped up to them. Her arm twisted in the air and her hand found her hip. She stuck it out. Her elbow mirrored the motion as her eyes bulged at the girls. "You are not doing what I know you're doing."

They both tried to look bored. Only one succeeded. The other's chest was rising too quickly, and she wouldn't look away from Jesse. Her eyes widened and her mouth dropped to a small O. Then Hannah purposely moved to block her view. I moved to the side and saw the girl looked ready to piss her pants, but the first yawned, "Can you get out of my breathing space? You're sucking all the air in."

Tiffany stepped next to her sister. That was when I learned where Hannah had gotten some of her fighting ways. The two looked so similar, almost like twins, as they turned their noses up at the other two. Well, Tiffany tilted her head back so she was snubbing the two. Hannah had her head bent and her eyes were locked on her target. If she could've drilled holes into the girl, she would've. Tiffany and Hannah were a unified front.

I was just thankful they had never teamed up against me.

Beth sighed as she locked elbows with both of her cousins. "Come on. This is stupid. If they find out where we're going, they're going to find out. Let's go."

"No way." Hannah dug her feet in.

"Tiffany."

She swept a hand to the girls. "I'm supporting my sister. I'm trying a new leaf, too. Join, not judge. I'm a supportive sister."

Beth's eyebrows shot up. I frowned. Hannah's mouth dropped. "You're doing what?" But she didn't wait. She rolled her eyes and grabbed her sister's arm. "Let's go. I'll text everyone directions from the car. No way are these two riding coattails."

The one harrumphed. The second one's teeth started chattering. She was still holding her breath.

Everyone separated into cars. Beth and Hannah rode with Jesse and me. Cord and his date went with Jamie and Tiffany. Derek and Kara took their own vehicle. When we got into the vehicles, the two girls from my floor hurried into their own car.

"I should slice their tires," Hannah grumbled.

"Don't. You'll get into more trouble."

She shot her cousin a glare and stuck her bottom lip out. "Whatever. Jesse, go fast. Those two pariahs are going to tell everyone where you're going."

"No, they won't," Beth corrected her. "They want him to themselves. They won't tell a soul."

After we got directions to Rowdy's, Jesse grinned when he pulled into the parking lot. There was a line outside the single door to a small dive bar. Three giant-sized security guards were in front checking drivers' licenses.

"Nice one, Hannah," Beth griped. "They're checking IDs; no one in this car is twenty-one."

"Shut up. I'll call Emerson. He's in the band. I'm sure he can get us in."

"Wait." Jesse twisted around. "You said Emerson?"

She nodded, holding her breath at suddenly being Jesse's sole focus. "Uh, yeah. He's my boyfriend."

"Bald?"

She nodded.

"Scar across his face?"

Another nod.

Jesse grinned. "Attitude up his ass?"

"You know him." She didn't look happy about that.

"Yeah. We'll get in just fine." Then he got out of the car and made a phone call. A minute later, a girl opened a back door. It'd been overlooked since it was hidden behind two large dumpsters. She waved at Jesse, who gestured back.

As I got out of the car, I saw Bri holding the door open for us.

"Hey, Bri. The guys are playing tonight?" Jesse asked, giving her small wave.

She rolled her eyes and swiped back some of her hair. Tiffany instantly lifted her top lip in a faint snarl. Hannah was all smiles, wiggling her fingers at the girl. Eyeing Hannah cautiously, recognition flared in her depths when she switched to me. "Hi. You're..."

"Alex. From the—"

"Yeah," she cut me off, skirting a nervous glance to the others. "I remember. Luke texted you, Jesse?"

"Nope. Not this time." He gestured to Hannah, who linked elbows with me. "She's a friend of Alex's. I believe she's dating your cousin."

"Yeah." No warmth traveled to her gaze as she lingered on our linked arms. "That's too bad."

Beth started laughing. Hannah stiffened and Jamie snorted. "Even she knows you're a whore, Hannah."

Before she could twist around and slap him, I tugged Hannah with me into the overcrowded bar. As we passed by Bri, I murmured, "Thanks for letting us in like this."

She shrugged. "Luke really likes Jesse. It's no problem." After everyone was inside, she shoved through the crowd back to our side. "Just don't get in trouble since you're underage and don't—"

But whatever else she was going to say was cut off. A guy from the bar shouted her name, "Brielle! Help please!"

She groaned. "I have to go. If you need drinks, come to the edge of the bar. Only you two." She pointed to Jesse and me. "I only like you two. Gotta go."

Then, she was swallowed up by the crowd. Expecting her to emerge from behind the bar, I was surprised when she merely climbed on top of a barstool. A large muscular guy from behind the counter lifted her over the bar and set her down beside him. He ruffled her hair, which she slapped away and then she started filling orders right away.

Jamie sidled up next to Jesse. "Holy shit! That's Sustain on stage."

Tiffany stood next to him. She was captivated by something beside the stage. I followed her gaze, and saw Hannah had already taken root there. Beth was next to her, biting her lip, and casting wary looks at the crowd behind them. More than a few scantily clad girls were pushing forward for a better spot.

"Oh my God," Tiffany groaned. "She's dating a rock star? Those guys are the worst guys to date."

Her boyfriend threw his arm over her shoulder and pulled her close. He shrugged. "They're a match made in heaven. Hannah doesn't stick with the same guy two nights in a row, and my guess is that he doesn't keep the same girl long. I heard they're all manwhores in the band."

"Something you have in common with them?" Cord joined

the conversation. His date looked unable to form words, much less thoughts. Her eyes were bulging out at the band.

"Not anymore." Tiffany gave him the snarl instead. "That's changed since I caught him with my sister."

Jamie had the decency to show a little shame. He pressed a kiss to his girlfriend's forehead. "She's the only one I want anyway."

Jesse had been quiet beside me, but Luke caught sight of him. Still singing, he lifted his head in an acknowledgement. Jesse gave one back. Everyone caught the shared greeting. Cord was the one who asked, "You know the band?"

"Remember that night I almost got arrested because I helped a guy out in a fight?"

"Yeah."

"Luke was that guy."

"Holy shit!" Jamie exclaimed again and shook his head in irritation. "What? Do all you famous and rich people know each other? Who else do you know? I want to know them."

"I'll make a list."

"Good. I want to be rich and famous someday."

"He was being sarcastic, asshole." Cord shot him a dark look.

Jamie frowned but kept quiet. His arm tightened around Tiffany, and an awkward moment filtered among the group. Derek and Kara were the first ones to break it as he gestured to the back area. "We're going to go look for a booth back there."

"I want to be closer to the stage."

Everyone knew Tiffany wanted to keep an eye on her sister.

Derek said again, "We'll look for a booth in the back."

She looked ready to argue, but Kara leaned forward and whispered something in her ear. After a few seconds, the elder Chatsworth's shoulders loosened and dropped in defeat. She nodded and was tugged behind Kara. Their fingers were interlaced. Derek cast a shrewd glance over Cord to Jamie but followed the girls. As they disappeared, Jamie frowned and asked, "What's your problem, man?"

"Nothing." But Cord took his date and went after them.

Jamie looked to us. "What'd I do?"

Jesse shrugged and clapped him on the shoulder. "Don't worry about it. Cord's been off lately. Just give him space."

"I give everybody space. Am I that bad to be around?"

The cockiness fell away, and a flash of vulnerability replaced it. I was given an image of a five-year-old version of Jamie. It was as if he'd lost his favorite puppy as he waited for our answer. I held my breath, but Jesse spoke up, "You're asking me that? You just got back into the house."

"Oh yeah." The little boy was gone, and he winked, full of his old self, all slimy again. "Never mind then. That's awesome that you know Sustain. Really awesome. Thank God, too. I didn't want to have to be nice to Hannah to get in an introduction. All right. I'm off for shots. You guys want some?"

Jesse shook his head. "No, but take a bunch to those guys back there and stay away from Cord."

As Jamie left, I moved closer to him. "What's wrong with Cord?"

He shrugged and put both of his arms around my waist. He pressed a kiss to my forehead. His lips brushed against me as he answered, "He gets like this sometimes. These are the nights when he winds up in jail."

I frowned. "Why?"

"I don't know. We've never talked about it. Why?" He moved away so he could peer down at me. "Are you worried about Cord?"

"No, but he's helped me. And I know he's the closest guy friend you have here."

"Oh." His expression softened, and he pulled me close again. He rested his cheek against my forehead. "He's not family, Alex."

Warmth filled me. He meant Ethan and me. At that thought,

the small grin slipped. I had tried blocking all thoughts of my brother over the last month, but they snuck in. This wasn't a time to start dwelling so I pulled away. "I'm going to get some drinks."

Jesse frowned but didn't say anything. Instead, his hand held mine firm as he led us through the crowd. We went to the edge of the bar. It was where the other staff could go behind the bar, but Brielle saw us right away. We had our drinks almost as soon as we told them to her. She flashed two fingers in a greeting to us before she was off, filling more orders. Jesse gave her a five for a tip before we went in search for the others.

28

The band took a break an hour into their set, but I was drunk by then. After our entire group settled into a table closer to the stage, Hannah and Jamie declared themselves in charge of drinks. She kept putting shots in front of me. Jamie tried, but I slid those over to Jesse. When he reminded me that he was the sober driver, I pushed them to Hannah instead. She took half and made Beth take the other half. It wasn't long before Beth disappeared. When I asked her cousin where she went, she leaned close and yelled into my ear, "She called her fuck buddy. He came to get her. He's not working at Club T tonight."

I still wanted to know who he was, but I was starting to figure out that Beth would never tell me. Only Hannah knew, but she wasn't told. She'd followed her cousin one night to find out.

Thinking about that, I started giggling. I couldn't stop. Even when Jesse pulled me onto his lap and nuzzled underneath my ear, I kept going. That was when the band descended on us, or Emerson swooped in on Hannah. She'd been dancing by our table and he merely lifted her in the air and carried her through the bar.

Luke came over and extended his arm to Jesse. The two shook hands as the lead singer slipped into my abandoned seat. He folded his arms over the table and leaned forward. I didn't know if he was hoping for incognito. It wasn't working. Every set of eyes at our table was on him. "I wasn't expecting to see you guys here tonight."

"Your guitarist is dating one of Alex's friends."

Luke grimaced. "Sorry about that, too."

"Bri had the same sentiment."

"Emerson doesn't do girlfriends. Not in the committed sense."

Bri shoved her way through the crowd and plopped a pitcher on the table. When Luke moved to pay, she shook her head. "It's on me. Just do me a favor and keep my brother out of my hair. He's already in the back trying to bartend."

Luke grinned. "He's getting in the way?"

"He tried to use the megaphone to start a stripping contest. I'm not having one of those again."

"Yeah. Tell him I need to talk to him. He'll come over here."

She nodded and turned, the crowd parting for her as she went. It wasn't long before the drummer sauntered over. His shirt was gone. I started giggling. I thought he'd been wearing one on stage. Images of girls ripping it off him came to me, and I pressed my nose against Jesse's chest. I couldn't hold the laughter back. As Jesse adjusted so I was more comfortable on him, he leaned back, and I heard Luke comment, "I met your dad the other day."

Jesse stiffened underneath me. "Oh yeah?"

"We're doing a song for one of his movies."

His tension only doubled before he heard the drummer comment, "Your dad's a dick, man."

"Braden."

"What? He is. Makes total sense why your dude hangs out at The Shack with us."

I was the one that had stiffened then. Had Jesse been going there again? Without me? He swept a hand down my back as if sensing my concerns and murmured in my ear, "Only once when you weren't talking to me. I got drunk with these guys that night."

The drummer spoke up, laughing, "And we met his new girlfriend. She's a piece."

"Braden, you're drunk."

"Whatever, Luke. You said he was a dick, too."

"And you're talking to his son. We don't want to piss him off."

"You said Jesse was cool."

"It's fine, Luke." Jesse's voice rumbled from deep in his chest. "And you're right. My dad is a dick. I hope he wasn't too much of a douchebag to you guys."

"Nah." Luke sounded relieved. "His girlfriend's a fan, and when he found out I knew you, he was really nice. Not that he's going to be mean to us, you know. We're doing the theme song for his movie."

"Hey, man." I heard Jamie interrupt. He sounded like a gushing schoolgirl. "Can I get your autograph? I've been trying to hint to Jesse to get it, but he's not taking the hint."

"On purpose."

"Yeah, whatever. So how about it? My girlfriend would really love it."

"I'm sitting right here," Tiffany chimed in. She sounded annoyed but also dazed at the same time.

I finally looked up, but when I did my eyes landed on the drummer. He had the same glazed look in his eyes and he still wasn't wearing a shirt. A fresh batch of laughter bubbled up. I doubled over. I didn't know what was wrong with me, but I couldn't stop laughing.

"Uh." Kara got up from her chair and came over to us. She took my arm. "I'll take care of her. Excuse us."

She pulled me to the bathroom and into a stall. There was only one empty, the rest were full, and she darted in front of the line. Ignoring the curses and yells, she locked the door and then said loudly, "I have explosive diarrhea. Back off."

That set me off, and I was wiping tears as more giggles rippled from me.

"Kara? Alex?"

Tiffany pounded on the door. It was unlocked again, and she hurried inside. As the door swung open, I saw the line had moved down a foot. They were now only waiting on the other two stalls. Ours was ignored.

More chuckles came from me. I shook my head. I couldn't stop them.

Tiffany wrinkled her nose as she smoothed out her dress. "What's wrong with her?" She ran her fingers through her hair before tossing it back over her shoulders. "Did you hear Jamie out there? Autograph my ass. He wanted that autograph. Although, I wouldn't mind more than an autograph from those two. Holy shit. I can't believe Jesse knows them. Alex, how'd they meet again?"

"Tiffany." Kara took a deep breath. "Be nice."

"I am. Aren't I?"

Kara gestured to me. I was sniffling, trying to muffle my laughter into a roll of toilet paper. "She's been like this since she got drunk."

"So. Hannah gets horny when she's drunk. Alex will be fine." She swung her gaze to me. "Right? You'll be fine. She'll go to bed, make sweet, sweet love to that fine man of hers, and tomorrow she'll act like none of this happened."

"Tiffany!"

"What?" She shrugged. "That's what she does. I mean, my God, it's been a month since that fiasco with her parents, and she hasn't broken stride. The chick is a survivor. She can handle worse."

Kara pressed her lips together. "You're not being supportive."

"Yes I am. I'm here." Then she frowned. "Scoot over. Since we're here, I need to pee."

We shuffled to the side and Tiffany took a squat. As she peed, she looked up. I caught a little glaze in her eyes as well and chuckled, "You're drunk, too."

"Yeah." The corners of her lips curved up. "I'm like Hannah. I get horny too."

Kara burst out laughing alongside of me.

Tiffany scowled. "When I'm drunk. When I'm drunk! My sister's always horny." Then she grew somber. "That's how she copes. It's not good. Not me. I cope by being a bitch."

More laughter boiled up in me. I couldn't stand upright and I started sliding against the wall. Kara gasped and grabbed for me. "You can't sit on the floor. That's disgusting."

"Yeah." Tiffany was still so somber. "That is disgusting. Oh God. I'm drunk."

Kara sighed. She had a firm hold on my arm. When Tiffany was done, she steered both of us out of the stall. I meant to ask what had been the point, but I couldn't get the words out. We were ordered to wash our hands, and then we shuffled back to the table. Cord and his date were gone. Derek was frowning at Jamie, who had a worshipful expression on his face. He was listening to the conversation between Jesse and the drummer. His head was even propped on his hands. He looked ready to propose marriage.

Kara went over to Jesse. Her hand was still firm on my arm. "Your girlfriend needs to go home. She tried sitting on the floor in there."

Jesse grinned and scooped me into his lap. "She's fine. She's just letting off steam."

"Yeah, well." She sighed. "Derek, I think I'm ready to go."

Jesse turned to him. "Take Jamie and Tiffany."

"What?" Jamie protested. "No way, man. The night's just starting."

Tiffany swayed on her feet, giving him a sultry grin. That was all it took. He stood. "Never mind, I recognize that look. I'm going to get lucky with my girlfriend. It's been a damn while."

She giggled when he pulled her close and the four of them left. As Jesse held me on his lap, he rubbed a hand up and down my back. The giggles eventually faded, and my eyelids grew heavy. I must've fallen asleep because when I woke, he was carrying me outside. When he buckled me into the seat, I asked, "What time is it?"

"It's late. Bar closed an hour ago."

"Where are we?"

"Leaving the bar."

"That makes no sense," I mumbled, but I didn't care. I fell back asleep. When I woke again, Jesse was carrying me into the house. My arm curved around his neck, and I pressed a kiss there. "I had fun tonight."

"Good." He kissed me back.

"Kara called me your girlfriend," I whispered. It was important, but I was so damn tired. I wanted to go back to sleep. I loved when he held me. I felt safe.

"Because you are. And you are safe."

I frowned. I hadn't meant to say that last bit aloud.

"It's fine." Jesse kicked open his door and set me on the bed. As he did, my eyes opened farther. I was still struggling to keep them focused. He didn't turn the light on. I was so thankful for that. I could hear him moving around before he moved me underneath the sheets and crawled in beside me. I thought I was too tired to do anything except snuggle into him, but he skimmed a hand down my arm and went to my waist before lifting my shirt up.

I was suddenly wide-awake. Desire built in me and I moved to help the shirt off.

Then we were kissing. I pulled Jesse on top of me, and it wasn't long until he was sliding inside of me. Arching my back, I closed my eyes and gave into the sensations. I loved him. Everything would be fine. I loved him.

He lingered over my lips and whispered back as he continued thrusting into me, "I love you too."

My eyelids flew open. I hadn't meant to say that, again, but I was caught by his gaze. I saw the love in him as he quickened the tempo. Something settled in my chest. Peace. Contentment. Whatever it was, it felt good. It felt right.

When we were done, I murmured without thinking, "I can't think about what Ethan did."

His arms tightened around me, but he only kissed my shoulder.

My chest filled. The pain was right there. I let it go. I had to. "I don't want to think about him wanting to kill himself. That's not the brother I knew. The one I knew watched over me. He took care of me. He wouldn't want to hurt me, and dying was the worst way to do that. I can't think of him like that."

"He was sick, Alex."

I heard the thick emotion in his voice. I didn't look up. I was swallowing my own back.

His voice was rough as he continued, "He went into a dark depression. He wouldn't get help. I tried to push him, but Ethan refused. He stopped talking to me toward the end."

My eyes closed. An invisible hand was on my chest, pushing down. My ribcage felt like it was going to break. "That was when he started hanging out with Jeremy Benson and Barbie?"

"Yeah." His chest rose up and down as he took a deep breath. "Yeah."

Flashes of him came to me. As he ruffled my hair, the same way the bartender had done to Bri's hair earlier. As he rolled his eyes at something our mom said or how he smacked a towel against my butt when we were forced to do the dishes together. I gasped. More pain flooded in. I couldn't hold it back and the tears started. They slid down my face, down to Jesse's arm that he had wrapped around me. He felt them, but neither of us said a word.

"I miss him."

"I do, too."

"I can't think of him sick. I can't think of him like that. It breaks me, Jesse. I can't do it. I have to think about him as he was to me. I loved my brother." I corrected myself, "I love my brother."

I love you, too.

I never heard those words, but I imagined them.

Then I took another deep breath and tried to push some of that pain away. I moved on to the next topic, one that I figured would always leave a hole in me. "My parents are never going to be there for me. I know this now." My voice grew hoarse, and I faltered. My lungs filled with air. My throat burned at the same time. "I don't know why my dad acts how he does. I have no idea, but I can't love them. They don't love me. It's going to be hard, but I have to somehow move on without them in my life. I just won't have parents. That's the best way for me to handle it. They're never going to get better. They're never going to want me in their lives and dote on me like loving parents should. That's just not who they are. It might've been them before, but not anymore. Ethan's death changed everything. I think it broke my mom. It almost broke me."

Tiffany had called me a survivor.

I'd survive. I had to.

"You have me."

"I know."

My heart split again, but not from pain. It split from over-whelming warmth. I had Jesse. It was the first time I allowed myself to trust in him. He wouldn't leave me. He hadn't, even though I always felt like he would go. Angie had been wrong so long ago. I'd been wrong. But there was one thing I'd been afraid to ask. Biting my lip, I asked it now, "Jesse?"

"Hmmm?"

I felt his answer rumble through his chest and my back. It soothed me for some reason. "Why didn't you tell me about

Ethan? I know I said I can't think of him like that, but why didn't you ever say anything?"

"I felt guilty."

"Why?"

"Because I should've stopped him."

"What do you mean?"

"I knew about Claire and the baby. I knew how your parents handled it, and that your dad scared Claire away, but I never spoke up. I should've helped somehow and then you didn't know. I couldn't tell you. I mean, I knew about the baby and Ethan didn't want you to know, but I should've told you."

"That he killed himself or about his baby?"

"About both. I was scared that you'd blame me and I'd lose you."

My heart began pounding. I swore he felt it through my back. I couldn't stop it. "Why would I blame you?"

"Because I'm the reason he got in that car."

I froze. My heart stopped.

He felt it, tensing as he said further, "Claire went into labor that night. I called him to tell him. He got in the car to go to her."

"What?" The word ripped from me. "What are you saying?"

"He took drugs that night. He was going to intentionally overdose, but when I called him, he decided to try to get to the hospital. He wanted to see his baby before he died."

My mouth gaped open. No sound came out. None could come out. Searing pain rippled through me, and it paralyzed me. I couldn't do anything but lay there in his arms. Then Jesse finished, his voice thick with guilt, "I didn't know he had taken drugs. I thought maybe he had, but I had no idea he was going to kill himself. I should've called the cops on him. I should've done something, but I didn't. I went to the hospital to meet him. I thought he was in the room when she gave birth, but he wasn't. I didn't realize it until later that he'd been in the ER the whole time. He had already crashed by the time I left Sarah's and got to the hospital. He died from the car accident before they realized his body had already shut down from drugs. I didn't know. I'm sorry, Alex."

I couldn't move. I couldn't do anything, but imagine that night again. And I cried. I didn't stop the entire night.

29

It was another month before I finally called Ethan's lawyers. They wanted verification of my name. I sent them a copy of my passport. It was another month after that when they told me they wouldn't be able to give me Ethan's inheritance. The spelling wasn't correct. I didn't understand it, not at first. His will and testament said all of his monetary assets would go to Alexandra Claira Connors.

I never blamed Jesse for any of my family problems. It took me a while to fully understand that Ethan had been sick. He wanted to die. I remembered the day of his graduation when he hugged me. It had been long, and he wouldn't let go of me. He'd been saying good-bye in his way. I never remembered it until recently. It woke me during the night, but Jesse was with me. He held me the rest of the night. We had a lot of those nights. I'd remember new information about that last year with Ethan.

It would send me spinning.

I'd cry and tell Jesse about it as he told me how much my brother loved me. It helped me accept that my brother was gone in a new way. It was different ever since I learned the truth about him. I would never accept that he killed himself. That wasn't right, but I accepted that he was gone. It probably didn't make sense to anyone else, so I never tried to explain it. It was how I coped with it.

I eventually moved back in with Jesse. And because I was on better terms with Tiffany, I started going to the games with her and Kara. Chandra joined us as well, but she never got with Cord again. He continued to have a new girl every few weeks. One night, when he was drunk, he confided to me that there was a girl from our school that he always loved. She never reciprocated his feelings, or at least that was what he told me. I wondered if he knew for certain that she didn't. He refused to tell me who it was, but she was the reason he never settled down.

Marissa and Angie came a few times for basketball games. She had hit on Cord, but he never took her up on her invitation. I was thankful that she never brought Sarah around. I didn't want to deal with another round with Jesse's ex-girlfriend. Justin stayed behind and the two planned girls' weekend with me. They remained cautious around Beth and Hannah. Beth never talked to them and Hannah was the opposite. She got into people's faces too much. Eventually they asked not to hang out with them. That was fine. Beth and Hannah told me they were fake. The dislike was reciprocated.

Jamie and Tiffany broke up at the end of the year. He cheated on her, which hadn't surprised me. Hannah started taking care of her sister instead, and Tiffany fought back like Hannah had earlier in the year. The two bickered almost daily.

Jesse's sister came to his championship game. She sat beside me this time instead of her father, who sat courtside with my parents. She was relieved when I told her I wouldn't be going to the dinner afterward. Then she confided that night had been too much for her.

Unlike her mother, she liked normalcy and quiet moments. She stayed at the house a few weekends, and I came to learn she really was a quiet girl. Oh, and she pretty much worshiped her brother. When she applied for Grant West the following year, I wasn't surprised. I caught Jesse staring at her at random moments. It was as if he was trying to figure her out, but maybe that was how Ethan stared at me, too. Jesse never had a real relationship with his biological family, but he did with her. He took her home one weekend and introduced her to Mary, who fell in love with the girl and promised to watch out for her.

I told him one night that it was ironic. He had grown up as if he didn't have a family, but now he did. I was the opposite. I had grown up with a family, but now I didn't. He rolled his eyes and lifted me on top of him. Then he proceeded to undress me and show me how I was still his family, no matter what.

It was the day of my last final and I was headed grab my bag when a shout stopped me.

"Alexi, come back here."

A little girl was running down the sidewalk toward me. A high-pitched giggle came from her as she pumped her arms harder. Her legs went too fast, and fierce determination came over her next. A slender girl raced after her. They shared the same blonde curls, but when the little girl saw me, she braked suddenly. Her eyes got big, and her cheeks puffed out. The mother hurried and caught up, lifting the girl in her arms. Fat arms and chubby legs wrapped around her, but she twisted back to me. Her eyes didn't look away. Her thumb slipped up and popped in her mouth. Her other hand caught hold of some of her curls and she hung there. She pulled on her hair as she continued sucking her thumb, all while she never looked away from me.

I couldn't either.

I felt the breath knocked out of me. Someone took a sledgehammer to my chest. I was batting practice.

This was Ethan. Or she was Ethan. This was his little girl. I knew it. Every cell in my body told me that, and I jerked forward. The mom started to turn, but I called out, "Wait!"

She turned back, frowning at me. Her free hand went to cover her eyes. As she saw me, her eyes got big. Her mouth fell open to form a small O, and she suddenly went rigid.

This was Claire.

My eyes shifted to the daughter. That was Alexi.

I hurried toward them, fearful she'd decide to scramble. I caught up before she could have that thought, and I stuck my hand out. My heart was pounding out of my chest. I hoped my voice was sturdy as I said, "I'm Alex. I'm Ethan's sister."

She chewed on her lip for a moment and then she nodded. She never shook my hand. "I know."

"You're Claire." But my gaze couldn't leave the little girl. She had Ethan's eyes. She had Ethan's mouth. She was Ethan. I just knew it. It was like my brother was back with me and not in a haunting presence anymore. "And who are you?"

She smiled, still sucking her thumb, before she twisted and buried her head into her mother's shoulder. Claire's smile was sad as she covered her daughter's head. She blinked away some tears and cleared her throat before she could say, "This is Alexi." Regret flared over in a second and she amended, "Alexandra. Her name is Alexandra."

A huge knot formed at the base of my throat. Did she mean . . .

"We talked about names, Ethan and me. He wanted her named after his little sister." She rolled her eyes, but in a good way. A small grin came over her. "He always talked about you. He adored you, you know."

I bit my lip. I was trying to keep from sobbing. I had done so much over the last few years.

"Anyway," she took a deep breath and forced a brighter smile. "I came here to introduce you to your niece. This is Alexandra Claira Connors."

"You gave her his name?"

She nodded and then shrugged before she turned away. "He wanted that. I wanted my daughter to have a piece of her daddy. Stupid, I know, considering that I haven't wanted anything to do with your family, but whatever. I came here to tell you not to blame Jesse. I threatened him if he told you about us. I knew Ethan hadn't. I threatened him, too. Both of them wanted you to know, but I couldn't handle it. Not then, anyway. I can barely handle it now."

I was struck speechless.

"Listen . . ." She brushed at her eye.

Alexi turned back. She hunched down between her shoulders before she darted back to her mother's shoulders. She was playing peek-a-boo with me.

I tried to keep from grinning too much.

Her mom took on a serious tone. "Jesse's been begging me to tell you about Alexi, but I refused. I thought you were like your parents, and I don't want them anywhere near her."

I nodded.

She turned away again. Her jaw was trembling, and she bit her lip again. "Anyway, I threatened Jesse. I knew about all of the affairs Malcolm had when he was married to Evelyn. My dad worked with Malcolm for years. I said I'd go to the press and ruin his mom's memory if he said anything to you. To give him credit, I think he stayed quiet out of loyalty to Ethan, but I knew it was hurting him. He loves you. He always has. Ethan talked about it. I was sick and tired of hearing him moan about his best friend and his sister. Once we got pregnant, he stopped caring so much about that. But anyway. God, what am I doing here? That's right." She hoisted her daughter higher up, adjusting for a better hold on her. "So this is your niece. Alexandra Claira Connors. I'm a sap." She gave her daughter a soft smile, one that showed her love as she tucked some of Alexi's curls behind her ear before she fanned herself. "I'm just rambling. I'm so nervous. You're not what I thought you'd be."

My own nervousness came out and a strained laugh bubbled up.

Her eyes pinned to mine. She heard it and relaxed. She was able to breathe normal again. "Do you want to be her godmother?"

My eyes got big again. My chest was starting to hurt, too much to speak.

It wasn't a problem. Claire kept going, "I know it's late. Three years late, almost, but we're having a birthday party at my mom's. She helps out a lot. I live with her and go to the community college in Clarkson. That's where we live. I do what I can. I'd love if you and Jesse would come. Please not your mom. Your mother hasn't stopped calling me for the last two months. I can't handle it anymore. I think that's another reason why I came here. Can you talk to her? Although Jesse said you don't see them, either. I think that's when I decided to reach out. Maybe you're not like them. Ethan always said you weren't. He said you were so kind and so gentle. He said you're nice. There are so many people who aren't nice. So many people are so selfish, but I can see he was right. And I'm kicking myself for not listening to him. I was so mad at your family. Then I was mad at Ethan. We broke up, and he never tried to see me—"

My hand grasped her arm. "He did."

"What?" She fell silent.

"He did. Jesse called him when you gave birth. He was coming to see you." I swallowed back the pain. "I think he was coming to save himself, too." I never said those words to Jesse, but I wondered. It felt right to say it to her now.

Her bottom lip started trembling. Her throat strained, and I could tell she was trying not to lose it. Then she rushed out, "Can you take her?"

"What?"

But Alexi came to me willingly. Her mother turned away. A hand was pressed to her mouth, and she walked a few steps away.

As her shoulder started shaking, I knew what she was doing, and I turned to give my niece the brightest smile I could muster. "You're so pretty!"

A toothy smile was my reward. Little fingers reached out, and she grabbed hold of my cheeks and started yanking my face back and forth. It was the best feeling. Her eyes darkened, and she grew serious then. Leaning forward, she plucked at my lip. My hair was attacked next. I didn't care. She could yank all she wanted.

When Claire remained away, still crying and wiping at her face, I took Alexi to a nearby bench. I was bouncing her on my knee when Hannah and Beth appeared at my side. Beth frowned at the little girl. When she reached for her, Beth took two staggering steps backward. The little girl grew more determined, but grabbed Hannah's knee instead.

Hannah gestured at her. "Who's the kid?"

"My niece."

I didn't bat an eyelash. I didn't hesitate. I was so damn proud. Ethan created this little girl. She would've been the love of his life.

"Oh. Wow."

I looked up and squinted against the sunlight. There were no sarcastic remarks. Even Beth looked close to tears. She took the seat beside me and held a finger out. Alexi grabbed on and twisted. As Beth cried out in pain, Hannah snorted. "Dumb—"

She caught my look.

And finished, "head. Dumb head."

"I'm better now." Claire joined us, her voice still wobbly. She knelt and took Alexi from me. "Thanks for holding her." Then she glanced at Beth and Hannah.

"These are my friends."

"Oh, right. Angie and Marissa. Ethan told me about them."

"Hannah and Beth."

"Oh." She flushed. "Sorry. Of course. You're at college. Who goes to college with their high school friends?"

"I did." Hannah threw her arm around Beth's shoulders. "Actually, I coerced my cousin to come here after me. Couldn't live another year without her."

"Shut up," Beth mumbled. Her eyes were glued to Alexi before she turned away. "Let's go. This is a private moment."

"Oh man."

"Shut it, Chatsworth!"

"Shutting it." Hannah winked at me as she followed Beth to the dorm.

"They're, uh, nice?"

"They're like me." I stood from the bench. "Not everyone gets us."

"So, um, the birthday party. Yes? We're having it in two weeks. Did I say that before? Two weeks at my mother's. Jesse knows the address. Bring him, too. I haven't been all that nice to him, but I've started to realize that he's not the bad guy I always thought he was."

I grinned. I understood that as well.

"It's not going to be anything special. I mean, I can't afford much, and I don't like letting my mother dish out money all the time. Free rent is good enough, you know." She rolled her eyes and sucked in her breath. She puffed out her cheeks. "Sorry. You don't need to know all about that. I just feel bad. Seeing you, I know I've been wrong the last three years. I was so angry with your dad, and I took it out on everyone. Alexi, too. She'd probably love meeting your mom, huh? What am I doing here?" She choked out next, "Thank you for telling me about Ethan. I never knew. They only said he died in a car accident. That was it."

I stopped her as I put my hand on her arm, the girl was beautiful and sweet but obviously a nervous talker. "Do you mind if I ask, but how do you spell Alexi's middle name?" I needed to make sure.

"Oh." She blinked in her confusion, but rambled out, "C-L-A-I-R-A. I wanted it to be a bit different. My aunt's name is Claira, too. I thought I was taking care of three birds with one stone. Okay. I have no idea what I was thinking. I didn't want her to be just like me or just like you. All right." She forced out another deep breath. "I am so nervous right now. You are so beautiful. Ethan told me you were pretty, but I had no idea."

It was my turn to be confused. Jesse always told me that I was hot. My mother mentioned I was beautiful, but the truth of it hit when Claire said it. I was touched. The tears started forming.

"Okay. I'm going to go. I'll be in contact. I really will. This wasn't some form of drive by and meet your niece sort of thing. You know what I mean. I'm just having a hard time keeping it together. You're not what I expected. Jesse said that's your dorm over there. I've been waiting all day to catch you. I almost left. Alexi needs to eat and take a nap, but then she took off running. I have no idea why. She'd been fine with me under the tree, but all of a sudden she took off. It was like she was chasing something. I don't know. She does that at times. She'll suddenly start talking to someone in the room, but no one is there. And I'm rambling again."

She darted forward and gave me a hug. Her skinny arms wrapped around me before she let me go. Then she gave me an awkward wave and hurried to the parking lot. Alexi hung over her shoulder. Her dark eyes didn't look away. Before they got into their car, she lifted her tiny hand and waved.

I bit my own lip. The tears were starting to spill.

I missed my brother so goddamn much in that moment.

30

"Hey!"

I looked over and saw Hannah and Beth crossing the lawn to me. Instead of the skintight ensemble Hannah usually wore, I was surprised that she was in jeans and a lightweight white shirt. She almost looked like me. I glanced down, but my jeans were ripped at the knees, and a shirt Jesse had stretched one night while trying to get a better view of my cleavage. I was now the scantily clad one, but I was comforted at Beth's usual apparel. All black. A new tattoo peeked out from underneath her neckline. It looked like the tip of a bird's wing. Then I glanced around. "Where'd you park?"

"On the street." Hannah gestured to the red Camaro. "We figured everyone's moving back in so there wouldn't be enough room." She glanced around and saw two other cars. "Maybe I was wrong."

"No." I sighed and bent forward to grab my boxes. "Jamie just got here. Cord moved back last week. And their new roommate isn't here yet."

"You guys got a new roommate?"

I nodded. As both of them grabbed a box, I headed into Jesse's house. Jamie had put all his boxes in the foyer and dining room so we sidestepped his stuff and placed my boxes in the living room. "Yeah," I answered Beth as we headed back out. "Derek and Kara got their own place since she's not a resident advisor this year."

"I can't believe you're really living with Jesse now."

Beth frowned at her cousin. "Why not? She basically did last year."

"Yeah, but she still had a place of her own. What if something happens? What if she needs somewhere to go?"

I grinned while Beth punched her cousin's arm. "Good thing I have your place to go to."

"Go to?" Hannah froze as if she hadn't thought about that. "But we only have a two bedroom apartment. And her boy toy doesn't work at Club T anymore. He's got a new job, so I know he'll be sleeping over more. And I—"

"We all know your sex life hasn't really dwindled." Beth spoke over her cousin, giving her a meaningful look.

"What? It has. I'm not dating Scarred Baldy anymore."

I grinned, reaching into my car for another box. The other two followed suit, and we headed back inside. As we got there, Jamie had jumped from the stairs. He landed in the foyer and scooped one of his boxes. When he noticed who else was with me, the slight warmth chilled.

"Oh. You."

"Oh. You." Hannah sent him a snarl.

Beth sighed and moved around her cousin to put her box down. Hannah lingered in the foyer, skimming a disgusted eye up and down Jamie. "Have you gained weight over the summer?"

"No." He looked insulted. "I've been lifting over the summer." Then he cast a shrewd eye over her figure. "You're not the normal whore that you usually are. What's up with that? Are you in costume today? Practicing for Halloween? We've still got two months to go."

"Shut up, and what are you doing, gaining weight? That's only going to slow you down on the basketball court."

I frowned and handed my box to Beth so I could take the one Hannah was holding. She looked ready to throw it at him.

"It's none of your business. You're just hot for me. That's the only reason you give a damn."

Her top lip curved even higher in a sneer as she tossed her platinum hair back. "You're just jealous because my sister dumped your ass in May. Good one. Classy move cheating on her."

He stiffened, looking ready to throw his box at her now. "I was set up. Your sister wanted me to cheat on her."

Her mouth dropped open and her eyes bulged out. "Are you kidding me? That's the lamest excuse I've ever heard."

He rolled his eyes. "Whatever. I don't give a shit what you think. Alex."

My back stiffened at the abrupt call. "Yeah?"

"Who's the new roommate?"

I sucked in my breath and shook my head. No way was I getting involved with that one. "Jesse's almost home. You can ask him."

"What?"

I hurried out of there. I wasn't looking forward to hearing Hannah's reaction either when the new roommate did show up. Then, because karma hated me, Tiffany's Mazda pulled into the driveway. She got out, flashed me a friendly wave, and grabbed two large suitcases before she crossed the lawn. "Hi!"

This wasn't going to go well. I gestured toward the house. "He doesn't know. And neither does she."

Tiffany went rigid. "My sister's here?"

I nodded. No words were needed.

Beth stepped out from the door. She saw the packed car, her

other cousin, and the luggage. She turned around and went back inside. Emerging a moment later, she had Hannah's keys in her hand and she waved at us as she crossed the street. The red Camaro took off a second later.

Tiffany grinned as she pushed her pink sunglasses on top of her head. "She's smarter than I give her credit for."

I grunted. "I was starting to like you until that comment."

She shrugged. "That doesn't bother me, either." Nodding toward the house, she asked, "So who's all in there? I see Cord and Jamie's cars."

"I just got here ten minutes ago. I had to go back home to finalize the sale on my house."

"Oh, that's right. The one your parents left you."

I nodded. It was better in someone else's hands and I didn't want it. Plus, with the monthly allowance my father was still paying and the inheritance I got from my grandfather, the money from the house wasn't that much. Still, I figured I'd find good use for it somewhere down the line. For the next three years, Jesse wanted me to stay in his house. He said even if we broke up, he still wanted me there. If that happened, he was family no matter what. He had to be. We needed each other.

"Where's Jesse?"

"What? Oh. He was called in for a meeting with the coach. He just texted. He was going to help me move the last of my stuff, but he'll be here in a few minutes."

"So I have Derek's old room?"

I nodded. The unspoken question was if she was still across the hall from her ex-boyfriend, and yes. She was.

She took a deep breath and surveyed the house as if we were heading into enemy territory. "This is going to be interesting."

"Yep."

That was an understatement.

"All right." She flashed me a perfect smile. "Are you coming in after me? Or am I—"

I waved her off. "Oh. You're going in there alone. I'm staying back. I'll go to the back to move in if I have to."

She frowned and for a second, fear flashed in her crystal blue depths. She wavered before she rolled back her shoulders and her hands tightened their grips on the luggage. The Grant West Royal Princess was back in the building.

Hannah and Jamie were still bickering, but as Tiffany stepped inside, I only heard him scoff, "Oh hell no!"

Then the bickering tripled.

Another car pulled into the driveway. This time, a girl came out. She was dressed in a tight black halter-top and overly tight jeans that showcased every muscle in her legs. Dark almond eyes landed on me and she flipped a strand of sleek black hair over her shoulder. She was the darker version of Tiffany. I only hoped she wasn't there for Jamie.

"Hi." She moved over to me. Her eyes crinkled a bit as she studied me before she asked, "Do you know Cord Tatum?"

I let out a small breath of air in relief. "Yeah, but you might want to call him out. I wouldn't step inside if I were you."

"Oh." She frowned at me for a second before she pulled out her phone. Leaning next to me against my car, she quickly texted him.

"Like fuck you are!" Jamie shouted over the sisters.

"Oh." Her head craned back and her eyes shifted to me, a small smile on her lips. "I understand now."

I nodded.

And we waited. No further introductions were made. This girl struck me as a type that didn't lower herself to being the first one who gave her name, and I didn't care enough to be polite. She was another in a long line. She'd be gone after a week.

A momentary lapse in the fighting occurred. Cord popped out of the door. He lifted his hand to wave her over, but then he saw me and lowered it instead. Stuffing his hands in his pockets, he sauntered across the yard to my car. "Hey."

The girl flashed perfect white teeth and he turned to me. "I didn't know you were back."

"Yeah. Ten minutes ago."

"When did that start?" He jerked a thumb over his shoulder.

"Five minutes ago."

"Oh." He skimmed his date up and down but spoke to me. "Is Jesse headed back soon?"

I nodded. "You know what the coach wanted?"

He grinned at me. "That's team confidential. What's wrong with you?"

I shrugged. "I'd appreciate a heads up if it's going to be a problem for him later on."

"Oh. No. It's nothing like that. The pros are already watching Jesse. That's what it was about. I was just teasing before."

"Gotcha. And thanks for telling me."

I could feel the girl reevaluating me. It was always the same. Tiffany had underestimated me as well.

Cord asked, "Is everything situated with your mom and niece?"

My gut dropped. I hadn't expected that question, at least not in front of one of his girls. Sucking my breath in, I couldn't stop my hand from clenching around the bag strap in it. Then I forced my head to nod. I tried to sound normal as I responded, "Yeah. The lawyers notified Claire of the inheritance. They thought it was typo."

Cord nodded. "And the original lawyer never told them, right? He quit after your brother died?"

"Something like that. Yeah." I narrowed my eyes at him. Why was he dredging this up? And in front of a stranger?

He turned and glanced back at the house. "They seemed to have come to an impasse. We could dart in and not get hit by any crossfire." He jerked his head at the girl, and she followed him eagerly.

After they disappeared inside, I released the breath I'd been holding. My stomach was in knots. It was rolling and twisting. I knew I wouldn't be able to calm myself, not for a while, not after hearing my mother brought up in a casual way.

Turning, the relief hit me hard when I saw Jesse's black Ferrari pulling up on the driveway. He turned the engine off and put the windows up before he darted over to me. I already knew I couldn't hide it so I didn't even try. He stopped. "What's wrong?"

My knees were folding under. I could only shake my head.

"Hey." He came over and touched my chin. Raising it, my eyes found his. That was all it took. His calm came into me. I breathed it in. "What happened?"

"Cord brought up my mom and Alexi."

"Oh." He looked alarmed as he raked a hand through his hair. It had grown out an inch, so it stuck up in the air when he ran his fingers through it. "I didn't tell him about your mom and dad. I swear."

"He might've heard from someone else. I think Marissa still calls him."

"She does?"

"I think she's trying to slither in as a friend, hoping he'll get drunk one night and sleep with her."

Jesse grinned. "He probably will."

"Then her plan will be a success."

He frowned again as he heard the bite in my tone. "Is it your mom?"

After three months of no word, she called me two weeks ago. She had left my father, and she felt the need to report that information over Jesse's landline. She knew my cell phone. She knew my email. She even knew my mailing address, but she could only call me over his landline. It irked me. And then she dropped the additional bomb that she was moving to Clarkson. She wanted to be close to her granddaughter. I was supposed to pave the way since I had grown close to Alexi and Claire.

That hadn't gone over well with me. I hung up on her.

She called a second time. I hung up again. After the fifth time, I finally listened to her and regretted it immediately. She ended up moving a small house on the same street Claire's mom lived on. It was still touch and go with them. It was less than that with me. I couldn't stomach an entire conversation with her, not after all she'd done to me.

He swept a hand through my hair, tucking it behind my ear, and he pulled me against his chest. Wrapping an arm around me, he pressed a kiss to my forehead. "I'm sorry your mom's a bitch."

It was so much more than that, but I sighed. "I'm trying to forgive them. I have no idea how, but I'm trying. Ethan would want that."

"Yeah, he would."

The bickering started again inside. This time something thumped against a wall, and we heard glass shattering.

"Fucking hell," Jesse bit out. He clenched his jaw and headed inside. As he disappeared through the door, I heard him yell, "What the hell is going on? Stop trashing my place!"

"He started it!" Hannah shrieked back. "Do you know what he called me?"

"I don't care. Put the damn vase down."

"But—"

"NOW!"

I grinned to myself and shook my head. These were my friends. This was my family.

Cord poked his head out and held his phone in the air. "We're going to order pizza. You in?"

I sighed and started toward him. "I wouldn't be anywhere else." And as I stepped through the door, he closed it behind me before moving around me. He and his girl were positioned in the living room. Hannah and Jamie were in the dining room. Tiffany was sitting on the stairs and Jesse had his back turned to me. It was rigid as he continued to yell at Jamie, who had taken the condom bowl from its hiding spot. He'd been throwing condoms at Hannah. They were all over the floor.

I glanced up to the portrait. I felt Ethan laughing down at me. I could only imagine him saying, "And you love your new family. You know it."

The corners of my lips curved up. He was right.

EPILOGUE

JESSE

I t's about ten years later now.

I wanted to pop back in and let everyone know how we're doing and when I say we're doing good, we're doing *good*. I'm coaching basketball and track (don't ask how I got roped into that sport, I just did somehow), and I'm shocked at how much I'm loving it. Who knew I'd enjoy kids one day, but I do.

Though, I'm not an idiot. I know that's Alex's influence on me.

She and I lived together for the rest of college. There were ups and downs, but not between us. I never fucked that up (not after I'd already fucked it up so much before I even got the girl.) The dramatics were our friends and roommates. To give an update on them, Jamie's in prison, but it's one of those day-camp kinds. I've ceased talking to him, so I have no idea what else is new in his life.

The girls all keep in touch with Alex. Most are married with kids. A couple are newly single, but I'll be honest that I mostly don't care about them. I know her friend Beth hooked up with a drug dealer dude from Grant West, but they've since broken up.

And I can share that because I remember Alex talking to her just last night on the phone.

As for Alex and myself, we have two little boys and a girl on the way. Ethan and Connor. Alex got a kick out of naming our little boy Connor since he's Connor Hunt. The little girl is going to be named Claire.

So yeah. We're doing good.

This might not be the update you're hoping for, but I'm not the best at the verbiage. Alex doesn't let me do the Christmas letters because it tends to not be anything.

And hey, if you feel like checking out Alex's website, hit her up. She runs a program for adolescents. Youth come in, do paintings, and Alex sells them. They have other options. She works with a bunch of social services and occupational therapists, but the paintings are the big draw. Some are okay, but some are fucking good. She hosts events for them, does the whole nine yards to get 'em in local papers and business newsletters. It's called the Ethan Connors Foundation. It's amazing and makes me damn proud of my woman.

Peace out.

I gotta go and stop this kid. He's trying to windmill dunk when he's not even learned the right footwork for an easy layup.

— Jesse Hunt

If you enjoyed Broken and Screwed 2, please leave a review! They truly help so much.

ACKNOWLEDGMENTS

Thank you to all the readers who have continued to read and love on the Broken and Screwed characters!! These were some of the first books I wrote and published so they have a special place in my heart.

ALSO BY TIJAN

Standalones:

Sustain

Ryan's Bed

Enemies

Teardrop Shot

And many more at

www.tijansbooks.com

CPSIA information can be obtained
at www.ICGtesting.com
Printed in the USA
BVHW081011130121
597716BV00001B/76